DECEIT

DOCTOR WHO – THE NEW ADVENTURES

Also available:

THE NEW

DOCTOR WHO

ADVENTURES

DECEIT

Peter Darvill-Evans

First published in 1993 by
Doctor Who Books
an imprint of Virgin Publishing Ltd
332 Ladbroke Grove
London W10 5AH

Cover illustration by Luis Rey

Phototypeset by Intype, London

Printed and bound in Great Britain by
Cox & Wyman Ltd, Reading, Berkshire

ISBN 0 426 20387 9

For
Ian Briggs and Sophie Aldred

—thanks, and I hope you
both still like her

Contents

Prologue

FIVE YEARS AGO

He rose from the couch, scratching an itch on his left arm. At the doorway he pulled aside a flimsy purple curtain – ugly colour – that had not been there when he had gone to bed.

He shuffled across the room. Once again, it seemed wider. He crossed the Telepathic Net. Better than a brisk shower. He stood for a moment, enjoying the comforting tingle. At his console, screens were pixillating into life; subdued monitor lights began to glow.

Settling into his chair, he ran the usual unnecessary systems checks. As the reports came in for processing from all corners of the station, he sat back and surveyed his quarters.

He had been asleep only five hours, but the changes were noticeable. There seemed to be more columns and archways. Some of the pillars had been decorated in a spiral pattern. Not pleasing to the eye. Gaudy colours. He'd have to—

He sensed impatience in the Net. He reached for the cranial harness hovering above his head. He drew it down until its central plug touched the socket in the neural implant on the top of his shaven scalp.

One more glance across the room. Once it had been a bare space, he remembered, a functional area for work and rest. Now it was a labyrinth of gauze-curtained alcoves and dusty cul-de-sacs between frankly rather unaesthetic architectural features. It was partly his fault. And he kept forgetting to reprogramme the cleaners. The archways gaped like portals to infinite gulfs. He had a premonition, a lurching physical fear. There was nothing to be afraid of. He closed his eyes, tugged on the harness, and felt the plug slide into the socket.

3

He would never get used to that sensation of falling.

'Good morning, Bertrand. We welcome you. You're a little perturbed today.'

Good morning. It's nothing, don't worry. But I want a word with you about those twisted candy-striped columns that are littering my room.

'You don't like them. We thought you might find them intriguing.'

Leave the interior decor to me, and you stick to number-crunching, how about that? Talking of which, how's the latest projection?

'We have just completed the final phase of the calculation.'

And? He felt anticipation. Or was it anxiety?

Voices in his head expressed wordless, soothing thoughts, but could not disguise their own excitement. 'We must accelerate the experiment. We now have only six years and four months, Earth time, in which to complete it.'

But that's impossible.

A soundless chuckle. 'Leave the number-crunching to us. We have assessed the resource statistics and incorporated them into the calculations. It can be done.'

Can you summarize the reasons for urgency? Surely this war will last long enough for our purposes?

'A war is a unique event. Until the hostilities started, we had insufficient data. Therefore our initial projections were optimistic. It is now clear that although the war will last almost as long as we first calculated, the later stages will be sporadic.'

And who will win?

'Win?' There was a moment of absence. 'Earth will win. It is of little consequence to the experiment. We will of course use our influence to prolong the conflict, but nothing we can do will maintain the Daleks at viable deep-space battle strength for more than six years. Thereafter we will experience political interference.'

From Earth?

'Yes. Interestingly, our hypothetical calculations show that we would suffer in the same way from the Daleks

4

were they to emerge victorious, and on a slightly shorter time-scale. We cannot allow interference before the experiment is concluded.'

We need another ten years.

'We can accomplish our priority objectives in less.'

Then of course I will be proud to help to my utmost. He gasped, his mind drowning in waves of unspoken concern.

'Bertrand, consider this carefully. You have already given so much, so many years. You have almost become one of us, but you are not yet ready. You must not neglect your physical needs. You are frail, Bertrand. You know you no longer have the strength to make your rounds of the station.'

It was so unfair. It was they who continuously enlarged the working space. But he knew they were right. His life had become nothing but sleep and the neural link. His body was prematurely aged.

I want only to serve.

'We appreciate your loyalty, Bertrand. You know that we do.'

He basked in a tide of gratitude. He could have wept.

A single voice now, querulous and dogmatic. Hiroto's voice. 'You can continue to serve us. We want you to. We will need your help for many years to come. You must train your successor.'

Bertrand recalled his own induction. Hiroto had been exhausted, too. A shrivelled husk, shrunken and crumpled in stature, his voice a whisper. He had taken great pains to tutor Bertrand. He had held Bertrand's hand as the neural implant was fitted, and again during Bertrand's first link. Strange how such a simple physical contact had been so important. And then Hiroto had died. Bertrand knew he had one more duty to perform before his own body expired.

Of course. I must educate a successor. There are some promising candidates among the research teams.

He presented a list of names – a list that he realized he had been preparing, subconsciously, for many years. He provided a visual image of a face to match each name.

The station's research scientists were recruited from the postgraduates of Earth, Astral, and the university planet Academia; Bertrand's short-list was the pick of the crop. He began to enumerate their various qualifications.

'Stop, Bertrand. We know our staff. You have selected well. But there is one other whom we should consider.'

Another? Who? But he knew, before the facial image was placed in his mind. He wouldn't have that face inside his head. He wouldn't let them sense his shame and fear.

He tore the cranial harness from his head.

Slumped across the console, his head in his hands, he began to recover from the shock of separation. Recovery brought no relief. With it came memories and regrets, and long-buried guilt.

He had been younger then. Much older than her, and old enough to know better. But he hadn't known much: he was innocent beyond his years, and she had been precocious.

She had led him on, seduced him. Yes; but that didn't excuse what he had done. He knew now that it hadn't been an unnatural act, not compared to the stories he had heard since. But he had been younger then. He suspected, now, that it had distressed her far less than she had claimed. She had been precocious. His remorse had been very real. And she had used his guilt. He had lied, tampered with the records, his dissimulations leaving a more glittering trail of slime than the original deed could ever have done.

He had maintained his mental defences ever since. He had tried to have her transferred to another posting. Why had she clung like a limpet? What did she want? Hadn't he paid her enough, over and over again? Her telepathic shields were even better than his own. She had a will of steel. He had shut her out, buried the memories, buried himself in the link to avoid her – and now they wanted him to train her as his successor.

He opened his eyes. That face again. He wasn't surprised. She was in his room.

She had been pretty once. Or his lust had convinced him so. Now the wide eyes were disquieting, not appealing. The half-smile was mocking, no longer coy. The hairless skull shocked him.

She ducked her head. He glimpsed the bulbous shape, the glint of metal.

'Bertrand. Look what your money paid for, lover. I had it fitted on Earth. Nothing but the best. And now I've come to take over.'

'Never!' What was wrong with his voice? 'I – won't – let you.'

She opened her hand. Lying on the palm was a plasti-graft applicator.

'A few milligrams of Dezeldox, while you were asleep. Time to go bye-byes again, Bertrand. This time you won't wake up.'

The link. He tried to grasp the harness, but it was hovering out of reach. His limbs were too heavy. His muscles were too weak. The drug was doing its work.

'The – link. Must – connect. Must – drain – please . . . '

She laughed. Standing, she plucked the harness from the air. 'There's only one person capable of maintaining the link now. They know it, I know it – and now you know it, too. Good-bye, Bertrand. This is the start of a new era.'

She placed the harness over her head.

Part One

FIVE WEEKS AWAY

A small starship flits through warp space. One of its networked picoprocessors carries the mail: its ROM-store contains a stack of silvery needles embedded in non-conductive plastic. Each needle is rectangular in cross-section – this can just be discerned by eye – and with the aid of a microscope it could be seen to resemble a swiss roll: a structured filament of organic molecules sandwiched between equally thin layers of inorganic material, folded and refolded. The needle has been electronically configured into blocks. There are eight thousand blocks along the length of one needle. Each block consists of enough data-recording medium to store the information contained in a set of encyclopedias. The entire contents of the library of Alexandria would occupy only a couple of needles. There are three hundred needles in the ROM-store.

All of the needles are nearly empty. Each one represents a destination planet, and although the recordings will not be transferred physically, the picoprocessors of all the ships in this part of the galaxy have been set up to encode each needle as a separate planet.

Therefore each needle contains only a few memos and reports – market research for the sales director, personnel records with salary updates, the half-yearly profit and loss account, copies of local correspondence – and some personal mail.

In one of the starship's cabins, someone seated at the communications station has retrieved an item from the mail: a personal message from Britta Hoffmann. The addressee's private security code has been invoked to access the recording; this is illegal. The lights have been dimmed. The holographic projectors glow, and in the darkened cabin appears . . .

11

. . . a school of fish. An almost-vertical, wavy line of a dozen silvery-purple little fish, hardly moving, just trembling in the darkness, quivering enough to set their silver scales scintillating.

They move, slowly at first, not going anywhere, shifting back and forth against the blackness, the column undulating. Their movement becomes rhythmic, insistent.

A stifled giggle breaks the silence.

'Here we see the indigenous life-forms of the planet Ellanon.' It is a woman's voice, breathless and excited. 'Remember the day we went snorkelling? Those little fishes went everywhere! And here they are again. Take a good look! Lights on!'

A flash of brilliance. Blurred shapes condense into crispness as the holovid recorder adjusts to the sudden glow of artificial illumination. In the claustrophobic surrounding of a holographic representation of a starship cabin that fits inside the real one like a hand inside a glove, a woman stands naked. Her eyes shine as brightly as the scales of the fishes that are tattooed in a line from her left breast to her right hip.

She is young, slim, lithe. She stands on tiptoe and twirls, her long, blond hair lifting in a golden arc.

If she had been wealthy, one would assume that gene selection had had a part in creating her appearance. But the wealthy don't have to travel between the stars to find their fortunes. She is as natural as she looks.

As she spins, she plucks up a robe, and as she slows to face the recorder, she pulls it tightly round her body.

'That's enough peeking,' she says. 'No point in getting you all worked up when we're this far apart.' Her eyes are bright with excitement – or are those tears?

'Hello, soldier boy.' Her voice is quiet now, her hands awkward in each other's company. 'Oh, Dimitri. I'm already missing you so much. I've been saving up so many things to say to you, and now the time's come and I can't think of anything.

'We're going to dock at the station soon. A bit of excitement at last. I can't wait to get down to some real work again. But I wish you were here with me. And not just for that, stupid: I know what you're thinking. It's because I'm a bit nervous. Butterflies, at this stage, isn't it ridiculous? It's not like me at all. I wish you were here though, Dimitri, just to tell me I'm being silly.'

She looks, suddenly, straight at the recorder. Her pale eyes are huge, beseeching. Then she shrugs, a one-shouldered movement, her head tilting to one side, her eyelids lowered over glittering eyes. Her smile is once again radiant.

'And I am being silly, I know I am. I'm so lucky, really. There are people in the company who'd kill to get this posting. Everyone's madly jealous. All the high-ups have been posted here at some time or other. It's the big project, apparently – all the serious research is done here. So it's the passport to success, prestige, riches, lots of holidays with lots of snorkelling! But the funny thing is . . .'

She pulls the silky material more tightly, and shivers. 'This is going to sound really dumb. But the funny thing is, when I talked to some of the project co-ordinators and station managers, before I left – people who'd been posted here in the past – none of them reacted as I'd expected. Some of them laughed: you know, "Ha!", like that, very cynical. And some of them looked so sad. They wouldn't tell me anything about it. And I've been having such weird dreams, coming here on the ship. Yes, I know you can get weird dreams in warp space, but I don't, usually. And it's the same thing, over and over again. Dreams of being eaten. Eaten alive. It's horrible.

'But I suppose it's just anxiety. That dreadful woman waiting to interview me, perhaps the moment I arrive. Only an hour or so away now. What can she be like, Dimitri? She sounds so – so cold.

'Anyway, that's enough of my paranoia. I'm happy really – see? Except that I'm missing you so much. No more to say. Love you. Don't get yourself killed, it'd be very thoughtless of you, especially now all the real fighting's over. Think about me every day, won't you?

'I'll send this holovid back on an X-ship. It'll take an

age, but you'll still see it months before you see me again. Oh, Dimitri . . . '

She blows a kiss at the recorder. She waves. She says 'Record off,' and disappears.

In the X-ship cabin, a voice says 'Override. Delete.' The holovid recording is erased from the ROM-store memory. Dimitri will never receive his letter.

The image of Troheim crossed her legs. That was to show she was agitated, but Celescu suspected it was also to show her legs. He sighed. Some holograms, he thought, are nice and easy on the eye. She was whispering urgent instructions to her terminal, which was beyond the visual field.

She was slim, and she was wearing a shimmersuit that would have knocked a hole in Celescu's credit rating. Her hair was tiger-striped; Celescu assumed this was the latest fashion on the core worlds. Her dark eyes were implausibly large. Through the transmission interference, she looked no more than twenty-five years old. Celescu wondered what she really looked like. Did the Spinward Corporation think that a Spacefleet officer was going to be distracted by a holosynth?

Troheim turned to face him. She blinked her black, scintillating lashes. 'Our records indicate that our Arcadia base has no fastline facility, Commander Celescu. I'm so sorry.'

'Our records indicate otherwise.'

Troheim ignored him. 'Of course, we despatched an X-ship from Belmos base as soon as we received your earlier communication but, as you know, Arcadia is three weeks from Belmos, so we can't expect any news for at least a month.'

'You don't have a fastline on your X-ship?'

'It's an old model, Commander. That's all we have at Belmos.' She ducked her head and smiled up at him. 'We fully support Earth Central's directive that the military should have priority in communications technology.'

'So you've got no idea what's happening on Arcadia?'

14

'I don't think anything untoward is happening, Commander.'

Celescu's finger, the quivering focal point of his suppressed rage, hovered over the cancel button. 'Then where in the galaxy are Agent Dixon and his team?'

'I really couldn't say, Commander, but when the X-ship—'

Celescu's finger jabbed the button. Wynette Troheim's image dissolved into splinters of fading, coloured light. Celescu swivelled his chair to face the black-suited woman sitting on the other side of his desk. She lifted her shoulders and the corners of her pale lips.

Celescu glared at her. Enforcement Agents were, in his experience, only slightly less duplicitous than the executives of the Spinward Corporation. 'They're lying!' he said, bringing his fist down on the marble desk-top.

'We know they're lying, Commander,' Agent Defries replied. 'But we don't know what they're hiding. And that's what I have to find out.'

Without thinking, he glanced at the three-dimensional resources display that was scrolling on stand-by across the rimward curve of his office wall. He cursed inwardly as he realized that Defries would not have missed the significance of the gesture. 'I suppose you'll need back-up,' he growled.

Defries raised the squat glass from the arm of her chair, and took a sip of the amber contents. 'Whiskey,' she said, after an appreciative pause. 'From Earth?'

'The best. Scotch. From South America.'

'My parental community had a distillery. On Thrapos 3. We didn't make anything like this, though.' She put down the glass and leaned forward. Her eyes were pale blue, scanning his face. 'Can you spare a troopship and a full complement of troopers?'

Celescu took a deep breath. He rubbed a hand across his eyes. He'd been expecting her to ask for a flash-fry squad and a couple of X-ships at most. 'Do I have any choice?'

'Not really. You could kick it back to the Centre and

15

ask Vice-Admiral Pirrado. He'd tell you to let me have the troopship.'

I'm slowing down, Celescu thought. Missing the obvious. 'So you don't actually have a warrant to requisition a troopship, Agent?'

Direct hit. Defries's eyes shifted momentarily, before her face set in an expressionless mask. 'I have the authority to request whatever support I deem necessary, Commander.' For an instant she looked tired, hunted, bitter. 'I need that ship. I need those troopers.'

He noticed that Defries had unconsciously allowed her fingers to stray to the holster at her belt. 'You must be expecting trouble on Arcadia,' he said mildly. He was suddenly intrigued.

'We don't know what to expect, Commander. We've had Agents in just about all of Spinward Corp's other settlements, and they look legal.'

'Legal?'

'More so than most. And yet Spinward have been conspicuously successful – they beat the rush back into the equities market when the war ended, for instance, and their colonies suffered less than others from the plagues. But it could be a run of luck. There's no Arcadia connection that we can detect.'

'So why do you need a troopship to go visiting?'

'You know why, Commander. It's the Spinward planet we know least about. It's the only Spinward planet where we lost an Enforcement team. I'm going to find out what's going on there, even if no-one else gives a damn.'

So that's it. She's had obstruction at Central. Spinward influence. Political machinations. Celescu had had his share of that kind of problem, too.

'I suppose,' she was saying, 'that you haven't taken the trouble to find out what the Fleet datanet has?'

Celescu didn't voice-switch the monitor. He didn't need to. His Tech Officer had already come close to mutiny because of Celescu's demands for information – any information at all. 'Nothing. Colony founded three hundred years ago, give or take. One of the first Spinward settlements. No immigration records. No emigration records.

No trade records, except the usual goods and equipment. No Fleet survey, of course. All data courtesy of the Spinward Corporation.'

'We have about the same.' Defries waited, twisting the glass on the leather upholstery. The silence lengthened.

'You can have a troopship,' Celescu said at last. 'The *Admiral Raistrick* has just been through re-fit. Captain Toko and his crew are on stand-by. But the nearest troopers are on Hurgal, two weeks away.'

'I need to move quickly, Commander. You have troopers in the Hai Dow system.'

'They're on a pirate hunt, Agent!' Celescu knew he had to sound reasonable. 'We are close to the culmination of a year's work. I can't pull them out now. If speed is essential—' His mind raced, caught an idea, rejected it immediately, returned to it, worried it. 'We have an entire division of troops here, on stand-by. But they're Irregular Auxiliaries.'

'Why didn't you say so, Commander? I thought you were disbanding the Irregulars as fast as you could. But they'll do. I think I can just about stand to be cooped up with a shipload of Auxies. It's only five weeks to Arcadia from here.'

'What about your secret weapon?'

'I'll keep him in cryo till we reach the system. Better to have Auxies around when he thaws out. They are reputed to be the most dangerous arm of the military.'

Celescu scowled. 'Often more dangerous to us than to the enemy. They'd rather fight their own officers than anyone else – except Daleks, of course.'

'Then I'll tell them there are Daleks on Arcadia.'

'They won't appreciate being duped.'

'If I know Spinward Corp, they'll have enough weapons on Arcadia to equip a SYSDIDS. When the spikes and clusters start shooting up towards us out of the forceshells, those Auxies'll have to fight – or die. I'll promise the survivors that they'll get Daleks to kill next time.'

Celescu surprised himself: he was beginning to like Agent Defries. 'I'll let you have the best of the bunch,' he said. 'We can't find enough Dalek nests to keep them happy these days. The mopping-up's about done. They'll be ready to go at ten hundred tomorrow.'

'Thank you, Commander. You've been very helpful.' Defries stood, saluted, and turned to go.

Celescu grunted. 'Well. Good luck, Agent. I don't envy you the drop with the Auxies. And Arcadia sounds like it'll be hell with a warp drive.'

The afternoon sunshine gave a golden glow to the white limestone walls. Atop the burnished towers of Castle Beaufort, pennants hung limply above conical roofs and crenellated battlements. Below the keep, the greensward of the outer bailey was deserted but for two tired donkeys. Two curtain walls arced from the castle like a pair of arms, embracing the red-roofed town that jumbled down the hill from the gatehouse to the river.

The town was as sleepy as the castle. Smoke curled skyward from a few fires: the second batch of loaves was baking, the potter had given his day's work to the kiln, the smith's brazier was hot, but his anvil was silent. Barges were moored at the wharf, but none disturbed the still, metallic sheen of the river. No carts rumbled across the bridge, but here and there along the parapets a stationary angler could be discerned, a slumbering shadow at the base of a curving rod.

The fields, full of ripening crops, made a ragged chessboard with copses of dark trees. Forested hilltops ringed the horizon, except to the north, where a herd of wild ponies flicked their tails in the inadequate shade of thorny shrubs.

The turquoise sky was cloudless, but smudged with bands of darker colour, like distant smoke. The bands were too regular to be natural. The sky was not like Earth's. The moon was already up: a brilliant, jagged rock, like a tiny, rough-edged coin in the firmament. The moon was not like Earth's.

Shafts of sunlight lanced through the tall windows of the castle library. Alone, surrounded by towers of books on shelves, a robed scribe sat writing. He had started to transcribe the words from a book lying open on his desk, but having written only three sentences he had succumbed to the heat and was merely doodling in the margin of his copy. In any case, the book secreted in his lap was more interesting than the one he was supposed to copy from. He read furtively, his right hand inscribing repetitive, curving shapes.

A bell chimed. The scribe started and the book fell from his lap to the floor. He picked it up, thrust it under a pile of other volumes, and bent over his work. Another sentence was copied. The bell clanged again.

The scribe shook his head, put down his pen, and crossed his arms. He waited, and watched motes of dust dance in the sunbeams. The silence was broken by the bell: an insistent peal of chimes.

There was still no clatter of footsteps, no creaking of opening doors. The scribe stood and stretched. He was a tall young man with a face as sharp as a quill nib. He sauntered to the half-open doors of the chamber.

'Hubert! Hubert, are you there?' He directed his stage whisper down the spiral stairway. There was no answer. He raised his voice. 'Hubert! There's someone at the gate. Answer it, there's a good chap.' The only answer was another clamour of bells from the darkness below.

The scribe shook his head, gathered his robe in his hands, and started down the steps. The bell was tolling repeatedly now, and the scribe tried to match the rhythm with his footsteps and his speech.

'Library's on the third floor, other side from the town. Why? So we aren't disturbed. Who comes to the West Gate? No-one comes to the West Gate. But if someone should happen to turn up, who's supposed to answer the bell? Not me. But round and round and round I go, until I reach the bottom—'

As he jumped from the final step his foot caught in the hem of his robe and he fell with a loud and indelicate exclamation against the timbers of the West Gate. The ringing of the bell suddenly ceased.

The scribe pulled himself to his feet and, doubled over and gasping for breath, he fumbled at the heavy bolts. The gate swung inwards, and the young man straightened to find himself staring into the shadowy depths of a black cowl. Two eyes regarded him steadily from within the hood.

He refused to feel fear. 'Greetings, Humble Counsellor,' he said, standing aside. 'Please enter. May I ask why we have the honour of your presence?' In other words, who's died? Let it not be someone – someone I know, he thought. Could it be true that Counsellors could read thoughts?

'The honour is mine,' the Humble Counsellor mumbled, sweeping past the Scribe. 'I would beg an audience with his Highness.'

The scribe gave a sigh of relief. You're a supercilious trickster, he thought, and his Highness daren't refuse to see you. As he closed the gate, he hesitated, peering at the lawns beyond the courtyard. No hoofprints. How did the Counsellors travel from Landfall? He turned to find the cloaked figure standing in front of him, a thin form draped in black silk.

'May I ask your name?' the Humble Counsellor said, gargling the fateful question as if through a mouthful of mud.

Now the young man felt afraid. He tried to think of an answer; he couldn't summon a plausible untruth. 'Francis,' he said.

'And what is your occupation, Master Francis?'

Surely the ground was slipping away like a sand dune in a dust-storm? Surely the beams of the ceiling were collapsing into the room? No: the gatehouse anteroom was silent and still, the flagstones were firm beneath his feet. He found he could smile, and did so.

'I am a Scribe, Humble Counsellor. And not a Master yet; a mere Apprentice.'

'Ah. That explains it. I thought I had not seen you at Landfall. But surely you are advanced in years for Apprenticeship? Is it not time you became a Master?'

'Thank you for your concern, Humble Counsellor.' Why is he toying with me? Francis could have wept with anger and frustration. 'I must admit that I have been remiss. I have lingered, I confess it. The journey to Landfall is said to be long and hard. It is well know that not all who attempt it survive.'

'But Francis!' The Counsellor inhaled noisily, as if about to spit. 'Think of the rewards for those who return! Would you not exchange your Apprentice's cell for the apartment of a Master Scribe? Do you not long for the perquisites of office? The fees, the rewards from grateful nobles?'

Leave me alone, Francis begged silently. I'm happy as I am.

'You must come to Landfall. I will mention it to his Highness. Would you be so kind as to accompany me and present me at the audience chamber?'

Francis pushed open the inner door and led the way across the cobbled courtyard.

'Is your fastline secure, Commander?'

Defries leaned back in her chair and imagined Celescu's features struggling to retain an expression of calm politeness. His voice, filtered through the station's comms net, had a metallic edge.

'We took delivery of this system only three days ago, Agent. You brought it with you, as I'm sure you remember. I don't see how anyone could have interfered with—'

'Patch me in,' Defries said, and Celescu's voice was cut off as the fastline overrode the station net. Defries sat watching the blank screen of her terminal. It remained blank for half a minute.

Fastline, she thought. About as fast as a decommissioned refuelling tub. She stood up and paced back and forth across the three-metre width of her cabin. She glanced at the screen. Still blank. She ordered a coffee from the dispenser, drumming her fingers on the plastic fascia as the brown liquid hissed into a cup. She took a sip, stopped herself from looking back at the terminal, took another sip. She lingered over the five steps it took to re-cross the room. Earth Central's identifier code was flashing on the screen, along with a request for her password.

Settling back into her chair, she said her name and her

identity code, and then leaned forward for the retina scan. The screen stopped flashing. More seconds passed. At last, an image began to form in the air above the desk. The floating pixels coalesced into the barely identifiable face of No-Go Joe. Joe was the holographic face of the Director's security software.

'I'm sorry,' Joe said, insincerely and indistinctly, 'you have connected with an unauthorized party. Please disconnect immediately.'

'Cut it out, Joe. This is Agent Defries. Get me the Director. And I don't care what time of night it is wherever on Earth he is right now. This is clearance double zero.'

Joe's face registered sardonic surprise before fading. Defries grinned; the guys in the programming department were getting good.

An even grainier image collected itself together: the round, pale-eyed face of the Director of External Operations. The face's mouth opened and closed. A few seconds later, the Director's voice arrived.

'Agent Defries. Considerate of you to call between the hors d'oevres and the entrée. How's it going, Belle?'

'Your digestion is my prime concern as always, boss. Since when did you forget how to lip-sync?'

Another pause while the Director's words caught up with his facial movements.

'You look pretty stupid too, Belle. And I can see at least three of you.'

'And this is supposed to be the pinnacle of human technological achievement?'

'Even radio was rough when it was first invented, Belle. You're six hundred light years away and we're talking as if we're in adjacent rooms – well, almost. They'll fix the lip-sync.'

Repetition of a key word was the signal. Defries pressed the palm of her hand on the box she'd plugged into her terminal. The Director's face froze while the system ran the handprint scan.

Almost as immobile as the Director's face, Defries waited. The scrambler hook-up was old technology, but this one had modifications and it hadn't been tested. If it were to malfunction . . .

The static hologram suddenly dissolved, and then re-formed. The Director appeared to be sitting in a blizzard. His voice sounded as if he was whispering to her in a gale-force wind.

'Belle? Can you hear me?'

'Just about. This may not confuse the enemy, but it surely confuses me.'

'Cures the lip-sync glitch, anyway. I can't see your lips any more. Are you ready to receive the data?'

Defries checked the terminal's subsidiary display. 'Ready and waiting,' she said.

'OK. Downloading now. Don't worry if it takes a while. Some of this stuff had to be digitized. It's coming to you in good old binary.'

'Digitized? You mean, it was only on paper?'

'Microfiche, in fact. Don't bother to ask. Same as paper, as far as we're concerned. Spinward's an old Corporation. One of the first to leave the home system. The name's new – they changed it after the Cyber Wars – but the core company originated on Earth back in the 2100s. It's all in the data. You'll see. How are you getting on with Commander Celescu?'

'He'll survive. He's the kind of soldier who doesn't like obeying orders from Fleet, so he's not exactly jumping to help us.'

'But you got the back-up you need?'

Defries hoped the Director could see her smile. 'No problem, boss. A whole troopship. Hand-picked by yours truly and ready to warp tomorrow morning. They're Auxiliaries, kicking their heels. Dalek hunters.'

'Well done, Belle. I knew you could do it. And the weapon?'

'Already on board, and sound asleep.'

'Excellent. Now listen.' The shape of the Director's body shifted. His windswept voice was louder and more urgent. 'I've had three Ministers on to me today, advising me to refrain from taking an interest in Spinward's affairs. An hour ago I received a Presidential order to omit Arcadia from our security operations. The Spinward Corporation has influence here. We knew that. I've junked all records relating to your mission. You're on leave, as of three weeks ago. You have no authority and no power.'

'Except for a ship full of Auxies.'

'Exactly. Good luck, Belle. When the data transmission ceases, this fastline will go down. And the scrambler will take down every other fastline in your sector. You're on your own. Find Dixon and his team. Take Arcadia apart if you have to. And if there's an innocent explanation, we can both look forward to a lifetime posting to a plague planet. So be clever.'

The indistinct hologram faded. The screen was blank.

From a horizontal position, Commander Celescu stared at his terminal. It was bad enough to be woken up to receive a top priority fastline call from Fleet, but he'd barely kicked his brain into consciousness when the fastline had abruptly failed.

'Replay,' he growled. 'On screen. Complete.' He struggled from beneath the bedcover and padded naked to the terminal to watch the recorded data appear.

'Fastlines!' he muttered, as if expelling something unpleasant from his mouth. 'Why can't they wait until they get it right? Why do they issue this garbage if it doesn't work yet? At least X-ships are reliable. Mostly.' He watched the wording of the Fleet datanet protocol stream across the screen. The only important words would be in the last line: a warrant for the immediate arrest and imprisonment of . . .

He had been sure, while listening to the message as it infiltrated his sleep, that he had heard *arrest and imprisonment of Agent Defries* just before the communication ended with a squawk of ruptured programming. But the name had not been recorded. According to the screen – and therefore according to the station's log – the message had ended before the name of the party to be arrested had been relayed.

Celescu smiled. He went back to bed.

* * *

24

The Halls of Crystal were deserted. Francis zigzagged through an ambulatory, between scintillating pillars as wide as houses, following one of the twisting paths of jewelled emblems set into the onyx floor. The trail of ruby coronets led him into the main chamber of the Octagonal Court, and as always he paused to stare upwards at the coloured glass of the dome, set so high above the tiers of galleries that it looked like the patterned disc at the end of a kaleidoscope. The Humble Counsellor, less impressed by grandiose architecture, stepped on the heel of Francis's shoe.

Francis muttered an apology and hurried on, wondering not for the first time why a Counsellor's footsteps sounded like the scurrying of mice. On the far side of the Octagonal Court, within sight now but still further than Francis could throw a stone, the Throne Room doors were slightly ajar, and unattended. Francis slowed the pace of his progress across the vast, bejewelled floor and began to glance from side to side. Ushers and men-at-arms had a habit of disappearing just when they were required. A thousand mirrors multiplied and remultiplied images of the Apprentice Scribe and the Humble Counsellor, but otherwise the hall was empty.

In theory the Prince's audience was open to any visitor. Francis knew that in practice His Highness was only too pleased to end an audience early if business was light; he also knew, from embarrassing experience, that it was unwise to bring a visitor unannounced into the Prince's presence. Therefore Francis stopped in front of the Throne Room door; plucked up the courage to ask the Counsellor to wait for a few moments; and turned to find that the black-robed figure was already scuttling to sit on one of the velvet-covered Supplicants' Benches that occupied the wide niches between the silver statues lining the fascia of the Throne Room.

Francis studied his reflection in the nearest mirror, adjusting stray curls of his black hair and straightening the lapels of his robe. He practised his expression – the respectful yet friendly smile with a hint of debonair sophistication – and pushed the door a little further open.

The audience was over. From within the Throne Room, Francis could hear shouting, laughter, high-pitched giggles and someone playing a harpsichord badly. He tapped on one of the doors.

'Who the blazes is that?' It was the Prince's voice. The other noises in the room continued unabated. 'Go away, whoever you are. Audience is over. Come back tomorrow, eh?'

Francis felt sick with apprehension. If he was unlucky, he was about to disturb the Prince and some of the courtiers in the middle of a game of forfeits. He stepped through the doorway.

Yes, he was unlucky. The throne, set on its stepped pyramid of black marble at the centre of the semicircular apse at the far end of the room, was empty except for the Prince's crown and staff. The Prince had descended to lounge on a brocade-covered couch in one of the side-aisles; he was holding a goblet in one hand and Lady Christina in the other, and was guffawing at the antics of the courtiers.

As Francis shuffled across the turquoise carpets, he became more and more convinced that he would prefer to be anywhere else. Master Henry the Goldsmith, one of the Prince's closest companions, was embracing one of the stone columns for which he had himself designed the gilt decoration, and reciting an epic poem. Mistress Mary, the Prince's favourite clothier, was seated at the harpsichord, and was playing badly because she was blindfolded. Lady Fiona was standing on a small table, holding a rose between her clenched teeth, and attempting to make lascivious dance movements to the harpsichord's halting rhythms. Half a dozen other courtiers, some of them not entirely clothed, were surrounding the performers and making loud comments that the whole company found hugely amusing.

Lady Christina was the first to see Francis approaching. He stopped and gestured frantically towards the door, trying to indicate that he had brought a visitor for the Prince. Lady Christina smiled, nodded, and inclined her head toward the royal ear beside her.

Francis expelled a sigh of relief and began to retrace his steps.

'Francis the Scribe!' It was the Prince's voice.

Francis arranged his features into the rehearsed smile and turned again. 'Your Highness?'

'Come here, Francis. That's right, closer. Don't be bashful, young fellow. Christina tells me you're not usually bashful. Not usually bashful, are you, eh? Like a game of forfeits, so I'm told, eh?'

Francis had reached what he considered to be a respectful distance from the Prince's couch. He bowed. 'Under certain circumstances, your Highness.' He hoped Christina had not had time to tell the Prince about all the games that she and Francis had played. 'But perhaps not when there's a Humble Counsellor waiting outside on a Supplicants' Bench.'

'What! A Counsellor? Here? Waiting to see me? Why didn't you say so earlier? Send him in, send him in!'

The courtiers melted away silently. Francis started on the long walk back to the Supplicants' Door.

'Not yet, Francis, not yet. Let me get back to the throne. You were a promising young chap once, Francis. But you're neglecting your proper duties these days, aren't you, eh? Never mind, never mind. Show the Counsellor in. And don't forget to close the door!'

Isabelle Defries rested her head in her hands. She rubbed her eyes with the balls of her thumbs. She needed hard information, not a history lesson. 'More,' she said, and then, after taking one look at the antique handwriting that appeared on the screen, 'Digest.'

Spinward Corporation, founding of. Merger 2107 of two trading organizations, both rated as small for period.

Eurogen Company: genetics; research and development of improved crop and livestock strains. Expansion due to requirements of planetary colonists.

Butler Institute: artificial intelligence; modelling and forecasting. Weather systems expertise employed in Earth meteorological control; decline thereafter in Institute's for-

tunes reversed by need for similar analysis on colony worlds.

Merged companies formed EB Corporation. First warpship commissioned 2112.

Defries shook her head. It was late, and she had to go into warpspace tomorrow. Correction: later today. In a few hours. She took another sip of the fruit-flavoured stimulant she'd started drinking when the coffee had stopped keeping her awake. If she could just keep sipping the stuff for a few more hours, she could take something to put her to sleep in warp. 'More,' she said.

Transcript of advertising broadcast follows.

ARCADIA: THE PARADISE PLANET

At last you can really get away from it all. Have you ever looked round at this small planet we inhabit? Have you ever wondered how it came to be so dirty, so crowded, so damaged and ravaged? Do you hate the bustle and rush, the noise and the machinery? Do you long for a simpler life, a life in tune with the rhythms of nature, the life our forefathers led before we lost our way?

You can make a fresh start on Arcadia, the paradise planet. Arcadia offers you a new life, a new beginning, thanks to the pioneering labours of the EB Corporation. Leave your worries on Earth, and fly with EB to the new world of your dreams. Just sign your name – one stroke of the pen – to EB's transfer of ownership document, and all those material possessions that tie you to this tired old planet will simply melt away. In return you will receive a berth on the luxury warship Back To Nature, *plus a landholding in the heart of Arcadia's fertile and temperate countryside.*

No machines. No computers. No cities. No crowds. Nothing unnatural. Simply paradise. Arcadia.

Defries read it twice. It made no more sense the second time. She knew, intellectually, that Earth had been through some unpleasant times. The Industrial Crisis and the Dalek Plague and Invasion were taught in schools that were hundreds of light years from Earth. But she also knew that Earth had always been the wealthiest and most exclusive of the planets: she'd never earn enough in her lifetime to buy even a timeshare in a hut in Siberia.

The advertisement must have meant something to people on Earth back then, when the first warpships were leaving. It was supposed to have been a time of idealism and innovation: the breakout to the stars, primitive ships full of brave adventurers guided by pioneering astronauts. But nothing changes, Defries thought. It's always the same motivations: fear and greed. Not brave adventurers, but desperate nobodies; not pioneering astronauts, but the faceless executives of the EB Corporation.

And even if the sales pitch had been true; even if Arcadia had started as a bountiful wilderness: what's it like now?

If it's anything like the other Spinward planets we've surveyed, it's a one-product factory planet. The population live on tidy estates of pretty little corporation houses, they never think of going off-planet because it's too expensive and anyway they get six weeks a year at the corporation's luxury seaside resort. They read their news from the corporation datanet, they go shopping at the corporation store, and they think they're doing well because they can buy a brand-new airspeeder every year.

They don't talk about politics, at least not in public, because if they do the corporation can always arrange to have them transferred to a less congenial posting. Arctic weather stations are always full of dissidents on Spinward planets. And Spinward's a long way from being the worst.

Defries smiled. 'Well, well,' she said to herself. 'Still got a few of those high ideals, after all these years in External Ops.'

And this particular planet? Arcadia, the one world above all others that Spinward don't want outsiders to see? System Defence In Strength at the very least, Defries thought. If it comes to a fight, Captain Toko can probably get the *Raistrick* past the satellite defences. But we'll find every Arcadian armed to the teeth. Just hope I've got myself enough firepower.

Edward – Prince of Beaufort, Elector of Verdany,

Warden of the Northern Marches and High Alderman – settled himself at the apex of the royal dais and straightened the crown on his head. He raised his sceptre.

Francis was a hundred paces away, standing in the narrow gap between the two main doors. He was concentrating on remembering which of the narrow corridors he had seen the Lady Christina use to leave the Throne Room, and almost missed the Prince's signal. He hurried to fetch the Counsellor.

For a moment, Francis watched the black shape as it lurched and tottered towards the throne; then he dashed into a side aisle and through a small doorway.

He was in the wrong corridor. The way was dark, musty, and contained no hint of the Lady Christina's spicy cologne. Francis cursed silently. To return, and stumble into the Throne Room, would be ignominious. He would have to press on.

There was just enough illumination to see the staircase, curving upwards beyond an archway in the right-hand wall of the passage. Francis climbed it, and emerged into a small, circular chamber with dust-filled sunbeams streaming through crevices in the domed ceiling.

'Counsellor!' The voice – the Prince's voice – seemed to be coming from the floor. 'This is most unexpected – I mean, a most unexpected pleasure.'

Francis looked down at his robe, decided that a little more dirt would make no difference now, and knelt on the floor. He found himself looking through a knot-hole in a wooden trapdoor. The trapdoor was immediately above the throne. Francis could see the Prince's bald patch encircled by his crown. The Counsellor was at the foot of the marble steps, his limbs twitching under their covering of black silk.

'It is an honour to attend on your Highness,' the Counsellor said.

'Has someone . . . ?' The Prince's hand gestured vaguely. 'Has there been a bereavement of any, ah, particular note?'

'By no means, Prince. I have come with an important message from the High Counsellor at Landfall. But first

– that overgrown Apprentice Scribe who brought me to your presence . . .'

'Apprentice? Francis?' In the chamber above the Prince's head, Francis's stomach contracted with fear. 'I suppose he is still an Apprentice,' the Prince said. 'What of him?'

'The path of the Scribe is ordained,' the Counsellor said, his robe shaking agitatedly. 'It passes through Landfall. Few are blessed with a talent for letters. It must be nurtured in the correct manner.'

'Yes. Francis is highly gifted, Counsellor.'

'All the more reason.'

'Master Percy relies on him, you know.'

'Percy is a fool. Apologies, Highness. Allow me a moment's thought.'

Francis looked down at the black-robed shape. It remained motionless for several minutes. The Prince's fingers began drumming on the velvet arm-rests of the throne.

With a twitch of the limbs and a viscous clearing of the throat, the Counsellor spoke again. 'Master Percy has allowed the apprentice Francis to assist him in Master's tasks. Percy should not have permitted this. Francis can have no understanding of the rituals. It is imperative that he leaves for Landfall immediately.'

What rituals? Francis could have wept with frustration. Don't listen to him, your stupid Highness. He's bamboozling you. There are no rituals. There are just books. Yes, I read some of the ones I'm not supposed to. But I've been doing that for years. I don't want to end up like poor Percy. Don't send me to Landfall!

'I'll send him to Landfall, of course,' the Prince said. 'I'll give him the instruction myself. Now – didn't you say you had an important message?'

Francis rolled over and lay on his back, staring unseeingly at the punctured ceiling. There was no point in thinking any more, but he couldn't stop. His books, his discoveries, his little herb garden, his carefully planned flirtations, his comfortable, complicated life at court – it was all about to crumble.

A few of the words from the Throne Room below penetrated his despair. A terrible crisis was threatening the whole world, according to the Humble Counsellor. Francis listened more closely. Every Prince was, at that moment, receiving a visit and an identical message from a Counsellor.

The dull monotone emanating from the depths of the cowl could not disguise the drama of the news. There was rarely any information from off-world; most people gave other colonies not a thought. The Counsellor was talking of things that Francis had heard of only from the books he was not supposed to have read.

Throughout the colonized galaxy, the Counsellor said, humankind had been devastated. Men and Daleks had almost wiped each other out in a conflict of cataclysmic proportions, and the war was still raging. Only the policy of quarantine, as advised and maintained by the Counsellors, had prevented this world from being ravaged by one or other side. The same policy had protected the planet from contamination by the plagues that the Daleks had unleashed, and which had so affected the galaxy that all other colonies had been reduced to destitution.

All this the Counsellors at Landfall had discovered through their occasional use of communications devices (like carrier pigeons, but much faster, crossing the void between the worlds, the Counsellor explained to the Prince).

In the same way, they had found out about the impending danger: a starship, full of soldiers, on its way to the planet – and everyone on board infected with a Dalek plague.

'And if it were to – to come here,' the Prince said. 'If it alights on our world?'

'Perhaps it will be destroyed as it crosses the void, before it reaches us,' the Counsellor said. 'Perhaps it will land badly, and be burnt. Perhaps those on board will have died by the time the vessel reaches us. But all of these things are unlikely.'

'What, then? What are we to do?'

'Arm your people. Train them in the arts of war. We

will help you to do this. Then, when the starship arrives, make sure there are no survivors.'

'You don't mean . . . ?'

'They are plague carriers. Every one must die.'

There was a long silence. Francis had almost forgotten his personal fears. He knew that he should be appalled, horrified; in fact he was excited. Something was going to happen – something big, something unprecedented.

He looked through the knot-hole. The Prince was slumped on the throne. 'We have had so many centuries of peace,' he said slowly. 'And now violence has come at last to Arcadia.'

Stronty Lopecs and her field artillery team had been drinking vodka and Burn-up. They were standing on one of the few upright tables, supporting each other, and bellowing the artillery chant.

'We're going to grill the Daleks,' they bellowed, 'we'll fricassee the Daleks, we'll roast them, we'll bake them, we'll boil them in a bag.'

The same thing, over and over again.

Sitting in a corner in a pool of spilt beer, one of the troopship mechanics was bawling a tuneless rendition of *My Dalek Lover is a Sex Machine*, his voice rising to a crescendo on the filthiest words.

Everyone else was just yelling, laughing, or breaking furniture. The decibel level was dangerous. A whole troopship-load of auxiliaries were celebrating their last night before embarkation and warp. The space station's canteen wasn't big enough to hold them, but they were determined to soak up every drop of alcohol they wouldn't be able to smuggle aboard ship.

There wasn't room to lift a plastic beaker without losing half of its contents. Second Tracker Reynald Yesti was elbowing his way through the shifting jungle of bodies. He'd collected four cans of Triple-Z, and he was determined that most of the liquid should go down his throat and not down the front of his shirt. He barged towards the exit.

The corridor was scarcely less crowded. To the left,

33

a crowd had gathered to watch a fire-extinguisher duel between Bodylouse Oboke and The Fur-lined Zapper. Yesti would have put money on the Zapper, but he turned away. In the other direction the corridor was passable, because a lot of the bodies were horizontal. Yesti stepped over outstretched legs and arms. The four cans were still almost full.

He reached a man-sized piece of wall. It was clean; there was no blood or vomit on the floor here, and only a little beer. He put his back against the paintwork and slid down until the seat of his pants rested on the short-pile carpet. One by one, the four cans were arranged in a neat row between his knees. He picked up the first, and began to drink.

After a while, when the roof of his mouth felt comfortably numb and a tingling vibration had reached his extremeties, Yesti looked around. On one side of him, a wired-up named Tragg was snoring. Someone had painted a lipstick kiss on the metal plate in his forehead. Yesti turned his head. He could still do that, and the world didn't spin. He needed another Triple-Z.

On his other side, he could see over the rim of the second can, was a more attractive prospect than Tragg. This trooper was awake, female, and quite a looker. Yesti was a sucker for dolls with big brown eyes.

She noticed him. 'Have I got two heads?' she said.

Yesti considered this for a moment – a moment too long.

'So stop staring. I didn't ask for company.'

Yesti liked a challenge. 'Don't mope, kid. You didn't get to go tomorrow, right?'

She looked at her boots, ran a hand through her long dark hair. She had a wide mouth, and full lips. She was sort of pouting, and Yesti thought it suited her. He wanted to see her smile, too, and then he started to wonder what those lips would be like to kiss. He took another gulp from the can. She seemed to have forgotten him.

'You good with your mouth?' he said.

'You what?'

34

He grinned. He had a grin that could charm the ladies, he knew that. He waved the can. 'The booze talking. Ignore it. Listen, doll, we can't all get picked for this trip. Some you win, some you lose. I've seen you around, but I don't know you, do I?'

She turned to face him. Now she was holding a stun-gun in her right hand. 'You don't know me, creep, and you're not going to get the chance – unless . . .'

It was as if she had only just seen him. Her big eyes widened, and adopted a puzzled expression. Yesti smiled and winked; he had that effect on women, sometimes, when they looked him in the eye for the first time.

'Are you going, tomorrow?' she asked. Her voice was softer.

'Sure. No better Tracker than Reynald Yesti. They can't do without me.'

'A Tracker? Hey, that's something. You must be a clever guy.'

Play this very cool, Yesti told himself. No more Triple-Z. I'm going into warp tomorrow, and I want so badly to get lucky tonight. What do I do next? Think! Wow, those lips. Yeah, got it – be interested in her. 'And so what d'you do in this bunch, pretty girl like you?' he said.

It looked like she was giggling. Maybe she was on something. All the better.

'Explosives,' she said. 'I'm on – er, secondment, I suppose you'd call it, from IMC. Now in Special Weapons, attached to the First Infantry. Or I was until now.'

'You're kidding.' No, she wasn't. Don't get her angry. 'Well, that's great, doll. Because I like a big bang myself.' He winked again.

'I bet you do,' she said. 'And you're really on the ship tomorrow?'

He fumbled in his breast pocket. 'I got the papers, see? Signed by ice-queen Defries herself.'

She took the document, looked at it, handed it back, and gazed at him. 'They say it's going to be rough. This could be your last night of fun, soldier.'

'I guess so.' It didn't worry him. But she seemed pretty worked up about it. She wanted him, he could see that.

There was something in her eyes – something feral, a deep hunger. The twins he'd met in that bar on Novaport, they'd been wild. But this woman was something else again.

'This place stinks,' she said. 'Let's go to my cabin.'

It took a while to register. He took a gulp of Triple-Z. 'Now?'

'Now. Come up and see my etchings.'

She was already on her feet. He took her outstretched hand. 'What?'

'A very old joke. Come on, soldier. I need you.'

She needs me. You're a clever bastard, Yesti. You're going to get yourself one hell of a send-off tonight.

Far away – five weeks away at warp speed – Francis was feeling ridiculous. And hot. He was sheltering from the hazy sunlight in a grove of apple trees beside the road, but he was still too hot. He hated the prickly sensation of perspiration breaking out on his skin, but he couldn't risk doffing his incognito. The long robe and wide-brimmed hat were damnably uncomfortable.

He peered once again between the grey-brown trunks towards the russet walls and shimmering rooftops of Beaufort. And this time he saw, emerging from the shadow of the gatehouse, a trap pulled by two black horses. The driver shook the reins, and the trap sped towards the grove.

Francis stepped out on to the raised kerbstone and watched the trap approach. Christina, resplendent in a hooded cape of aquamarine, handled the vehicle with confident ease. She reined in the horses, and Francis leapt on to the seat beside her. She threw back her hood, kissed him, and cracked the reins. With hardly a tremor, the trap accelerated along the highway, the paving stones blurring to an unbroken grey beneath the clopping hooves.

With one hand holding his hat on his head and the other resting on Christina's knee, Francis stared without interest at the passing countryside. Fields of wheat and maize gave way to terraces of vines. They passed cottages

36

with neat gardens. They crossed a bridge; next to it a mill-wheel turned slowly. Chickens, goats and pigs foraged beneath plantations of olives and walnuts. There were a few carts on the road, laden with produce and pulled by donkeys or oxen. Farmers were walking or riding to and from their fields. The horns of huntsmen sounded in the distant parkland. Everything was as it had always been. Francis glanced up at the misty blue sky: what would a ship from another world look like? What sort of plague could it bring?

The trap slowed as the road wound up into the hills. Here the fields were smaller, partitioned by hedges and low walls of stone. Cows and sheep grazed unconcernedly. Dark woodlands concealed mysterious depths.

Christina urged the horses off the road and on to a rutted track between tall hedgerows. This was the way to the Clearwater Cataract. This was not the first time she had brought Francis to this secluded corner of her family's estate.

They trundled beneath trailing boughs and into the forest. Christina, laughing, ducked her head to avoid pendant clusters of wild cherries. The horses were walking now, and the path was becoming steep. Christina steered the trap off the track and into a clearing. The horses knew the place, stopped, and began to nibble the sun-dappled grasses and the loganberries. Christina jumped from the seat and loosely tied the reins to the loganberry bush.

Francis watched the horses' nodding heads for a while before following his blue-green mistress along the foot-path.

They stopped, as usual, in the middle of the bridge that arched over the cataract. Far below them, water was tumbling over rocks, making a continuous noise but hardly visible through the leaves and fronds that overhung the stream. Before them and behind them the gorge widened from this narrow chasm. Behind them the banks fell away and opened into the Clearwater Vale, whose waters fed the Slow Brochet that wound round the walls of Beaufort; in front of them the cliffs rose like walls, dripping with foliage, parting to reveal the glittering spout of ice-cold water falling vertically from a tree-shrouded source and landing with a roll of unending thunder in a turbulent pool of inky blackness.

They held hands and watched the water plummet. At last, she turned to him with shining eyes. He felt his heart falter. Was this sorrow, or premonition, or guilt? He didn't even know which of the two of them he felt more sorry for. He had never before experienced such disquiet at finding and taking an easy way out.

'This place is so exciting!' she whispered. 'Come on – let's go down to the bottom.'

After a scramble up and down a narrow path, they reached a greensward beside the dark pool. The roar of the waterfall filled the funnel of vegetation that yawned above them. Here, the pool was almost unnaturally calm, a black mirror sprinkled with gently bobbing lilies; only a stone's throw away, it was a maelstrom of falling, churning water, throwing up a fine mist in which miniature rainbows lived and died in seconds. Quicksilver fish leapt and dived in a complicated dance.

They stood a little apart. Francis knew she was trying to catch his eye. It was up to him to make the move now, and he couldn't. He would have to tell her. He couldn't.

'Look,' he said, 'maize. It must have seeded itself. Funny to find it down here. Are you hungry?' He tugged the head from the stalk.

'Francis,' she said, 'don't be silly. Come here.'

He peeled away the leaves. 'It's not ripe. It should be, by now. Everything's late this year, have you noticed? Even later than last year. If it carries on like this, they say there'll be only one harvest next year.'

'Since when did you take the slightest interest in raising crops?' She had moved closer, behind him. He felt her hands slide under his arms. 'The grass is quite dry. Now come here!'

She pulled, and they fell down together, laughing. She landed on top of him and sat on his stomach, pinning him down. He watched, feeling strangely indifferent, as she unlaced her cape and then the bodice of her gown.

38

He ran his hands from her shoulders to her hips, then tightened his grip to stop her moving.

'It's no good, Christina. Stop it, you incorrigible woman. I don't think I can . . .'

'Francis! And you're always such a reliable little cock sparrow.'

'I mean it, Tina. Stop that.' The thundering waters made everything seem distant. 'The Prince is sending me to Landfall.'

'Oh.' She rolled sideways and lay beside him. Her hand found his.

After a while, she said: 'Have they found out—'

'About us? I don't know.'

'My father used to go hunting with the old Prince. Edward wouldn't dare make a fuss about anything I want to do.' She moved her head on to his shoulder and started to kiss him.

Francis closed his eyes. Christina was beautiful and playful, as well as wealthy and well-connected, but for some weeks he had been trying to think of a way to loosen the seductive silken robes which she had entwined about him. At least he no longer had to worry about that.

'I don't think it's anything to do with us,' he said. 'It's just me. Percy let me help him with writing reports and writing letters. And there are books in the Master Scribe's library that I'm not supposed to see . . .'

'You and your secret books.' She nuzzled his neck and ran the back of a fingernail down his ribs. 'Sometimes I think we'd all be better off if you Scribes were as uneducated as the rest of us. There are some things you can't learn from books, you know. Like this . . .'

He sat up. 'The volumes I gave you – they're still safe? I know Percy hasn't missed them.'

'They're at the bottom of my linen chest,' she said, 'hidden underneath my finest silk unmentionables. Even Elaine won't find them there.'

He stroked her hair. 'That sister of yours is capable of anything. I don't suppose I'll ever be able to finish teaching the two of you how to read now.'

'But when you come back from Landfall . . .'

39

'If I come back. How many Apprentice Scribes are there? And how many Masters? Something must happen to the – unsuccessful candidates.'

'You'll come back. You're so clever.'

'Is Percy clever? He's always in a daze. If I come back, I'll be different.'

'You won't be my clever little cock sparrow?' At last she seemed to realize that he was saying goodbye. She stood suddenly, shrugging off her unfastened garments as if they were the inconvenient complexities of her life. Her golden skin glowed in a shaft of sunlight.

She had never looked more beautiful. Francis felt his eyes sting with incipient tears. 'Thank you for – for everything, my Lady,' he said. 'I'll remember you.'

'Don't be silly,' she said. She paced back and forth beside the pool. 'I won't let this happen. I'll talk to Edward. You'll see.'

'The Counsellors want me,' he sighed. 'There's nothing the Prince can do about it.'

She spun to face him. 'We've got to try something. Or are you expecting help from the people on those other worlds that you're always talking about? Is a Prince from another planet on his way to save you?'

'It's all in the books, Christina. The ones I gave to you. You can read them for yourself. How old are you?'

She shook her head, surprised by the question. 'I'm getting on.' She pulled a face. 'I'll be thirty soon. Not long to go, I suppose.'

'On other worlds, Christina, men and women live for a hundred years.'

'Impossible.'

'It's true. Or it used to be. It's in the books. That's one of the things that the Counsellors don't tell us. They say they're protecting us, but what are they really up to? Why do people on Arcadia die so young? What are they doing to us?'

And none of it matters anyway, he thought. The plague's coming. Or is it? 'Christina, I don't know what to do.'

'Well I do. Hand me my things. We're going back

40

home. And I'm going to have a few words with the Prince.'

Francis supervised her dressing. Normally, he delighted in adjusting the pleats and laces. This time, nothing. Nothing but fear and foreboding.

The dark-haired doll had disappeared into the wash cubicle to freshen up. Yesti could hear running water, and splashing. He liked a woman who took care about personal hygiene.

The cabin was exactly the same as all the others on the station. Just about the same as all the others on every other station and every ship, too. As much character as a plastic cup, and room for two people if they didn't mind being very intimate. Yesti didn't mind at all.

He sat on the bunk, angled his head, and pulled open the overhead locker. Empty. He reached down and tugged at the drawer units under the bunk. Nothing but trousers and shirts and vests, old but clean and carefully folded. This baby travels light, he thought. Then he saw the backpack, hanging on the back of the door.

On target. All women carry tons of junk around with them, Yesti knew that. This one just kept it all in a battered old bag. It was all in here: badges, coins and tourist tat from dozens of worlds. Some of the stuff looked ultra-weird, even to Yesti, who'd done quite some travelling. There was a small arsenal of hand-delivery bombs and grenades: timed, heat-seeking, programmable, and just plain powerful. There was a strange metal box.

He was staring at it as she emerged from the cubicle to stand next to him.

'What is this thing?' he said, and then looked up. The first thing he saw was that she wasn't wearing anything except a towel; then he noticed that she wasn't looking friendly.

'Put it back,' she said, with a smile that didn't reassure him.

'Just looking, OK? What is it, anyway? It's metal, right? But it's transparent – except you can't see through it. What the hell is it?'

41

'It's called a tesseract. It was a present. From a guy I travelled with for a while.'

Yesti felt that he was back on familiar ground. 'Sister, if that's all you got, you got yourself screwed. You could hold out for heavy credit with a body like yours.'

He made a grab for the towel. She let him take it. He watched her body as she pushed it against him and folded her arms around his neck.

'You know,' she said, ruffling the spiky hair on the back of his head, 'until now I really hadn't decided about you.'

'But you're sure now, right?' he said thickly, into her damp and sweet-smelling hair.

'Oh, I'm sure now,' she said.

He felt a sharp pain on his right shoulder. 'What's happening?' he said. His legs felt unsteady. He dropped to the bunk. Looking up was difficult. The girl was still there, in front of him.

She held her hand in front of his face. There was something in the palm. He couldn't see clearly.

'Injector pad,' she said. 'Just a local anaesthetic. But on top of a can of Triple-Z – I don't think you'll be going anywhere for a few days, Romeo.'

He tried to stand. Nothing happened. He couldn't even feel his legs.

'Bitch!' he said. He could hardly hear his own voice. She had something else in her hand now. Something shiny.

'Keep still,' she said brightly. 'Not that you've got any choice. You won't feel a thing, and I mean that most sincerely.'

It was a knife! He tried to shout, but heard himself croaking. This was worse than a nightmare. This was worse than a horrorholo.

'Don't panic, soldier. I won't damage your manhood, although God knows someone ought to. I just want your ID implant.'

She worked with the knife, close to his chest. He hoped she was only cutting through his shirt. He felt nothing, not even when she pulled her hand away and he could

42

see, between her finger and thumb, the small, pink plastic square that had been buried under layers of skin.

He could breathe. He could hear. He could open and close his eyes. He could feel his heart beating.

The woman didn't move away. She was squatting next to the bunk. She wanted him to see what she was doing. She was using the knife to remove her own ID chip, slicing through the epidermis between her breasts, slowly and carefully making tiny incisions that would free the implant without drawing blood. She took her time, glancing up at him from time to time, smiling lasciviously.

'That's it,' she said. 'And now you become me.' She pressed her ID chip against his chest, and sprayed the area with an atomizer. 'Plastigraft,' she said. 'You already look as good as new. And now I become . . .'

She took the papers from his shirt pocket. 'I become Reynald Yesti. Second Tracker – what a come-down. Never mind, eh? It's only temporary. Just until I get on board that troopship and we're into warp.' She fondled the atomizer and licked her lips as she squirted artificial skin into her cleavage. 'Well. That was wonderful, darling. How was it for you?'

He fell sideways on to the bunk. 'Who?' he managed to say.

She dropped the metallic cube into her backpack, and slung the pack over her shoulder. 'You deaf, or something? I'm you, of course. And you – for a while, anyway – are Ace, who blows things up. Now – I'm off to join the celebrations. And then I'm going to Arcadia to kill Daleks. Sleep well.'

Dear Diary,

Well, that looks ridiculous, for a start.

But it's how people used to do it: Dear Diary, *as if you were writing to a friend.*

I wish I were.

It's so slow, writing on paper like this. Out of practice. I suppose I'll get faster. Assuming I continue with it. Assuming I don't have to stop. For some reason.

This is the last will and testament of Britta Hoffmann. I

am in sound mind, but perhaps not for much longer. When I die, I hope to go to Arcadia. How convenient.

That's not funny.

Down to business. Dear Diary, I'm writing this by hand because I don't trust any of the station comms systems. And I'm writing a diary because – well, because I've no-one to talk to.

That sounds awful. It's not as bad as that. I've been here only two days, so it's hardly surprising that I'm a bit disoriented and homesick.

Everyone's very friendly, but a bit guarded. Formal. They all work hard. Very dedicated. There's not much social life. Good sports facilities – this place is so big! It's mind-boggling: a swimming pool on a space station. And tennis courts, and amazing speedball courts with everything done holographically, even opponents if you want.

And I've hardly seen any of it yet. There are loads more levels I haven't seen. Actually, I think I'm not allowed into most of them. The security system is complicated, to say the least.

And the androids are spooky. They're the best I've seen, in many ways: almost perfect speech and movement. But they don't look quite right. Each one's different, and that's unusual with any batch of androids. The robots are even weirder. Bloomveld told me that the ones on our level are the normal-looking ones! I don't like him. He's like the others, only worse. Always insinuating that there are secrets that he knows and I don't. They all do it.

I haven't met Lacuna yet. Doctor Van Holblad called me into his office for a chat, but he's in charge of just our research team. There doesn't seem to be anyone in command of the whole station, but everyone talks about Lacuna – usually in hushed tones. She must be quite something.

'Does it continue like this for very much longer, Lau-Po?'

The lines of text stopped scrolling down the wall screen, and then were replaced by Britta Hoffmann in close-up and in slow motion, her brow furrowing gradually as she lowered her pencil inexorably to the waiting paper.

'At considerable length, Madam. And the visual boxes aren't quite up to deciphering the handwriting, so I've had to spend three hours squinting at the video recordings.'

'You poor thing. Are your duties becoming too onerous, Superintendent?'

The threat was obvious. 'Not at all, Madam. I am many years from retirement.'

'Let us hope so. Now then – what about this young woman?'

'She seems harmless. A very average research scientist. Bio-chemist. She'll do her stint and leave, I reckon. Not management material.'

'I seem to remember that you entered much the same report about me, some years ago.'

Lau-Po tensed, then relaxed. She seemed genuinely amused by the recollection. 'Yes, Madam. Perhaps so. But in this case, further surveillance is unnecessary. There is always the Net.'

Britta's face covered all of one wall. She blinked. The closing and opening of her eyes took several seconds. Her lips opened, as slowly as a dawn-wakened flower. The pencil rising towards them moved as cautiously as a ship manoeuvring into dock.

'No, Lau-Po. I want this one watched. Continuous surveillance. And tag all the data with my priority code. Understood?'

'Of course, Madam,' he said. Poor little girl, he thought. Welcome to the asylum.

Part Two

FIVE DAYS TO GO

He cut.

He cut a hole.

'She has not said a word since – you know, since it happened.'

'She was in the room. It must have been a shock.'

'But not a word. She hasn't even wept.'

'She's little more than a child. She just needs some rest. Peace and quiet.'

He cut a hole.

Professor Bernice Summerfield was worried. She was going to win. And that was worrying, quite apart from everything else.

The three-dimensional display was hovering above the tapestry carpet in the centre of her room. She walked round it, several times, watching the movements of the pieces as the TARDIS executed the best-options program based on the premise that the Doctor's next move would be to bring the queen's bishop forward from three moves previously and upwards five cubes to block her rook's imminent attack.

The pieces stopped moving. As Bernice had predicted, the Doctor's move would be futile. She was going to win. Checkmate in two moves, against any defence. She'd never beaten him at four-dimensional chess, and she had never expected to. A Time Lord, she reasoned, would always have a better understanding than her of a game in which the pieces could move temporally as well as spatially.

The pieces shifted again, recreating the position after her last move. Her fingers toyed with the buttons on the hand-held keypad. What if the Doctor had something up his sleeve from more than three moves previously? Impossible: he'd use up too many energy points, he'd have nothing left for any movement on the board. So unless he's got checkmate in one . . . But the TARDIS had already run that what-if program twice. What was the Doctor going to do?

And why was he taking so long to make his move?

'Take it like a man, Doc,' Bernice called out. 'Or like a Time Lord, anyway. Are you listening? I've got you. Checkmate in two. You owe me a trip to Club Outrageous on Bacchanalia Two, that was the deal.'

There was no reply. The soothing hum of the TARDIS was the only noise. The pieces in the display remained stationary.

The trouble is, Bernice said to herself, when you don't know what's normal, you can't tell when things are going wrong. When you find yourself travelling through time and space in a craft that looks like a blue crate on the outside and seems to be infinitely large on the inside, you tend to take the bizarre for granted.

But, looking back, the bizarre had been getting quirkier for some time. Ace's decision to leave the TARDIS hadn't been taken only because she'd fallen for that wide-boy traveller on Heaven who'd died destroying the Hoothi. It hadn't even been just because she blamed the Doctor for his death. She'd said that the TARDIS was getting 'well weird'.

Weird was right. It was getting worse, and it was getting downright dangerous.

Bernice had tried for several days to persuade the Doctor to tell her where the TARDIS was going to materialize next. She was sure he needed a rest; she sure as hell needed one. His replies had varied from the noncommittal to the indignant, but had contained no information. Had he been affected by the destruction of the Seven Planets? Millions had died. He had been powerless to prevent it. His presence had almost made things much worse. She didn't like to ask him. He didn't mention it. Bernice had slipped into the control room and queried the navigational console: as she had suspected, the TARDIS was going nowhere.

The next time she had managed to track him down, the Doctor had been standing in a fountain, up to his ankles in water in one of the rooms full of gothic follies in what she thought of as the back of the third level of the TARDIS interior – although orienteering inside the TARDIS was another thing that had become increasingly difficult.

He had been staring up at the vaulted stone ceiling.

'Most people take off their shoes and socks before paddling,' she had said. 'I only mention it. Friendly advice.'

He hadn't heard her.

'And another thing,' she had said, waving her hand in front of his eyes, 'the corridors keep changing. Left turns have become right turns. And vice versa. Some of the corridors are just blocked off.'

'Benny!' the Doctor had said. 'Hello. Who are you waving at? Too late! They've already gone.'

'And so have you, Doctor. Now look, about the corridors—'

'If I were you, Romana,' the Doctor had said, conspiratorially, 'I should stay in your room for a bit. Much better, while these changes are going on. Why don't you configure the four-dimensional chess again? I'll give you another game.'

Bernice had wanted to know who on earth Romana was, but reckoned she'd get more sense out of the TARDIS data store than the Doctor. She had returned to her room, and had set up the chess program. She had expected a short game: it had never taken the Doctor more than five days to beat her.

And now, only three days later, she had won. She was very worried.

If the Doctor tells you to stay in your room, she thought, what do you do? What would Ace have done?

She picked up her shoulder bag and marched towards the door, almost breaking her nose when it failed to open automatically. She hit it. It opened.

Outside, the corridor which had always run both right
and left now ended at a wall just to the left of her door.
She turned right and strode off.

I only wanted to look at the books again. The secret books.
And yes, I did try on some of her clothes.
That was naughty.
But it wasn't my fault.
He cut.
He cut a hole.
'She's a daughter of the house of Delahaye. Why
doesn't she snap out of it.'
'Don't shout, Gerald. You'll make her worse. She's to
have complete rest while she's wearing the comfrey and
henbane poultice. Help me pull the curtains, the room
must be dark.'
Dark. It was dark.
I heard someone coming. I hid in the wardrobe. It was
dark.
She was beautiful, but she was unhappy.
He cut a hole.

Dear Diary,
Well, I went to the edge to look at the planet anyway.
And getting to the edge was quite an expedition. I expected
to come across lots of security doors that my code wouldn't
open, and there were certainly plenty of those. But then
there were all the dead-end corridors that seemed to go
nowhere. And there were staircases – I've never come
across stairs in a space station before. And the signs were
confusing, because so many of them are out of date. It was
like working my way outwards through the skins of an
onion: I'd reach a viewing gallery, only to find that it had
been turned into a hydroponics plantation, or a warehouse,
or a robot repair shop, because it wasn't on the outside
any more, because the station has been extended so many
times. It felt as though the station was being built faster
than I could find my way through it!
I'm getting used to the strange, twisting corridors and
the oddly-shaped rooms in this place. But some of the

things I found! There are passages that are too small to get into – complete with lighting, and carpets, and doors off, and everything, but too small for people or robots. And huge empty spaces, so big and dark you can't see the other side. Actually they're less frightening than the illuminated ones, when you just open a door and find nothing on the other side except the lights of galleries that must be kilo-metres away. Sometimes there are structures in these spaces, complicated metal things that curve away like the framework of a half-finished starship. Then there are corri-dors that stretch across the empty spaces, supported by rickety-looking girders. Some of them lead to blocks of rooms that are just suspended in mid-air. I didn't explore any of those.

The funny thing is, I didn't come across many robots actually building anything. In fact, I don't think there are enough robots on the station to do this much construction work. Maybe they all come out and do their welding while we're all asleep! I don't understand it, but then there are so many things I don't understand about this place.

I was exhausted, and thinking about turning back, when I finally reached the edge. I walked into yet another tiny hallway – this one was decorated with green and red liquid-lights that seemed to spell out meaningless words (typical decor in this place!) – and then I walked down some steps and suddenly I was in a kind of tear-shaped pod on the outside of the station. And set into the skin of the pod, in a sort of abstract pattern, were strips of vitreous, so I could see out. And there was the planet!

Arcadia is so big and beautiful. We must be in a very low orbit. The planet covers almost half of the sky. It looks like pictures of Earth. The oceans are blue, the land is green and brown, the clouds are white and fluffy and look close enough to touch. We're so low that you can see rivers and forests and lakes and the snow on the mountains. I just stood there looking at it for hours.

Appearances can be so deceptive. It's ironic, really, that such a lovely-looking planet with such a lovely name can't support human life. I wonder what happened to the colon-

ists who came here all those years ago. I suppose the Corporation resettled them somewhere else.

All the same, Arcadia is a perfect research site. I looked for Landfall, the manned surface station, but I couldn't find it. Like looking for a needle in a haystack, trying to find one small speck of humanity in that amount of uninhabited wilderness.

It took me ages to find my way back to the biochemistry department. I skipped dinner and came back here to write this.

What else can I say? The research is going well. The others are more friendly now. The computers are quite simply amazing – the most powerful I've ever worked with. I sometimes feel that I'm helping them, not the other way round. We get a steady supply of samples from the ground station at Landfall, so we can analyze the changes in the plant life on a day to day basis. It's becoming clear that the effect of stopping fertilization is accelerating. I feel so privileged to be part of a long-term trial like this. Imported plants, and the whole changed ecology of Arcadia, have been nurtured for hundreds of years. I don't know of any other Corporation that would set up such extended experiments. This will be the first measurement of the effect of ceasing to support an imported ecology.

And the results seem to be clear: partial terraforming isn't stable. No fertilizers have been added to rainwater for four Arcadian months, and already some of the fastest-reproducing imported species are showing genetic deterioration. Even the indigenous species are producing lower yields of seeds.

Of course, it doesn't help that other teams are working on other experiments at the same time. It's sheer madness, actually. Some of them interfere with our data – in particular the project that's designed to assess the effects of a reduction in the amount of sunlight. Or I assume that's what it's for. That's one of the most secretive of the research teams. I don't even know who's in charge of it. Maybe it's this chap Pool I've heard people talking about.

Later.

Well, talking of people in charge, Doctor Van Holblad

called me into his office today – just a few minutes ago, in fact. It was a strange interview. He didn't want to get to the point. He started off by telling me that his term in post was coming to an end soon, as if that wasn't common knowledge. For want of something to say, I asked him if he would be pleased to leave.

'Perhaps I'll find a way to stay,' he said, mysteriously.

'Would that be allowed?' I said.

'I expect it can be arranged,' he said, and then he started saying very odd things. 'It will involve some small sacrifices, no doubt. But it will all be worthwhile. To become one with the ocean, to become that within which the fishes swim and breed, to become the material from which the coral build their intricate and towering reefs. I have been granted a glimpse of that existence, young woman. Who wouldn't choose it, when the alternative is inevitable decline into unending darkness?'

I said I didn't understand what he was talking about.

'You will,' he said. 'You will. I have been asked to send you to Lacuna. This is an honour for you, I must say. You will go to her quarters this evening. And don't be afraid.'

Why did he have to say that? I'm getting nervous already, and I don't know why.

Everything was going just fine. It wasn't impossible to intercept a ship in warp space, but nothing had disturbed the progress of the *Admiral Raistrick*. It was very nearly too late to stop them now.

Defries had spent much of the last few weeks asleep, letting the ship's medics prepare her for whatever she might have to be prepared for. She'd had a detox programme; she'd had a dietary supplement implant; she'd had three different kinds of nanosurgical virus. She felt about the same as she had before.

Today, she had decided to start wearing combat gear instead of dress uniform: every little gesture helped to nudge the troops from warp boredom into battle readiness. In any case, black suited her. She pulled the webbing more tightly around her waist and smoothed the pleats of her non-reflective blast vest. The smell of the chemical treatments that permeated combat clothes always excited her. She smiled at herself, almost shyly, in the long mirror. You're dressed to kill, Isabelle Defries.

Natural adrenalin. There's nothing quite like it. She flexed her hand and her blaster jumped to meet it. Reluctantly, she reholstered the gun. A few more days to go, she told herself. A few more days of killing nothing but time.

She called for a visual display of discipline violations and strode to her desk. Only two fights in the last twelve hours: the auxies weren't getting too restless just yet. That still left the problem of the stowaway. Defries had been prevaricating about this one, she admitted it. The more data she gathered, the less sure she felt about the case. Returning the culprit to Commander Celescu's jurisdiction was out of the question; that left only imprisonment for the duration of the mission, which would tie up human and systems resources, or ejection in a life-pod, which would be a waste of a trooper.

There was a knock on the door. Such old-fashioned courtesy. How were you supposed to respond?

'Come in, please,' Defries ventured.

The door slid open and the stowaway walked in. She too was wearing combat blacks and had been, Defries knew, throughout the flight. She was grinning, as if pleased with herself. The door closed behind her. She was stationary but not motionless: she was poised on the balls of her feet, she tossed her head to throw back her long dark hair, her eyes scanned Defries's office – and then came to rest on Defries. The two women studied each other.

She's not perfect, Defries thought. Never had cosmetic nanosurgery, let alone genetic beautifiers. So she's sort of lopsided. But she looks fit. She looks good. She looks tough. And black suits her. No side gun. I suspect that makes her no less dangerous. This situation could become difficult. So much for old-fashioned door-opening protocol.

The stowaway stepped forward and thrust out a hand. 'Hi,' she said. 'I'm Ace.'

Defries had suppressed the urged to step back. 'I'm Agent Defries, trooper,' she said, ignoring the hand. 'You'll salute when you see me, keep zipped unless you're spoken to, and address me as Ma'am. You're in big trouble.'

Unbelievably, the stowaway laughed; the amusement was so genuine that Defries found herself almost smiling.

'If you only knew, Agent Defries, how many times I've been told I'm in big trouble. What is it this time? Summary execution? Vivisection by cannibals? The death of a thousand military tribunals?'

The stowaway had an attitude that was as unusual as her name and her accent. Defries was intrigued. 'The other auxies have spent the last month in deep-sleep, or using up the booze and other substances I let them smuggle on board. You've been working out every day, you've been using the ship's datanet, and most of the time you've been on the bridge getting friendly with Captain Toko and his crew.'

'I like the stars.'

'We're in warp space, trooper.'

'But I know they're there. I like to know we've moving.'

Defries realized that at some time during this brief meeting she had taken the decision not to invoke military discipline. 'What's that – that big stick?' she said.

In a fluid overarm movement, Ace pulled the weapon from the pack at her shoulder and brought it down in an arc of blue sparks. This time Defries did step back. The metal club hovered, crackling ominously, a centimetre above the desk.

'Now that's how to tell someone they're in big trouble,' Ace said, and laughed again. 'Good, isn't it? Back where I come from, folks call this a baseball bat. This one's got added extra super pizzazz.' The bat arced upwards and was replaced in the pack with less ease than it had been drawn out.

'And where, exactly, is back home?' Having decided

57

to keep this auxiliary in the mission squad, Defries applied herself to the matter of deploying her new resource.

'Here and there,' Ace said. 'I was in Special Weapons.'

'I'm not surprised,' Defries said. She wasn't unimpressed, either. 'If we're lucky, we won't need you, of course.'

'But you'll feel better knowing I'm around,' Ace said.

'Right.' The interview seemed to have ended. Defries needed time to think before allocating her new explosives expert to a squad.

Ace made no move to leave. 'There's a lot of talk,' she said.

'There always is.'

'About your Special Weapon. The big secret. In the weapons hold.'

'Not there. In the medical suite. Don't even think of peeking. It's secret. And it's guarded.'

'Doesn't worry me, Agent Defries.' Defries didn't know whether this remark reassured her or worried her. 'See you on the bridge when we come out of warp.' Now Ace was backing towards the door.

'I'll be there,' Defries said, and raised her voice slightly. 'But you'll be in your quarters, trooper.'

'Got an invitation from the Captain, haven't I? And I wouldn't miss it for anything.' The door slid closed, and Ace had gone.

I couldn't move.

If I could have moved . . .

She was unhappy. I think she'd been crying.

I should have said something. But I couldn't move.

I was frightened, in the dark.

Frightened to come out, too. She was angry and unhappy. My big sister.

I should have said something. But I was frightened.

She lay on the bed. She hit the pillows, hard. She was definitely crying.

Then she slept.

She looked so beautiful.

My big sister.

Don't wake up, Christina.

Don't wake up, and I'll tiptoe away.

Don't wake up, there's someone coming.

Don't wake up, something's happening.

Don't wake up, oh no, don't wake up, please, don't wake up, don't wake up, don't wake up, don't wake up, don't wake up.

'Great heavens, Clarissa, how long has she been like this? Like a demented rocking horse. Has she gone stark mad?'

'I think it might be a good sign, Gerald. Perhaps the result of the hot and cold compresses. At least she's moving. A sign of life.'

'Too much life, I'd say. She's said nothing, I suppose? No, of course not. She's too far gone. As if I didn't have enough to worry about.'

'The archery practice?'

'Waste of time. Three fellows with a good eye – the ones who hunt, of course. The rest couldn't hit the castle if they were standing in it.'

'Did Edward come?'

'Edward? Yes, he was there. Encouraging his subjects. About as much use as a gelding at stud. Seems to think we'll have no trouble finishing off these mysterious plague carriers of his. I think he's off his head.'

'Francis was here again. He's a bit calmer now, poor boy.'

'He should have been training with us. He's always been a shirker. Don't know what Christina saw in him.'

'He's going to Landfall. He seemed very scared. It was as if he thought – well, you know, that it had something to do with him. As if he was in danger.'

'Fanciful nonsense.'

'But what if – what if it wasn't accidental, Gerald?'

'Don't be ridiculous. She'd had her time, that's all. She wasn't young.'

Don't wake up, Christina. There's something round the bed. Something like a golden cloud. All around.

She woke up. She was shouting. Then she started screaming. I could see her. But there was no sound.

Only the footsteps coming.

He found a mirror in one of the rooms. He studied his reflection.

He saw a short, slight figure, of indeterminate age. He thought he probably looked a little comical, with those tartan trousers, the paisley patterned scarf and tie, the battered straw hat and the dusty jacket. The eyes that stared back at him were brooding, troubled. And not surprisingly, he thought. Who was he? The question mark motif, endlessly repeated across his pullover and reiterated in the handle of his umbrella, seemed peculiarly appropriate.

He sighed, and shook his head. He essayed a jaunty flourish with the brolly. The mirror reflected the half-hearted gesture. He left the room.

Another corridor. He wandered along it. If only the structure of the place would give him a clue. Not all the corridors were of the same design, but most of them were similar: plain colours, often a muted white, set with circular recesses or protruberances. He felt that the place should be familiar. But it wasn't. No signposts, of course, no labels on the doors.

He had taken to looking into every room he passed. It was as if he were searching for something, but he couldn't imagine what it might be. Sometimes he would find cupboards, sometimes domestic accommodation, occasionally a vast panorama of countryside. He was puzzled that none of it surprised him. But none of it seemed familiar. Nothing seemed significant.

Most of the corridors were long and straight. Some were short, a few were curved. Some were dead ends, most ended at junctions.

He was standing at a crossroads when the vision came again. If he was suffering from amnesia, this was his only memory. A young man, clean shaven, clearly ill, was barely conscious in a bath chair. A young woman – short, with elfin features, chestnut curls and soft brown clothes – was struggling to push the chair along a corridor very like these; another woman, taller, a little older, dressed in some sort of uniform, was a few steps further on, looking back and frowning.

The image seemed important, but he had no idea why.

He turned left. Another corridor, more doors. The man in the bath chair remained in his mind's eye. He felt something like a sense of purpose as he strode to the nearest door.

But if I find what I'm looking for, whatever it is, he thought, how will I know I've found it?

Brave heart, he told himself as the door opened.

The android walked surprisingly quickly. It seemed to have something wrong with its legs, and it shuffled awkwardly, tilted forward as if it might fall over at any moment. Britta couldn't see the structure of its lower limbs: the androids that worked in the interior sections of the station wore long, loose garments that covered them from neck to feet. In any case, she had to concentrate on keeping up with it. She was trekking through sections to which her security code allowed no access, but she scarcely had time to glance at the strange embellishments of the passages and rooms through which she passed.

She hurried round yet another shadowy corner and found herself at one end of a long, straight, dimly-lit corridor. She couldn't see the far end. The android had disappeared. She hesitated, waiting for instructions or the return of her guide. Silence. The corridor seemed to be watching her. She set off along it and, although there were no doors or side passages, the feeling grew that she was being observed. When at last she discerned the end of the corridor, she almost ran towards the sliding door that blocked her path.

She pressed the door sensor, and recoiled suddenly: the sensor pad was soft and warm. And it was a face, she realized as her eyes adjusted to the gloom: soft plastic moulded into the shape of a small, human face. The door remained closed.

Her heart was beating fast. She told herself that it was because of the long march through the station. She told herself that no-one could blame her if she turned back and tried to retrace her steps to the research station.

The door moved. It split. It peeled open from the centre like a ripe fruit, like membranes of flesh. Beyond the doorway lay a deep darkness. And somewhere in it, Britta knew, Lacuna was waiting for her.

You'll see. That was all that anyone would say in answer to her questions about the station's controller. She suspected that most of her colleagues knew as little as she did. Lacuna – was it even a name? Or was it a title? Could Lacuna be an android, or an artificial intelligence? Britta knew only that she was about to find out. She stepped forward.

Britta had never been to Earth, and so she had never seen or been inside a real cathedral, a place of worship built in the pre-industrial, superstitious interlude between the stone age and the stars. But she had seen pictures, as she had experienced travel holoshows. This was what it must have felt like: the chill, the convoluted columns and confusing aisles and galleries, the deep shadows in every corner that obscured height, depth, distance. The sense of entering a sacred place. The heavy silence.

It didn't occur to her to wonder at finding structures made of stone at the heart of a space station. Her concerns were only to avoid the areas of inky shadow and to reach the central source of the pale light that gleamed through inaccessible clerestory windows and was filtered through massive carved screens. When she noticed the stonework it was only to retreat from a leering caryatid or to peer through a sculpted aperture.

She was trembling. She was cold, but her hands were clammy with sweat. This was fear of a sort that she had not experienced in her remembered lifetime. This was eons-old fear. Waiting for the results of her diploma examinations; daring to ask Dimitri for that first dance; her first warp trip – these were fears of a different, lesser order. Tiptoeing through the nighted architecture of Lacuna's lair induced follicle-lifting, heart-racing terror: the fear of the dark, of the unknown, of the unseen, of the hungry predator; the fear that resides in the hypothalamus and is an inheritance from ancestors who swam in pre-Cambrian oceans.

And then she entered a circular chamber, and found the source of the light. The fear changed, but did not diminish. Lacuna was waiting.

Lacuna looked almost normal. That made it worse, somehow. Lacuna was a slim, tall woman, dressed in voile robes – but her head was hairless, huge and bulbously bivalved, the cranium shining like the wing-cases of a beetle. Inserted in the cleft was a metal implant. And worst of all, she was smiling: a vulpine rictus. Her eyes stared unwaveringly at Britta.

'I can feel your fear.'

The taut, grinning lips had not moved. It took several seconds for Britta to realize she had heard no sound. The voice had been in her mind.

'I have strengthened the Net,' the soundless voice said. 'I cast it ever more widely each day. Does my appearance alarm you?'

Britta put her hand to her head, as if to touch the intruder. She managed to nod.

'I no longer need the physical apparatus of the link.' One of the woman's slender arms snaked upward. Her hand caressed the metal cylinder lodged in her cloven scalp. 'I wear it as a sign, a badge. I am Lacuna.'

'Link?' The fear was thawing. Britta found herself able to think, and to speak. 'Link with what?'

'I will tell you as much as you will understand,' Lacuna said, the voice in Britta's head now echoed by whispered syllables from the scarcely-moving mouth, 'later. Now we must attend to this.'

Britta felt the voice leave her mind. Lacuna's eyes closed. The walls of the circular chamber glowed, and suddenly the surface was covered with words.

The handwriting writhed as it flowed across the wall, and Britta didn't recognize it immediately. She turned, trying to catch a tail, a beginning or end somewhere in the script-filled cylinder.

Well, I went to the edge to look at the planet anyway.

The writing was hers. Her diary.

'This must stop,' Lacuna said. 'The physical record has already been destroyed. The Corporation has an archive in which employees can store data. The maintenance of private recordings is not permitted.'

The words whirled faster and faster. They curled inwards, a spinning vortex with Britta at its centre. She was surrounded by her diary, it formed a shrinking cylinder that enclosed her like a rotating prison. The words overlapped and intertwined, trapping her inside a lattice that solidified as it shrank.

Britta could see nothing through the spinning wall of words. She was standing inside a tube. The turbulent air caught her hair and her clothes. She pulled in her shoulders, but still the cylinder contracted. It would crush her. It brushed against her arms, turning her, tearing the cloth of her jacket. Her legs twisted. Her legs were lifted from the floor. She began to spin. She screamed.

The tube disappeared. Britta fell on her hands and knees.

'A warning,' Lacuna's voice again, in Britta's mind and in the chamber. 'You have been chosen to help our work. The rewards are great. Beyond your comprehension. Disobedience will not be tolerated.'

Britta looked up. Lacuna was staring at her, eyes bright with excitement, a smile of genuine pleasure on her face. Under the circumstances, Britta found the sight reassuring. 'How,' she said, pulling herself to her feet, 'how did you do that?'

'You misunderstand, my dear. The power is not mine. I am merely a maidservant. I am Lacuna. A sensory organ of the Corporation.'

Something about the tone of Lacuna's voice, or a slight inclination of the misshapen head, gave Britta the clue.

'The Corporation,' she said. 'The Spinward Corporation is – here? On Arcadia station?'

'Well, well. Not just beauty, but also a brain. You have much to contribute.'

The idea of resistance died as quickly as resentment had flared, but Britta could think of no strategy other than defiance. 'What makes you think I'll even want to contribute?' she said, with more confidence than she felt. 'And who is Pool?'

'You are under contract,' Lacuna replied. 'You have no choice. And your consent is not required. You have experienced a demonstration of the Corporation's might. You are not ready to meet Pool. Few ever do. But let me show you something.' Lids dropped over the intense eyes.

Something was inside Britta's mind again. And then Britta was inside somewhere else, a place that she somehow knew was vaster than she could imagine. She was disembodied, an incorporeal observer in the darkness.

And yet it wasn't exactly dark. And it wasn't an empty vastness. Gentle light was everywhere, revealing the outlines of shapes. It was like being underwater and able to discern the submarine rock formations. But there was no sense of up or down; just a viscous medium crowded in every direction with more solid shapes.

Britta knew, without knowing how she knew, that she could see only a tiny part of whatever she was in. She moved effortlessly through streams of colour, moving between structures that varied in size from a cube no larger than a fist to a rippled, curving cliff-face whose edges were beyond sight. Some of the shapes were regular, others were nebulous. Many were translucent, some were black, a few were bright with colours. And the shapes were moving, too, meeting each other and parting again, but also changing their formations. She saw a polyhedron become a sphere, and then an ovoid, as she passed it.

Bright streaks of light, like comets, flashed playfully between the shapes and, Britta saw, moved equally freely inside the translucent bodies. They left glittering silver trails in their wakes as they darted back and forth. In some places there were no streaks of light at all, in others there were lone sparks, while round and between some of the shapes the swooping and zooming fireflies were as thick as bees swarming round a hive.

Britta sensed something else. She caught sight of a movement, a darker presence at the edge of her vision.

She turned, but it had gone. For the first time since finding herself in this strange environment, she felt the touch of fear.

And she was back in the circular chamber, under Lacuna's unwavering gaze.

'Where was I?' Britta said.

'You were inside an analogy,' Lacuna said. 'A model. A paradigm. It is as close as you – or I – can come to experiencing the reality. Was it not magnificent?'

'Yes. Yes, it really was. But what was it?'

'You haven't understood, have you?'

'Oh. I think I see. That was – that's the Spinward Corporation, isn't it?'

He cut a hole.

I couldn't move. I was so scared. I wanted to shout, but my mouth felt blocked up.

I wet myself.

She was screaming, but there was no noise. She was in a golden cloud, it was killing her.

She was twisting like a tree in a storm. I saw a goldfish die once, flapping from side to side. She was like that, on her bed, inside a golden cloud.

He was getting nearer. You can always tell. Those footsteps.

He cut a hole.

'She's improving, Gerald. Surely you can see that? She's making sounds again.'

'You call that an improvement? I said the leeches were a waste of time. Old wives' tales. Look at her. Gibbering like a monkey.'

'The chirurgeon says the shock could have brought on pressure in the brain. He says we should consider drastic action, whatever that means.'

He cut a hole.

Ace lay nonchalantly on the couch, trying not to look as though she was craning her neck and squinting through nearly closed eyes.

Only one door was marked *No Admittance – Medical Personnel Only*. That had to be the one.

One of the other doors opened and the ship's doctor walked into the diagnostic bay. He was youthful-looking, but Ace knew that was no indicator of age. He was plump and smooth-skinned, with watery eyes and a vacant smile. Ace knew that vacuity of expression could conceal acuity of mind: it was one of her own favourite techniques.

The doctor started to remove the detector pads from Ace's head, neck and arms.

'Don't tell me, doc. Let me guess. There's nothing wrong, right? I'm as clean as a Tarian asteroid.'

'On the contrary, trooper. You're suffering from a viral infection.'

'What?' Ace was seriously alarmed. 'But that's not supposed to be possible. That shot you gave me before we jumped—'

'No trace of it. Quite remarkable. But then, your virus is unusually pervasive. Every cell in your body is infected, according to my machines.'

'Oh.' Ace thought about illness for a while. Something didn't add up. When in doubt, muck about, that was Ace's motto. 'So – how long have I got, doc? And should I leave my body to science?'

The doctor's smile widened. 'I didn't say you were ill. Your virus appears to be benign. Have you noticed any unusual symptoms lately?'

Ace sat up on the couch and combed her hair with her fingers while she pondered. That was something she was doing more and more these days: thinking before opening her mouth. Had she been feeling sick? No – not at all. Not so much as a head cold or a hangover. Not for years. Not since before she left—

'Doctor,' she said softly, 'what have you done to me?'

'Done? What do you mean? These were diagnostic tests.'

Ace burst out laughing. 'Not you, doctor. A different Doctor.' She could hardly speak for laughing. 'He made sure I got my jabs before I went travelling in foreign parts, didn't he?'

'Jabs? What are you talking about?'

Ace swept back her hair and gave him one of her most devastating smiles. 'Like you said, it's a benign virus. It looks after me. Keeps my cells on the straight and narrow, I suppose.'

'But non-specific.' The doctor's voice was pensive, but his eyes were now anything but vague. 'So it can't work by recognizing specific pathogens. It's an inversion of a benign virus. It must recognize every aspect – every possible aspect – of a healthy cell. It can't be done, of course. Where did you say this doctor of yours practises?'

'He travels. Very hard to track him down. Perhaps you'd better make sure you've made a private file copy of the test results.'

The doctor turned to go, and then swung back with a knowing smile. 'You wouldn't be trying to get me out of the way, would you? It's just that you're the fifteenth trooper I've had in here for a routine and completely unnecessary check-up. And every one of the previous fourteen has tried to get through the medical security door over there.'

Wide-eyed, Ace shook her head. The doctor wasn't fooled for a moment.

'So, to save my time and your military conduct record: Defries's weapon is in there, in a cryo pod. But the door is locked. And an alarm sounds if anyone attempts to enter without the correct security code.'

'And I'll bet you know the code, don't you?' Ace jumped from the couch.

The doctor backed away. 'Yes,' he said. 'Yes, I do, But I won't help you. There are guards just outside. I only have to shout.'

Ace held up her open hands and blew him a kiss. She continued to advance. The doctor retreated until he was backed against a tissue regrowth cabinet. Ace leant forward and placed her hands flat against the cabinet, one on each side of the doctor's head.

'Would you like a little bit of me?' she said. 'In return for that code.'

'Are you suggesting – oh, I see.' His mouth resumed

its accustomed smile. He giggled. 'Oh yes, trooper. I'd like nothing more than a little bit of you. A small blood sample would be most satisfactory. You and I are going to make medical history.'

But Ace had already realized the flaw in her plan. Don't leave anything behind, that's what the Doctor had always told her. Particularly anachronisms. And particularly advanced technology in less than advanced civilizations. And here she was, about to leave some Gallifreyan super-bug in the hands of a doctor who probably knew just about enough to realize what he was dealing with. And to spread it all over Earth-colonized space in the twenty-fifth century. It was just a drop of blood, but Ace couldn't imagine that de-inventing the wheel would mess up the course of history in a more fundamental sort of fashion.

'Don't be so eager, doctor,' she said. 'You and I have different priorities. The door open, and you make yourself busy elsewhere, now. Blood sample when this mission's over.'

'I wouldn't wish to spoil your war, trooper, but you must admit there's a chance you won't survive to complete the deal.'

'That's true. Then again, I'm not easy to kill. And your blood storage units aren't invulnerable, either, if the ship takes a hit. I reckon my blood's safest in me, until this thing is all over.'

The doctor raised a pudgy hand and touched Ace's cheek. It was a strange gesture, as if he needed to be sure that she was real. 'You'll let me take a sample, if we both get through this?'

Ace nodded gravely.

'Then we have a deal,' the doctor said.

Ace crossed the first two fingers of her right hand and presented the hand as if in a salute.

'And what does that mean?' the doctor said.

Ace grinned. 'It means we have a deal.'

'Corridors are supposed to go somewhere!

Bernice stood with her hands on her hips, as if daring anyone to refute her assertion.

'You're supposed to be long in relation to your width. You're supposed to have a plethora of doors and other corridors leading off you. I look to you for choices, for opportunities, for the possibility of randomness in an otherwise linear existence.'

She strode from one end of the short passage to the other, passing the only door in it. She glared at the blank, white expanse that sealed off the corridor.

'And it's all your fault!' There was a hint of hysteria in her voice now. 'I was here only five minutes ago. You weren't. This was a corridor that went somewhere once. Just five minutes ago. And now. It doesn't. And it's all. Your. Fault.' She struck the unyielding surface with her fists, again and again, until she started sobbing.

The TARDIS was closing in on her. Soon there would be no corridors, no rooms: just endless little, sealed compartments. And one of them would contain her.

She turned and faced the stump of passageway.

'Bernice Summerfield,' she said, loudly and distinctly, 'you will achieve nothing by shouting at a wall. As long as there is still a door, there is hope. Run!'

She ran. The door opened, and she fell through it. It didn't close behind her. She looked back. The door had disappeared. Where there had been a door, there was now a blank wall. She ran.

Round a corner. Another dead end. But another door. Even as it started to open, she saw the gap beginning to mist over. She jumped into the space, feeling the molecules tingle and sizzle as they accumulated.

The doorway became a solid wall. But she had pushed through and fallen on the other side. She looked up. She was in the control room.

Gasping sobs of breath caught in her throat. She'd made it. She'd reached a safe place. A familiar place. She dragged herself to her hands and knees. She couldn't tell whether she was laughing or crying.

Both equally useless, she said to herself. And inappropriate. Nothing was amiss in the control room. It exuded its usual smug air of calm normality. The time rotor rose and fell in a slow rhythm. Around it, the six banks of instruments and lights flickered intermittently. None of the red warning lights was flashing. The only sound was the usual pervasive humming. The TARDIS was in flight, somewhere between here and there, somewhere between time was and time to be.

The big double doors were closed, but they were still doors. But there was no longer a door leading to the interior of the TARDIS.

Bernice almost succumbed to the temptation to curl up and sleep on the warm, gently vibrating floor. Instead she forced herself to stand, and to walk steadily to the hexagonal console.

The destination indicator was still blank. The TARDIS was still going nowhere, hovering in the Vortex. She could enter some figures – any figures – and materialize the ship's physical shell somewhere and at some time in the real universe. Then she could open the big doors, and escape. The TARDIS had been going wrong since before she had started travelling in it; now it was obviously beyond repair. The Doctor must have become trapped, as she almost had been, between the proliferating partitions in his collapsing time machine. It was up to her to do something.

She dismissed the idea. The TARDIS's battered blue box might materialize anywhere: on an airless asteroid, a poisonous gas giant, a planet falling into its sun. She might find herself stepping out of the frying pan and literally into the fire. And she couldn't abandon the Doctor. If he was still alive.

The control room was not a room for relaxing in. It contained only one chair, and Bernice had remarked to the Doctor on several occasions that it was only marginally more comfortable than a bar stool. Now, however, as Bernice fell into it, the chair seemed blissfully soft and accommodating. She could do nothing but wait, anyway.

She fell asleep.

Lacuna was waiting. Watching her, silently waiting. Britta

turned her head, averting her gaze, but couldn't help looking up to make sure that the tall woman's hungry eyes were still on her.

It was a long time since Dimitri had looked at her like that. It was a long time since she had seen Dimitri. He might be dead by now.

She was surprised at the thoughts that were crowding into her mind. She remembered the bitter and unexpected disappointment of the meeting with her father. He had survived the plague after the attack on Yalmur. One of only a handful. Hundreds of thousands had died. She had never seen him before, and had never sought him since. She remembered the sense of relief when the awkward interview ended, the clumsy hug, his bewildered eyes, the lightness of her step as she returned to her dormitory in the Corporation's Institute of Sciences.

Her diploma. The blushing, stammering, groping boys whom she had disdained. The handsome Captain in the Security Corps whom she had courted and won. His posting to Spacefleet. Her posting to Arcadia station. Regret, but again that feeling of relief.

In his first holo from the war, Dimitri had described the lives of the new settlers arriving on a planet liberated from the Daleks. She remembered the sudden stab of panic: did he want to go there, with her, after the war? He hadn't even mentioned the idea. But how could she go with him, if he wanted to do that? She served the Spinward Corporation. The Corporation gave her knowledge, provided the means to further her career.

And now she was looking up at the biggest step. Spinward wanted her. She was being offered the key to mysteries whose existence she had not suspected. She glanced again at Lacuna. Lacuna wanted her.

There had been something biochemical about the underwater-like scene that Lacuna had inserted into her mind. Is that what had stimulated her curiosity? A straightforward appeal to her scientific training? Or had these thoughts of gratitude towards a benevolent Corporation been planted in her? But if she could imagine

72

that possibility, surely there could have been no interference?

She needed to know more.

She was aware that terror had subsided to mere trepi-
dation. It's like learning to swim, she thought: once
you've survived immersion, your fear is balanced by a
sense of achievement.

She knew, also, that the reprieve was temporary. She
expected to be scared witless again. But now, in this silent
interlude, under Lacuna's gaze, she was able to think
clearly. There was no way out. It was sink or swim.

She wanted to know more.

'Lacuna.'

'Yes, my child?'

How could such a cold voice contain such warm concern? Britta trembled, sensing the same thrill she experienced whenever her screens started flashing up the results
of a successful experiment.

'Belmos – all those colonists, the system station as big
as a planet – isn't that the Corporation's main base?'

'Administration. Trading. Finance. Personnel. Of
course. All on Belmos. Other corporations exist only to
fulfil those functions. The Spinward Corporation has a
higher purpose. That purpose is here. Pool is here.'

'But Arcadia is so isolated. There's nothing here. And
it's so distant from the other Spinward worlds.'

'Is it? Think again, child. Can it not be seen as the
central point of the hemisphere of the Spinward systems?
Or perhaps we should think of the Spinward systems as
a shield, behind which Arcadia and this station shelter
from the intrusive attentions of Earth, and other corporations.'

'But why, Lacuna? What's so special about this station?
Is it something to do with Arcadia itself?'

Lacuna closed her eyes. Britta felt a sudden pang of
panic. Something was going to happen.

'Come here, my child. They are growing bored with
your questions. They wish to see you now.'

The words were innocuous, but somehow menacing. I
could turn now, and run away, Britta thought. But she

walked slowly across the circular chamber. Lacuna was waiting with outstretched arms.

'They have sacrificed much in the pursuit of knowledge,' Lacuna said, almost chanting the phrases. 'They have lost in order to gain. They are unlocking the doors of creation itself, but they have no eyes, no ears, no mouths, no fingertips. I serve them. I am content to be their sensory organs. Through me they experience the beautiful, the delicious, the sublime. Kneel before me!' Lacuna's eyes blazed icily down into Britta's. 'Now I will show them beauty.'

Britta knelt. She tried to look up, but her eyes filled with tears. Lacuna's long fingers gripped her chin. The great bulbous head descended towards her. She flinched.

'Keep still, child,' Lacuna said sharply, and continued in her declamatory tone. 'You see her eyes, blue and so bright, so brilliant with tears? Feel the softness of this cheek, the wetness of her weeping, the heat of her burning shame. Is she not beautiful? The most beautiful I have brought to you?'

This was worse than making a holo, worse than performing in one of the Institute's stupid end of term plays. Lacuna's eyes were penetrating her, peeling her open for the pleasure of an unseen, unknown audience. Britta pulled back, but Lacuna's fingers were in her hair.

'Strands of spun gold! Feel it twining in my hands like rope made of sun's rays. See how the slightest little tug brings forth another liquid jewel from her eye.'

Lacuna chuckled. The sound was so unexpected that for a moment Britta forgot her shame. 'They like you, my child. Theirs is a universe of abstractions. You and I will show them the world of the senses. Smile a little.'

Britta managed to lift the corners of her mouth.

'So pretty,' Lacuna said, and clenched another handful of golden hair. Britta gasped with pain.

'Prettier. They see you as I see you, my child. I will show them everything about you. And as I enjoy you, so will they. There are dangerous currents affecting them. There have been delays. They need to see beautiful things. They need to touch beauty. You will be with me at every moment, my child. You will be at my side at all times, ready to serve the Corporation.' Lacuna shivered. 'That expression – your face – that was the most delicious yet. You have much to give.'

What kind of weapon has to be kept in a cryo capsule? Something alive. And something too dangerous to unfreeze on board ship.

Ace shivered. The cryogenics store was maintained at a lower temperature than the rest of the medical suite, but Ace didn't kid herself. These were Iceworld-sized goosebumps, and the store wasn't that cold. She was shivering because she was spooked.

The medic who wanted to sample her virally-protected body had locked the door behind her. 'The alarm kicks in if the door's left unlocked for more than five minutes,' he had said. 'And I have to stay out here in case the guards look into the surgery. Don't worry, I'll let you out in ten.'

Ten minutes is about as much as I could take, Ace thought, and about as much as I'll need. The room was dimly lit and partitioned with metal racking, but Ace could see it was almost empty.

There was one capsule on each section of racking. The larger capsules, including two coffin-shaped body pods, were at the back of the store. The smaller boxes on the nearer shelves looked more promising. Ace didn't know what she was looking for, but she was expecting to find something like a new strain of smart bacteria, or maybe one of the sentient blasters that were supposed to have been outlawed centuries ago.

The capsules were Spacefleet standards. Ace grinned: hacking the built-in monitor system of a cryo capsule had been the first thing she'd done on her first Spacefleet combat trip. Then, of course, she'd been supplementing her rations by defrosting some of the ship's cryogenically preserved foodstuffs. But the principle was the same.

She tapped a sequence of numbers into the monitor of the nearest box. Ignoring the *AUDIO INPUT?* reminder that flashed on the miniscreen, she pushed more buttons until the words suddenly stopped flashing and stayed still on the screen. Then she spoke, very clearly. 'Vice Admiral, er – Vice Admiral,' she said, and closed her eyes.

She dared a one-eyed glance at the screen. *SECURITY CLEARANCE APPROVED – ALL LEVELS* was the message on the screen. Ace smiled and said 'Yow!'

UNKNOWN AUDIO INPUT, the screen said, *PLEASE REPEAT.*

'What's inside?' Ace said.

TISSUE SAMPLES, RAISTRICK CREW, appeared on the screen.

'Close,' Ace said, and moved to the next rack of shelving.

Several minutes later, Ace had interrogated the monitors of all of the smaller capsules. She had found litres of concentrated plasma-plus and enough skin regenerating cultures to clothe several skeletons, but she hadn't found a secret weapon. The box of intelligent, multi-headed, data-corrupting missiles had appealed to her, but she had resisted the temptation to pocket a few of the tiny darts: she didn't know what might happen when they thawed. And although effective against any electronic data-processing system, including the human brain, they were by no means secret.

That left the two coffin-shaped capsules.

Ace was beginning to feel shivery again. She forced herself to hurry. She had only a minute left. Her anxious eyes caught sight of their reflection in the dull sheen of the box's black lid, and she almost lost the numerical sequence she was loading. The screen told her she was in.

'What's – what's inside?' she said.

The coffin contained a body. Just a body. A trooper. She knew him by name, couldn't remember his face. Airlock accident. She remembered hearing about it. Ruptured lungs. In cryo awaiting surgery. Nothing out of the ordinary.

So it was in the other coffin. Whatever it was. Defries's secret weapon.

Ace stood for a few seconds, looking down at the blank, black box. She reached for the monitor, and started hitting the keys.

'What's inside?'

HUMAN MALE.

Ace laughed with relief, but stopped herself suddenly. This had to be the one. 'Injuries?' she asked.

PHYSICALLY INTACT.

That was a weird way of putting it. It begged too many questions, and most of them were spinning in Ace's head. But she needed basic information.

'Name?'

ABSLOM DAAK.

Abslom Daak. Ace had seen that name before. She knew something terrible about someone named Abslom Daak, but she couldn't remember what she knew.

More information was scrolling across the screen. *VERSION THREE. DALEK KILLER NUMBER ERASED.*

Abslom Daak. A Dalek Killer. Ace tried to jog her memory. Dalek Killers – DKs – were almost mythical. No-one ever met a DK, because DKs died quickly and a long way from home. They were criminals, the worst criminals, sentenced to exile on Dalek-controlled planets. Few survived the transmat. Those that got through could expect to live for a few hours. The more Daleks they killed, the longer they might last. Earth Central didn't much care either way.

And Defries was taking a DK to Arcadia. That didn't make much sense to Ace. Keeping the DK in the deep freeze, on the other hand, seemed eminently sensible. There was something about the name, though. Abslom Daak.

'How much longer in cryo?' Ace asked.

00.04.15.57 appeared on the screen.

Almost five days, Ace thought. So Defries isn't going to risk thawing him out before we drop out of warp. But I'd like to have a few words with this guy . . .

'Any problems with auto resuscitation?' Ace said.

AUTO RESUSCITATION SELECTED, the screen said, *2% ERROR PROBABILITY*.

So he's in good shape. OK then, let's give him an early alarm call. 'Implant post-resuscitation instruction to seek interview with trooper known as Ace,' Ace said, 'and reset resuscitation time to four days from now.'

RESET: 00.04.00.00 flashed on to the screen, and Ace heard a noise. She turned to see the youthful-looking doctor standing in the doorway.

'Did you find it?' he said. 'Come on, let's get you out of here. Those guards will think we're up to something. Come on, I said. Out!'

Ace shook her head and walked slowly to the door. She'd remembered where she had seen Abslom Daak's name before. The Dalek Killer was dead.

It was years ago, in the days when she'd been travelling with the Doctor. The days when her life was upside down and she hadn't known whether she was coming or going. She'd been leafing through the TARDIS memory store, using the terminal in her room (God, the chaos and crap she'd lived in then!) to follow references to the Doctor's activities. She'd wanted to know, for some reason, what he'd got up to when she wasn't around. She'd been a bit furtive about it, because although the information was readily available, what she was doing had felt like spying. It had been a frustrating exercise, anyway, because the relational aspects of the TARDIS's memory seemed almost completely arbitrary to a non-Gallifreyan. But she'd found a reference to Abslom Daak.

The Doctor had been with Daak when he had died. He'd made a crazy vow to kill every Dalek in the Galaxy. He had sacrificed himself in a suicidal attack on the central reactor of a Dalek Death Wheel. The Death Wheel had been blown apart, and an entire planet and all its inhabitants had been saved. Daak had been a hero.

But he must have died. He had died, according to the TARDIS. In which case how could he be frozen in a box in the medical suite of the *Admiral Raistrick*?

'Of course! I'm a nanobrain.'

'What?' The medic had moved away, and now turned back suddenly.

'Nothing.' Ace grinned at him. 'I was being stupid. The answer's time travel.'

Of course, it was very simple. The Doctor had met Daak in his – the Doctor's – past, but in the future from where Ace was standing now. So Daak, in his own time-line, had not yet met the Doctor. At some point in Daak's future (but the Doctor's past) Daak would launch himself into the reactor of a Dalek Death Wheel; the Doctor would witness the act of heroism; the record would be entered in the TARDIS memory; and then, still in the Doctor's past and also in Ace's past, Ace would look into the TARDIS's memory and discover how Daak died – how Daak will die.

Ace's head was spinning. No wonder she used to be confused in those days. There was something very worrying about knowing how someone is going to die.

The medic sealed the cryo store. 'Not so exciting, is it? Just a DK. I can't imagine why Defries thinks he'll make much differnce. She's got a shipload of homicidal auxies like you to use as Dalek fodder. But stay alive, won't you? I want to collect my part of our bargain.'

'Right,' Ace said, and left the medical suite. But she hadn't heard a word he'd said. She was thinking: Daak's going to wake up in four days. He'll jump out of that coffin like some deranged vampire, he'll knock on the door until someone lets him out, and he'll come looking for me. What do I say to him? *Hello, I know where you're going to die?*

Stop worrying, she told herself. He'll probably be a berserk, criminally insane psychopath anyway. Making conversation could easily be the least of my difficulties.

He cut a hole.

I hate them, they sound like insects moving. They sound like frogs talking.

But I thought he would help her, anyway.

The door was open. He came in. He saw her. He didn't see me. I was hiding. I was too scared.

Why didn't he help her? She was screaming. No noise,

but screaming. Inside a golden cloud. Shaking like leaves on a tree. Not pretty any more. Shaking and screaming.

He stood and watched.

'Gerald, the chirurgeon insisted. He says it's unavoidable.'

'Elaine is a Delahaye. And she's my niece. I won't have that butcher tampering with her.'

'Then what do you suggest? She's no better.'

'I can see that! Great heavens, it breaks my heart to look at her. I've spoken to the Prince.'

'The Prince! But Gerald – you know that Francis said we –'

'Has that young layabout been here again? I thought he was going to Landfall. Time he grew up. I don't care what nonsense he's been scaring you with. The Prince will help us. He needs something to do.'

'No sign of flying ships full of plague victims, then?'

'Of course not. Complete waste of time. Someone's idea of a hoax, I'd say.'

The *Admiral Raistrick* was three days from the Arcadia system. Ace was in her cabin, looking at her reflections in the tesseract.

The cube fascinated her; she could look into it for hours. From its surface, her face looked back at her, serious, frowning. But there were other reflections, inside the cube, smaller and smaller versions of Ace. She could see herself in profile. She could see the back of her head. She could see herself smiling, and that would make her smile, and then the reflection would be accurate.

Could it tell what she was going to do? She shrugged. It was a Time Lord gift, after all.

Abslom Daak would seek her out. For the first time in many months, Ace wanted to see the Doctor. For all his faults, he knew the answers to difficult questions. Sometimes he was prepared to share what he knew. She could do with a chat. She missed him.

Ace was never able to work out whether it was the Doctor's need for her, or her need for him, that made it happen. Perhaps the tesseract made the decision. Perhaps it had been waiting to link the moments of mutual wanting. It started to unfold.

Each face of the cube fell open, and each face was itself a cube, itself opening into other cubes. It expanded in all directions, like a metallic crystal forming out of a super-saturated solution.

Ace could feel the box-like shape in her hands, she was still looking into its heart, but it was also all around her. She glanced up: she was inside the proliferating structure, her cabin was a distorted, fragmented shadow seen through crystal prisms.

She looked back into the centre of the tesseract. A corridor of cubes corkscrewed away into infinity. In the distance, at the end of the tunnel, there was a tiny image. Like something seen through the wrong end of a telescope, the picture had an impossible clarity.

It was the Doctor, sitting on a white bench.

I might have guessed, Ace thought. I'd better go and see how he's been getting on without me. Very *Alice in Wonderland*, this.

Her hands parted as she stood and moved towards the tesseract's centre. She was suddenly in the tunnel, and the Doctor was suddenly close. He looked up.

She was in a bare, white room. It contained nothing but the Doctor and the bench he sat on. She looked behind her: the tesseract tunnel was there, too, spiralling away towards a distant image of her empty cabin.

She turned back to the Doctor, and grinned.

'Who are you?' he said.

'I know it's been a long time, Professor, but do me a favour.'

The Doctor's hands massaged the rim of his hat. It was an uncharacteristic gesture. 'Professor? Yes, there was someone . . . '

'It's me, Ace.' Ace struck a pose, pulled faces. 'You know, as in "Hello, I'm the Doctor, and this is my friend Ace".'

Unfathomable expressions crossed the Doctor's face. He tried the words. 'Hello, I'm the Doctor. And this is my friend – Ace?'

81

She waited. Confusion clouded the Doctor's eyes again. 'Something's happened, hasn't it?' she said. 'What have you gone and done to yourself this time?'

'You're – you're Ace!'

'Yes! Well done, Doc!' This is like training a parrot to talk, she thought. A kilo of birdseed would come in handy. 'Are we in the TARDIS?'

'TARDIS.' The Doctor considered this carefully. 'Yes. I think I remember the word TARDIS.'

Ace sighed. 'Budge up, Professor, and let me sit down. I think this might take some time.'

Ace was wrong. She had only to supply a few more reminders, and the Doctor was able to begin to restore his memories. He chortled and exclaimed as he unearthed treasures at an accelerating rate.

'Memories. They're all in here, you know. Somewhere. Ace. Yes, that's you of course. Mel. Peri. Spectrox – nasty stuff. Nil by mouth, I'd say. Daleks. Ah yes. And Davros. Earth, London. Twice. Three times. Oh. Susan. Susan. Well, that's enough of that. They're all there, anyway. Knowledge. Yes, it's all here. Oh – temporal engineering.'

Wide-eyed, he stopped chattering. He took a deep breath. 'You know, I've never seen it quite like that before. It's like being away from home and then coming back and seeing your furniture as if for the first time. I always knew it was big, of course. But it's so – symmetrical. Do you know what I mean?'

'No. Look, are you better now, or not?'

'I think so. There are grey areas. Block transfer computations, for instance. Something to do with chameleon circuits, whatever they are.'

'Don't worry about it, Doctor. It can't be any greyer than it used to be.'

'But I think it's all there. Ask me a question.'

'A question?'

'Yes. Something really challenging. N-dimensional geometries, that sort of thing.'

Ace looked at him. 'How long is a piece of string?' she said.

The Doctor frowned. 'That's a tricky one,' he said. 'Infinite-regression mathematics was never my strong subject. Let me think.'

He started counting on his fingers. Ace shook her head sadly. He'd flipped.

'It depends,' he said at last. 'How long was the original string of which the piece in question is a piece?'

Ace started to protest, and then caught sight of the barely-controlled twitching of his pursed lips. 'Alright,' she said. 'You're definitely back to your old self. Just spare me the Time Lord jokes, OK?'

'Don't be so miserable, Ace. It's not every day you get the chance to restore an entire mind. Certainly not a mind as full as mine. It's like visiting a museum.' He pointed to his head. 'I'm going up and down staircases, opening cupboards full of information, throwing open doors that lead to entire store rooms of data—'

'Talking of throwing open doors, Doctor,' Ace interrupted, 'have you noticed that there aren't any? In this room, I mean. Are you a prisoner?'

The Doctor thought, and then slumped with his head in his hands. 'I don't know,' he said quietly. 'I can't remember. Where am I?'

'You're asking me?' Ace said. And then she realized why the tesseract had brought her to the Doctor. The most important doors in his mind were still closed, and only someone who knew him could unlock them.

She stood up and walked round the bare room. 'This must be in the TARDIS,' she said. 'The walls aren't typical, but they're made of the same stuff. You told me once about a room you had to ditch. A very useful room, insulated from everything, even from the rest of the TARDIS. You had to use it, years ago, when one of your regenerations went wrong. You remember?'

The Doctor nodded slowly. 'Nyssa,' he said. 'Tegan. They helped. Pushed me in a chair.'

Ace clenched her fists. This was it! She was right. 'You called it the Zero Room. That's where we are. We're in a new Zero Room.'

The Doctor jumped to his feet and lifted his arms above

his head. 'Yes!' he shouted. 'Ace, how can I ever thank you? I did it. The plan worked. I knew it would, if only I could stop myself thinking about it.'

'That sounds completely typical. Now would you like to tell me about it?'

'Of course I will, Ace. Where would you like me to start?'

'How am I supposed to know? You never used to tell me what was going on.'

The Doctor contrived to look shocked, hurt and reproving simultaneously.

'And don't give me that,' Ace said. Restoring the Doctor's memories had stirred forgotten emotions. 'You were being even more stroppy than normal. I don't know what was wrong with you. Everything should have been OK. You remember the TARDIS was destroyed? And then there was that business in Turkey and New York and all that. And then we went to that Tir-na-n-Og place, and got the stuff to finish fixing the TARDIS. After that, everything should have been fine.'

'And in fact, Ace, that's precisely when something else went wrong.'

'You're not kidding. After that you went moping round the Yorkshire Moors. You know I made sure the TARDIS didn't have a gas oven, just in case you thought of putting your head in it? I got you out of that mess at the radio telescope, and did I get any thanks? No, I got my heart broken instead. No, I didn't. But maybe Robin did. And then—' She paused for breath.

'There's more?'

'And then you hardly spoke to me at all on Heaven. And I met Jan. And you let him die.' She couldn't say any more. She hated herself for sounding like a kid again. She hated him for making her remember.

'And that's when you left me. Yes, I remember. But I had to do it, Ace, believe me.' He looked at her with a pleading smile. 'It was all part of the plan.'

She froze. She couldn't bear it. He was doing it all over again. 'What plan?' she managed to say.

'You see, the TARDIS was contaminated,' he said eagerly. 'There was an impurity in the organic matter I used to refuel the link with the Eye of Harmony. The protoplasm from Tir-na-n-Og must have contained a small fragment of one of Goibhnie's experiments. Ace, are you listening? It infected the TARDIS, you see. And that meant it was in my mind, too. I couldn't make any conscious plans to get rid of it, because it always knew everything I knew. You must understand how serious the situation was. I've had to shut down the TARDIS and myself. Ace?'

'And what about me, Doctor? I was so young in those days. You needed me, so you stopped me staying with Robin. You needed me, so you let Jan die. And then you made me leave the TARDIS. I thought I was making the decision! But you wanted me out, and so out I went!'

The Doctor turned away from her. His voice was low and tight. 'You haven't changed, have you, Ace. You always do this to me. I've only just got my mind back. It wasn't a game. I've made – mistakes, recently. People have died. Now, for the first time since I repaired the link, I am free of the presence that has been riding inside me. Is it any wonder that I was bad-tempered? And all you can do is blame me for your boyfriend problems.'

Ace opened her mouth to yell at him, and found herself laughing instead. She'd made him angry, and that still gave her a perverse buzz. And he was quite right, of course: she'd long ago consigned both Robin and his bicycle, and Jan and his snake tattoo, to the lucky escape category of old lovers.

'Never mind, Doc. It was all a long time ago.'

The Doctor looked quizzically over his shoulder. 'Was it?' he said.

'Two, probably three Earth years, I guess.'

'Surely not. It doesn't seem as long as that.'

'This is a time machine, Professor. It can be five minutes for you, fifty years for me. Or the other way round.'

'But the tesseract was programmed to react as soon as I entered the Zero Room.'

'And it did. It just found me three years further on in my time. It's no big deal.'

'But that isn't how I set it up. You know, Ace, I feel as though I'm being manipulated again.'

'You feel like you're being manipulated! That's rich, Professor, it really is.'

The Doctor was listening intently, his head cocked to one side. When he didn't reply, Ace realized that he was listening to something other than her voice. Then she heard it too: a low rumbling and a high-pitched whine, rising and falling but gradually becoming louder. Within seconds it sounded as if an X-ship was firing up to escape velocity in the neighbouring room.

'Ace! Move away from the wall!' the Doctor shouted.

Ace threw herself behind the bench and watched one of the Zero Room's white walls vibrate into non-existence while, at the same time, something materialized in its place.

The wall was now grey, and appeared to be made of stone blocks. Sprouting horizontally from it, and occupying much of the space in the room, was a hexagonal column with a huge, six-sided shield at its end. It was like a hexagonal stone mushroom, growing sideways into the room. Although the shape was familiar, the unusual orientation confused Ace for a moment.

'It's a control console,' she said. 'It's the console from the tertiary control room, isn't it? What's it doing here? And sideways?'

'Oh, it's all in the plan,' the Doctor said airily. 'Using the tesseract triggered a minor reconfiguration. I need a console to filter the TARDIS through.'

Ace decided that the Doctor's last remark could wait. 'But why sideways?'

'Really, Ace. I was working under considerable pressure. I had to input a succession of contingency commands without letting myself think about why I was doing it. It's hardly surprising that I made a few small errors. But you see,' he gestured grandly at the horizontal mushroom, 'I succeeded in fooling myself!'

Ace laughed again. 'You don't half talk some nonsense, Doc. So what happens next?'

'Next, Ace, I put the TARDIS to rights.' He stood on the bench, from which position he could with some difficulty reach all of the console controls, and began to flick switches in what looked to Ace like an alarmingly random fashion.

Ace stepped on to the bench beside him. She was taller than him, she realized; she remembered him as being the taller of them. The black combat gear, with deflector pads on the upper arms, a reinforced comms collar, and long powerboots, made her look much larger than the Doctor. She waited until he became aware of her.

'And what am I supposed to do next?' she said. She had a nasty feeling she knew the answer.

'Next?' he said vaguely, as he scribbled a list of numbers in the notebook he'd pulled from one of his pockets. 'Do? Well, there's not much left to do, is there. Have a look round. See the old place again.'

Ace had jumped down from the bench before she remembered. 'Doctor. There are no doors, are there?'

'What? Oh – no, of course not. Just let me . . . And then I'll . . . ' He was lost in his work again.

Ace made a slow circuit of the small room. She stopped next to the impossible shape of the unfolded tesseract; peering into it she saw that her cabin on the *Raistrick* was still there, tiny but distinct. It looked miles away, but to get there would take only one step. Would the Doctor even notice if she went?

She walked to the console and looked up at him.

'Doctor?'

'Mm?'

'If I know how someone dies, and then I meet him – I mean before he dies – I can't tell him how he's going to die, can I?'

'No. Or is it yes? What did you say?'

Ace repeated the question. With a sigh, the Doctor closed his pencil-stub inside his notebook. 'You're quite right, Ace. Knowledge of the probable destiny of individuals is one of the burdens a time traveller has to bear. Whom do you have in mind?'

'Oh – just someone I think I'm going to have to talk to. I read about him in the TARDIS data files. So I can't tell him what's going to happen to him?'

'Of course not, Ace. Particularly if there's any chance that his future actions might prove to have a significant effect on the time lines. If you give him foreknowledge of his death, he might change his behaviour. And that might alter the course of events. And then I'd have to try to sort it out.'

'And that might make things even worse.'

'That was uncalled for. And you've made me forget where I was up to. I'll have to start again from the beginning.'

'Pardon me for existing, I'm sure.'

'What? Oh, really, Ace, if you can't make yourself useful then you might as well—'

'What, Doctor?'

He sighed. 'I don't mean to be inhospitable, Ace, but I am attempting to perform an almost impossible task. If I make the slightest mistake I may destroy some or all of the TARDIS's circuits. And I'm trying to do it while standing on tip-toe. I need to concentrate.'

'So what's the big problem? I mean, what exactly are you trying to do?'

The Doctor pulled a large white handkerchief from his trouser pocket and wiped his brow. 'If I tell you,' he said, 'will you leave me in peace?'

'No,' Ace said, 'but tell me anyway.'

'Although my mind is now free of contamination—'

'Because of the Zero Room, right?'

'Exactly. But the TARDIS's circuits and data stores are still infected. Therefore there is still a certain random element in any operation that the TARDIS performs. Not only that, if I step outside the Zero Room before the TARDIS is decontaminated, the bug will probably re-infect me.'

'Because of your symbiotic link with the TARDIS.'

'Precisely. Therefore I have to set up a decontamination

system through which I can feed every particle of data contained within the TARDIS. And that includes electronic impulses, magnetically stored data, the biochemical synaptic systems, the sub-viral networks that plug into the biochemical systems, and the contents of the solid-state inorganic crystal computers. Among others. The interior of the TARDIS, basically.'

'And you couldn't do any of this before, because the bug would always know you were going to do it.'

'Just so. It's not a clever fragment of intelligence. It's not even really malevolent. But it has a strong sense of self-preservation. It's used all kinds of tricks to stop me getting rid of it.'

'You mean, just when you were about to enter the commands that would finish it off, it could read your mind and stop you?'

'Yes. It was simply reacting instinctively. Sometimes it would give me a blinding headache; at other times it would cause a localized gravity fluctuation. Anything to disturb my concentration. Now it's gone from my mind. But I've got you instead.'

'Thanks very much. I still don't see the problem.'

The Doctor ran his hands through his untidy hair. 'I've got to filter the TARDIS – the whole interior, in coded form – through the decontamination system I have just created on this console. It's like – well, imagine trying to lift a cauldron that's too heavy and full to the brim with water and then trying to pour a constant dribble of the liquid through a moving sieve without spilling a drop. That's what I have to do next. So will you please let me concentrate.'

Ace thought for a while. Just as the Doctor was about to push a button on the console, she said: 'I wouldn't bother.'

The Doctor was shaking with suppressed impatience. 'What?' he said.

'I wouldn't bother trying to lift the cauldron. I'd use a jug, and filter a jugful of water at a time. Now don't interrupt, Doctor. Hear me out. I know you couldn't do that normally, because the TARDIS circuits are all integrated. But they're not integrated at the moment, are they? You told me, they're all split up and isolated, because you closed everything down when you closed your mind down. So use a jug. Filter the TARDIS a room at a time.'

The Doctor stood lost in thought for a moment. He leant across the console and touched a few buttons. Lights started flashing in rhythmic sequences.

The Doctor turned to Ace. 'The system's running,' he said. 'It'll take half an hour or so to process all the rooms. I remember why you used to be so helpful on our little trips, Ace. It wasn't just the blind aggression. Sometimes you can be nothing short of brilliant.'

'Glad to be of help, Doc.' Ace felt oddly embarrassed. A silence developed. She wondered whether she should disappear into the tesseract and leave the Doctor to his newly-restored home.

'So – um – where are you, Ace?' the Doctor asked suddenly. 'I mean, what are you up to these days?'

Ace explained.

'Daleks?' The Doctor seemed amused. 'Yes, you always did have a way with our metal-skinned friends. But are you sure you're going to Arcadia?'

'Of course I'm sure, Doctor. Astro-navigation's not my specialty, but I can read a star chart. And I've been up on the bridge every day since we went into warp. We're going to Arcadia.'

'Well, you're going to be disappointed. There are no Daleks in the Arcadia system. Not in the twenty-fifth century, or any other century that I can think of. It's a backwater system, at least in your time. I can't remember anything remarkable about it. It'll be a dull trip. You might as well stay here.'

Ace looked at him. He was pretending to be engrossed in reading dials and screens. She wasn't fooled. Something strange was happening on Arcadia, that was for sure. And she was willing to bet that the Doctor was going to set the co-ordinates for Arcadia as soon as the decontamination system had finished its work.

And then there was Abslom Daak. Escaping on the

TARDIS would be an easy way out of a potentially difficult situation. But she hated to leave unfinished business.

'I'll tell you what, Doctor,' she said. 'I'll see you there, OK? Last one to Arcadia buys the drinks.'

The Doctor looked up and smiled mischievously.

'And that reminds me,' Ace said, as she stepped into the mouth of the tesseract tunnel, 'what happened to Benny?'

'Benny!' The Doctor looked very worried for a moment. 'I'd forgotten – but it's all right. I told her to stay in her room. She must be safe. I'll let her stay there until we land on Arcadia, I think.'

'Give her my love,' Ace said, and disappeared into the crystalline corridor. It started to fold inwards behind her. She was in her cabin on the *Raistrick*. On her bunk, the last metacubes were folding into each other. The tesseract, restored to its cubic shape, glittered as it disappeared into nothing.

If it hadn't all been a dream, she had a rendezvous with the Doctor on Arcadia.

He stood and watched. He watched until she stopped moving. Then he cut a hole. A big hole.

He didn't try to save her. He just stood and watched.

You never see their faces. Just blackness under the hood. You never see what they look like under those cloaks.

They sound horrible.

Everyone says they're kind to us. They give us things, do things for us.

So why did he just stand and watch?

It was better when she stopped moving. She looked peaceful. The cloud disappeared. I don't know how.

She was just lying on the bed.

I didn't know. I thought it was all over. I wanted to come out of the wardrobe. I started to come out. Then he had something in his hand.

He cut a hole.

He cut a big hole in the top of her head.

Her beautiful hair.

'No improvement, I suppose?'

'She's had a little warm milk. She won't look at me. She's thinking, though, I'm sure of it. Her eyes move.'

'Well, it's not our problem any more.'

'Gerald?'

'I spoke to the Prince. He spoke to his Counsellor. Apparently the case has caused quite a stir at Landfall. They think they can do something for her. So in three days a Humble Counsellor will come to take her off our hands.'

'Gerald, I'm not sure . . . '

'Well, I am. Good riddance, quite frankly. Look at the commotion she's making now. She's going frantic. Landfall's the best place for her.'

Part Three

ET IN ARCADIA . . .

It was too early. Defries wasn't even awake, but she knew it was too early. She mumbled 'Lights' and rolled over in her bed.

Yes. It was the comms alarm. Shielding her eyes, she struggled to sit up.

'Alarm off,' she said. 'Audio.'

'Good morning, Agent. Rise and shine.'

'Morning, Toko. Don't sound so bloody cheerful. What's up?'

The Captain hesitated. 'Do you want the good news,' his voice said from the comms speaker, 'or the bad news?'

'You've just woken me up, Toko. What could be worse?'

'One of the cryo pods in the medical suite has defrosted early. Guess which.'

'Damn. How did—? Forget it. When?'

'Your weapon will be active in about five minutes, Agent. Shall I send in the guards?'

'What? Hell, no. No point in wasting personnel. And I don't want the DK armed. I don't want him to pick up so much as a fork from the galley.'

'Then what?'

Defries was out of bed now, pulling on her combat gear. 'I'll be on the bridge in two minutes. Just clear the corridors, and monitor his movements. It'll be interesting to see where he goes.'

'OK, Belle. You got it. I'm just glad he's your responsibility.'

'Don't go, Toko. You mentioned good news?'

'Oh yeah. We made good time in warp. We can drop into the Arcadia system any time, from about thirty minutes on.'

Defries grinned. Action at last. The DK hadn't defrosted too early, after all. She tightened the straps of her webbing. Her skin tingled as the cool lining of her tunic moulded itself to her body.

'Belle? Did you get that?'

'Sorry, Toko. Just enjoying the adrenalin rush. Yes, let's hit the system as soon as we can. I'll run the muster from the bridge. I'm on my way now. And keep an eye on Daak.'

It was a mirror. Britta had been dreaming: she was in the shallows, surrounded by waving fronds of weed, and looking up she saw herself, floating naked, face down, gazing at the sea bed.

But it wasn't a dream. It was a mirror, suspended from the ceiling of the alcove which was now her bedroom. The mirror hadn't been there when she'd gone to sleep, but Britta was becoming accustomed to the instability of her new environment.

She stretched her arms above her head, and watched her stomach tauten and her breasts rise across her ribcage. A secretive smile appeared on the face of her reflection. She frowned: she hadn't been aware of smiling.

Her reflection didn't frown. Its smile widened. It spoke to Britta. Its voice was Lacuna's.

'Time to wake up, pretty little Britta. Today is a big day. We might have visitors, so you must look your best. Get dressed.'

Now Britta smiled, sleepily. Her reflection was now wearing the short voile dress that had been her usual uniform in her few days in Lacuna's domain. It was impractical and a bit daring: the sort of clothing she never used to wear. She couldn't understand why she liked wearing it here.

How was it possible to feel comfortable and frightened at the same time? It had taken all her courage to undress in front of Dimitri, that first time. Now, according to Lacuna, she was displaying herself through Lacuna's eyes to the innermost circle of the Corporation.

Even when Lacuna made her do the most disgusting

things, when she couldn't stop herself bursting into tears while Lacuna crooned hateful descriptions of her, she felt a sort of pride. The Corporation needed her, Lacuna said, and it was strangely exciting to be so important, to know that her suffering and her shame were a necessary part of the Corporation's grandest scheme.

As she dropped the soft material round her shoulders and tied the sash, she wondered what Lacuna would do to her today. Something horrible: it was something horrible every day. Visitors, Lacuna had said. A big day. Britta felt a fluttering in her stomach: fear, but also anticipation.

This morning there were no garish cosmetics waiting for her on the lop-sided glass structure that served as her dressing table. She brushed out her hair quickly, checked her reflection in the mirrors that lined her sleeping quarters, and pulled aside the satin curtain.

She almost fell down the new steps. During the night, the area beyond her alcove had been remodelled as a sunken grotto. Twisting stalagmites of phosphorescent crystal illuminated a path that wound between walls of folded rock. As she picked her way past luminous boulders, she heard the tinkle of falling water.

She felt she was being watched. She looked up – and saw herself. A three-dimensional representation of her face, like a death-mask carved in stone, was set into the wall. The face's eyes were wide with fear; the lips were slightly parted. The path was lined with her face: every few steps she came upon another image of herself, another exact replica of her face. Britta grimacing; Britta protesting; Britta blindfolded, her mouth open. The grotto was a shrine to the indignities she had endured.

The path ended by dividing into two sets of steps, leading upwards. Between them a fountain played: its centrepiece was a statue of Britta, naked, half crouching, arms outstretched as if in supplication. The statue's face was a picture of misery. The tinkling water was a trickle of tears that fell ceaselessly from its eyes into the bowl in which the statue stood.

Britta knew that she should feel disturbed, but her scientific training demanded to know how the grotto had been constructed so quickly, and how the likenesses of her had been created so accurately. And she also felt pride: all this had been made for her. She reached towards the statue's hands, but didn't dare to touch; anyway, Lacuna was waiting for her.

The corridors at the top of the steps had been altered again, split into junctions, ramps and stairways, proliferating like fractal images. It isn't possible, Britta thought. The original chamber isn't big enough to contain this maze of paths and junctions. How can it keep growing? How will I find the centre?

As usual, finding the centre was a matter of heading for the central source of light. This was more difficult than it had been before, but it was possible.

It is beautiful, in a weird sort of way, Britta thought as she passed a stepped bridge that shrank in size to an infinitesimal point in its short span across a lower walkway. But what is it all for? I'm out of my depth in this place. Lacuna says that I'm beautiful, but she likes to make me look – well, twisted and unhappy. She says they like to see me that way. Whoever they are. But I think it's her. She's a bit peculiar, really. I hope I am being useful. She says I'm helping a lot. She says they like me.

And I suppose it must be true. All those faces, and the statue. Someone appreciates me.

Lacuna was waiting in the clear space at the centre of the chamber. As Britta stepped out of the darkness, Lacuna's eyes snapped open. She smiled her voracious smile.

'Our visitors might arrive today,' she said, 'if they have made good speed. They will be too late.'

'What visitors, Lacuna? And too late for what?'

Lacuna ignored the questions. 'You are as lovely as ever,' she said. 'Are you ready to show our masters some more of the ways in which you can express your loveliness?'

Britta felt the shiver of fear and anticipation again. She knew now that whenever Lacuna started talking like that, something nasty and shameful would happen.

'Good,' Lacuna said. 'That is one of your best expressions, my dear. I show them all such moments, you know. They have such a desire to see beautiful things. There are – negative factors in the depths.'

Britta had given up expecting answers, but her curiosity was undiminished. 'Negative factors?' she prompted.

Lacuna's mouth tightened. 'It doesn't matter. This phase of the project is almost completed. The planetary experiment has reached the end of its useful life. Shutdown is imminent.'

'We're going to close the base on the planet?'

'Of course. It has generated enough material. We will cull the remaining stock and bring the more adaptable of the androids back up to the station.'

'And the planet will be abandoned? Shouldn't we restore it to its pre-experimental ecology? We've introduced off-world species, haven't we?'

Lacuna smiled again. 'How delightfully naive. You silly girl, the planet will be destroyed, and everything on it too. Its mass is needed to fuel the second phase.'

Britta frowned. The answeres were more perplexing than the questions. She changed direction. 'And who are the visitors?'

'Intruders from Earth. Nothing to worry about.'

'Earth? But the holovid reports said—'

'Stupid! The Corporation filters and adjusts the news for the benefit of its staff, you foolish child. Did you think we would allow distractions? The war is over, or as good as. Earth has survived. And they are sending investigators to interrupt our work here. But all this was predicted long ago. Our visitors are expected, and we have made preparations to welcome them.'

'Oh. That's alright then, I suppose,' Britta said.

'Of course it is, my dear. Now, I have work to do this morning. But shall we give our masters a treat first?'

'Yes, Lacuna,' Britta said, trembling.

'Have you bathed this morning, pretty Britta?'

You know I haven't, Britta thought. 'No, Lacuna.'

'Then let's see what games we can play in the water, shall we?' Lacuna pointed to an archway: Britta saw, beyond the arch, rippling liquid reflected on a blue ceiling. 'Come into my bathroom, my dear.'

'How – how do you know the expedition from Earth won't trouble us?' Britta said. She had no fear of water, but she knew that Lacuna would toy with her until she panicked, for the benefit of the watching Corporation. The smallest delay was worthwhile.

'It has all been predicted,' Lacuna snapped. 'Their strength is unknown, of course, but our defences can defeat any feasible combination of Spacefleet and External Operations forces. Our work here is secure from everything.'

'Except the unpredictable,' Britta thought aloud.

'Get into the bathroom,' Lacuna said. 'I'm going to make you suffer beautifully.'

'If it doesn't hurt it isn't working,' Bernice said, rubbing her stiff neck and trying to remember where she'd picked up such an idiotic phrase.

She had woken up in the chair in the TARDIS control room, and was rather surprised to find everything except her muscles and joints exactly as it had been when she had fallen asleep.

'I need coffee,' she announced to the empty room. 'Tea would do. Even Eridanian brandy. Why has the Doctor never put a food dispenser in the control room?'

There was still a blank wall where there used to be a door to the interior of the TARDIS. The double doors were still closed. The console lights were still glowing reassuringly. Then she noticed that the time rotor had stopped moving.

We've landed, she thought. Doctor, where are you? Come to that, where am I?

She stood, stretched, and walked stiffly to the console. Wherever the TARDIS had materialized, the gravity was near Earth normal, according to the instruments. Not that the instruments could be relied on, in her experience. The atmosphere, too, was breathable – almost suspiciously suitable for humans.

'Let's see what you look like, then,' Bernice said, and

operated the scanner switch. She turned to the screen, and whistled as she drew in a breath. The TARDIS had landed on paradise.

Rolling green grassland undulated up to tree-covered hillsides. Beyond the hills, the distant peaks of blue mountains were crowned with snow. Cotton-wool clouds hung in a deep turquoise sky. In the foreground, a herd of small deer trotted out of a copse of broad-leaved trees.

Either I'm watching a promotional vid for a vacation planet, Bernice thought, or we've landed in someone's safari park. Either way, I'm going to have to take a look.

She pulled the door switch, and one of the embossed wall panels swung open. She stepped outside.

It was real. The air was warm, and full of the scents of leaves and wild flowers. Only the buzzing of insects disturbed the silence. Bernice couldn't resist it: she ran down a slope, threw herself into the long fronds of grass, and rolled over and over, laughing.

Then she lay on her back, clutching a clump of leaves in each hand, staring up at the clouds and basking in the touch of the sun on her face. Travelling in the space-time vortex was all very well, but after a brush with mortality and a bad night's sleep nothing felt as good as being on solid ground.

But she still needed coffee. And food, her stomach told her. She sat up.

The far-off mountaintops were still white-tipped, the dark forest still covered the hills and patched the grassland. The deer were a little further away now, nibbling tree-shoots and casting nervous glances in Bernice's direction.

Most grazing animals are edible, she thought. But my blaster's somewhere in the TARDIS. And I'm not sure I could live with the guilt, anyway.

She climbed back up the slope, past the incongruous police telephone box, and reached the crest of the hillock. She shook her head in disbelief. The planet was inhabited, after all.

A river meandered between fields and orchards. The snaking black ribbon of a road curved upwards from the riverside, and passed close to the mound on which Bernice was standing. And at the place, in the distance, where the road met the river, there was a huddle of red rooftops and a wisp of rising smoke.

Bernice looked back to the TARDIS. She couldn't think how she could communicate with the Doctor, still less release him from the interior of his walled-up time machine. And, she reasoned, she wouldn't be any use to anyone if she allowed herself to starve. 'You'll know where I've gone, won't you, Doc?' she said quietly. An animal bellowed mournfully from the fields below. Bernice set off for the town.

Among the crops that she recognized as she strode past the groves and fields were apples, pears, grapes, cherries and apricots; maize, wheat, courgettes, cabbages and olives; there were hives of bees, and huge clumps of rosemary, thyme and laurel. Everything looked ripe and perfect: the fruit was unblemished, the vegetables were vast.

She didn't resist the temptation. By the time she was half-way to the town she was considerably less hungry, and was able to confirm that the planet's produce tasted as wholesome as it looked.

She had lost sight of the town when she had descended into the rolling patchwork of fields and groves. And her preoccupation with satisfying her hunger had kept at the back of her mind her awareness that she had not seen a single agricultural machine. When she trudged to the summit of a hill planted with olive trees, therefore, and saw the town again, now only a kilometre distant, she was not prepared for the sight that met her eyes.

A structure of ycllowy-white stone rose above the red rooftops. It was a castle. Bernice sat on the hilltop and stared at it.

As a child she'd seen images of fairy-tale castles in story vids. Her history studies had included medieval Europe: the *Tres Riches Heures* of the Duc de Berri contained gloriously-coloured paintings of landscapes similar to the view before her. As an archeology student she had reconstructed three-dimensional images from recorded measurements of the low, worn walls that were all that remained of the stone fortresses that had existed a thousand years previously on Earth. But she had never seen a real castle before.

She needed a vid recorder. She needed her surveying pack. Everything was in her inaccessible room in the TARDIS. She took her notebook from the pocket of her jacket and started to write.

I've landed in archeologists' heaven. The TARDIS has brought us to Earth. Europe, in the Middle Ages.

But even as she wrote the words, she started to doubt them. It was a long time – fifteen years – since she'd been on Earth, but it hadn't been quite like this. The sky . . .

The turqoise firmament – well, it might have been like that, once. Before the pollution and the clean-up and weather control. But this sky wasn't clear, anyway. It was hazy, so thick with smog that you could look straight at the sun. And the sun was bigger and yellower than she remembered it.

The creature that crawled on to her left boot clinched it. Bernice took it for a beetle, at first, and went to brush it away. Her hand stopped in mid-air: the thing wasn't a beetle, it wasn't an insect of any sort. It had four legs and a long, forked tail connected to its hindmost body segment; a small middle section carried four rows of spiky feelers; and the head was a featureless wedge. She flipped it over: on the underside of the head were the mouth, a pair of mandibles, and two round eyes like those of a fish. Nothing like it had ever evolved on Earth.

'You're an indigenous life-form, aren't you?' Bernice said to it. 'This planet – or this part of it – has been terraformed. You've more right to be here than these olive trees.' She flicked it off her boot.

'So if this isn't Earth, where in the galaxy is it? And what's a medieval castle doing on a terraformed planet? And why am I asking myself these questions when I could ask those chaps in the brown suits?'

Bernice stood up and made towards the group of four men she had spotted walking across a field below her.

They were trudging cross-country towards the town,

and hadn't seen her. As she hurried to catch up with them, she tried to work out what they were wearing. They were dressed in similar smocks of coarse, brown cloth, with laced leggings and leather boots. Two of them wore wide-brimmed hats. Each man was carrying an implement: a wooden staff with a metal attachment. Bernice suddenly realized that the poles were tools.

'Call yourself a historian, Summerfield?' she said to herself. 'You're looking at real live agricultural labourers.'

But they're reassuringly human, she thought. Curiously pale-skinned, though. In fact, they look like medieval Europeans must have looked, in the days before mass communications on Earth. Perhaps this is one of the early colonies – perhaps a colony that's reverted to a pre-industrial level. Perhaps after a catastrophe – perhaps they've lost contact with other worlds.

'Too many hypotheses,' she told herself, 'and not enough evidence.' The men were close to the town's battlemented walls now, but Bernice wasn't far behind them. 'Hello!' she shouted. 'Do you know where I can find a cup of coffee?'

The men stopped, turned to look at her, exchanged a few words, and started to run towards the walls.

How does the Doctor do it, Bernice thought, as she followed them. People stop and talk to him.

As they reached the twin-towered gateway, the men started shouting. A small crowd of townspeople emerged through the open gates and stared at Bernice. A contingent of them were wearing metal helmets and carrying crossbows. They watched Bernice nervously as they slotted bolts into their bows and cranked up the firing mechanisms.

'Read all about it,' Bernice shouted, lifting her hands in what she hoped was a universally recognized gesture of peaceful intent. 'Town terrorized by unarmed archeologist in scruffy jeans and old jacket.'

She was only a dozen paces from the guards now. They were little more than boys. They lifted their bows. The townspeople huddled in the gateway.

'What's the matter?' she said. 'Look, no hidden weapons, OK? I give in, I surrender. Take me to your leader, and all that.'

She could hear some of the advice that the townspeople were calling to the guards. 'From another planet,' she heard several times. Also the word 'plague'. The demand, 'Don't let her in', was taken up almost as an incantation; as the guards hesitated, the chant changed to 'Kill her, kill her now.'

Hell and damnation, they're going to shoot those things, Bernice realized. She couldn't think of anything to do or say.

She heard one of the guards say 'All right, lads. Now.' And she saw fingers curl round crossbow triggers.

Back on Garaman, the Spacefleet station, a policeman with mutton-chop whiskers had discovered the contents of Ace's security locker.

Ace knew that this was impossible. She even suspected that she might be dreaming. But it all seemed horribly real.

Everything she'd collected during her various tours of duty was being laid out in rows and labelled. Drums of nitro-nine and its derivatives; the logic crystals she'd smuggled out of the Procyon system; various hand-held weapons, variously modified by Ace, and the tripod-mounted surface-to-air cannon; the bales of circuit membrane she'd bought for a song from the tailor on Antonius just before the Daleks arrived; even the converted X-ship in which she was gradually buying a quarter share.

Most of it hadn't been in her locker on the station, anyway. Most of it was stored in an anonymous container in a warehouse on Zantir, and the X-ship was being refitted by a dealer on Harato who owed Ace a favour. So Ace knew it was all a dream.

Nonetheless, the police sergeant had arrived at her door to disturb her sleep.

'Open up!' he shouted, as Ace tossed on the bunk. 'Open up in the name of the law!'

And then he started banging on the door, hitting it so

hard that Ace could feel the vibrations through the structure of the cabin. Her conscious mind strove to overcome her subconscious. When your dreams get this noisy, she told herself, it's time to wake up.

She woke up.

Someone was still banging on the door of her cabin.

'Who is it?' she called, and started climbing into her black combat clothes.

There was no reply. The banging was replaced by a series of heavy thuds, each of which caused the door to buckle inwards a little more.

'That door's Spacefleet property,' Ace yelled. She backed to the far wall and picked up her blaster.

The thudding continued. Ace ran her fingers through her hair and tied it loosely behind her neck. She touched the comms button on her collar, but didn't use it. She'd handled Daleks on her own; why not a DK?

'Open,' she said, and the door started to slide. It stuck half-way, but a muscular, hairy arm appeared in the opening and forced the buckled panel further into its recess.

The Dalek Killer stood on the threshold.

He was tall: his head almost touched the lintel. His long, black hair was loose, and hung straight down his back. His scarred and muscular torso was hardly covered by his torn, ill-fitting singlet; his trousers were equally distressed and figure-hugging. His fists were clenched, his eyes were burning under furrowed brows, and his face was twisted into a leering grin.

Ace thought he looked gross. He'd obviously been wearing the same clothes and gone without a shave for weeks before he went into the cryo pod.

'I'm Daak,' he said.

Ace couldn't believe her luck: it was a dream feed. 'Donald or Daffy?' she said, wide-eyed.

'I'm looking for someone name of Ace,' Daak said, oblivious to Ace's verbal dexterity.

'I'm Ace.'

'You?' Daak was momentarily nonplussed. His post-cryo instructions were completed. He snarled to cover his discomposure. 'Then you're the one I'm looking for, girl. You're going to start giving me some answers.'

'Sure,' Ace said, lifting her blaster, 'but don't call me "girl", OK?'

Daak acted before Ace had finished her sentence. He dived to the floor of the cabin, rolled forward, jumped up and snatched the weapon from Ace's hand.

His grin even wider, he backed away from Ace and kept the blaster trained unwaveringly on her midriff.

'I like it better this way,' he said. 'With me holding the gun. Now start talking.'

Ace sighed and folded her arms. 'What would you like to talk about? Lovely weather for the time of year, isn't it?'

Daak scowled. 'Cut it out, girl. This is a ship, right? So what ship? Where are we going? And why? I want to know everything you know.'

Ace told him, but she didn't tell him everything. She didn't tell him that she knew that he was going to die by self-immolation, that he was destined to be destroyed himself while destroying the Daleks' instrument of planet-wide genocide.

She told him the name of the ship and its captain. She said that it was a troopship, bound for the Spinward Corporation planet Arcadia, and that the troops were auxiliaries under the command of Agent Isabelle Defries of the Office of External Operations.

Daak's eyes gleamed ferociously when Ace mentioned the OEO, but this was as nothing compared to his reaction when Ace told him that their mission was a Dalek hunt.

'Tin-plated vermin!' he shouted, waving Ace's blaster above his head. 'I'll slice 'em open. I'll stew 'em in their tins.'

Ace was looking forward to giving him the bad news.

'Just give me my chain sword and put me on that planet,' Daak exulted. 'You auxies can sit and watch the fun. I'll slice up every one of those metal monsters. And don't give me that look, girl. You think I can't do it?'

'You look crazy enough,' Ace said. 'There's just one small problem: I think this mission's a cover. We're here

107

on false pretences. You included. There are no Daleks on Arcadia.'

Daak's eyes narrowed. For the first time since he'd broken into her cabin, Ace felt in real danger. Daak's imposing body was as still as a statue – except for his right hand, which slowly lifted the blaster to point straight into Ace's eyes.

'No Daleks?' he said quietly. 'Don't tell me that, girl.'

'Then I'll tell you this,' Ace said, pulling back the sleeve of her jacket to reveal the device strapped to her right forearm. 'This is a voice-activated dart gun.'

Daak didn't move. 'I can dodge a needle,' he said. 'Think you can outrun a laser?'

'I'm in Special Weapons. These darts are heat seeking, and each one has a warhead that will blow through steel carbide armour. That blaster, on the other hand, has a deactivated power cell. I let you take it, spongehead. Now shut up and keep still. I don't want to have to redecorate my cabin walls with your insides.'

And I can't, she thought, because if I do you won't live to destroy the Daleks' Death Wheel. God, have I got to spend my time worrying about keeping this creep alive?

But Daak had understood. The blaster hung limply in his hand. He looked deflated. His shoulders slumped, he moved his head from side to side like a dazed bull facing a matador.

Now what? Ace thought. And the comms link in her collar buzzed.

'Ace? This is Defries. I'm told you have a visitor.'

'Yeah,' Ace said. 'We're getting acquainted. No problems.'

Defries chuckled. 'Well, bring him up to the bridge. We're about to drop into the Arcadia system.'

'Great! Don't start without me, OK?' She touched the off button and made for the door, brushing past the Dalek Killer. 'Come on, big boy. Don't hang about. Let's go and look at this planet we've come to see.'

Daak swung round with a curse and followed Ace into the corridor.

* * *

If Francis had taken the direct way, he would never have come across the big, blue box. But he told himself that he needed time to think; he told himself that to walk on the hard road would hurt his feet; he told himself anything to avoid admitting that he wanted to put off his arrival at Landfall for as long as possible.

Since Christina's death, his life had become an indistinct nightmare. He had no evidence that she had died other than naturally; after all, she hadn't been young. She hadn't been ill, either, but it wasn't unusual for anyone, once he or she had reached the third decade of life, to be taken suddenly.

His suspicions seemed to others to result from an unhealthy obsession. Christina's family had rejected him when he had become a nuisance. The Delahayes were a proud house, and they had trouble enough with Elaine, driven mad with grief at her sister's death.

He couldn't blame Caroline and little Antoinette, either. One or other of them might have taken back Francis the troubadour, Francis the handsome, witty flirt. But why should they spare a thought for a Francis preoccupied with the death of another, more recent lover?

He had had no-one else to turn to, and the Counsellors had come every day to urge his departure to Landfall. They had never threatened; they merely made a point of offering, at length and frequently, their condolences on the death of Francis's lady friend.

When the Counsellors had stopped coming to see him, Francis became scared. He had spoken to no-one for two days, and he found himself starting at every noise from the street outside his cell. He was going mad, he was sure of it.

He had reached some kind of decision, however. If Beaufort and its inhabitants offered no comfort or security, going to Landfall became comparatively less threatening. He was in danger anywhere.

He would at least set off from the town. The Counsellors would see that he was following their strictures. And the change of air might restore his spirits.

He had started walking at dawn, avoiding the road and

following instead the farmers' paths through the fields and orchards. To his surprise, he found that the birdsong-filled groves and the scented meadows did, slowly, steal into his heavy reveries and lift his heart.

By the time he was striding across the low hills from the brows of which Beaufort was no more than a smudge of rooftops in a valley, Francis felt fully restored. His head was up, his mind was clear, his step was confident.

He knew he wasn't going mad.

Then he saw the big, blue box.

He staggered, recovered his balance, decided that face-down in long grass was the safest place to be, and allowed himself to fall.

He lifted his head, cautiously. The box was still there, motionless and silent. This was the stranger of the two strange sights he had seen that morning. The first, the tall woman, he had convinced himself was an insignificant phantom of his imagination. This was less easy to dismiss. Perhaps he was losing his mind, after all.

Or perhaps this was the off-world ship. The warnings had come so long ago that the Prince's frantic prep-arations against attack had become the subject of tavern jokes. But the woman, if she had been real, had been strangely attired, as he supposed an off-worlder might be. And now this: whatever it was, it was like nothing Francis had seen before. And it must have arrived only recently.

Everyone had imagined that a ship from another world would resemble – a ship. This was just a box, and not large enough to carry a force of plague-infected soldiers. But where could it have come from, if it hadn't dropped from the sky? And it was big enough to contain a few people: the side facing Francis contained a doorway, and the door was ajar.

And even as Francis lay in the grass and stared, a man stepped out of the box and closed the door behind him.

Francis knew everyone in Beaufort by sight, and many people from Clairy, Grandbourg, Fauville and beyond. He had never seen this little man before. In fact, he had never seen anyone like this little man. He was obviously an off-worlder.

Do all the people on other worlds wear such eccentric clothes, Francis wondered. Do they all carry parasols? He upbraided himself for worrying about trivia. Had he not discovered the invaders' ship? Was he not witnessing the evidence – the first, incontrovertible evidence – that people lived on other worlds beyond the sky, and could travel between worlds, as the books had told him

The little man was walking towards him. 'Benny!' the man shouted, suddenly, and Francis tried to bury himself in the grass. 'Benny, where are you? Bernice! Professor!'

The off-worlder didn't sound threatening. Worried, perhaps, and a little melancholy, Francis thought, but not dangerous. Francis risked another peek above the waving stems.

The little man had stopped in his tracks and was staring up at the sky. Francis followed his gaze, but could see nothing out of the ordinary: just the haze, which was normal these days, and the usual bands of darkness crossing the turquoise sky. The off-worlder seemed to find the heavens fascinating, however, and worrying. 'Oh no,' Francis heard him say. 'Oh dear me, no. This won't do at all. Just as well as I turned up.'

If the off-worlder was suffering from a plague, then the disease could only be of the mind, Francis thought. The fellow looked healthy enough, but his mood seemed to change by the minute, and he talked to himself continuously.

Now he was smiling like a loon, casting glances over his shoulder at the blue box, and chuckling. 'But she's back to normal,' he was saying to himself. 'Shipshape and Bristol fashion. Not quite as good as new, I'll admit, but a perfect landing. Right on target. If only I could find Bernice.' He put his hand against his forehead and scanned the countryside. 'Bernice!' he shouted. 'Benny!'

Francis was coming to a decision. The off-worlder appeared to be unarmed, and if it came to fisticuffs Francis was the larger. Francis also doubted whether the stranger was infectious – and anyway there should be no necessity to touch him. If Francis could bring the off-worlder to Landfall, he would surely reap some reward:

perhaps, if the stranger or his blue box proved useful to the Counsellors, they would allow Francis to remain in his apprenticeship.

And if the off-worlder had no malign intent towards Arcadia, surely he would want to visit Landfall?

Francis once again peered through the grass. The little man was looking straight at him.

'Hello,' the stranger said, doffing his hat. 'I'm the Doctor, and this is – a lovely day, isn't it? I do hope I haven't alarmed you?'

'Oh – er, no,' Francis said, getting to his feet and brushing grass seeds from his cloak. 'I'm pleased to meet you. My name's Francis, the Scribe. Well, I'm only an apprentice, really, but I work as a Scribe. I'm from Beaufort, the town in the valley over there.'

The stranger – the Doctor – smiled, twirled his multicoloured parasol, and glanced in the direction Francis had indicated.

'Ah yes,' he said, his intense gaze returning to the Scribe's face. 'And what, I wonder, takes you so far from your scriptorium?'

'Christina's dead,' he said, wondering, as he heard himself say the words, why he was spilling his thoughts for this curious Doctor. 'And the Counsellors say I must go to Landfall. I'm on my way there now.' He shook his head, and looked away from the Doctor's piercing eyes. He took a deep breath. 'And you are my prisoner,' he added.

'Am I?' the Doctor said, sounding genuinely surprised. 'Well, in that case, it won't matter if you tell me everything that's been going on, will it? I get the impression you've been having a trying time.'

Francis and the Doctor walked side by side across the grassy hillocks and down to the road. As they walked, Francis spoke of his eternal love for the Lady Christina, an aristocrat separated from him by age and by society's conventions, but united with him forever in mutual devotion, and now cruelly taken from him. He decided to gloss over the facts that Christina had never taken him very seriously, that she had only recently become the most

112

important of his several lovers, and that he had already started to become bored with her.

Into this story he wove an account of his difficulties with the Humble Counsellors, and with the Prince who was the Counsellors' catspaw. He wanted only to remain a simple apprentice, he said, and he didn't relish the prospect of disappearing or losing his mind, which seemed to be the fate of Apprentice Scribes who went to Landfall. As an afterthought, he mentioned that he suspected the Counsellors of having something to do with Christina's death, because she complained to the Prince about losing Francis.

As he finished speaking, he realized that his tale lacked all conviction. He knew that to the Doctor's ears he must sound like a pusillanimous, love-sick swain, throwing wild accusations at everyone in authority, more because of fear of the challenges of Mastership than in reaction to his lover's sudden death.

And I still haven't told the Doctor that I saw his friend this morning, Francis thought. Bernice, for whom he was calling, must be the tall woman I spied in the fields. I should tell him that she was heading towards Beaufort. And I should continue to Landfall alone.

'Here we are,' the Doctor said. 'The rolling road, the reeling road, that rambles round the shire . . . ' He prodded the smooth, black surface with the tip of his parasol. 'But this sort of thing wasn't constructed before the Roman came to Rye, was it?' He turned to Francis. 'You did say your society was at a level consistent with the technology of pre-industrial Earth, didn't you? Or words to that effect,' he added, noticing the incomprehension on Francis's face.

'No matter,' the Doctor continued. 'It goes in two directions, and therefore fulfills the most important requirement of a road. Landfall is – that way?' He pointed into the hills. Francis nodded, and started to speak, but the Doctor cut him off. 'Then I'd better come with you, I think. I am your prisoner, after all. And I'm most anxious to meet a Humble Counsellor or two. They've got some explaining to do.'

The Doctor was already striding off in his chosen direction. Francis hurried after him. 'But – Bernice?' he said.

'Ah – you heard me calling, then. Professor Summerfield is a very resourceful woman. I'm sure she can look after herself.'

Everything had slowed. The shouting voices had receded into a confused hum of noise. Bernice could see nothing but the glinting tips of the crossbow bolts. Her mind was racing, but like a cat chasing its tail, her thoughts were futile and circular.

I never wanted to die like this.

That's stupid. Do something, now.

What can I do? I never thought I'd die like this.

It seemed as though hours had passed. Bernice realized very gradually that the bolts were wavering, drifting away from their aim. The guards were lowering their weapons. A voice was shouting above the hubbub.

'I said hold your fire, you idiots. She's alone; she's unarmed. We'll hold her and let the Prince decide.'

The thing not to do, Bernice ordered herself, is to faint. But I really think I must sit down . . .

She sat in the dust with her head in her hands until her heart had stopped thudding. When she looked up, the guards were shuffling aside to make way for a young man who strode through the gateway and stopped a sword's length in front of her. Bernice knew he was exactly a sword's length away because the point of his sword was almost touching her nose.

Some of the townspeople were brightly dressed, but this young man was a peacock. His velvet doublet was slashed to reveal the silk shirt beneath. His coat was brocaded, and trimmed with lace. He wore gold and jewels on his fingers, round his throat, at his waist, and on the buckles of his shoes.

Henry VIII at the Field of the Cloth of Gold, Bernice thought. And they used to tell me it was a waste of time studying history. 'Hello,' she said. 'Give me a hand up, would you. I seem to have lost the use of my legs.'

'It pains me to be so discourteous,' he said, 'but there

114

is a chance that you are contaminated with plague. I must ask you to rise by yourself.'

Bernice struggled to her feet and beat the dust out of her jeans. He wasn't speaking Common, she realized, but some antiquated dialect. It was like twentieth century English, but not exactly the same. The TARDIS's instant translation systems were undeniably miraculous, but Bernice found that because of them she almost failed to notice when she was hearing and speaking languages other than her own.

'This sounds a ridiculous question,' the man was saying, 'but I assume you are from another planet?'

'I think I must be,' Bernice said. 'Home was never like this. Where is this, exactly? And what year is it?'

'This is the town of Beaufort, in the province of Verdany. The year is three hundred and seventy-nine.'

'Oh,' Bernice said. Very helpful, I don't think. She looked again at the turrets of the castle towering over the town's battlements. Medieval, without a doubt. But he knew I could be from another planet.

An ornate, four-wheeled carriage trundled out of the gateway. The black gelding pulling it was the largest horse Bernice had ever seen.

'My coach will take you to my villa at the edge of the town,' the young man said. 'It is both secure and secluded. I will ride and interview you there shortly.'

The coachman muttered agitatedly about plague as Bernice reached up to pet the horse's nose. 'And who are you?' Bernice, turning on the step of the carriage, addressed the young man. 'From the top drawer, I'd say, judging from the fancy duds.'

'Duds?' He was momentarily nonplussed. 'Young woman, I am Gerald, Lord Delahaye, Privy Councillor to his Highness. Have no fear: you are under the protection of one of the noblest families of Verdany.'

Struggling to free herself from Lacuna's insistent towelling, Britta caught site of her reflection in the mirrored wall.

Shivering, hunched, limbs white with cold, face red

115

from weeping, hair hanging damp in strands. A miserable, pale doll. Bathtime plaything of the tall, thin woman with the misshapen head.

'Are they seeing me now, Lacuna? Are they?'

'Hush, pretty one. Let me dry you. Softly, gently. There. And there. They are pleased with you, don't worry. I am pleased with you.'

'You're showing me to them now, aren't you? And you let them feel what I feel, don't you? Why, Lacuna? Why don't you show them things that are really beautiful? Why don't you show them nice things?'

'Nice things!' Lacuna spat. She shuddered, as if the concept of niceness disgusted her. 'I am above such considerations, silly little Britta, and they are more above me than you can imagine. They concern themselves with abstracts and absolutes. Power. Structure. Theory. My role is to provide the element of the senses. I cannot hope to reach their level of pure thought. But I strive to give them sensual clarity.'

'But why – why that sort of thing? Like,' Britta's voice faltered, 'like what you did to me in the bath?'

'They chose me to be their eyes, ears and senses. I was – I am – the strongest intellect on this station. I show them what pleases me.' Lacuna's voice became a warm purr. 'You please me, Britta. See? I can make you smile, can't I, little one? I can make you blush so prettily.'

Lacuna cocooned Britta in the towel. Britta rested her head against Lacuna's shoulder and closed her eyes. It was so peaceful and comfortable – afterwards. She couldn't analyze her emotions.

'So you're in charge of them, in a way, aren't you?' she said sleepily.

Lacuna shook her gently. 'Not a bit of it, silly Britta. They are the collected brains of the Corporation. From this station, they control the most successful businesses in human space. And that is as nothing compared to their research activities here. They are the mind; I am but their hands, eyes and ears. And the mind always controls the senses.'

Britta turned her head and stared up at Lacuna's visionary eyes. Did she really believe that? 'No,' Britta said. 'Not always. I don't think so.'

'It must be so!' Lacuna pushed Britta away, tearing the towel from her body. Britta stumbled and fell, naked, to the tiled floor. Tears filled her eyes.

'The mind controls the senses. It must be so. If it were otherwise . . . ' Lacuna's voice weakened. 'If it were otherwise, then I would be responsible for – for all that. And for . . . No! They chose me. They control me. This must be what they require.'

Britta sobbed. Lacuna smiled suddenly, and held out her arms. 'Come here, pretty one,' she said. 'Let's show them something else now, shall we?'

The lights went out. A second later they flared again. Britta saw that Lacuna had dropped the towel and was standing as still as a statue, with eyes closed. Sniffing, Britta pulled on and belted her costume.

Lacuna's eyes snapped open. 'Dressed? Good. I must work. Our guests are arriving. And there is something on the planet.'

'Something?'

'Yes!' Lacuna hissed. Britta had never seen her worried before. 'Something has appeared on the planet. It's too big – too complex – for Pool to analyze. We'll have to rely on the droids at Landfall. And this time Pool will have to rely on us.'

Britta followed Lacuna into the central area of the chamber. Conical spirals of tracery-thin metal had grown from the ceiling almost to the floor. They chimed dissonantly and shattered into tiny shards as the two women brushed past them.

Lacuna plucked a leering statuette from an alcove and started to smash it against the faces of an obsidian pyramid. 'Don't just stand there!' she shouted at Britta. 'Help me. The two-D screens are somewhere behind those purple curtains. Get them clear.'

Great flakes of stone fell from the pyramid. Through the thinning obsidian, Britta could see indicator lights winking dimly in the heart of the structure.

'We need manual communications, you silly girl,'

Lacuna grunted between swings of the statuette. 'The link won't be enough. Clear those screens!'

Britta ran to pull down the curtains. The chamber filled with sounds of crashing stone and tinkling metal. Everywhere, carvings were toppling to the floor as stone archways lurched like drunkards. The lighting pulsed erratically.

A hologram of the Arcadia system coalesced in the shadows beneath the ceiling. Britta felt drops of moisture fall on her hair and shoulders. Looking up, she saw that in place of the planet Arcadia, a strange blue box was rotating slowly in orbit about the representation of the system's sun. And where there should have been a hologram of the space station, a tiny image of Britta's face was orbiting the planet, and weeping real tears.

The bridge of the *Admiral Raistrick* was a typical, three-tiered circle. Ace had seen dozens like it. The lowest of the three concentric rings was the hologram display, and it was still dark as Ace, with the DK cursing behind her, pushed through the opening doorway and into the controlled excitement of the crowded bridge.

The ship's officers, along with Agent Defries and Jerval Johannsen, the auxiliaries' elected spokesman, occupied the wide, middle tier. Captain Toko sat at his command console, isolated on a lip of blue carpet that rose slightly from the manned deck and protruded over the hologram pit, giving him a view of the entire bridge. The voices of the men and women seated at the control modules all round the deck were subdued and efficient, but the atmosphere was electric with excitement.

'Two minutes, Captain,' one of the officers said.

'Belts, everyone,' said Toko's amplified voice, and the officers strapped themselves into their seats without taking their eyes from the banks of instruments.

Above the control consoles, the circular wall of the bridge sloped away to give all the personnel a view of the third tier, which consisted of a plain screen like the inside of a shallow drum. The domed ceiling of the bridge rose seamlessly from the third tier. The drum and dome made up the visual screen. It was dark and blank now, as the ship was still in warp space.

'Coming in like a dream,' announced a voice over the comms net. 'Drop-out now at two-forty mill kilometres. Closing to two-thirty.'

'Get strapped in, you two,' Toko called to Ace and Daak, who had moved to stand behind Defries and Johannsen. Ace sat in an armchair next to Defries's.

'I'll stand,' Daak growled.

Ace caught Defries's glance and lifted her eyes to the ceiling in mock despair. 'Can't we re-freeze him until we're on the planet?' she said, loudly.

'You woke him up, trooper,' Defries said. 'He's your responsibility now.'

'Thanks,' Ace said, and then called to Toko. 'Hey, Captain! Let's have the screens on.'

'Against regulations until we're out of warp,' Toko laughed. 'But the hologram's on auto. Warp status, Lieutenant Rikov?'

'Steady, Captain.'

'Estimated distance, Henriks?'

'One ninety mill kilometres, sir.'

'Then let's go.' There was a moment of absolute silence. 'Ion drive on.'

'Sir.'

'Close down warp systems.'

'Sir.'

Lights flickered all round the bridge as the ship's processors issued thousands of interrelated commands and responded to millions of feedback signals. In the pit below the bridge deck, a hologram of the Arcadia system twinkled into existence. That, and a slight tremor, were the only signs that the *Admiral Raistrick* had materialized in real space.

Ace had time to spot the tiny red light that represented the ship, just inside a band of white cloud that circled the entire system. Then the ship bucked like a ketch in a tempest, and the Dalek Killer fell across her chair.

Red warning lights were flashing on every console, but Toko and his crew appeared unconcerned.

'Rikov?' the Captain said.

'Thrusters cut in, sir. We dropped out too close to that asteroid belt.'

The dot of red light in the hologram display was now visibly moving further into the planetary system, away from the cloudy ring.

'Damage report,' Toko said.

'Negative, sir.'

'You can get up now,' Ace said, trying to shift her legs under the weight of the recumbent Daak.

He moaned theatrically, and tried to lift himself off her chair. He succeeded only in jamming his right hand between her thighs and giving her a broad grin before he collapsed again.

'Re-freeze him!' Ace hissed at Defries.

Defries smiled sweetly. 'I think he likes you,' she said.

With a grimace of distaste, Ace moved aside Daak's mane of hair and placed her wrist against his exposed neck. 'Off,' she said, 'or I'll blow your head away.'

Daak wriggled the fingers of his trapped right hand, and slowly pulled himself upright. He had a wide smile on his face. He moved his right hand, slowly and ostentatiously, only after he was standing again, and he shook it and blew on his fingers to indicate that his hand had been somewhere very hot.

Every one of Toko's officers was watching his or her console.

'A couple of years ago I would have killed you for that,' Ace said to Daak. 'You're just lucky no-one saw it. Don't ever touch me again.'

Daak grinned. 'You're a hell of a girl,' he said. 'Remind me of someone, too. I think it was—'

'Spare me,' Ace said. 'Captain, can we have the screens on now?'

'My pleasure, Ace.'

Light flooded the bridge as the panorama of space appeared across the drum and dome. The Captain's chair faced the front of the ship, and all eyes turned in that same direction.

The system's sun was almost directly ahead, a startlingly

bright disc with only a hint of yellow. Experienced travellers – in other words, almost every person on the bridge – immediately classified it as an F8 or F9 main sequence star, a little smaller and brighter than Earth's sun.

There were two planets between the *Raistrick* and the sun. The innermost planet was too small to see on the screen: according to the hologram display it was on the far side of the sun. The second planet was, according to Starfleet's limited intelligence, the site of the Spinward Corporation colony.

'There it is!' someone shouted, and fingers all over the bridge were soon pointing to the greeny-blue sphere just to the right of the sun. 'Arcadia!'

But Ace had a rule never to enter an unknown room without first checking behind the door, and as soon as the screens had come on she had looked backwards, over her shoulder. Daak, Defries and Johannsen had done the same. All four of them were now transfixed by what they saw.

'Bloody hell,' Ace said at last. 'Captain, take a look at this asteroid belt we almost hit.'

Toko, and then everyone on the bridge, turned towards the rear of the ship. The gasps of shock were audible, and were the only sounds to break the silence for several minutes.

The asteroid belt was a wide ribbon lying at a slight diagonal across the entire breadth of the screen at the rear of the bridge and thinning as it curved forwards until on the front-facing screens it was a barely-visible line that disappeared behind the sun. The *Raistrick* had now moved sufficiently far inside the parabola of the belt for the individual rocks and boulders to be indistinguishable. And therefore the larger patterns were all the more obvious.

The lumps of space rock had been arranged.

It was impossible. But they could all see it.

Rough chunks of stone and metal, some as big as a planet's moon, most no larger than boulders, had been grouped together into distinct aggregations.

And each aggregation of rocks had been organized to resemble a human face.

And each face was grotesque and contorted.

The closest face, the one directly behind the troopship, the one they had almost hit when dropping out of warp space, was lopsided, with huge filigree ears and an expression of mournful anguish.

Sick, Ace thought. Elephant man.

'Rikov,' the Captain said quietly, 'cut acceleration. Steady speed.'

Isabelle Defries unbuckled her seat belt. 'Battle stations, Captain?' she said as she stood.

'No, Agent. I don't want your gunners to see this yet. Let's find out what it is. Henriks, radar scan. Materials analysis. Throw some radiation at it and see what bounces off, eh?'

Ace was out of her seat now, and scanning the length of the asteroid belt. All of it, as far into the distance of its orbit as she could see, had been arranged to make faces staring inwards at the sun.

It wasn't impossible, she realized. You'd need a lot of big ships, and a mega-computer – and force-field technology that humans wouldn't discover for hundreds of years.

But someone had done it.

'Zoom in on the nearest face,' Toko said.

The screen blanked, and came to life again with the lopsided face filling half of the drum and dome. But it was no longer a face: seen this close, it was just a collection of rocks.

'Scan report, Captain,' Navigator Henriks said. 'Nothing out of the ordinary. They're typical asteroids. Solid. High levels of silica, iron and nickel.'

'What's holding them together, Henriks? What's keeping them in those – shapes?'

'Gravity, Captain,' Henriks said. Amplified over the comms net, he sounded almost offended at having to state the obvious. 'I mean, there are no structures or fields that I can detect between the asteroids.'

'That's what I was afraid of,' Toko said. 'It would have

been so much easier to accept if they'd just been glued together.'

Ace turned towards Toko's command console. 'Captain,' she said, pointing with her thumb over her shoulder at Daak, 'isn't this the right time to launch a completely futile, suicidal, one-man expedition in an unarmed shuttle?'

'You volunteering, Ace?' Toko said.

Daak spun round. 'I'll go,' he shouted. 'Where's my chainsword?'

'Nobody's going,' Toko laughed. 'Our business is on Arcadia. There's nothing here.'

'There's something further out, Captain.' It was Henriks, frantically checking the figures that had appeared on his console screen. 'Some sort of barrier. No detectable mass, but it reflects most forms of radiation. And it's closing in.'

It was Ace who realized first. 'The stars,' she said, staring up at the dome. 'The stars have gone.'

'It's the barrier,' Henriks said, his voice an eerie whisper. 'Jesus, Buddah and Lenin, it's a complete sphere. All round the system.'

'How fast is it contracting, Navigator?' Toko said.

Henriks ran a finger across his screen, and visibly relaxed. 'Nine hundred kilometres a second, approximately. No problem.'

'Unless it starts to accelerate,' Toko said. 'And the longer we stay in the system, the less room we have to manoeuvre in.'

The Captain didn't need to state the obvious. Everyone on the bridge knew the dangers of jumping into warp while travelling towards a nearby sun. And by the time the ion drive could turn the ship to face out of the system, the contracting barrier would be upon them.

'Well, Rikov, Henriks. What do you think? Could we get through it in real space?'

The two officers looked at each other across the hologram pit. Rikov shook his head. Henriks shrugged. 'We don't even know what it is, Captain.'

Toko smiled grimly. 'And we can't see through it. So

123

we don't know what might be waiting for us on the other side.' He stood up suddenly, and looked along the line of grotesque asteroid-faces that stretched away into nothingness round the drum, against a background of empty, starless black. 'You might as well run the estimate, Navigator,' he said. 'If it continues to contract at its present rate, have we got room to jump into warp?'

'Already done it, Captain. We can't jump unless we ignore the usual safety parameters. And,' he gulped, 'the rate of contraction has started to increase.'

'Monitor it,' Toko said. He strode round the bridge to where Defries, Johannsen, Ace and Daak were standing.

'We've fallen into a trap, haven't we, Captain?' Defries said.

'And it looks like our chances of getting out are getting slimmer by the second. It's your show, Belle. I'm just the chauffeur. Do you want to pull out now?'

'No!' Daak roared. For once Ace agreed with him.

'Keep him quiet, trooper,' Defries said to Ace. 'Captain, I don't know much about space physics, but I reckon anyone who can turn an asteroid belt into a portrait gallery and create a barrier across all wavelengths round an entire solar system probably has the means to prevent this ship leaving.'

'I reckon I agree, Agent,' Toko said. 'Can probably crush a troopship, too, like I could crush a flea.' He pinched together a finger and thumb.

'So we lose either way.' Defries laughed suddenly, and stretched her arms above her head. 'What do you say, Jerval? What would your people do?'

A thin smile appeared on the tall, slim trooper's normally expressionless face. 'Let's put it like this,' he said thoughtfully. 'If they ever find out how much shit you've got us into, they'll probably try to kill you. But it's a safe bet they'd rather die fighting something than suddenly, out here in space, without knowing what it is we're up against.'

Ace had never heard Johannsen say so many words in one speech. Defries thanked him for his opinion, but Ace didn't believe she needed it. Ace suspected that Defries had no choice: not a single fastline communication had been received on the bridge – Toko had commented on it – and that meant Defries was on her own. Spinward was a big corporation, everyone knew that. Defries had to come back with proof of something illegal, or not bother to come back at all.

'Damnation!' Abslom Daak thrust himself between Defries and Toko. 'Are we going to stand around talking until that barrier strangles us? Let's get down to that planet and find something to kill.'

'Agreed,' said Johannsen.

'Sounds OK to me,' Ace said.

'Your decision,' Toko reminded Defries.

'Then let's go,' Defries said. 'Would you issue the call to battle stations, Captain?'

Sirens on every deck summoned gunners to their consoles and landing parties to transmat stations. Weapons lockers on the bridge were broken open and small arms were handed out. Iris valves opened at intervals around the circular deck as escape pods were put on stand-by.

Daak thumped a protective hand on to Ace's shoulder. Ace shook it off.

The red dot in the hologram display inched closer to the green sphere that represented the planet Arcadia.

Every now and then the roar of falling masonry echoed in the chamber. Soon the circular space would be empty but for the barely-visible prisms, and prisms within prisms, that showed where the interior dimensions had been folded in upon themselves. Britta avoided them. The dust of the decaying stonework swirled round her feet.

The old and long-disused instrument panels were all visible now. Britta was struggling to cope with the antiquated, manually-operated controls of a monitoring station. Ten small, two-D screens in front of her displayed visual signals from the planet's surface.

She didn't know who she was communicating with; she didn't know how she knew where to direct the search. Something on the edge of her consciousness nudged her towards the right location. You're in the Net, Lacuna had told her; just do as you're told.

Lacuna was a few metres away, surrounded by arrays of dials and screens. Frequently she would throw her misshapen head back and gaze intently at the holographic display: things were moving among the planets and moons, things that were not naturally part of the star system, and only one of the things was the intruding ship.

At other times she would freeze, suddenly, and close her eyes. At these moments Britta felt the presence in her mind retreat slightly, and she guessed that the Corporation and Lacuna were in telepathic conference.

And when not transfixed by the hologram or communing silently with her masters, Lacuna was dashing from one console to another, reading dials, jabbing buttons, kicking recalcitrant machines and screaming curses.

Britta dared to interrupt her.

'Lacuna,' she called. She scanned the video screens again. 'Lacuna, there are people on the planet. It's inhabited.'

'What? Drown them all, where are the X-ship droids when you need them?' She poked frantically at a keyboard. 'Of course it's inhabited, little fool. The programme required it.'

'But everyone up here thinks . . . And everyone on Belmos . . . It's an abandoned colony, isn't it?' Britta stopped to order her thoughts. Everything she'd ever learnt or believed was being upended. 'There are people on the planet, Lacuna. Who are they? They look – primitive. And what will happen to them? The experiment's ending.'

'Get on with the search, child. Those – those people are unimportant. They are part of the programme. They are dispensible now. Pool is almost at optimum. Remaining stock will be culled, as I told you before. Some will be brought here for Pool, the rest will be left on the planet.'

Britta looked at the flickering images on her screens. They were young men and women. Children, too. All in old-fashioned clothes. They were remaining stock. They were to be culled. She fastened on the least distressing of her thoughts. 'Pool?' she said. 'Who is Pool?'

'Questions!' Lacuna broke off her attempt to insert a new sub-routine into the station's defence system. She threw herself across the room towards Britta. 'Enough questions,' she said. Britta backed away from Lacuna's flailing hands. 'Pool is their name. Pool is the corporate mind of the Corporation. A mind as wide and deep as yours is narrow and shallow. Pool controls us all. Pool can alter reality by the power of thought. Pool knows all. Except – '

Lacuna stopped. Something on one of the screens had caught her eye.

'Found it!' she said. 'One of the droids has found it.'

Britta took her hands away from her face. The anomaly was obvious. On one of the screens, in the middle of an otherwise ordinary rural landscape, stood a large, blue box.

'Such a small physical manifestation for such an intractable paradox,' Lacuna mused. 'Britta, summon more droids to that location. Whatever that thing is, we'll learn its secrets if we have to break it into pieces.'

'Yes, Lacuna,' Britta said. 'Do you think – do you think the box contains any people?'

'If they're still inside, Pool will deal with them. If they're on the planet, they can stay there and die.' Lacuna's eyelids fell. Two seconds later, her eyes snapped open again. 'No,' she said. 'There is another impenetrable conundrum on the planet. It is one of two life-forms that emerged from the box. One was human, and is of no consequence. Pool cannot analyze the other. It must be found. It will be used, or destroyed. Bring the box here, and continue the search.'

'Perhaps we should have used the TARDIS,' the Doctor said, as the first drops of rain fell from the dark grey clouds that had rolled across the sky.

Francis, as usual, didn't understand what the strange little man was talking about. Perhaps he was insane. He had walked for miles under the morning sun without bothering to shelter beneath his parasol; now that the sun had disappeared, he had opened the brightly-striped device and was using it to protect himself from the rain.

'It's not a parasol,' the Doctor had snapped at him. 'It's an umbrella. The technology's the same. Which do you think is the more useful application?'

Francis had to admit that the Doctor had a point. His cloak was already heavy with water. He pulled the hood over his head. 'It doesn't rain in the middle of the day,' he said. 'Not usually. The weather has been very bad this year.'

The Doctor stopped and looked up at the sky. 'It will get worse,' he said. 'I wish I could see what was going on up there.'

Francis could almost believe that the Doctor's hard gaze could pierce the clouds. He touched the Doctor's sleeve. 'The forest is hard by the road ahead,' he said. 'We could take shelter.'

'A hard rain,' the Doctor said quietly, letting the drops of water roll down his face. He turned his sharp eyes to Francis. 'There is no shelter!' he said angrily. 'You humans are always ready to ignore or deny unpalatable truths, but you never think to question pleasing false-hoods. This place,' he revolved on his heels holding his umbrella as a pointer, 'this whole planet is just one long, lazy, relaxing soak in a warm and scented bath. And now someone's pulled the plug out.' He shook his dripping hat. 'Let's shelter under those trees.'

By the time they reached the margin of the forest, the sky was a quilt of black and grey. The rain was falling in sheets, billowed by gusts of icy wind. The interior of the forest was quiet, so quiet that Francis could hear the smack of the occasional raindrop that found its way through the broad-leaved canopy to fall on the carpet of dry leaves.

He pulled his cloak more tightly round his shivering body and pushed through some brambles. Every step into the dark took him further from the wind and the rain. He realized that the Doctor was no longer following him.

'Francis!' the Doctor called. 'Is the forest safe?' He was

standing between two massive trunks, silhouetted against the wild sky, flapping his umbrella.

'Safe?' Francis shouted back. 'What do you mean?' It was obvious that the Doctor had no intention of moving. Francis sighed, and plodded back to the forest's edge. I'll catch my death of cold, he thought.

The Doctor was examining the woodland plants, his eyes darting from fern to tree to bramble, and then suddenly to Francis. 'Wild animals?' he suggested.

Francis shook his head angrily. 'Of course there are wild animals,' he said. 'Fox, boar, badger, weasel, squirrel. Nothing to fear. Now let us—'

'Imported fauna,' the Doctor interrupted quietly, and pointed to a tree. 'What do you call this?'

I'm cold, I'm wet, I'm on a journey I don't want to make to a destination I don't want to reach. Now I'm being interrogated by a madman. I should go on alone.

'It's a beech tree,' Francis said.

'And this?'

'Nettles!' Francis almost shouted. 'Stinging nettles.'

'And what about that?'

Francis turned to follow the Doctor's pointing umbrella. He hesitated. 'Holly. Some sort of holly?'

The Doctor's umbrella pointed unwaveringly at a low bush with convoluted leaves. 'Try again,' he said.

'Laurel. It could be laurel. Or myrtle. I'm not a woodsman, Doctor. Let us continue into the forest.'

'In a minute. I'd like you to fetch a small branch of that shrub for me, please.'

Francis shrugged and stepped towards the bush. It must be some variety of holly, he said to himself. But you know it isn't, he thought. It's one of those plants you never really notice. They seem to be cropping up all over the place these days. Ugly things. Not quite right, somehow.

He arrived at the bush. Yes, there were more of them: bigger ones, different ones, deeper in the forest. He looked down at the long, purple leaves. They seemed to move independently of the gusts of wind.

He remembered sunlight. Christina. Their last day together, at the waterfall. Maize growing wild in the grasses. These things growing in the forests. The purple leaves were fleshy, like a baby's fingers. What was the Doctor trying to make him see?

'I can't,' he said, and turned back to the Doctor. 'What is it?'

'It belongs here,' the Doctor said. 'The beech trees and the nettles don't. Neither do you.'

'I know that,' Francis said, suddenly angry. Had the little madman listened to nothing he had told him? 'We are descended from people who came from another world. We came in ships from the sky, many years ago. The proof is in the books which I discovered.'

The Doctor stared at him. 'Are you trying to tell me, Francis,' he said, 'that the rest of the population is even less curious and inquisitive than you? You're all being used for – for something.' He scratched his head. 'The ground is dry here. Let's sit down, have a rest, and wait for the rain to stop. How much further do we have to travel?'

'A long way. The road to Landfall is long and perilous . . . ' Francis noticed the Doctor's impatience. 'I don't know. I found maps, but they are incomplete. The Humble Counsellors tell us only the things we need to know.'

'They tell you everything but,' the Doctor said.

They sat side by side on the exposed roots of a tree, gazing in silence at the rain slanting across the fields.

In the depths of the forest behind them they heard a noise. A roar, and a crashing of undergrowth.

'Wild boar?' the Doctor said.

Francis shrugged.

A fountain played in the pool in the centre of the square atrium. Its tinkling sound was drowned by the noise of the rain falling on the tiles that covered the terrace, where Bernice was sitting in a wicker armchair. She wasn't cold: each of the romanesque arches that cloistered the paved atrium and supported the terrace roof contained glazed doors which kept out the wind and the rain. And the flagstones beneath her feet were warm.

Under-floor heating, she thought. And damned good mulled wine. Comfortable cushions, with fine damask covers. And a view of fountains in the rain, surrounded by vast terracotta pots sprouting orange trees. It's all rather hypnotic.

She brought the goblet to her face and inhaled cinnamon and clove with the alcoholic fumes.

Medieval life wasn't so dreadful after all. Perhaps the text books were wrong. During her drive through the town of Beaufort she'd seen no dung in the streets, no beggars or cripples, no houses made of anything but straight timbers, well-laid courses of bricks, and dressed stone.

The Delahaye villa – the smallest of the family's residences, Lord Gerald had pointed out, and not at present being used by the household – was situated in a quiet suburb of Beaufort. It was the perfect place to house a visitor who might be a plague carrier and who might need protection from a fearful mob. The neighbouring villas were set wide apart, each in its own walled grounds, and most were as unoccupied as the Delahayes'. The suburb was the only part of the town on the eastern bank of the river known as the Slow Brochet, and the only way to reach it was across an arching stone bridge with its own crenellated guardhouse and mail-clad guards.

Bernice was alone in the villa. There must be servants, she supposed: someone must bring in fresh food, and fuel for the heating. But she hadn't seen anyone yet.

Lord Gerald had opened a room for her. She was sitting outside it now, watching the rain fall in the courtyard. It was bigger than her room in the TARDIS. The bed was a four-poster, like the ones she'd seen in books, with a mattress as soft as marshmallow and curtains of shot silk. Lord Gerald, apologizing stiffly for the absence of domestic staff, had managed to locate clean sheets and towels, new items of what he called feminine attire (and which Bernice classified as very fancy fancy dress), and a tray of bread, cheeses, grapes and mulled wine.

When he had departed, promising to return soon, Bernice had rolled up the slatted shutters to look out on a walled orchard of fruit trees and cropped grass. The rain had just started, rustling the leaves.

I could get to like it here, Bernice thought, as she took another swig of the wine, if it weren't for the bars at the window of my room. I really ought to start feeling guilty about not being much help to the Doctor. But this is more than just a touch more comfortable and interesting than the average prison. The architecture's fascinating. Very fine carvings on those arches. Almost impossibly regular. Must have a closer look. In a minute.

She wriggled deeper into the cushions, closed her eyes, and listened to the falling rain. She started to sing, a lullaby that her father had sung to her. The raindrops seemed to fall into the rhythm of the tune.

She stopped, suddenly alert, eyes open. It wasn't the sound of the rain. Somewhere in the villa, somewhere above the ceiling, a muffled knocking continued the slow rhythm of the song.

It stopped.

There's something in here with me, Bernice thought. She shivered. She listed the possible candidates for imprisonment in a medieval society: dangerous animals, lunatics, criminals, and the infectiously ill. She couldn't decide which she'd rather share a prison with.

Doctor, if you're as telepathic as you make out, this is a distress call, right? Maybe you'd better come and get me out of this.

Francis spoke again. 'Doctor?'

'Hm? Sorry. Thought I heard something.'

'So did I. It's that noise again. Listen.'

Above the noise of the falling rain, Francis could hear a scratching, rustling sound. Something was moving through the forest.

'Ah yes,' the Doctor said. 'It sounds quite large, doesn't it?'

Bilious fear bubbled in Francis's gut. He didn't want to be here, in the rain, in the forest, in the cold, with this manic off-worlder and with something unseen among the dark trees. His life was books. Books and beds.

'I don't know!' he almost shouted. 'I'm just an Apprentice Scribe. Don't ask me.'

The Doctor stared at him, a schoolmaster staring at a wayward pupil. 'You've had a better education than most on this benighted planet,' he said. 'Use it. What can live in the forest? Only creatures that can survive on the forest plants and on smaller forest creatures.'

'A boar, then,' Francis said. He had to admit that the Doctor was right: when he started thinking, the fear subsided. 'Perhaps a fox.'

'There are no wolves? Or bears?'

Francis knew the words. He couldn't picture the animals. He shook his head slowly, trying to remember. 'No,' he said. 'Only in books. But, Doctor . . . ' The fear had gripped him again. He could hardly speak. 'If the squirrels eat the nuts from the trees. And the boars eat the shoots and roots of the bushes . . . '

'Yes?' The Doctor was almost smiling now.

'That plant – the one you showed me. The one I couldn't touch.'

'Yes?'

'What sort of creature lives on that, Doctor?'

'Well done,' the Doctor said. 'I was wondering when you'd work it out.'

There was another crashing of undergrowth. The noises were getting closer.

'More to the point,' the Doctor added, 'what kind of creature lives by predation on the animals that live on that plant?'

'I really don't want to find out.'

The Doctor looked disappointed. 'Perhaps you're right,' he said. 'The rain might be the lesser of the two inconveniences. Time to move on, I think.'

They stood up. As Francis walked away from the wide trunk of the tree that had given them shelter, he saw something move in the bushes beside him.

The Doctor came up and whispered in his ear. 'Don't dawdle, Francis,' he said. 'Run!'

Footsteps were approaching. Bernice shrank into the armchair. The door in the corner of the cloister started to open.

Gerald, Lord Delahaye, stepped through the doorway, smiling.

Bernice was so relieved she could have run up to him and hugged him.

'I have informed His Highness about you,' he boomed as he strode along the terrace towards her. 'He approves of my decision to offer you hospitality here until he has had time to confer with the Counsellors.'

'Am I going to meet him?' Bernice babbled. 'Just fancy, a real Prince. This could be the start of a fairy-tale romance. Will I have to wear my new frock?'

Gerald continued to smile indulgently. 'An audience may be granted,' he said, toying with the gold chains at his chest. 'The Prince will doubtless proceed according to the advice of the Counsellors.'

The subject appeared to be closed, and for a moment the nobleman seemed at a loss. 'Are you comfortable here?' he asked. 'Do you require anything?'

I could do with getting out of here and finding the Doctor, Bernice thought. I'd like to know what made the noises upstairs. I don't understand how a pre-technological society can manufacture blocks of dressed stone that are as completely uniform as the ones this building is made of. I'd like to know, even approximately, where and when I am.

'Do you always wear enough gold and jewels to fill the average treasure chest?' she said.

Lord Gerald stepped back. 'I am accoutred according to my rank as head of the Delahayes,' he said, obviously mystified by her question. 'Metals and gems are surely not remarkable? But of course: you are from another world.' He nodded his head sympathetically. 'The Counsellors tell us that Arcadia is furnished more plentifully than any other place. They tell us where to dig; they train the Masters of the Guilds in the arts of metalwork and gem cutting. Our forefathers came here to escape death and disease, misery and violence.'

Arcadia. Bernice didn't recognize the name. But she

had some idea, at last, of what was going on. This was, as she had suspected, a colony on a terraformed planet. A colony that thrived in blissful ignorance of the rest of the galaxy. Perhaps the Counsellors were an elite corps of administrators, a team of corporation bureaucrats who were in the know and who maintained the planet as a medieval paradise. Now the question was: why?

'I'm an archaeologist,' she said. Lord Gerald looked blank. 'A historian – a historian of buildings. Could I possibly inspect the villa? It's absolutely fascinating. I'd like to look in all the rooms.'

Lord Gerald's eyes darted upwards for a moment. He smiled gracefully. 'I regret that it's not possible. Most of the doors are locked. And my chamberlain has the keys. The house is unoccupied at the moment, you see.' He paused for emphasis. 'You are quite alone here.'

'I see. It's just that . . . Well, never mind. I'll just have to sit and watch the rain, won't I?'

The nobleman stared through the glass doors at the growing puddles in the paved courtyard. He looked worried. 'I apologize most sincerely for the inclement weather,' he said. 'It really is most unusual. Or it used to be. The Counsellors have no explanation. Most unusual.'

He made a slight bow and hurried away, frowning.

Bernice heard the outer doors open and then close. She started to sing again, softly at first, and then more loudly.

Above her, in one of the rooms above the terrace, the knocking started. The sounds were not equally loud, and sometimes strayed from the rhythm of her song. She didn't like to imagine what kind of wounds or mental impairment would cause someone to keep time so badly. Still singing, she rose from the chair. She was going to investigate.

Francis ran. Something was coming out of the undergrowth. Something big.

A sharp pain cut his ankle. As he fell face forward he had time to realize he had snagged his foot in a loop of thorns. He gasped for breath. The thing was upon him.

He looked up, ready to cry out. The scream died in his throat.

A vision from a nightmare stood over him.

He saw four legs, straight and bristling with hairs. He saw a huge head, flat-fronted and grey. Two blank eyes as big as plates. A round mouth filled with spines.

'Fascinating,' the Doctor said.

The creature hissed as the Doctor lunged at it with his umbrella.

Francis felt the Doctor's hand on his shoulder, pulling him up with surprising strength.

'He's hungry,' the Doctor said, holding on to the Scribe as he retreated step by step. 'A long way from his hunting grounds. He won't venture into the open.'

Francis felt the rain on his head and sobbed with relief. They were out of the forest. The Doctor's hand released its grip and Francis fell into the wet grass, shuddering. He rolled on to his back and stared up at the dark, writhing lumps of cloud. The cold, driving rain was as sweet as a summer shower.

Some time later he shook himself, and looked around. The Doctor was standing nearby, under the opened umbrella, watching the shadows under the trees. 'You'd better get up,' he said. 'Catching your death of cold is as bad as being eaten by an alien carnivore.'

'Doctor. I have to tell you . . . '

'Get up, man.'

Francis struggled to stand. His cloak was waterlogged. 'Doctor, I've been very foolish. I knew – or I suspected. I found books in the library. Books I shouldn't have read. Things are wrong here. Things have been wrong since the beginning. And getting worse. I was the only one who realized. And I didn't let myself believe . . . '

'Don't blame yourself,' the Doctor said cheerily, holding the umbrella over both of them. 'It's very common, particularly in your species. Ignorance is just ignorance. You need knowledge to achieve self-delusion. And more knowledge still for enlightenment.' A distant look appeared in his eyes. 'Sometimes it seems there is never enough knowledge.'

'But I didn't tell you. I saw your friend.'

'Bernice?'

'Yes. She was walking towards Beaufort.'

'Good.' To Francis's surprise and relief, the Doctor seemed suddenly cheerful.

'Good?'

'Francis, let me tell you something. Very little has pleased me since the TARDIS landed here. My companion has wandered off, almost certainly into danger. Something terrible and inexorable is going on here, and I can't tell what it is. But I have a nasty feeling that it might be my fault, in a way. I have been under telepathic siege for the past few hours. And I fear that the TARDIS is no longer where I left her. Now I know, at least, where Professor Summerfield is. And,' he added, flapping his umbrella, 'it's stopped raining. Shall we return to the town and rescue Benny?'

'I don't think so, Doctor. Look.'

Francis pointed across the fields. Two black-robed figures had appeared as if by magic, and were advancing towards them with ungainly haste. Glancing behind him, Francis saw two more Counsellors standing beneath the trees and barring a flight into the forest.

'I think we're going to be escorted to Landfall,' he said.

The Doctor's face twisted in anger. 'All right,' he shouted. 'I really don't care. I just want some answers!'

Weak, watery sunlight fell in thin stripes through the row of shuttered windows. Peering through the slats, Bernice looked down on the rain-spangled fruit trees in the orchard.

Good. She was in the right place. This narrow corridor ran above the wing of the villa that contained her bedroom. The dust on the floorboards was thick, but not undisturbed. Someone had been here, recently.

The scuffed footprints led to one of the doors opposite the windows. Bernice tiptoed along the corridor until she reached the door.

Now that the last drops of rain had been wrung from the clouds, the silence was absolute. Bernice could hear only the beating of her own heart. She pulled a stupid face, with crossed eyes and protruding jaw. No point in taking danger too seriously. She started to hum the lullaby.

And the knocking started almost immediately. The noise was still muffled, hardly louder than it had sounded on the terrace, and still irregular.

Now what? Bernice wondered. I can't stand here humming at a door forever.

She touched the handle. The door swung open.

Bernice stepped back, half expecting something to leap at her from the gaping darkness. The knocking stopped.

Nothing else happened.

Bernice stepped into the doorway.

The room was in darkness, its window shuttered and curtained. It smelt inhabited: Bernice wrinkled her nose at the odour of sweat and excrement.

As her eyes became accustomed to the gloom, she saw that the room was bare: floorboards, plastered walls, beams and rafters criss-crossing under the slope of the roof-tiles. Nothing else – except for a bundle on the floor in one corner.

Bernice hummed again. The bundle moved.

It wasn't a big bundle. It was smaller than Bernice.

Never pick on someone your own size, she reminded herself. It's easier to head-butt downhill.

She walked across the room, pulled aside the curtain, threw open the shutters, and spun round to look at the bundle.

It didn't move. It still looked like a roughly-rolled blanket. She stepped towards it, avoiding the scattered pieces of filth and discarded food.

She stopped when she saw the chain. A ring of iron was set into the wall, and a chain ran from it and disappeared into the bundle.

A wild animal, Bernice thought. You might chain a wild animal. But why keep it in an upstairs room?

She stepped forward again. She was close enough to touch the bundle. She hummed the tune, and the bundle jerked, as if surprised or frightened to hear a voice so nearby.

Bernice rested her hand on the rough cloth. The bundle lay still.

Human. It was a small human. Bernice could make out the shape of thin legs through the outer layer of cloth. She peeled back the material, and let out a gasp that sounded like a cry of pain.

She blinked back the tears that welled in her eyes, and lowered herself to sit on the wooden floor. She no longer trusted her legs to support her.

The bundle contained a young girl, naked and dirty from the waist down. The girl's torso was constricted inside a linen garment with elongated sleeves that were tied together behind the back. The chain was connected to a ring in the collar. A leather bag, tied tight at the neck, enclosed the girl's head.

Bernice stretched out a shaking hand and touched the girl's shoulder. The bound body jerked again.

Bernice couldn't help it. She let tears stream down her face and sobs burst from her lungs as she tore frantically at the buckles and knots.

The girl would have been pretty, normally. Now she was emaciated and dirty. Her eyes were wide open, staring at nothing. Her cracked lips were slackly parted. She made no noise. She was free from her shackles, but she hardly moved.

Bernice cradled the girl's head in her lap and rocked gently back and forth, crying occasionally as she stroked the greasy, matted hair.

She started to sing the lullaby again, and gradually the girl's face came to life. Her eyes focused on Bernice's face. Bernice smiled through her tears, and sang more loudly.

The girl's lips started to move, as if she was trying to speak. Bernice caressed her face, and murmured words of comfort.

A choking noise came from the girl's throat. Bernice hushed her, but she began to move her arms and legs agitatedly. And suddenly she jerked out of Bernice's arms, and sat bolt upright with her eyes wide. She brought her hands to her face, and started to scream – abrupt cries of pain, as if in response to repeated and swift thrusts of a dagger.

She didn't stop screaming, even after Bernice had wrapped her arms round the skinny, rigid body, but she did eventually quieten. And at last the cries became softer and less regular as Bernice hugged and stroked her, until Bernice was sure she could make out words among the anguished moans.

'He . . . He did . . . '

'What is it, my sweetheart,' Bernice whispered. 'What are you trying to say?'

'He killed her,' the girl shouted. 'He cut a hole.'

The Doctor seemed delighted with the Humble Counsellors. Francis had never liked them: he remembered having bad dreams about them in his childhood, and he was sure that in those days the Counsellors had been less ungainly than they had become in recent years. One at a time they were disconcerting enough, and being surrounded by four made Francis twitch with apprehension. He was glad the Doctor was with him.

They travelled quickly into the hills. The Doctor was apparently tireless, and Francis was the slowest of the group. The Counsellors hissed and croaked disapprovingly whenever he insisted on a rest.

Panting as he sat on a boulder half-way up a rocky slope, Francis tried to analyze his dislike for the hooded advisers. They seldom spoke to him, so the horrible gargling sounds they made could cause only a small part of his distaste. He decided it was the way they walked.

Each one was different, he realized now that he could see four at once. One had a spine so curved that his head hung level with his chest; another seemed to be extremely thin except at his hips, where the black silk bulged strangely. Francis knew, from his illicit studies, that deformed babies used to be born, back in the bad old days on Earth. Everyone thought that none were born on Arcadia, but perhaps the malformed children disappear to be trained as Counsellors, he thought. All of them moved oddly, as if their legs were making irregular movements under their robes. But they could certainly move quickly, even over difficult terrain. He looked up the slope and groaned.

The Doctor sauntered over and jumped lightly to stand on the boulder next to Francis's.

'I've been trying to take a look at our hooded friends,' he said.

'I know,' Francis replied. 'You've been running in circles round them. I don't know where you get the energy from.'

'Gallifrey,' the Doctor said absently. 'They're not human, you know,' he added.

'What?'

'I don't think they're human. They're organic, but I think they're constructs. It's the differences that intrigue me. Most androids are disappointingly standardized. Mass production, you know; economies of scale, and so forth. Shall we have a closer look?'

Francis was about to decline the offer, but the Doctor had already jumped down and was walking towards the nearest Counsellor. He tapped the figure on the back of its head and, when it turned round, he beckoned it towards Francis.

The other three Counsellors remained standing like statues on the hillside. Francis had to admit that the Doctor was probably right, and that he should have recognized the fact himself years ago: the Counsellors weren't human.

Stationary, and silent except for its wheezing breath, the chosen Counsellor stood before the Doctor and Francis. The Doctor paced around the still figure.

'What I would like to know,' he said, his words coming in bursts as he increased the speed of his circling, 'is why no-one, ever, in the history of this unadventurous planet, has ever done this before.' And he stopped behind the Counsellor and yanked its hood backwards.

Francis was almost getting used to shocks. This was no

worse than the beast in the forest; slightly easier to look at, in fact, because it might once have been almost human.

But it wasn't human. It had a head, with eyes, ears and a mouth, but it wasn't human. The worst of it was the scalp: it was hairless, but it wasn't a smooth, bald dome. It had ridges, nodules, horns and spirals, shapes that Francis's eye couldn't follow, that seemed to turn in on themselves. Some of the crinkled, soft matter that nestled in the heart of these shapes, Francis realized with nausea, was like bits of a brain.

The coarse skin, black and purple and green, was almost normal by comparison. The facial features, though distorted and unbalanced, were roughly of the same shapes and in the same places as a human's. Francis was particularly intrigued by the curls and folds of the thing's right ear, which seemed to become more complicated the longer he stared at them. The creature was odious, certainly, but Francis had no difficulty in stifling his exclamations of horror.

The Doctor, to Francis's surprise, was speechless, and grey with shock.

'Oh no,' Francis heard him say at last. 'This is worse than I thought.'

The Doctor placed himself a mere hand's breadth in front of the Counsellor's repellent face. 'Let me look into your eyes,' he said. 'I want to communicate with your masters.'

The creature's eyes glowed red, and then became blank white discs. The Doctor's brow creased with the effort of concentrating. His eyes were chips of blue ice.

'Yes,' he said at last, the word escaping from his lips like a sigh. 'I see. I can't read you, and you can't read me.'

He turned away from the Counsellor and bowed his head.

'Doctor?' Francis hadn't seen the Doctor look defeated before. 'Is everything . . . '

'All right? Oh yes. Everything's splendid. Couldn't be better. I'm just a prize idiot, that's all.' He clenched his fists and threw back his head. 'By the Rod and the Sash,

142

what have I done this time?' he shouted at the sky. 'I was only trying to help,' he added bitterly, 'as usual.'

They were in Bernice's bedroom when Lord Gerald returned. In between bathing and feeding the girl, Bernice had coaxed from her a name, Elaine, and a garbled story that added considerably to Bernice's suspicions about the world called Arcadia.

Bernice had taken a pair of scissors to the costume that had been provided for her. Elaine had smiled her first smile on seeing her reflection dressed in the cut-down finery, and Bernice had almost wept again. She had just swept the girl into a hug when there was a peremptory knock and the door flew open.

Elaine's body froze in Bernice's arms.

Lord Gerald stood on the threshold, too surprised to speak.

Bernice had no such difficulty. Her anger gave her the strength to lift Elaine with one arm. She advanced towards the door with the scissors in her free hand.

'What have you done?' She didn't know what she wanted: answers, revenge, an apology. 'How could you do that to a child? Talk, you aristocratic bastard. What did you think you were doing?'

'Lady, be peaceful,' Lord Gerald said. 'My niece was—'

'Your niece? You did this to your own niece?'

'I am the head of the family, it was my responsibility to care for her.'

'Care? That's what you call care?'

Lord Gerald was standing against one of the columns of the terrace now, with the scissors at his throat. Bernice was beginning to control her anger, and she had to admit he was keeping his cool.

'My niece was out of her senses,' he said, with deliberate calm. 'We did everything we could. We tried purging and bleeding. We used poultices. We plunged her into hot and cold baths. We – '

'Don't go on,' Bernice said. She dropped the scissors

143

and wrapped both arms round Elaine. 'She just needed time, you idiot. Time and a bit of affection.'

Lord Gerald shook his head sadly and spread his hands. 'We didn't know what to do. We did our best. We followed the best advice.'

'Something bad is going on.' Bernice spoke slowly and carefully. 'You know that, don't you? Don't just shake your head. Think! The truth is being kept from you. Elaine is still very frightened, but I believe what she says. She saw the murder of her sister.'

'Murder?' Lord Gerald was incredulous. 'You must be mistaken, I assure you. She was in the room, I know, and it must have been a terrible shock, but there's no question of murder. None at all. It was a natural death, and not untimely. The Humble Counsellors always know.'

Elaine had started to wail. Bernice comforted her, and Lord Gerald took the opportunity to retreat along the terrace.

Bernice became aware of strange noise: shuffling, irregular footsteps, and laboured breathing. She felt Elaine's body go rigid with fear.

'I have not yet had a chance to tell you,' Lord Gerald called from the end of the terrace, 'that both you and Elaine are to be moved from here. The Counsellors say that we risk an epidemic if you stay in the town. My niece needs some sort of special treatment, apparently. So you're both to go to Landfall. The Counsellors are here to take you.'

The door behind him opened. Three thin figures, robed and hooded in black, advanced towards Bernice and Elaine.

'It's all right, sweetheart,' Bernice said, fighting down a wave of panic. 'I'll look after you.'

Now it was the Doctor who slowed their progress. Francis was by no means ungrateful for the change in pace, but the change in the Doctor's demeanour worried him. The usually piercing blue eyes were shadowed; the Doctor looked neither to right nor left, but seemed to be staring

144

at his shoes as they dragged him across fields of scree and hummocks of mountain grass.

The Counsellors were apparently prepared to match the Doctor's pace. They staggered, wheezing, over the rough terrain, maintaining a square formation around the Doctor and Francis.

The Scribe had no idea how many hours they had been stumbling up and down rocky slopes. He was exhausted, hungry and thirsty, and he was sure that the soles of his sandals had worn perilously thin. When he glanced behind him, he saw that the comforting vista of fertile valley and wooded hillsides had disappeared, cut off from his sight by the sharp ridges the party had crossed.

Ahead, the view was the same, or worse: crags of rock, boulder-strewn plateaus, and occasional gulleys containing trickling streams and dense, thorny, scrub. A steady wind stung his eyes and stole the warmth from within his cloak. At least half of the sparse vegetation, he realized with a shock, was unfamiliar – no, it was worse than unfamiliar, it looked wrong, misshapen, unnatural. He didn't like to look at the plants, but they held an awful fascination. He tried to imagine meadows of the stuff, forests of giant specimens; it was all too easy to visualize such places, and all too obvious that men and women wouldn't survive there.

There were no signs of people on the slopes ahead, no obvious places to rest or take shelter, and no hint that the going would become any easier. The consolation, from Francis's point of view, was that there was no indication that they were approaching Landfall, either.

The Doctor walked past. His step had recovered some of its former liveliness, and his eyes were scanning the horizon.

'Doctor,' Francis said, hurrying to catch up, 'are you well?'

'I've done some thinking. It usually helps, even in the worst situations. Do your people keep hamsters?'

'Hamsters?'

'Small, furry rodents. White mice, perhaps? Gerbils? In cages? With wheels inside?'

'Mice, yes. Children like to keep them as pets. The cage usually has a spoked double wheel, like a water wheel. The mice run in it. They seem to like the exercise.'

'I know what they feel like.' The Doctor sighed. 'I used to think I liked it, too. But the trouble is, the harder you run, the faster the wheel spins. And the faster the wheel spins, the harder you have to run. You see what I mean?'

Francis had no idea. 'I think so,' he said. 'You think you're to blame, in some manner, for – all this?'

'In some manner. I've been sifting through the time lines. It's more difficult outside the TARDIS, but I think I've identified where this anomaly comes from. And it comes from something I did on Earth. I thought it was very clever and successful at the time.'

'I don't understand, Doctor.'

'Well, I saved humanity again. Good old Doctor, riding to the rescue as usual. But you can't make omelettes without breaking eggs. I looked ahead, of course. Couldn't detect any tremors. Only four centuries. Less than a thousand light-years from Earth. It wasn't very far away. And I missed it. I was under a lot of strain at the time. So was the TARDIS, poor old dear. I pulled you out of the frying pan then, but it looks like you're in the fire now as a result. Am I making myself clear?'

Francis looked sideways at the Doctor, and tripped over a stone. 'Is it something to do with cooking?' he said.

The Doctor's frown of annoyance suddenly turned into a wide grin. 'You're right,' he said. 'It doesn't do to take things too seriously. Nor should we jump to conclusions. The genetic manipulation isn't anachronistic. The block transfer mathematics is, but perhaps it's not intrinsically damaging. But the mind that's capable of carrying out the computations – that's what worries me. It shouldn't be possible, you see. It knows I'm here. And I have no idea what it is.'

'Will it be waiting for us at Landfall?'

'Quite possibly. I'm looking forward to the meeting. There's no reason to expect the worst. I sense a mind not unlike mine. A deep mind. A mind that perceives the currents. Let's press on.'

The Doctor strode ahead, almost overtaking the vanguard Counsellor. Francis struggled to keep up.

'Restrain your optimism, Doctor,' he said. 'If this thing, this mind that you expect to find, it unfriendly, then we are walking to what could be our deaths.'

'Or worse. On the other hand, it wouldn't do to assume evil when we have evidence only of great power.'

'But we are alone, Doctor. We can hope for no prospect of help.'

The Doctor chuckled. 'Do you know,' he said, 'I'd quite forgotten. A friend of mine should be dropping in at any moment.'

He looked up at the sky, as if he expected some sort of assistance to break through the rolling clouds.

The sirens had been turned off, but the red lights were still flashing every five minutes. In the hologram pit, the red dot that represented the *Raistrick* was still inching towards the green golfball of Arcadia. The ghostly sphere that represented the unidentifiable barrier was shrinking inwards, confining the troopship to a smaller and smaller ball of space. On the forward screen the planet was now dead ahead, and getting close enough to show continents and cloud patterns. The rearward screen was blank.

There wasn't much talking. There wasn't much to do except wait, but the ship's officers ran endless systems checks. Defries and Johannsen were together at a terminal, issuing orders to the auxiliaries' section leaders. Heavy weapons were being assembled and programmed, combat suits and power armour were being donned, medicines and provisions were being allocated, drug and hormone implants were being triggered, transmat bays were being filled with battle-crazed troopers.

Ace wanted to be down on the landing decks, amid the fear and excitement, the shouting and crowding, the smell of hot circuitry and berserkaloid plastigraft, the whine and thump of the armoured infantry, the chittering of a thousand personal comms speakers.

But she also wanted to find out what was happening, and so the bridge was the only place to be. She and Captain Toko were the only still, silent figures on the bridge: both sat, apparently relaxed, their eyes glancing continually from the screen to the hologram and back again.

Abslom Daak was pacing back and forth behind Ace's chair. Defries had reluctantly allowed him to have back his personal weapon, a chainsword capable of cutting through a Dalek's steel carbide casing. Ace thought it was primitive. Every few minutes he pulled the trigger and the weapon made a noise like a dentist's drill. Ace was beginning to get used to it, but she made a mental note to keep well away from Daak in a fight. He gave no indication that he would be careful about precisely who he scythed down.

It was Daak who saw them first, even before the ship's defence system had reported.

'Fighters,' he said. The bridge fell silent. Daak pointed at the screen. 'There. Coming from behind the planet.'

Ace couldn't see them. She guessed that Daak had augmented eyesight. But the *Raistrick* had picked them up: a dozen red dots appeared in the hologram display, spreading out as they curved round the planet and headed towards the troopship. They were moving faster than the *Raistrick*.

'Steady, everyone,' Toko said. 'This isn't a problem. Agent Defries, are your people ready at the pipes?'

'Yes, Captain. Are we going to use the fast-guided missiles?'

'Only if we have to, Belle.' He laughed. 'We can handle this with nuts and bolts technology. I don't entirely trust a weapons sytem with a range that's bigger than a solar system. Henriks, patch the bridge comms through to all sub-stations.'

'OK, Captain.'

'Hear this, everybody.' Toko raised his voice, as if addressing a crowded room. 'This is Captain Toko on the bridge. We're going to get some action at last. So far it's only a dozen fighters, so don't get too excited. We'll use drones and torpedoes. I'll put the hologram through the terminal screens so you can watch the fun, and I'll leave this channel open. Stand by for some fireworks.'

He rubbed his hands together and stared at the forward screen. Twelve silver specks were just visible now.

'Launch six drones, Desoto,' he said. 'Forward, of course. Random distribution. And ready twelve torpedoes.'

There was no noise or vibration to indicate that the drones had been launched. Ace gripped the arms of her chair and gaped. Six troopships, identical in appearance to the *Raistrick*, had appeared on the forward screens in a scattered formation. Ace had seen drones used as decoys many times in space battles, but she had never seen drones that were as big as their parent ship. It wasn't possible.

'Captain?' she called.

Toko waved in acknowledgement. 'It's the latest thing, Ace. Little devils are no bigger than you are, but even our own visual enhancement can't tell they're not troopships. As far as those fighters are concerned, they've got seven *Raistricks* to kill.'

Ace didn't reply. She had felt – something. Something in her mind. It was like passing through a weak energy field, or stepping out of a warm room into a cold evening. But there was no physical sensation. She sensed that she had crossed some sort of boundary.

She looked at Daak just as he was turning to look at her. He grinned, as usual, but then raised a questioning eyebrow. Ace nodded. He'd felt it too.

'Fire torpedoes,' Toko said confidently. 'Keep them back behind the drones until I give the word.'

On the forward screen, twelve darts flashed into view and hung in space behind the huge images of the drones. A cheer went up from all round the bridge.

The fighters from Arcadia didn't stand a chance. They were too small to carry many missiles, and the drones would take the entire payload. In Ace's opinion, Toko was being over-protective: three or four of these new super-drones would have been enough. And not one of the fighters would get back to base: a Starfleet torpedo would, unless intercepted or scrambled, pursue and destroy the fastest and biggest Dalek battle saucer.

Ace preferred a slightly more even fight, but that wasn't why she felt troubled. Something was wrong.

She looked at the hologram. Nothing had changed, except . . . She squinted at the display. There was a vague shadow behind the red dot that was the *Raistrick*, as if that area of the display was overlaid with haze.

She spun her chair and looked at the rearward screen. 'Bloody hell,' she breathed.

The fighter attack had been a feint. The real danger was behind the troopship. Ace didn't know what it was. It looked like a face. A face that dwarfed the *Raistrick*. The face of a beautiful young woman with streaming, golden hair.

Ace found her voice. 'Captain,' she said. She heard his chair turn.

'Well, well, well,' Toko said, after a long silence. 'Desoto, send those torpedoes out. Henriks, what is this thing behind us?'

Ace turned her head in disgust. The head was changing. At first the widening of the eyes and the opening of the mouth seemed to be a normal facial expression. It looked attractive; Ace thought it might be a greeting.

But the eyes grew into circles, and the mouth extended into a gaping beak, and the hair that spread like a halo round the face congealed into fibrous strands that started to wriggle towards the *Raistrick* like eels.

'It's not there, Captain,' Henriks said. 'I mean, there's nothing physical. There's some diffuse radiation, indicating that energy's being used. But nothing physical. Not even a cloud of dust.'

Toko swore and stood up. 'There must be something there. We can all see it. You can all see the same thing, I take it? It used to be a face, but it's getting horribly like a giant squid, right?'

Everyone on the bridge murmured agreement.

'In that case,' Toko went on, 'it's real. Unless we're suffering from a mass hallucination. And if it's real, we

150

can damage it. Desoto, fire a torpedo from one of the rear pipes.'

The thing's tentacles were so close that Ace imagined they might reach through the screen. The torpedo appeared, flashing along the undulating tunnel of tentacles towards the thing's beak.

'Impact,' said Desoto.

The torpedo struck the centre of the face, and disappeared.

'Dammit, Desoto, where's it gone?' Toko said.

Henriks replied. 'It went straight through, Captain. Like I said, there's nothing there.'

Ace was out of her chair. Something terrible was about to happen. The face was nearer now, and the tentacles were streaming along both sides of the ship, their tips almost meeting across the forward screens.

'Captain!' she yelled, but when Toko spun round she had no idea what to say.

Abslom Daak was moving. Ace had the breath knocked from her body as he ran into her and pushed her forward, towards the rim of the bridge. She stumbled, and he pulled her upright.

'Escape pod, girl!' he snarled.

Ace didn't argue. 'Defries and Johannsen,' she gasped. The couple were standing by the nearest iris door, staring up at the enveloping tendrils.

'You get Defries,' Daak said, 'I'll grab the auxie.'

Defries and Johannsen were five paces away. The escape pod door was another five.

Ace heard something slide across the ship's hull. The floor rocked. Sirens started to blare.

'Don't argue,' Ace said as she grabbed the front of Defries's collar. The ship lurched.

Defries, off balance, failed to disable Ace with her instinctive open-hand blow. The chop glanced off Ace's upper arm. Ace kicked and punched and shoved and screamed, and Defries stumbled backwards into the open iris valve.

'Get in!' Daak roared from behind. Ace leapt through the doorway and landed on top of Defries. Johannsen, tossed through the doorway by Daak, landed on top of Ace.

For a moment there was a strange silence. Then the ship lurched again, and Daak fell through the doorway. Ace thought she glimpsed a tentacle snaking down the tiers of the bridge. The grating noise of metal being torn was cut off as Daak's hand found the door button and the iris valve slid shut.

The automatic systems cut in. The floor moved, and the four evacuees found themselves sliding through a second doorway, which closed behind them.

They were in a cylindrical space with eight couches. There were no windows.

'Lie down and fasten the safety straps,' said a mechanical voice. 'Emergency lift-off with maximum thrust in ten seconds.'

Johannsen was the first to move. He climbed on to one of the couches. 'Thanks, Daak,' he said. 'Come on, get strapped in. This is just the same as drill, but it's for real.'

'Five seconds,' the voice said. Ace, Daak and Defries threw themselves into position.

There was a loud explosion, and Ace felt herself being thrown upwards while her stomach plummetted downwards. This was the part of emergency evacuation that wasn't in the drill.

Later, she felt able to speak again.

'Everyone OK?'

There were three sets of grunts and groans.

'Looks like we made it,' Johannsen said.

'What about the others?' Ace said. She hadn't had enough time with this division of auxiliaries to make any strong friendships, but some of them had been good fun. And she'd like Toko.

'Not a chance,' Daak growled. 'The ship was coming apart as the escape hatch closed.'

'The transmats?' Ace said, but she knew that there would have been no time for even an emergency transmission.

Defries was still white-faced, and seemed to be making

an effort to control her words. 'Does anyone have any idea what that thing was?'

Ace could almost have smiled. 'Not a lot of shape-changing giant squids in space,' she said. 'You're not going to believe it, but that thing was an illusion. Induced, across the entire ship, and from a distance. Plus a complex pattern of energy fields. That's what ripped the ship apart.'

Defries laughed, harshly and too loudly. 'Telepathy and force fields!' she said. 'Ace, you've been vidding too much science fiction.'

Ace started to protest, but Johannsen cut in. 'It's not so far-fetched,' he said. 'I've done a few weather station postings. Used to be a troublemaker, see. Weather control – that's some kind of force field technology, I guess. And who made every single one of those intelligent systems? Spinward Corporation, that's who.'

'Is that supposed to make me feel better?' Defries blazed. Ace guessed she was back to normal 'I've failed, dammit. The mission's over.'

'You're alive,' Ace pointed out.

'And we're not finished yet,' Johannsen said. 'These things are programmed to put down on the nearest planet. That's Arcadia.'

Daak howled a wordless cheer. 'We get a chance to die fighting after all!'

Part Four

LANDFALL

Lacuna danced. She skipped in circles round the silent chamber, her great head bobbing like a bird's. Britta felt too drained to move, but she shared Lacuna's joy: she could hardly do otherwise, as fountains of jubilation were spilling into her mind, the overflowing bursts of mental energy broadcast by Pool.

She sensed other emotions, too: satisfaction, relief, anticlimax, and sorrow at the waste of so many healthy brains.

But above all triumph, and a revelling in the exercise of might.

Britta was still at her post, standing in the semicircle of two-D screens. Lacuna came to a stop behind her, and pulled her gently into an embrace that for once was nothing but tender. Lacuna's eyes were shining.

'Our enemies are crushed, pretty one,' she said. 'You're safe now. Pool is safe. The project will be accomplished as planned.'

'What happened?' Britta asked; she already knew, but the sudden calm after battle, the jumbled thoughts filling her head, and the sensation of Lacuna's strong arms around her combined to create a magical atmosphere that she wanted to prolong.

'They were doomed from the moment they entered the Net,' Lacuna said. 'I distracted them by launching our fighters. Pool generated a structure behind their ship. The calculations had been completed and stored many months ago. Fingers of energy, disguised – a felicitous whim – as strands of your golden hair. Pool closed the fingers into a fist. The ship was crushed.'

'What a horrible way to die.'

'The ones we want still live.' Lacuna closed her eyes,

and Britta felt her sudden absence. The eyes opened, and Lacuna had returned. 'The two indecipherable intelligences are on the planet, and in our grasp. There are two other minds that contain echoes of the unknown intelligences. Both are women. Pool wants them too. One of them is in the only escape pod that ejected from the starship. The pod will be allowed to land. The other is on the planet. Androids have been sent to locate her. We should be able to see her on one of your screens, my pretty.'

It was like drowning in candyfloss. Bernice could see, as if through a shimmering mist, the arcade of the terrace. She could see the three robed figures, watching impassively as she tried to force her hands through the gold-flecked cloud that surrounded her. She fought the futile urge to draw breath. Her lungs were empty; hoops of steel seemed to be contracting around her chest. Her hands encountered no resistance, but found no way through the fog.

She felt Elaine fall. She looked down. The girl's eyes were wide with fear. Her face was turning blue. A film of golden strands covered her mouth and nostrils.

Bernice sobbed, gasped for non-existent air, and felt the golden stuff invade her mouth. She panicked, clawed the mist. Her chest was about to burst; dark shadows closed in around her. She felt her legs give way, her body collapsing to the floor. She thought: this is my last thought.

The golden mist disappeared.

Bernice sucked in air with a rasping gasp that hurt her throat. She could see the timbers under the terrace roof. She could feel her heart banging like an old engine. She was alive.

She rolled over and grabbed Elaine. She tore the glittering strands from the girl's face, slapped her cheeks, tilted her head, pinched her nose, exhaled into her mouth, pummelled her chest.

Elaine jerked and coughed, inhaled with a ragged sigh, and began to breathe.

Bernice rolled on to her back and closed her eyes. She felt herself being picked up and carried, but she hadn't the strength to struggle.

In her short experience of travelling with the Doctor, she had found that being saved from certain death entailed the likelihood of suffering a fate that was even worse. But this time she didn't struggle. She didn't care where she was being taken. She concentrated on enjoying the sensation of air entering and leaving her lungs.

The pod started shuddering. Ace felt that her eyes were going to vibrate out of their sockets. And it was getting hot. The combat suit evaporated the perspiration that she felt springing out of her pores, but her face was blazing, as if she was staring into a furnace. In fact, she was staring at the ceiling of the escape pod.

I'd feel about one hundred per cent less claustrophobic without these safety straps, she thought. On the other hand, I'd be vibrated off the couch and all over the cabin.

She heard Johannsen's voice: 'Atmosphere. Good.'

'If the heat shields can take it,' Defries said.

Daak was pounding his couch with his fists. 'Trussed up tight as a smack-smuggler's arse!' he muttered. 'This is no way to land a ship. I'm going to find me some controls to fly this thing.' Ace heard clicks as buckles were unfastened.

'Daak! Stay where you are!' The pod was now shuddering so violently that Defries's voice was distorted. 'That's an order, Daak!'

The Dalek Killer winked at Ace as he staggered past her couch and towards the front of the little craft.

'I'm a DK, lady,' he said to Defries, grunting the words as he struggled to keep his footing on the juddering floor. 'I'm as good as dead already. But I don't want to die like an ice cube in a cocktail shaker.'

Ace unfastened her safety harness and clutched the sides of her shaking couch as she pulled herself into a sitting position. She saw that Defries and Johannsen were attempting the same manoeuvre. Daak was at the narrow front of the cabin. The muscles of his legs and arms bulged alarmingly and shone with sweat as he braced himself against the bulkheads to study the small control panel.

'Programmed,' Johannsen said. 'Better leave it.'

'You heard, Daak,' Defries said. Daak's hand swerved unsteadily towards the console. 'Don't touch it. You may not value your own life – ' she paused, then said: 'But do you want to kill Ace?'

'What?' Ace was outraged, but the worsening vibration made it almost impossible to speak coherently. 'Don't trouble yourself on my account, mate.'

But Daak had hesitated, and then pulled back his hand. He started to turn, with difficulty, to look back at Ace. The vibration stopped.

'Thank the stars,' Defries breathed. But even as she was speaking, Daak, in mid-turn and braced against the constant shuddering of the ship, lost his balance in the sudden calm and started to topple backwards.

Ace, Defries and Johannsen could only watch as, almost in slow motion, Daak thrust out a fist to support his weight – and pushed down half the switches on the control panel.

Nothing happened. The vibration didn't resume. The pod continued to fly straight and true. Daak shrugged, grinned, and started back towards the couches. Imperceptibly at first, the floor of the cabin began to tilt away from the horizontal. The right side dipped; the left side rose. By the time Daak managed to haul himself on to his couch, the floor was angled at forty-five degrees, and tilting faster.

'Strap yourselves in,' Defries said, 'and hold on tight. We're in for a crash-landing.'

As it sped groundwards through the Arcadian skies, the escape pod began to roll.

A large covered wagon was waiting in the forecourt of the Delahaye villa. Rainwater steamed off the backs of the two enormous horses in the shafts and glistened on the cobblestones. The only sounds were the whistling of the rising wind and the viscous breathing of the Counsellors.

Bernice was pushed between the canvas flaps at the back of the wagon. The interior was dark and gloomy. She didn't try to stand. The flaps parted again and Elaine was pushed inside. Bernice murmured, and the girl crawled to nestle alongside her.

The floor was cold: metal, not wood. There was still no sound. No clopping of hooves, and no sensation of movement. Bernice continued absently to stroke Elaine's forehead, but her eyes were becoming accustomed to the gloom, and she was puzzled.

I don't know much about horse-drawn transport, she thought, but I never read anywhere that horses were difficult to start. And this doesn't look like the inside of a covered wagon: this looks like the inside of a metal box.

It was a cube, less than three metres on each side. The floor and ceiling were flat, and the walls were corrugated, except on the side that consisted of the canvas covering of the back of the wagon. Bernice became aware of a humming, rising in pitch and volume, that seemed to come from all around. She stood up.

Elaine made a wordless cry of distress.

'It's all right, angel,' Bernice said, offering her hand and pulling the girl to her feet, 'I just want to take a look at this thing we're in. Not the workmanship of the Beaufort stonemason or metalsmith, I'd say.'

She squinted at the emblems imprinted on a panel in the ceiling.

'In fact, it says here that this was made in the Phobos factories of the HKI Industries Corporation. And see this sign? That's the logo of the Spinward Corporation. It's a strange thing to say in an empty tin box, but I suddenly feel almost at home.'

'Home?' Elaine said.

Bernice hugged her. 'You're still talking! I thought perhaps . . . But you're a brave girl, Elaine. I've been travelling in – no, I can't explain this. But I didn't know where or when I was. And now I've got some idea. Spinward and HKI were big corporations where and when I come from. So, give or take a couple of centuries and a

161

few hundred light years, I'm home. Don't worry: it confuses me too.'

Elaine smiled. 'That's good, Benny. But what's going to happen?'

The humming had reached a painful level of audibility. A chequerboard of ceiling panels was beginning to glow with a greenish light.

'The bad news,' Bernice said, 'is that HKI specialize in the manufacture of instant transit systems. We're in a transmat booth, and we're about to go on an instant journey.'

'Where to?'

'I never heard of a transmat with a range of more than a few thousand kilometres, so I'd say we're probably going somewhere else on this planet.'

'We're going to Landfall,' Elaine said gloomily. 'Gerald said so.' She looked at the canvas flaps. 'We could jump out.'

The green iridescence flooded the cubicle. 'It's too late,' Bernice said. 'We're on our way. Keep still and concentrate on holding your molecules together.'

'Will that help?'

'No, but it'll take your mind off the nausea and dizziness.'

The light began to pulse, faster and faster, and the metal walls shimmered out of existence.

The escape pod was rotating so rapidly that its four occupants were pinned against their couches.

People do this kind of thing for fun at fairgrounds, Ace thought. It's getting difficult to breathe. My face feels like it's flat. If we're lucky, the pressure'll kill us before we crash. Or would it be better the other way round?

She gulped air. It felt so good she laughed. And she realized she could move again, slightly. The craft's spin was slowing.

'What the hell's going on?' Daak grunted.

'Automatic system correction?' Defries suggested.

'Not possible,' Johannsen said. 'Daak overrode the automatics.'

The pod was stable again. Ace sensed that its forward speed had slowed too, and that its course was veering rightwards.

'Someone's bringing us down gently,' she said. 'Maybe we'll have a soft landing after all.'

The bottom of the escape pod hit something. The noise and the shock were like an explosion.

Half conscious, Ace felt a series of lesser shocks and bangs, and the anguished sound of tearing metal. The cabin filled with dust, smoke, and the smell of burning circuitry. Daak was shouting curses.

With a drawn-out screech, the pod vibrated to a standstill, rocked gently from side to side, and then rolled over.

Hanging helplessly in the safety straps, Ace looked down to see the cabin ceiling buckling and tearing. She was about to be impaled on jagged strips of metal.

Then the pod rolled again, and came to rest.

Ace found herself looking up at the sky. Billowing black clouds were racing above her. Raindrops stung her face.

There were long moments of silence.

'Everyone OK?' Defries said at last, shakily.

There were three grunts in reply.

'Then let's get out before this thing blows. We've got an emergency exit where we used to have a roof. Johannsen, Daak, you're tallest. Try to rig up a line through there and down the side of the pod. Ace, find the emergency rations and the patch-up kit. I'll get the weaponry.'

The pod didn't explode. Ace thought that was another suspiciously lucky break, but she had no complaints. Getting on to the remains of the top of the pod had been relatively straightforward, although Daak had tried to insist on being the last one out and she'd had to threaten him with troopers' oaths and a blaster to convince him that gallantry was inappropriate.

Getting down was another matter.

The pod had come to rest half-way down the side of a splintered ridge of rock. It was tilted to one side and nose down. The rear part of the hull, an impassable tangle of twisted metal, was embedded among outcropping boulders; the front of the craft was largely undamaged but was suspended over the steep slope of the ridge.

Defries, Johannsen, Ace and Daak had managed to climb on to the top of the pod's nose.

Ace stared morosely down at the rocks. 'Another unlikely stroke of luck,' she said. 'We're stuck in the only crevice along this whole mountainside. Another metre either way, and we'd have carried on rolling all the way down.'

'Don't worry,' Defries said. 'If the wind keeps rising the pod'll be blown down there. And don't stand so close to the edge.'

Ace stepped back, and almost fell over as the pod shuddered. Daak had jumped back into the cabin.

'Slughead!' she yelled. 'You trying to get me killed? Fairy footsteps from now on, OK?'

'Whatever you say, girlie. You want to give me a hand with this?' Daak was using his chainsword to slice safety straps from their moorings. 'Going to make us a rope.'

'Looks like you're handling it,' Ace called down to him. 'And being in a confined space with you and a chainsword isn't my idea of how to relieve stress.'

She joined Defries and Johannsen, who were vainly scanning the horizon for signs of life. Low clouds and squalls of driving rain concealed all but the local terrain, which consisted of rocky crags and gulleys. The only vegetation was scrubby trees and patches of coarse grass. Ace recognized some of the plants as similar to Earth species; the others, the weird-looking ones, she decided were native to the planet.

Johannsen spoke at last. 'Arcadia!' he said, and barked a laugh.

'Bit of a misnomer, isn't it?' Defries said.

'It won't all be like this,' Ace said confidently. 'I always manage to land in the least desirable areas. If the whole planet was one enormous Regent's Park, I'd come down in the zoo car park.'

Daak pulled himself through the crater in the top of the hull. A knotted skein of nylon straps was looped round his chest. He tied one end to the stub of a broken aerial housing.

'Well done, DK,' Defries said. 'I thought you were only interested in certain-death scenarios and fighting Daleks – which come to the same thing.'

'That's right, Agent,' Daak said. 'And sitting on a wrecked pod that's going to blow up if it doesn't blow away first is just way too safe for me. Let's get out of here and into something really dangerous.'

Ace dropped to a crouch. 'Down, everyone,' she urged, and pointed up the slope. 'Is that dangerous enough for you?'

Ten figures had appeared at the summit of the ridge. They were moving with difficulty, perhaps hampered by their long black cloaks, but they were coming downhill fast. East one was carrying a gun.

'My guess is: not friendly,' Defries said, unholstering her blaster. 'Get down that rope, all of you. I'll cover.'

'Rats scurrying down the anchor chain of a beached ship.'

'What?' Britta lifted her head from Lacuna's shoulder.

Lacuna pointed to one of the screens. 'We have found them, pretty one. They are on the doomed planet below. See them, swinging in the wind?'

Britta leant forward. On the screen, three tiny shapes were climbing down a thread. A fourth was crouched on the silvery carapace of the wreck above them. 'Are you going to attack them now?' Britta asked. She found the prospect strangely exciting.

'Soon. We must take care not to harm the one that Pool wants.'

The picture dissolved and was replaced by an image of the three climbers: almost at the end of the knotted rope, a slim man in black combat clothes, hanging with the agility of a spider, keen eyes scanning the gulley for cover; above him a young woman, similarly dressed, eyes bright with excitement, talking and gesticulating; and above her a giant of a man, his body barely covered by his torn clothing, waving a bizarre weapon, grinning like a wolf.

'The one in the middle. The girl,' Lacuna said.

The picture zoomed closer. The young woman's face filled the screen.

She's not really pretty, Britta thought. Not like me. Her mouth's too wide. Her hair's very straight and just an ordinary brown. I suppose it's practical, tied back like that. And look at her shouting at those poor men. She's obviously the bossy sort. But she looks as if she knows what she's doing.

'Isn't she magnificent, little Britta?' Lacuna was gazing at the screen. 'Fit, strong, capable, clever. Look at her: she's enjoying the danger. I can feel her excitement. The others have it too: the thin one and the other woman are experiencing a desire, a sensual thrill, and the big man is full of wild rage. But this woman has some of both of these feelings, as well as more fear than the others, and even the fear excites her. And above all of these emotions, there is a hunger to know the result of the conflict. It's as if she is conducting an experiment, with herself as one of the ingredients. She needs to know what's going to happen next. Fascinating. A remarkable woman.'

Britta said nothing.

Now all of the screens were showing the site of the pod's crash-landing. The pictures, Britta realized, were the views seen by the Counsellors as they scrambled down the slope towards the wrecked craft. One Counsellor had hung back, and positioned himself near the top of the ridge, above the mouth of the narrow gulley: his viewpoint gave the watchers in the space station a panorama of the area. Other Counsellors' viewpoints picked out the wrecked pod, various parts of the slope and the gulley, and the four human targets.

The slim man, the first to reach the floor of the ravine, had taken cover in a nest of boulders. Bursts of white light that shattered the rock showed that some of the Counsellors had started to direct their lasers towards him. Only the barrel of his blaster could be seen. Shafts of brilliant light issued from it continually. One of the screens went blank as he hit a Counsellor.

The big man and the woman were running up the

166

gulley, towards its narrow end. Boulders burst into fragments behind them. They disappeared from sight behind the root of the crag on which the pod was perched.

The older woman was sliding down the rope now. Her image grew larger and larger until her face filled the screen. One of the Counsellors had her in his sights. The pin-point brilliance of the targeting beam danced across her forehead. For a moment, she was looking directly out of the picture. Her blue eyes widened, and Britta was sure that her mouth formed the word *No!* Britta tensed: the woman was about to die. But instead, the screen blanked.

Britta scanned the remaining screens. The slim man? No: three Counsellors were concentrating on him, keeping him pinned behind his shield of stones. As Britta watched, one of the three screens flashed blinding white as one of the three Counsellors was hit.

There – at the narrow end of the gulley. A glint of metal behind a spur of rock. A flashing stream of light, almost too sudden to notice. The picture on the screen dissolved slowly. The young woman was sniping at the Counsellors. Had hit one.

Three screens were dark now. On one of the remaining seven, the woman jumped from the rope, crouched to fire two bursts of light up the slope, and ran zigzagging into a cleft on the opposite side of the gulley. Three screens showed views of the slim man's shelter of rocks, but all that could be seen of the target were the streams of laser fire that issued from his blaster. Two Counsellors had turned to scan the end of the ravine, where the young woman and the big man had taken cover. And the final screen continued to show a view of the entire valley: nine Counsellors were ranged in an erratic line along one slope. Three were still, their robes fluttering in the wind. The others continued to advance into the gulley, scuttling between outcrops of rock.

The big man appeared, suddenly. He leapt on to a boulder, waving his weapon above his head. He seemed to be shouting.

The young woman stood up, also shouting. The big

man turned to her, briefly, and then started to run upslope, jumping from rock to rock, towards the line of Counsellors. Flashes of light exploded around him as he ran.

The young woman shook her head, as if in disbelief, and set off after him. She moved more slowly, stopping every few paces to aim and fire her blaster. One, and then two screens picked her out. Bursts of brilliance began to flare around her. She was thrown to the ground, staggered upright, jumped into a hollow, emerged again to fire her blaster and move on.

Another screen went dark. The older woman had started to fire from the ravine.

The picture on another screen suddenly swerved. An out of focus close-up: a scarred, unshaven face, a feral grimace, the whirling blades of a chainsword – and then nothing. On yet another screen: the young woman, hands on hips, laughing; a brief impression of rotating metal, and then darkness.

Visible now only in the panoramic view, the young woman appeared to be throwing something towards the few remaining Counsellors. Explosions: red flames and chunks of rock spouted from the slopes where the Counsellors had been standing. All but one of the screens were now blank. The view of the gulley receded rapidly as the surviving Counsellor retreated towards its wider end.

'They – they killed the Counsellors.' Britta could hardly believe what she had seen.

'Droids are expendable,' Lacuna snapped. 'One is enough to lead them to Landfall.'

Four walls do not a prison make, Bernice reminded herself tentatively. Utter rubbish, she concluded. She was getting decidedly fed up.

And she was worried abut Elaine. The transmat journey had been as brief, uneventful and nauseating as she had expected. She had been still recovering her wits when Elaine had been taken from the booth by two more of the misshapen, black-robed, gurgling Counsellors. The girl had struggled at first, but Bernice had reassured her:

They'll bring me to you in just a minute, she'd said. But they hadn't.

The Counsellors had returned and, answering her questions with nothing but their phlegmy breathing, they had dragged he along corridors of metal and stone and into a large cell. There was no sign of Elaine.

Three of the room's walls were made of metal, and looked like the riveted bulkheads of a starship's cargo hold. But Bernice was sure she was still on the planet: the fourth wall and the floor consisted of blocks of masonry, and the gravity felt exactly the same as it had before the transmat trip.

Illumination came from a glowing sphere, recessed into the high ceiling and protected by a grille of thick, iron bars. There was one door: set into one of the metal walls, it had an electronic lock that, while not as sophisticated as the transmat, was certainly hundreds of years away from the medieval technology of Arcadia. Just as well the control panel's on the outside, Bernice told herself, saves me wasting my energies on a futile attempt to crack the combination.

There was no furniture.

The stone wall is probably the weakest, she reasoned. It's obviously an addition to the main structure. Best place to start my Count of Monte Cristo impersonation. It would be ironic to pick away at the mortar for a few decades only to break through into the next-door cell.

Elaine! It could contain Elaine.

Bernice knelt at the wall, pressing her ear against the stone. She could hear nothing.

She pounded on the masonry with her fist and then, after tearing at the fastenings round her right foot, with the heel of her boot.

'Elaine!' she shouted, heedless of attracting unwanted attention. 'Elaine! Are you there?' She beat the wall until her arm ached.

'Benny?' It was Elaine's voice, quavering and barely audible, from the other side of the wall. 'Benny, I'm scared.' She was crying, and trying not to, Bernice could tell. 'Benny, please come, please.'

'Don't worry,' Bernice said. 'I'm coming, all right? Just a few minutes.'

She pulled her boot back on. Her hands were trembling with anger. How could they do this to a little girl? It was inhuman.

The door opened. A Counsellor hobbled into the room. Another, holding a blaster, stood outside.

'What do you require?' the Counsellor gurgled.

Bernice strode towards him. She caught a glimpse of a disfigured, oddly proportioned face in the depths of the shadowy hood, but this wasn't enough to distract her from her purpose.

'What I require, Rasputin, is that you let me out of here and let me see Elaine.'

The Counsellor took a deep and viscous breath. 'You may have provisions. Food and water are available. Medicines are available. The light is controlled by voice command.'

'Deaf, are we? Or just plain stupid? I want to be with my friend Elaine.'

'Wait,' the Counsellor said, and stood silent for half a minute. 'Your request is not permitted,' he said at last. 'Provisions are available. Medicines are – '

'Yes, I know. You've told me. You're not very bright, are you? If I'm allowed to have food, why can't I have it in the same cell as Elaine?'

The Counsellor paused again before replying. 'You are the older female prisoner. You are to be kept alive. Provisions are available. Medicines are available. The other prisoner is of no importance.'

'Isn't she? I see.' Bernice was so angry she could hardly speak. 'If I thought you were even remotely human, dogface, I'd wring your neck. But as you're obviously something else, let's try this instead: what would happen to me if I take no food and water and medicine?'

The Counsellor pondered. 'Humans require provisions,' it said. 'You would die. You are to be kept alive.'

'Very good. Now hear this: I will take provisions only if you take me to Elaine and provide both of us with the things I ask for.'

Another pause. 'You will survive long enough without food and water,' the Counsellor said, and turned to leave.

'Wait!' Bernice said. 'I'll kill myself.'

The Counsellor turned to face her. She sensed disbelief in the tilt of its head.

'I'll hang myself from the bars under the light,' she said, desperate to sound convincing. 'I'll bash my head against the walls until I break my skull. I'll cut open my arteries.'

The silence was very long. What have I got myself into, Bernice thought. Now he'll come up with all sorts of bright ideas like tying me up or pumping me full of tranquillizers for my own safety.

'You may join the other prisoner.' The Counsellor stumbled towards the door. Bernice followed. 'What do you require?'

The Counsellor with the gun kept it trained on her while his colleague operated the lock of Elaine's cell.

'Coffee,' Bernice said. 'Black and strong. Bread, lightly toasted, and butter. A selection of local cheeses. Honey. Fruit. And a few centilitres of good whisky.'

The door opened. 'Bread and water are available,' the Counsellor said.

Bernice was too preoccupied to quibble. She ran into the cell. Elaine was sitting hunched in a corner, rocking back and forth, her head buried in her crossed arms.

The girl looked up as Bernice approached, and managed a small smile. Bernice could have yelled with relief. Instead she pirouetted and made a bow. 'Summerfield rescue service,' she said, 'as promised.'

'Are you going to rescue me, then?' Elaine asked, straight-faced.

'You're not feeling too bad, are you? No, angel,' Bernice said, sliding down the wall to sit beside Elaine. 'I can't think how to get us out of this one. I don't even know where we are.'

'I expect it's Landfall,' Elaine said confidently. 'That's where the Counsellors live.'

'Well, wherever it is, all we can do is wait. I wish the Doctor were here. He'd know what to do.'

* * *

'Well, well, well. I think we must have arrived at Landfall.'

The Doctor had reached the summit of yet another bleak ridge, and turned to make this announcement to Francis and the Counsellors, who were toiling upwards towards him in the face of a wind full of dust and hailstones.

Why doesn't his hat blow off, Francis wondered. All such speculations were banished by the sight that met his eyes as they followed the Doctor's pointing finger.

Landfall. The legendary retreat of the Counsellors. The secret, almost inaccessible haven where the black-robed savants hoarded the wisdom that sustained the people of Arcadia.

The land sloped gently downwards from Francis's feet, and from every rocky height that he could see, to form a vast oval bowl ringed with sharp-toothed mountains. The floor of the wide valley was carpeted with hummocky grass. The storms that threatened to pluck him from the summit where he stood barely rippled the grey waters of the lakes that were strung like pearls along the centre of the grassland far below. And in the midst of the valley, set on a plinth of rock that was like an island in a sea of green grass, stood Landfall.

Few Princes had ever made the journey to see the sight that Francis now gazed upon; few Princes, and hardly any of lesser rank. Only Apprentice Scribes were obliged to make pilgrimage to this unique seat of wisdom, and those that returned never spoke of it.

The four Counsellors had reached the top of the ridge and were standing stationary in a line, like four badly-constructed scarecrows, their robes billowing in the wind. They seemed in no hurry to escort their prisoners into the valley. The Doctor too was rapt, his keen eyes studying every detail of the scene.

'I could almost believe in magic,' Francis said, raising his voice above the howling storm. 'Or that Landfall was built by giants. The symmetry of the curtain wall! The width of the internal roadways, the vast stone archways! And the towers, so slender and graceful, dressed with beaten silver. Such wealth, such magnificence – such sheer size!'

The Doctor turned to him. 'How interesting,' he said. 'I take it that you see that architectural dog's dinner down there as a skilfully-planned structure – some sort of enormous palace.'

'The ruler of even the meanest Principality has a palace,' Francis said scornfully, 'and every one has a half-finished tower, or a carelessly added gatehouse in a different style. There,' he pointed downhill, 'is perfection. And not merely on the scale of a palace. Landfall is – a citadel.'

'I have to say I see it rather differently,' the Doctor said. 'Shall we make a move towards it, by the way? These androids don't feel the cold, but we'd be rather more comfortable off this wind-swept mountain-top, I'm sure.'

The Doctor set off down the slope. Francis caught up with him. 'Differently?' he asked.

'There are at least three separate periods of building,' the Doctor said, 'and the oldest-looking, all the monumental masonry made of weathered stone, is the most recent.'

Francis stopped and peered down at the complex of buildings. 'But the entire citadel is made of stone!' he said.

'No it isn't,' the Doctor snapped. 'Look again. The central structure, there.'

'The six hexagonal towers?'

'Yes. It's been built over, of course, but that is, unless I'm very much mistaken, the original survey camp. It would have been domed, at first. Nearly everything else follows the ground plan of the later, and much larger, colony base station. Runways and hard standing; hangars; warehousing. The thin towers aren't covered with silver, they're made of metal: they were rockets, once, presumably for emergency launching of satellites – perhaps even for defence. The stone walls are the last – Francis, are you listening?'

The scribe shook his head. 'I understand only a little of what you say. Landfall has always been. The Counsellors have always provided. This is their place. Their ancient home.'

'Use your eyes, Francis!' The Doctor's voice was low and angry. 'Use your brain. The whole complex is only a few hundred years old. Your forefathers landed here only a few generations ago. I know the Counsellors restrict your access to books, but there must be legends, stories handed down through the years. Didn't you hear tales of the first settlers from your father? From your grandfather?'

Francis was sullen. The four Counsellors had skittered down the slope and were harrying him to walk more quickly. The wind had dropped, and in spite of a thickening drizzle he felt hot and flustered.

'My father?' he said. 'I can hardly remember what he looked like. What is a grand father? My father wasn't grand.'

The Doctor stopped in his tracks. 'Of course! I'd forgotten the genetic manipulation. They've tampered with everything, including the colonists. Life expectancy as well.'

'Yes, Doctor,' Francis broke in. 'I told you. I discovered, in the forbidden books, that on other worlds men live for many decades.'

'Long life and literacy,' the Doctor mused, and then, when one of the Counsellors urged him forward with a shove, he yelled into the android's cowled face: 'Long life and literacy! The first and second means by which knowledge is transmitted. And your masters have robbed these people of both! You've created a society with no history, no culture. You can impose any laws and traditions you care to invent. No wonder Apprentice Scribes are vetted and brainwashed. But still . . . '

The Doctor turned and strode downhill, and once again Francis had to run to catch up. 'But what, Doctor?'

'Eh? I still don't know what it's all for, that's what. What's the point of it all? I hate not knowing—'

The Doctor was interrupted by a tearing, cracking noise that echoed around the ring of rocks, and rumbled into silence like dying thunder.

'Another storm?' Francis said.

The Doctor smiled secretively. 'You remember I mentioned I was expecting a friend? I rather think she's arrived.'

Defries touched the comms button on her collar, then struck it with the butt of her blaster. Still no response. She hadn't expected one. Spacefleet's personal R/T devices were supposed to be unjammable up to a range of two kilometres, but it was obvious that Spinward had technology in the Arcadia system that outclassed Spacefleet's latest equipment.

That makes it strategically important that I report back to Earth Central, Defries thought, *and of course it also makes it highly unlikely that I'll survive to do so.*

She risked standing, poised to duck back under the slab of rock if she saw even the shadow of a movement.

No enemy in sight. Johannsen and the DK were still clambering up the long diagonal slope to her left, almost level with her now. She waved, pointed to her collar, drew her finger across her throat. Johannsen raised an open hand: message received and understood. An unnecessary signal: the radios had been dead since the crash landing.

No sign of Ace. Defries scanned the serrated line of rocks above her. A red flash ruddied the belly of a cloud; the noise followed almost immediately, the roar of an explosion bouncing in decreasing waves of sound between the clouds and the ravines.

A moment of silence. Then the hiss of blaster fire, and the crack of breaking stone.

Defries glanced at Johannsen. He had taken cover, but bobbed up to shrug his long arms in answer to Defries's enquiring look. Daak was still moving uphill, faster now, towards the source of the noises.

Still no sign of the enemy. Still no Ace.

Defries looked upslope again, and there was Ace: a small figure leaping between two horns of rock at the summit. A second later, the rocks burst into fragments, but Ace was coming downhill now, sliding and rolling with an avalanche of stones and scree, her pony tail flying behind her and her blaster held above her head.

Boulders bounced round Defries's foxhole. Dust filled it. Trusting to the shock resistance of her combat gear, Defries jumped into the rain of rocks and braced her feet against a projecting shelf. 'Here!' she called, as loudly as she could. Ace was careering downwards. Defries was in her path.

Ace saw Defries, found time to grin, and angled her legs. She disappeared into the cloud of dust she created, but she was slowing. Defries extended an arm. Ace caught it, almost pulled Defries from her perch, released it, and rolled to a stop a few metres further down the slope.

Defries found her lying on her back, eyes open. For a moment she thought Ace was wounded, but as she slid down the slope Ace tilted her head back to watch her approach.

'It's a trap, Belle. Only a dozen or so of the creeps in the black nighties, but they've got heavy weapons. Heat seekers, random field, intelligent stuff. Three mobile platforms. Hover type. Well,' she grinned suddenly, 'only two now.'

'You're OK?'

'Don't worry. Still functioning.'

'Good. I can't afford to lose you.' Defries was silent, in thought, for a moment, but her eyes didn't cease scanning the rocks, and her hands were making automatic checks of her suit's status controls and of the weapons hanging at her waist.

'We've got the firepower to take them out,' Ace said, scrambling to her feet.

'Hold it, trooper,' Defries said. Two hotheads in a squad of four. That didn't help. 'They're better armed than us. And we're in a lousy tactical position. If we put our heads over the top they'll pick us off like ducks in a shooting gallery. If we stay put they can stay up there and fry the valley bottom, and us with it. If we move out we're even easier targets.'

'They've got longer reach than us. To have a chance we have to get up close.'

'Looks like your lover-boy has the same idea.' Defries pointed. Abslom Daak, his hair and ragged clothing streaming in the wind, had almost reached the top of the slope.

'He's not—' Ace abandoned the protest.

'Yeah, I know,' Defries said, but Ace had started to move. Gravel spurted from the heels of her boots as she crawled furiously up the cliff down which she had just slid.

Defries lifted her blaster. For a second she was on the point of executing Ace for insurbordination. Stupid. She needed the crazy auxie, and she needed the crazy auxie's armour-piercing grenades. And anyway, Ace was right: their only hope was to close with the enemy. So they had to get up the slope fast.

Swirls of dust stung her eyes. She waved to Johannsen, pointed uphill, made a wide circle in the air to indicate the size of the opposition, and signalled for him to advance. She set off up the scarp, using juts and ledges as a diagonal staircase to take her on a course that would bring her close to Johannsen when they both reached the top of the incline.

The wind howled louder as she climbed. Gobbets of ice sliced through the air. Even when a chip of hail cut her cheek, the worsening weather made her smile grimly: it would confuse heat-seeking and auditory shells. It all helped to even the odds.

A blast of gusting air carried Daak's shout to her. She looked up. There was Ace, almost at the summit, above her and to her right. Johannsen was twenty metres to her left, only a little further up the cliff than her: they both had some climbing still to do. And beyond Johannsen, Abslom Daak. He had reached the top: he was standing on a rock, he was brandishing his chainsword, he was roaring defiance at enemies Defries couldn't see.

He's a dead man, she thought.

Daak jumped from the rock just in time. Half a dozen beams of concentrated laser light converged on it, and it burst into fragments. Even at a distance, the noise hurt Defries's ears. Stars danced before her eyes.

She blinked. She couldn't see Daak. But she was sure she'd seen him jump.

The ground trembled. A fountain of shattered stone spouted into the air at the top of the cliff. A second explosion, and vast shards of the cliff lazily peeled away and tumbled down the slope. The enemy was using big weapons, shells or missiles, Defries couldn't tell which. She still couldn't see Daak. The barrage intensified: the explosions merged into a continuous crackling rumble of noise, the clifftop where Daak had stood was turned into a firework display of blinding flashes, and below it an avalanche of smoking rocks.

How could Daak survive?

Defries cursed. There was nothing she could do until she reached the top. She tried to shut out the wind, the explosions, the driving hail, the movement of the ground beneath her feet. She fixed her eyes on the jagged line of rocks to which she had to climb.

Ace was there now. If she's trying to draw the enemy's fire, she's not succeeding, Defries thought; but she's doing it exactly right.

Ace was running from boulder to boulder along the summit of the ridge, stopping wherever she found good cover, just long enough to hurl one of her primitive-looking grenades, or fire her blaster, or launch some kind of tiny projectile that Defries couldn't see clearly.

The air above and beyond the ridge became filled with wind-swirled smoke and the echoes of distant blasts. Defries climbed towards the battle.

Johannsen reached the summit ahead of her. She saw him fold his long body into a crack between two rocks that jutted like teeth along the ridge. The enemy had seen him: streams of light burst against the rocks, chunks of which flew off and rained down on Defries.

Defries pushed herself onwards. Johannsen was a true professional: ignoring the heat and noise all round him, he aimed his blaster and started to fire. Short bursts, each one destined for a chosen target.

Ace and Johannsen were clearly taking a toll: the enemy's fire was beginning to lessen. There was enough time between the explosions for Defries to hear the ringing in her ears.

But it must be too late to save Daak, she thought. Where he had reached the summit, the cliff had disappeared: it had been excavated by explosions, it was a hole ten metres wide. Red-hot rocks continued to slide from the place.

Then she saw him: further along the cliff, beyond the bleeding gap, the DK was struggling once again towards the top of the ridge. He reached it. He stood, legs apart, arms lifted above his head. Defries was sure he was shouting, although she could hear nothing but the thud of shells and the tinnitus inside her head.

The heat-seekers would be drawn by the steaming wound in the rock face, Defries realized; they'd ignore Daak. The smoke would confuse missiles with eyes. And if he didn't yell too loudly, the ones with ears would miss him too. Now if he'd just take cover and place some well-aimed bursts with his blaster . . .

He didn't. He thrust out his chainsword like a lance, and charged forward, into the smoke and explosions. He disappeared from sight.

Defries was only two metres below Johannsen now. Further along the ridge, Ace was still throwing high explosives. She kept moving, and the enemy fire kept missing her. She saw Defries, and paused long enough to make a curious gesture: a closed fist, and the thumb sticking upwards. Defries thought it looked a bit obscene; but then, perhaps that was appropriate. It was a quaint and arcane gesture, and seemed of a piece with Ace's sometimes archaic and obscure phrases.

Johannsen was in trouble: his shield of rocks had been reduced to a line of rubble, his combat suit had been torn, and his exposed skin had been wounded by flying splinters of stone. Blood streamed down his face and back. He couldn't see to aim.

'Johannsen!' Defries yelled in a gap between shell bursts. 'Get down here. You need patching up. I'll take over.'

He didn't hear. Defries jumped to a higher ledge and reached out to touch his foot. A flash of light turned everything white. The foot was suddenly not there. Next instant, Defries felt herself falling. Something had punched her chest; she felt the refrigeration unit of her suit cut in, she felt rather than heard the tearing, rippling, screaming boom of the explosion.

The smell of burning.

The impact of landing, breath knocked from lungs, pain.

It seemed like hours later. She knew it was only seconds. She opened her eyes. The light made her retch, but she could see. A dust-storm, clouds scurrying above.

She tried to move. Every limb worked. The suit had absorbed the impact. Only a few molecules thick, how did they build in so much padding? She'd send a thank-you to the manufacturers. No: they don't need it, do they. Rich bastards. Must have made a mint out of the wars.

Wish I knew whether my face was burnt. Ask Johannsen.

Johannsen.

She rolled over. The blast had picked her up and dropped her a couple of metres along the ridge. She was still near the top. She saw Ace, getting nearer, wide-eyed with concern, leaping from rock to rock. Jump; crouch; aim; fire. Jump; crouch; aim; fire. Explosions flared behind her.

Defries turned and looked in the other direction. Where Johannsen's shelter had been there was now a smoking crater. There was nothing left of Johannsen.

Yes there was. Defries realized that she was holding something in her right hand. She didn't want to look down. Of course. Johannsen's boot. And his foot.

She sat up. She wanted suddenly to continue the movement, to rest her head on her knees, curl up, cosy, comfortable, cry herself to sleep.

Ace's boots crunched closer. Defries turned towards her, lifted Johannsen's boot, and tossed it into the crater.

'OK?' mouthed Ace, her eyes veering from Defries's face to follow the trajectory of the boot.

'First casualty,' Defries said. 'Damn him. We can't afford losses. He was a good trooper.'

Ace was talking again. Defries shook her head. They couldn't hear each other. They did some smiling and signing, and Ace helped Defries to stand.

Explosions and laser fire were sporadic now, and seemed to be striking at random along the top of the ridge. Defries and Ace crawled up to a hollow, and peered cautiously over the lip.

Defries smiled. The enemy was in retreat.

The other side of the escarpment was a fractured plateau, a great, cracked slab of rock tilted away from the summit of the ridge. The widely-scattered smoke-swirls from destroyed weapons and vehicles showed that the enemy had advanced on a broad front.

Ace nudged Defries, grinned, and pointed proudly to the two largest pyres: they were the remains of two hover-speeders, presumably wrecked by Ace's grenades.

Fluttering rags revealed where Ace's and Johannsen's blaster fire had cut down the black-robed enemy personnel. Defries counted nine bodies. Some had been shot down singly, quite near the edge of the plateau, presumably while advancing. Others were in pairs, lying next to tangles of black metal that must have been mortars and missile launchers before Ace had destroyed them.

The survivors, three ungainly figures in robes whipped by the wind, were grouped on the remaining hover-speeder. One was in the cockpit, at the controls; the other two were standing on the rear platform, firing blasters at random towards the clifftop and overseeing the automatic fire of the hoverspeeder's cannon.

'They're going to get away!' Ace yelled into Defries's ear. Defries realized that her hearing was returning.

'Good! she shouted back. Her little squad had survived one firefight, but she'd already lost a quarter of her manpower and she was sure that the enemy had plenty of reserves They needed rest and medication, that was the first priority. Then, as soon as possible, move on again. Find a place to lie low. Avoid firefights. Guerrilla tactics.

Ace nudged her again, hard. Defries turned angrily, but her eyes were drawn to follow Ace's pointing finger.

On the plateau, as yet unseen by the black-robed figures, Daak was running towards the hoverspeeder.

Now they'd spotted him. Laser beams swept like searchlights, leaving smoking trails across the rock, as blasters were turned towards the approaching Dalek Killer.

He zigzagged. The beams missed him. And he was there, making the impossible leap from the ground to the moving platform, ducking beneath the barrel of the cannon, waving his chainsword in circles as if it weighed no more than a walking stick.

He cut one of the enemy in half. His weapon snagged in the cloak, and for a moment he was vulnerable. The second enemy took aim at point-blank range. Daak lifted the chainsword, and the cloak, and the upper half of the corpse it contained, and swung the whole mass. The second enemy fell from the platform and lay still.

The hoverspeeder started to accelerate. Its pilot had decided that he had to shake Daak off. Daak staggered, fell, slid towards the back of the platform.

The speeder slewed from side to side. Defries lifted her blaster, tracking the vehicle's erratic course. If the wind died for just a moment; if she could just get a clear sight of the cockpit . . .

Ace's hand blocked the viewfinder, pushed down the barrel of the gun. 'Don't be daft. You might kill him,' Ace yelled.

Defries lashed out: her blaster struck Ace's shoulder. Ace stumbled back, an unreadable expression on her face and her blaster half-raised.

'He's a dead man anyway,' Defries shouted. 'He hasn't got a chance. He's a DK. He's on borrowed time. He's a lousy soldier. But it's Johannsen who's dead. Johannsen who's in pieces. Johannsen . . .'

Shut up, Defries, she told herself. Shit, I sound like I was bunking with the guy. This crazy auxie is acting cooler than me. Take it easy.

'Take it easy, Belle,' Ace said, and smiled. 'Daak didn't kill Johannsen. The creeps in the black nighties did. Spinward did. Take it out on them.'

182

'I will.' Defries's gaze followed the careering hover-speeder. Suddenly, here, on the windswept rock, after the battle, she experienced certainty and settling, as if the clouds had parted and the sun had illuminated her. 'I'm not going to take this personally. I'm just going to wipe out everyone who stands between me and whoever's running this place. And then I'm going to wipe him out. Or her. Or it. Let's move.'

She vaulted over a boulder and started to jog across the plateau. She didn't turn round: she expected Ace to follow, and a few moments later she heard running footsteps behind her.

'Looks like the DK isn't easy to kill anyway,' Ace panted.

They ran on together. The hoverspeeder had completed an erratic circle, and was now moving away from them again. Daak was hanging from the rear platform, legs dangling, but he had embedded the teeth of the chainsword in one of the armour-plated side panels. He managed to glance over his shoulder, see Ace and Defries, and lift his left arm in greeting. Then he began to move.

He used the chainsword as a mountaineer uses an ice pick: he clung to the platform with his left hand, and brought the chainsword up and then down again, grinding it into the metal structure of the vehicle and pulling himself forward centimetre by centimetre.

The hoverspeeder turned again. Daak was almost at the front of the platform now, behind the vitreous bubble that protected the cockpit. He stood up, swaying. The pilot seemed to have forgotten his passenger: he had seen Ace and Defries. He turned the speeder towards them, and accelerated.

'Split up,' Defries gasped. 'Shoot to disable, if you can.'

Ace veered to the right.

Defries sprinted leftwards. Damn, she thought, that thing's after me. I get all the luck.

She scanned the gently sloping face of rock. Plenty of fissures, but nowhere to hide for anything bigger than a lizard. The thrumming of the speeder's engine was getting close. Much too close. Where's Ace? Shoot the damned thing, now!

Nothing for it. Defries stopped, turned, dropped full length on the ground, and aimed her blaster. The hover-speeder was only twenty metres away. It had looked kind of cute, from a distance. Now it looked like thirty tonnes of metal falling straight towards her.

If I'm very lucky, she thought, I might just avoid being turned into a long smear of guts and blood. She aimed at the cockpit – and saw Daak's chainsword.

The DK was no more than a shadow, seen through the reinforced glass sphere at the front of the speeder. His chainsword, lifted high above the dome, descended in an arc and stopped with a tortured howl as it hit the carbon-reinforced vitreous.

The glass shattered like an eggshell, and blew away. Daak leapt through the flying shards and into the cockpit. The chainsword rose again, and fell, and Defries ducked her head as the speeder suddenly banked and sliced through the air only a metre from where she lay.

She looked up again. The hoverspeed was swooping and diving as Daak wrestled with the controls. She stood up, instructed her legs to stop feeling like jelly, and set off after the machine.

Daak brought the speeder to a halt on the far side of the plateau, in Ace's path. Not a coincidence, Defries thought. Ace had stopped running, and now walked towards the hoverspeeder very slowly, as if waiting for Defries to catch her up before she reached it.

Daak spent a few minutes kicking the remains of the pilot out of the front of the cockpit, and then settled himself into the pilot's bucket seat and swivelled lazily from side to side, waiting for the women.

They arrived together, wind-worn and battle-weary, converging on the grounded speeder. Surrounded by gale-jangled remnants of the vitreous bubble, Daak sat like a lord and looked down, grinning, as they approached.

What an insufferable pig, Defries thought. I don't know what Ace sees in him. He's a hunk, sure, but some rough trade is just too coarse.

'What kept you, Daak?' she yelled, still five metres from the speeder. 'You took your time. Another five seconds and you'd have had to scrape me off the underside of this thing.'

'Or you could have kept down on the platform,' Ace added. 'I could have plugged the pilot if you hadn't been in the way.'

'Ungrateful bitches,' Daak said, still grinning. 'You could have plugged him that good?' He pointed down to the messy heap lying on the rock in front of the speeder.

Ace and Defries reached the place. Ace grimaced, reached down and hesitantly pulled aside the tattered sheet of black silk. The wind took it, and tore it fluttering from Ace's fingers. Ace turned her head away from the uncovered corpse. 'Jesus. He looks even worse than you do, Daak.' She looked again. 'In fact, I bet he wasn't much prettier when he was alive.'

'Android,' Defries said. 'There's not enough blood for a human. There's metal and circuitry mixed up in there. That's a relief.'

'You'd rather be up against androids?' Ace said.

'I'd rather not kill colonists.'

'That goes for me,' Daak threw in, to Defries's surprise.

'Me too, I suppose,' Ace said, as if she didn't care. 'Let's get off this rock and out of this weather.' She started to climb into the cockpit.

Defries went up to her, and stopped her climbing by placing a hand on her boot. That made Defries think of Johannsen. People were dying. Didn't Ace care why?

'Well?' Ace said, looking down.

'Sometimes I wonder, trooper, just who you're fighting for. Do you have any loyalties?'

Ace continued to look down at Defries. Her face showed no expression. For a moment Defries thought that Ace was going to kick her, but she just shook off Defries's restraining hand. 'You'd be surprised,' Ace murmured. She stepped into the cockpit, picked her way across it, and went to stand alone on the weapons platform.

When Defries pulled herself over the projecting fragments of glass and into the cockpit, Daak was still half out of the pilot's seat, staring at Ace's back and her wind-whipped hair. Defries swivelled his chair to face the front.

'You ever seen androids like that before?' she said.

'What? No, I guess not. I never mixed much with tin goons. My speciality's ripping them open.'

'So much less taxing than analytical thought,' Defries said. 'Well, I've never seen an android like that before. They're all pretty much alike, even from different manu-facturers. That one's a real freak.' She thought about it. Daak started looking over his shoulder towards the weapons platform. 'You did well, Dalek Killer,' she said, attracting his attention again. 'No kidding. You requisi-tioned us some transport. Now we'd better put some distance between us and here. I guess you've worked out how to fly this thing. So which way?'

She and Daak looked to the left, and then to the right, along the plateau. The view was about the same both ways.

'This way.' It was Ace's voice, from the back of the speeder. There was an urgency in the voice that made Defries and Daak turn and climb the three steps to the weapons platform.

They stood beside Ace, and took in the panorama that was laid out like a map below the edge of the plateau. Defries hardly noticed the lakes and the vegetation: she was studying the strange complex of structures that had been built on a vast slab of rock in the centre of the fertile valley.

'It's a colony base camp,' she whispered. 'Glorious Humanity, it's the original base. It's still here. And still in use. Look at the shuttle runways. But what are all those walls and staircases and ramps and towers? What are they made of?'

'It's stone, isn't it?' Ace said. 'Someone's dressed it up to look like a castle out of a fairy tale. Or a nightmare.'

'This could still be Spinward's main base on the planet,' Defries said. 'Maybe we've found what we're looking for.'

'Good,' Daak said, and started the motors of his chain-sword. 'Let's take it to pieces.'

'I give the orders,' Defries said. 'We're tired, hungry, in need of plastic skin here and there. If we were fit, a frontal assault would be suicide. As things are, I'd feel happier trying to eat that chainsword. We'll go and find a place to rest a while.'

'No,' Ace said.

'What? Trooper, if you won't obey a straight order . . . What is it?'

Ace's arm was outstretched, rigid, pointing to a road that meandered along the valley floor. Defries looked through the viewfinder of her blaster, found the convoy moving along the road, and increased the magnification.

Four of the black-robed androids were on foot, stumblingly escorting a big, open wagon pulled by a four gigantic horses. Roped upright in the wagon was a blue box. It was taller than a man, and big enough to accommodate four or five people inside. It had a shallow-pitched roof, with a blue light at the centre. It was oddly heavy – or perhaps the horses were very tired.

'What the hell is that?' Daak said, pre-empting Defries by about half a second.

'It's the TARDIS,' Ace replied, with a smile in which Defries detected more than a hint of malicious enjoyment of her audience's incomprehension. 'It belongs to a friend of mine. We arranged to meet here. He must be inside that tarted-up colony camp. He's probably in trouble, he usually is. He'll be expecting me to ride in with the cavalry. And all I've got is you two.'

'Cut out the clever crap, trooper.' Once again, Defries found herself having to ignore insubordination, this time in order to extract information. 'We're not going anywhere until I get some answers. Who is this guy? What is that blue box? And why in hell should we care?'

'He's called the Doctor. He looks human, but he's not. The TARDIS is his – well, he travels in it. And we need to find him because he'll be right in the middle of whatever's going on. He always is. And the TARDIS is our best hope of getting out of here.'

'Sounds like he's a loser,' Daak said. 'But – the Doctor. I think . . . Hell, I . . . ' He shook his head and snarled.

'Anyway, that chicken coop's not big enough for a one-man transmat.'

The DK was having memory trouble. Defries wondered whether it was the early defrost. Or maybe just a faulty copy. Didn't matter either way. He was already a dead man.

'It's deceptively spacious,' Ace said. She was still smiling, and still watching the cart as it crawled through a Gothic gatehouse and into the compound.

The crazy auxie was going to go down there, Defries realized, whatever Defries's orders were. And Daak would follow her. Defries shrugged. She'd just have to make the best of it. And anyway, she wanted to kill.

In the old days, Defries had read, when humankind was still stuck in one planetary system, when the Martians and the Cybermen came back, the soldiers were genetically manipulated to follow their leaders and implanted with intelligent chips that could be used to enforce military discipline. Desperate times, different priorities. Mostly, Defries thought that things had improved since the break-out. There was a lot wrong with the way the corporations ran the colonies. A lot. She'd seen things . . . But in general it was good for mankind to look outward to the stars. It lessened the tendency for people to fuck up their own heads and others' with neural implants, semi-organic picoprocessors, and viral drugs.

Yet sometimes, like now, she wanted a neural-driven transmitter that would send a signal that would send Ace and Daak into painful paroxysms if they so much as thought of questioning her instructions.

'Fifteen minutes,' she said. 'Daak, you see to the speeder. Engines, controls, fuel. It's the only transport we've got, and I don't want a breakdown. Ace, weapons check. Power levels, all three of us. Plus the cannon on the speeder. And see if you can rig up something forward-firing. I'll come round with the skin and some shots – protein and Zip should do it.'

'And then?' Ace said.

'Then we go in. One hoverspeeder against a fortification full of androids and heavy weapons.'

188

'My kind of fight,' Daak said.

'Doctor!'
'Benny!'
'Is it – Elaine!'
'Francis? Oh, Francis!'
The door clanged shut. The two pairs of prisoners
hardly noticed: they were too busy exchanging news.
Elaine, still holding Bernice's hand, had jumped into
Francis's arms. Benny tried to concentrate on the Doc-
tor's words while her eyes continually strayed towards
Elaine.

'Been having an interesting time?' The Doctor was the
same as ever. Rumpled clothes and unruffled demeanour.
It did her good to see him again. His ice-blue gaze darted
into every corner of the room.

'Mustn't grumble,' Bernice said. 'Two near-death situations, one rescue of a fellow-prisoner, several moments
of heart-stopping tension. You?'

'Oh, much the same. Intriguing planet, this.'

Elaine was chattering to the chap with the soulful face
as if she'd never forgotten how to talk. Bernice grinned.
'What? Oh yes, very. But – you must have escaped from
the TARDIS?'

'Escaped?'

Oh God, I've offended him.

'Professor Summerfield, you should never under-
estimate the guile of a Time Lord. I suppose you thought
I hadn't noticed the occasional vagaries in the systems?'

'Occasional vagaries? Doctor, both you and the
TARDIS have been going ga-ga for months. Ever since
I've been on board. I began to think it was something to
do with me.'

'I had to keep you in the dark. All part of the plan.
And it worked. The TARDIS is fully recovered. As good
as new. Well, as good as – as good as Sun Park.'

'Sun Park?'
'Everton.'
'What?'
'Stripy mints. One of my favourites.'

Bernice gave up. She hoped the TARDIS was in better shape than the Doctor. 'So all we have to do is get out of here, and get back to the TARDIS.'

'Unnecessary,' the Doctor said smugly. 'They're bringing her here.' He cocked his head, as if listening. 'Very close now.'

Bernice hardly heard him. Elaine's hand had started quivering in hers; the girl was sobbing. Bernice flashed an apologetic smile to the Doctor, and turned towards the young couple.

The young man was weeping, too. Francis. Hardly more than a boy, in fact. Slim, with sharp features and large, dark eyes. A look of corruptible innocence that Bernice found rather appealing. As many women would, she thought. But tears are a great leveller; everyone looks ugly with red-rimmed eyes and a screwed-up face.

'Christina!' Francis sobbed, and Elaine's cries rose in a crescendo and then subsided again.

'Christina!' Elaine stammered, and Francis wailed the name again and again.

Bernice watched helplessly. She squeezed Elaine's fingers, and placed a hand on Francis's shoulder. The weeping continued.

The Doctor seemed to find the scene embarrassing. When Bernice glanced over her shoulder, he averted his eyes and took a consuming interest in the door hinges.

Elaine and Francis stopped crying. Bernice gave them an encouraging smile, which they returned weakly, and detached herself from their embrace with one last squeeze and one last pat on the shoulder.

The Doctor was scowling at the door. As Bernice approached, he kicked it. The clang echoed in the empty room.

A tad theatrical, Doctor, Bernice thought.

'I don't understand why they're keeping us in here,' he grumbled. 'The usual routine is that I get frog-marched into the presence of the Topmost Panjandrum so that he can have a good gloat. I can't find out what's going on while I'm locked in the basement.'

'He might be a she, of course,' Bernice said.

'He might turn out to be set of sub-atomic particles bouncing around in a box in intelligent wave formations,' the Doctor fumed. 'He might be anything. That's the trouble. I just don't know. Hush!'

'I didn't – '

'Hush!' Concentration and worry creased the Doctor's forehead. 'Can you hear it?'

There was a continuous, low rumble, which Bernice sensed rather than heard. 'Old-fashioned rocket engine?'

'Two jets, with a rocket booster. A short-hop shuttle, probably.'

'It's taking off, isn't it?'

'Oh yes. It's certainly taking off. With a heavy cargo, I'd say. And we're not on it.'

He was getting angrier by the minute. Bernice didn't understand. Francis and Elaine, looking questioningly at the Doctor, wandered towards the door.

'What's the matter?' Francis said, unwisely in Bernice's opinion.

The Doctor spun round to face him. 'We're in the wrong place, that's what's the matter,' he said with ominous self-control. 'We are here. The Panjandrum is elsewhere. Would you like to start digging the tunnel, or shall I?'

'Cybershit and Dalek dung!' Defries wriggled backwards from the edge of the rock until she was out of sight from the base station below. Crouching, she ran back to the speeder. Ace wasn't going to like this.

Ace was at the front of the vehicle, using Daak's chainsword to hack at the metal-plated skirt. The DK was standing behind her, making comments that she ignored.

'Stop that!' Defries called. She reached the speeder. Ace and Daak turned to face her. 'They've launched the shuttle.'

'What?' Daak raised his fists as if he intended to box Defries's ears.

'Bang goes Plan A,' Ace said. 'It was a nice easy target. There it goes. And the TARDIS inside it.'

Defries followed Ace's gaze. The shuttle was already

no more than a streak of silver. It disappeared into the clouds.

'Escape trajectory,' Daak said.

'Yes, of course,' Defries said. 'Interesting. They're taking your friend's box to a space station. I suppose, Trooper Ace, that your advice would be to follow it?'

Ace smiled. 'Can't think of anything better. But we can't fly this old banger to a space station.'

'No problem.' Daak turned and hoisted himself into the speeder's cockpit. 'We'll go in and find us another shuttle.'

Defries couldn't see any alternative, but she felt obliged to point out the difficulties. 'They'll try to stop us,' she said. 'The original plan was just to get in there, and that was suicide. Now we have to get in, steal a shuttle, fly it out, and then take it off planet. If I say the words giant squid, does that remind you of what could be waiting for us out there?'

'What's the alternative?' Daak yelled.

'No alternative,' Defries said, and climbed up beside him. 'I just thought I ought to remind you that we're all doomed. But I've got a job to do.'

'And I want to stick close to the TARDIS,' Ace said, appearing on the stripped-down rear platform. 'You two remember to keep your heads down. This cannon has a three-sixty degree field now. And Belle: the front thruster's blocked. That lash-up pedal near your right foot releases it. We'll fly nose-down, but we can take a rough ride and it might just save you a laser shave when I start shooting. When you push the pedal, the thruster'll blow – straight out the front of the skirt. Wicked waste of fuel, but it'll fry anything close in front. Best I could do.'

'Quit talking.' Daak laughed, and hit the ignition button. 'I just want to kill something.'

The Doctor had been staring at the ceiling for a very long time. Bernice thought she detected more than a suggestion of injured pride in his rigid stance. Escaping from prisons was one of his specialities, but this time he had conspicuously failed. He hadn't said a word since his last attempt to bamboozle the androids who had brought them more bread and water.

Bernice was almost grateful for the hours of enforced idleness. Every change of scene, every sudden shock, had threatened to plunge Elaine back into catatonic silence. The cell, although uncomfortable and oppressive, made for a haven of quiet and stillness within which Bernice had been able to calm and draw out the traumatized girl. The arrival of Francis, apparently a trusted friend and obviously a gentle and intelligent young man, had augmented the therapy. While the Doctor stalked about the room, or fiddled with the door, or argued with the guards, the three others had sat on the floor and exchanged their stories. Elaine was now chatting happily with Francis, and Bernice had learnt more about the strangely anachronistic civilization of Arcadia.

She gave Elaine a hug and a smile, and stood up. 'Doctor!' she called softly, and walked towards him.

He made no reply until she was standing next to him. 'It's up there,' he said, still staring at the ceiling.

'The sky? Freedom? The pot of gold at the end of the rainbow?'

'The TARDIS. And whoever or whatever has taken it. Only a few miles, but it might as well be the other side of the galaxy.'

'The TARDIS? Oh – the shuttle we heard. A few miles?'

The Doctor turned to her at last. 'A space station, probably. It's hardly likely that the people in charge would want to share the fate of this unfortunate planet. It's getting less arcadian by the hour. Everything important is up there. And we're stuck down here.' He gazed upwards again.

'Doctor, I've been thinking about this planet. Did you know that everyone dies young? In their thirties, mainly. Elaine says that her sister was murdered by the Counsellors – the androids. And according to Francis, the Counsellors officiate at every death, and look after the bodies. Elaine keeps saying that they cut a hole in her sister. I'm going to try to get her to tell me more, but it all sounds dreadfully nasty. Wht's it all for? Doctor – Doctor, are you listening?'

'Damn and blast!' The Doctor jerked his head as if to avoid a blow. 'I still can't get through. Sorry, Benny; I've been trying to communicate with – with whatever it is that's up there. All I can detect is great size and power. There's a lot of data processing going on. A sense of yearning. But what is it? What does it want?'

Bernice folded her arms. He needed a talking-to. 'Doctor, while I can appreciate your academic enjoyment at finding an intellectual equal, I really think you might do better to devote at least some of your attention to the lesser mortals who have been caught up in—'

The Doctor suddenly smiled broadly. 'At last!' he said.

The door opened. Two androids could be seen waiting outside. Stiffly, they beckoned the prisoners.

'We're off to see the wizard on a magical mystery tour!' the Doctor announced, and while Benny was trying to untangle the references from mid-twentieth-century popular culture, he strode out of the room. 'Come along!'

Bernice sighed, shook her head, and turned to shepherd Francis and Elaine through the doorway.

She was on every screen. On some a small figure, seen from a distance, almost dancing across the platform at the back of the bucking hoverspeeder, spraying arcs of laser light that burst into explosions along the top of the perimeter wall, pausing only to hurl grenades that widened the hot smoking breach in the stonework. On others in close-up, her long pony tail swinging, laughing and shouting, eyes dark and glittering.

Britta glanced up at Lacuna. The tall woman's eyes swept from screen to screen. Britta shook her hair free of the long fingers and their slow stroking.

'Isn't she superb?' Lacuna hissed. 'Such vigour. Such excitement. It seems a shame to call off the droids. It's such fun to feel her passion as she destroys them. But we must let them through. We must let them steal the shuttle we've prepared for them. All the pieces are falling into place.'

'Oh,' Britta said. 'So you can feel her feelings too, can you?'

Lacuna laughed, and pinched Britta's ear. 'Not as keenly as I feel your jealousy, pretty one,' she said. 'But Pool is aware of everything in the Net. All thoughts and concepts, at least, except for the stranger and his blue box. And so, through the link, I receive an impression of Ace's thoughts, if Pool channels them to me.'

She's called Ace, Britta thought. Stupid name. 'Try to tell me again, Lacuna,' she asked, attempting to divert attention from the battle on the planet 'What exactly is Pool?'

'Look! They're through the wall. The man and the other woman have survived, unfortunately. No matter. The shuttle is theirs. They will join us soon.'

The screens blanked one by one. Lacuna sat beside Britta, and lifted the girl like a doll on to her lap. Britta hung her head, so that Lacuna had to brush aside her golden hair and turn her face with cold fingers. It made Britta feel like a child. She hated it. She loved it.

'Pool, my little baby, is the collective brains of the Corporation. At first, centuries ago, they were a research team. The Corporation's most senior scientists. They conducted an experiment, using semi-organic material to link their minds.' Lacuna giggled, shockingly. 'It must have looked like something from an old-fashioned horrorvid. All those thick cables, and helmets with lights and flickering displays. And it worked. They were able to merge their thoughts. Six very intelligent and powerful minds became one. And the whole was greater than the sum of its parts.'

'Oh.' Britta had been expecting something more exciting. Neural linkage, brain to brain and brain to computer, was old science, had been pushed to the limit in the years before mankind had reached out for the stars. 'I can see that it would help to run the Corporation more efficiently,' she said, 'although I'm sure there are artificial intelligences that would be as powerful. But some of the things I've seen are – well, that doesn't explain them.'

'Of course not, you silly. That was just the beginning.

They added to themselves over the years. They abandoned their bodies, and became Pool. They grew continuously, for centuries. And now they have mental powers that allow them to surpass physical laws.'

Britta still had no image of Pool. 'So – where is it?'

'Not it – they.' Lacuna stood, cradling Britta in her arms, and turned in a circle before setting the girl down. 'They are here. They are all around us.'

Britta felt dizzy. Suddenly she didn't want to know any more. But the walls of the circular chamber were changing, fading away, becoming transparent.

'There!' Lacuna said. 'Behold the physical reality. You have already been allowed to enter an abstract model of Pool. Now you see them as they are. They reach almost to the ceiling. They are at maximum capacity, optimum power.'

At first Britta could see nothing. The wall was as transparent as glass, but it was as if it revealed only another wall of uniform greyness. She turned in a complete circle. She was enclosed in grey, all round and from floor to ceiling.

She saw that the greyness was not quite opaque. She made out thick bundles of fibres. Some were pulsing regularly. Lumps of darker grey. Slight movement in the depths. It was a thick soup. Congealed.

Lacuna closed her eyes. Britta squealed: something was in her mind.

Hello, Britta, said a voice inside her head. Don't be alarmed. We are Pool. We know you well, and we are grateful to you. Now that you have seen us, you can imagine that we enjoy little in the way of sensory awareness. We exist in pure thought. Lacuna's pleasure in you provides great pleasure for us. When we calculated that we lacked aesthetic sensibility, we created the link. We have come to depend on Lacuna even more than we did on her predecessor, who was unfortunately unable to join us.

'But what are you?'

We are the collective brains of the Corporation. We were only six at first, but many hundreds of individuals have joined us since. All of the Corporation's ablest intellects. And, of course, we harness the cranial material of the descendants of the colonists. We erase the memories, disrupt and reconnect the synapses, and use the material for routine calculations. You have seen some of the things we can do with our power.

Cranial material. Of course. Britta was too amazed to feel shocked, or sickened. Lacuna's chamber was surrounded by a vat of human brain cells.

Part Five

POOL

Bernice could hear the Doctor's voice. At first he sounded distant, as if he was calling to her from the basement of a big house, but he came nearer very quickly and suddenly he was shouting in her ear.

'Do try to snap out of it, Professor Summerfield. I'd like to think that at least one of my travelling companions had a functioning intelligence.'

He sounded tetchy.

Bernice opened one eye. She couldn't identify what she could see. The main thing was, it wasn't rotating. She was lying on her back. The floor wasn't moving. Maybe she wasn't going to die, after all.

'To experience one transmat journey may be regarded as a misfortune,' she said. 'To experience two within the same day is no less than a catastrophe. If I try to sit up, do you promise that you'll keep the world still?'

She closed her eye again before she levered her body upright, reasoning that the movement of her head would produce more than enough sensory input for her brain to cope with.

She still wasn't going to die. In fact, sitting upright, she almost had a sense of balance. She opened both eyes.

Francis and Elaine were sitting in front of her, huddled together. It wasn't clear who was comforting whom. Elaine was pale, her eyes rolling independently. Francis sat clutching her, rigid with fear.

The Doctor had wandered along a shadowy coridor. Bernice could see him tapping his umbrella on the floor, pretending to study the walls, and glancing back impatiently as if he couldn't believe that his companions were still unable to follow him.

'Where are we?' Francis said, in a desolate voice.

'Doctor,' Bernice said, standing, 'why don't you come back here and answer some questions while I make sure no bits of my inner ear got left in the transmat.'

'We're on a space station, Francis,' the Doctor said. As he stepped back into the circle of dimming green light issuing from the door of the transmat booth he looked for a moment like some bizarre demon that Francis had summoned. 'An artificial world, in the sky above your planet.'

'Are you sure, Doctor?' In Bernice's experience, space stations were constructed from prefabricated metal units, bolted together and strung with bulkhead lights and systems ducting. The corridor that led from the transmat booth had a tiled floor, and plastered walls covered with a mural that Bernice felt she might be able to understand after three or four big glasses of strong rum.

'You mean – like the moon?' Francis said. His imagination had apparently overwhelmed his fear. 'It's as if we're in the moon?'

'Very good,' the Doctor said. 'In fact – what does the Arcadian moon look like?'

Francis was perplexed for a moment. 'It's – it's just the moon. Shiny. Sparkling. But not round like the sun. Jagged at the edges. Like a badly dented silver coin.' He seemed pleased with the analogy. Elaine had recovered enough to nod her agreement.

'That's probably where we are then,' the Doctor said, also pleased with himself. 'We're in the moon.'

'Point of order, Mr Chairman,' Bernice said. 'That's all very well, but why isn't there anyone here to meet us and take us into custody again?'

The Doctor pointed along the corridor, and set off in the direction indicated. The others followed him into the darkness. 'I imagine, Professor Summerfield,' his voice floated back to them, 'that it's because we are under surveillance, and in any case we can only go in one direction – oh.'

He had emerged into another pool of dim light at the far end of the corridor. Bernice, Francis and Elaine found him there, standing indecisively at the centre of a cross-roads of corridors.

'This way,' Bernice said, taking the right turn. She strode confidently along a featureless corridor and followed it round a bend. 'All these passages must lead to the same place.' She stopped. 'Then again, a good archaeologist is always receptive to alternative interpretations.' In front of her the corridor divided again, running to the left and the right. In the wall opposite her was a landing from which concrete steps spiralled up and down.

She turned to find that the Doctor, Francis and Elaine had followed her, and were staring glumly at the fourfold choice of paths.

The Doctor took his hat off and placed it on the floor in the centre of the junction. 'Right again,' he said, pointing with his umbrella. 'I have a nasty feeling that getting anywhere might take some time.'

In the deep of the space station, Lacuna was staring at a screen.

On the planet, unaware of being watched, Ace was laying explosive charges.

On other screens, the big Dalek Killer was drawing fire, hurling the damaged hoverspeeder towards the centre of the Landfall complex through a lattice of laser beams, attracting attention away from the Agent from External Operations, who had broken into a shuttle hangar.

But Lacuna barely glanced at the other screens. She was watching Ace, sharing with Pool her enjoyment of the grim smile on Ace's face and the anticipation of the impending explosions.

Ace kept moving, jogging round the inside of the base's perimeter wall, programming one mine after another as she ran. Some she placed by hand at the bases of the silver towers; others, with instructions to seek out metal structures in locations shielded from radio interference, she launched into the air.

'Very clever,' Lacuna said, without checking whether Britta was listening. 'Pool can read the coding, of course, and could defuse the charges. But she's getting round most of the planet-based scrambling systems. It would take them hours to deprogramme those instructions. Very clever. Pool won't help them. Let's all enjoy the fireworks.'

On screen, in close up, Ace's face was tense and excited. She had placed enough mines. Her smile turned into a feral grin as she glanced at her wrist computer. As she ran towards the shuttle hangar, the explosions started.

Landfall was suddenly ringed with volcanoes of metal. On every screen, thin silver towers were spouting flames, sections of stone wall were bulging and bursting like balloons.

'Magnificent,' Lacuna breathed. 'Pool enjoys you, Auxiliary Trooper Ace. Come to me quickly.'

Britta stood apart, staring unseeingly at a three-dimensional display of the space station. She felt cold. She felt ridiculous and awkward in her flimsy tunic, with her hair damp and unbrushed. She despised herself for caring. She wouldn't look. She wouldn't look at Lacuna.

It's just a job, she told herself, jabbing at the display controls.

'Britta, my pretty,' Lacuna said. Britta shivered. 'Is the blue box unloaded? Has the transmat party arrived?'

'I don't know.' She didn't care if Lacuna was angry. 'I can't tell. There are areas of the display that are unclear.' She pressed another button. The tiny image of the blue box, and all around it, dissolved into a grey mist.

'Let me see.' With two long strides Lacuna was standing beside Britta. She put an arm round the girl's waist. Britta pulled away.

'Well,' Lacuna said. 'We are going to have some fun when Ace joins us, I can see that. Pool will be very entertained.'

Britta hated her. Britta hated herself for wanting the arm to encircle her again.

'Pool has been altering the topography of the station again,' Lacuna said. 'Or part of Pool. While we were concentrating on the troopship and the fighting on the planet. We can't afford to divert this much processing power.'

Britta didn't understand, but she was reminded of her mind-trip inside the simulacrum of Pool. She remembered the dark movement she had seen just before the link had been severed. Disturbances in the depths. Something like a shark, lurking among the sea-bottom rocks.

'It doesn't matter,' Lacuna decided. 'The transmat party must be on the station. We will find them eventually. The box is more important. Pool wants to learn its secrets. Concentrate on finding the box.'

Britta filled her mind with thoughts of grey blankness, and kept her finger on the button she had pressed. 'I haven't found it yet,' she said. 'But I'll keep looking.'

'Good girl,' Lacuna said absently, and returned to sit at the bank of screens. Over her shoulder, Britta could see coils of smoke. Tongues of flame. The hoverspeeder. A shuttle, taxiing. Ace's face.

I hate you! Britta hurled the thought at Lacuna's back. Lacuna laughed, but didn't turn round.

It was sheer spitefulness, Britta knew that. Pool and Lacuna knew about everything she did, anyway. Didn't they? But Britta didn't care. She did it anyway. It took only a few seconds to order six droids and a goods transporter to the 65th level cargo bay. A few seconds more to instruct them to move the blue box.

Britta almost wanted Lacuna to notice. That would show her. But the double-domed head remained craning towards the screens. The red light of fires reflected from the hairless cranium.

Francis had lost count of the junctions and side-passages they had crossed. Bernice, the Doctor's rather overbearing friend, seemed fascinated by the paintings on the walls. Francis didn't like to study them too closely: they were even more disturbing than the strange plants that seemed to be growing everywhere on the planet. And even Bernice, for all that she was a Professor and obviously very learned, seemed unable to read any meaning into the convolutions of colour.

'Distasteful subject matter,' she had said, more than once. 'Bosch's *Garden of Delights* meets Picasso's *Guernica* in a pointillism cum blood-splatter style. But the workmanship is incredible. The detail. The materials. Images that fill the corridor, packed with images too small to see with the naked eye. The painting incorporates tiny imperfections in the building materials. It hardly seems possible.'

'It isn't,' the Doctor had said, looking up from his notebook, 'humanly.'

The Doctor was trying to make a map of their journey. Francis guessed, by the way that the Doctor's head-scratching and pencil-licking increased with every junction they reached, that the task was proving difficult.

'It would help,' the Doctor had announced several times, 'if the corridors were straight.'

Some of the corridors were straight, or at least ran straight for many metres. But most of them were curved, or meandering. At least one long passage must have been a spiral, because they had walked far enough round a uniform bend to accomplish two circles. That passage, like a few others, had ended at a stairway: up or down were the only choices. The Doctor had assured them that they were now on the same level as they had started on, but Francis wasn't convinced.

He resented the automatic assumption that he would look after Elaine, even though he had to admit that he was so tired and amazed that even scribbling in a notebook or commenting on the decoration were beyond his capabilities. In fact Elaine wasn't much trouble. And when he felt he couldn't walk another step, or wanted to question the wisdom of setting off down an unlit passage, he could always say *Elaine's so tired* or *Elaine's a bit nervous*.

There were no doors. There were no dead ends. Every corridor led to other corridors, or to stairs. They walked along corridors so narrow that they had to turn sideways, and through corridors as wide as barns. Corridors that sloped down more and more steeply, so that they had to sit and shuffle down the last few metres. Corridors that twisted upwards like corkscrews. Once they came upon

206

an irregularly-shaped room as wide as the grazing meadow on the east bank of the Slow Brochet; eleven passages led from it. But there were no dead ends.

'Look at this, Doctor.' Bernice was gazing at yet another painting in yet another curving corridor. 'I'm sure this is a representation of the Perseus myths. This could be Medusa, don't you think? And then here, much larger, Andromeda and the monster from the sea. He's very nasty. Mind you, I can't say I fancy this Perseus much, either. Doctor?'

'Hmm?' The Doctor looked up from his notebook. His face was mournful. 'I'm afraid we're completely lost.'

This seemed to Francis an opportune moment to slump to the floor. 'I don't suppose there's any chance we could have another bite of that cheese, is there, Benny? I'm worried about Elaine. She's almost exhausted.'

'No I'm not,' Elaine stated, destroying Francis's plans for an impromptu picnic. 'I want to see what's round the next corner.'

'That's the spirit,' Bernice said, grabbing Elaine's hand and skipping out of sight.

'Come along, Francis,' the Doctor said, and followed Bernice and Elaine.

Francis dragged himself to his feet and plodded round the bend.

He found the Doctor, Bernice and Elaine at the end of the corridor, staring aghast at the floor in the middle of the next junction of passages.

The Doctor's hat.

They had reached the place they'd started from.

Bernice stepped forward and picked up the hat.

'Damn!' she said. 'I thought I'd seen the last of this particular fashion accessory.'

The Doctor took it from her and placed it on his head. 'Mutually accessible centres,' he said, 'in three dimensions and with no dead ends. The worst kind of maze.' He looked glum. 'We might as well have a rest. Here's as good as anywhere else.' He sat down.

'Will we find the way out?' Elaine asked.

'Oh yes,' the Doctor said gloomily. 'But it might take

a few years. How much cheese did you managed to pocket as we left the cell, Benny?'

'Enough for another chunk each.'

'Then I can foresee some difficulties.'

Francis had a sudden, terrible realization. 'Perhaps there isn't a way out!'

The Doctor sighed and covered his face with his hands. 'Thank you, Francis,' he said. 'It might have been more diplomatic not to mention that possibility.'

Elaine started to cry.

The rain had started again. In the windless valley, it dropped from the sky in vertical sheets. Thunder rumbled among the tumbling bags of cloud.

It was cold, and drenching, even at first. Soon it was falling in icy, clattering streams, as if above the clouds the bottom of a reservoir had been suddenly pulled aside.

The fires continued to burn, but now they produced blankets of smoke as dark and dense as black treacle.

Visibility was so poor that Defries could hardly see the runway in front of her. She checked the pilot's array. OK for automatic lift-off. The filthy conditions wouldn't help: the droids probably had infra-red sight, and heat-seekers don't notice a rainstorm when they've got a rocket trail to home in on. And that assumed there wasn't a ground-controlled auto destruct.

The only hope was to get off-planet now, in the confusion of the explosions. Where in Hades were the others?

Ace appeared in the open doorway of the cabin. Her boots were muddy to the knees, her hair was dripping, and her face was covered with rain-borne streaks of black. 'I suppose this is what they call the fog of war,' she yelled. Defries could hardly hear her over the rain.

'OK to go?' Ace shouted, even more loudly. The runway lights came on, two lines of haloed yellow flares that faded as they converged into the curtains of rain and smoke. Searing streaks of laser light sizzled across the illuminated path.

Defries cursed. 'Runway lights off!' she ordered. 'Switch to voice reactive, you antiquated heap of shit, and get those runway lights off!' The lights stayed on. A beam flashed across the runway only a few metres away from the shuttle's nose.

Ace threw herself across the cabin. She studied the controls for a moment, then touched a button. The light went off.

'You wouldn't believe the age of some of the crates I've driven,' Ace said.

Defries didn't have time for talk. 'Where's Daak?' she snapped.

Ace struck her forehead with her fists. 'He isn't here?' She didn't wait for a reply. 'That stupid foamhead,' she said, and made for the door.

'Trooper!' Defries heard herself almost screaming with anger. 'Daak's a dead man. Leave him. Get back—' But Ace had jumped.

Defries punched the edge of the control panel. Her reinforced glove created a satisfying dent. She smiled grimly: nothing and nobody was going to stop her finding and fixing the Spinward bosses in the Arcadia system. She started pressing buttons: life support, fuel system, ignition system, navigation processors.

'Young love,' she muttered to herself. 'Gods, she must really like the big oaf. Should have defrosted him earlier. They could have rutted each other stupid on the *Raistrick*. Time and a place for everything. And this isn't it.

'Ready to roll. Nothing to do but sit here and wait to be fried. I'll give them three minutes. Then I'm going, with or without them.'

Ace ran through rain that hissed like radio static, through mud that sucked at her heels, through rolls of smoke that cloaked the camp with the darkness of night and parted only occasionally to reveal nothing but clouds, almost as dark, racing across the sky above.

There wasn't much blaster fire near her. She made for the fires and the sudden yellow flashes that lit up the central complex of buildings.

Now she'll be convinced I fancy him, Ace thought. Ice-queen Defries. I'll bet she goes for Cybermen. How can

she think I'd even consider a nanoceph like Daak? I'll
bet he's as useful in bed as a leaky hot-water bottle. All
those muscles are an obvious attempt to compensate. And
as for that chainsword . . . Still, he's handy with it. What
a mess.

She had reached the place where the Dalek Killer had
entered one of the six squat buildings that made up the
central complex. The hoverspeeder, its motors still idling,
was attempting to wedge itself into the hole in the wall
which Daak must have made with the vehicle's front thrusters. Dismembered androids, some still twitching, lay in
oily puddles on and around the speeder.

Ace couldn't see Daak. The speeder was blocking her
way into the building. She thought of crawling beneath
the vehicle's metal-plated skirt, but one faceful of ex-
haust-heated mud was enough to discourage her. She
wiped the filth out of her eyes and pulled herself into the
wreckage of the cockpit.

The motors whined as she put the speeder into reverse.
With a screech of metal and a shower of falling masonry,
the speeder suddenly jerked backwards.

Ace was about to shut off the power, abandon the
speeder and enter the smoking blackness of the building,
when she heard Daak's voice.

He was shouting, as usual. His voice was coming from
above. She couldn't see him, but she didn't have time to
consider many options. She put all the motors through
the vertical jets, and prayed that the speeder wouldn't
blow apart or shake to bits as it lurched up the side of
the building.

Someone on the roof started shooting at her. She shot
back. It passed the time.

Then she saw him. The Dalek Killer was on a balcony
– a flat, unwalled slab that projected from a wide opening
just below the top of the wall. It might have been a
loading bay, or a landing pad for one-person fliers.

He was shouting, but that was all. He was standing
hunched forward, facing into the building, his left arm
across his stomach. He was holding a blaster there, awkwardly, firing occasional and random beams into the

opening in front of him. The chainsword hung from his right hand. Ace could see dark liquid dripping from the motionless blades; she guessed it wasn't lubricating oil.

He staggered, then straightened with a yell. He shook his rain-sodden hair away from his face, and sent a spray of drops into the air. He was now only a step from the edge of the platform.

Ace was getting bored with her laser duel. They were never going to hit each other, anyway. She unpacked a self-locating mine, punched in her identifier and gave it a simple verbal instruction. As if in reply, it unfolded its triangular wings.

She hesitated before launching it. These little whizz-bangs were among her favourite weapons. They were more intelligent and versatile than most, and they reminded her of playing with paper aeroplanes during lessons at school. This was her last.

Even if there were weapons on the shuttle, there wouldn't be anything as advanced as the sleek little dart in her hand. She threw it upwards. It disappeared into the smoke.

Fifteen seconds.

The speeder was approaching the level of the platform. As it rose, the motors now screaming in protest, Ace could gradually see more of the opening from which the platform projected.

She didn't like what she saw. Three androids, apparently unscathed and in untattered robes of black silk, were standing just inside the doorway. Daak's shouted curses were becoming weaker, and it was obvious that he was unable to aim his blaster. The androids ignored the few bursts that issued from his gun and carved smoking scars in the wall.

Ten seconds.

The hoverspeeder's cockpit was now only a couple of metres below, and slightly to one side of, the platform.

'Daak!' Ace shouted. 'Daak, you musclebound prat, get down here. Jump! Or just fall over in this direction, for God's sake! Daak!'

He couldn't hear. Ace's voice was drowned by the

shriek of the speeder's motors. And Daak had apparently not heard the speeder, anyway. He was barely conscious.

Shit, Ace thought, I'll have to jump across and get him.

She checked the power level of her blaster, looked up – and saw the three androids simultaneously raise their hands and aim three blasters at the Dalek Killer.

Five seconds.

Too long, by about four seconds.

Ace threw herself at the speeder controls, stamping on the throttle override while wrenching the steering column forward.

The speeder froze in mid-air for just a moment, while its computers coped with the sudden assault on the automatic systems. Then it surged upwards and forwards with a noise like a washing machine spinning itself to oblivion, and crashed into the underside of the platform.

Ace fell over, and didn't even attempt to stand again. The floor of the cockpit was vibrating, the motors were screaming. Ace kept her foot rigid against the throttle override and lifted her head. The speeder's weapons platform was jammed up against the underside of the platform: somewhere in the middle of the sandwich was a crushed laser cannon. On the top side of the platform, Daak had fallen over. He looked unconscious. He could have been dead. The three androids had fallen over, too, but they were still functioning, and were beginning to aim their blasters.

'Come *on*,' Ace yelled, willing the motors to sacrifice their entire future lifetimes of useful work for just a few more horsepower *now* – and with a grinding, tearing, roaring noise the platform cracked, buckled, and was ripped from the side of the building.

The speeder, with Ace on the cockpit floor and Daak lying on a concrete slab lying on the weapons deck, soared skywards, into coils of choking smoke.

Zero.

The building's roof exploded, sending rays of ruddy light to gild the bulging bottoms of the clouds. The noise was like thunder, painfully loud but somehow indistinct. The speeder bucked and dived, and Ace struggled with the controls while chunks of hot stone and metal rained around her and sizzled in the ankle-deep puddles on the floor.

She got it down before the motors blew, and without tipping over. She told her wrist computer to give the speeder the settings for the shuttle hangar, and as the automatic pilot cut in she turned, intending to climb up to what was left of the weapons deck.

Daak was standing, swaying, at the back of the cockpit.

'Microbrain,' Ace said, 'you very very nearly got yourself killed.' She almost added *too soon*.

He didn't look well. There were deep gouges in his left forearm, and the only reason they weren't bleeding was that the flesh was also burnt. He was still holding his stomach, but Ace couldn't see the damage there. The most impressive wound was down the length of the upper part of his right arm, where the flesh had been sliced away. Ace thought she could see the bone. She could certainly see lots of blood.

'What you need,' she went on, 'is a month in sick bay and a steady supply of regen tissue. What you'll get is whatever we can find on the shuttle. If Defries hasn't gone without us.'

Daak shook his head, slowly, and took a step forward.

'Can you hear?' Ace suddenly realized he might have taken other damage. Head wounds. 'Try to say something. You could try "thank you" for a start.'

Daak took another painful step. His face twisted into a grin. 'Give us a kiss, girlie,' he said thickly.

'Get – ' Ace was cut off by the jolt of the speeder coming to rest. The shutting down of the motors was lost in the roar of louder engines. The shuttle was looming over them, a dark, angular shape in the darkness. Just beginning to taxi. The cabin door beginning to close.

'Belle!' Ace called. 'Defries! Cut the engines and get us aboard.'

The roar decreased in volume. The shuttle stopped, trembling, as if straining at a leash. A silhouette appeared against the light streaming through the cabin doorway.

'Ace?'

'Belle. I've got him. He needs help.'

'So do you. Psychotherapy.' The shuttle's emergency steps, with Defries balancing on the end of them, extended down to the speeder's cockpit. 'Black hole in Hades, Ace,' Defries said as she jumped from the steps, 'the Dalek Killer's more dead than alive. He'll slow us down.'

'I couldn't leave him, Belle. I can't let him die.'

Defries looked disgusted, but she helped Ace manhandle Daak on to the retractable steps. 'He's just a DK. He's already on borrowed time. And he isn't even – gods, but he's heavy. I'll explain some other time.'

Me too, Ace thought. She's got a nerve, banging on at me about not caring. Ice-queen Defries isn't the half of it. She makes that bastard Kane look like a social worker. What am I supposed to do, stand and watch while the droids fry him? Let him bleed to death?

They were in the cabin. The door slid shut. Defries turned to the controls. Ace felt the shuttle begin to move. 'Medical kit?' she said.

'See what you can find,' Defries said over her shoulder. 'He's your boyfriend. I'm getting us off this planet as fast as I can.'

Ace found painkillers, plastigraft, artificial blood. The shuttle trembled violently as it accelerated along the runway. With a lurch, the vibration ceased. The shuttle was airborne. Ace knew she had to work fast, before they all had to strap in.

'If I didn't need you, Defries,' she said, pumping drugs into Daak's arm, 'if I could get up there without you . . . '

Defries didn't even look round. 'Junk it, trooper. I've got a job to do. You're under orders to help me do it. Don't forget that. I've lost the *Raistrick*. I've lost Celescu's troops. I've lost Johannsen. I can't afford to fail now. I'm not going to. Those responsible will pay.'

Ace moved out of range of Daak's left hand and stood in thought for a moment, averting her eyes as the shuttle broke through the cloud cover. 'Yeah,' she said. 'OK, that's cool.'

214

Defries laughed. 'Don't you ever say "Yes, ma'am" when you acknowledge an order?'

'No, ma'am,' Ace said, 'seems like I never do.'

It's almost as if he knows where he's going, Bernice thought. Who does he think he's fooling? And if his whistling *Amazing Grace* is supposed to keep our spirits up, he needs a refresher course in building team morale. I suppose it's his idea of a pun.

The Doctor was being irritatingly cheerful. He would stride ahead to the next junction of corridors, twirling his umbrella, and then wait impatiently for the others to catch up. Usually he would choose the next direction without hesitation, but sometimes he would wait, head cocked, as if listening for far-off sounds. Once, he licked his finger and held it aloft in the airstream before lowering it to point decisively along a corridor that appeared to Bernice no different from the other two that also ran from the junction.

With a worried glance at Elaine and Francis, she hurried forward to walk alongside him.

'Doctor, you win, all right? You can have the gold medal. You can slow down now. Francis and Elaine can't keep up. Will you maintain a more reasonable pace if I bombard you with inane questions?'

He stopped. Bernice was deeply suspicious. The twinkle in his eyes looked genuine enough. But how could you tell with a Time Lord? Had he conceived of a scheme to lead them out of the maze?

'How about this,' Bernice said. 'In the transmat booth that brought me and Elaine from Beaufort to Landfall, I saw the logo of the Spinward Corporation.'

The Doctor, thinking deeply, tapped his front teeth with the crook of his umbrella.

'Well, that's right,' he said expansively, and started to stroll onwards along the corridor. 'Of course. Arcadia was a Spinward colony planet for centuries. It's all in the Matrix. Nothing wrong with that.'

'And another thing – '

'No,' the Doctor interrupted, 'but *this* is all wrong.' He

gestured dangerously with his brolly. 'I suppose I created the Spinward Corporation, in a way. Helped it along, anyway. Back then.'

'Back when?' Bernice said, her archaeologist's mind ever alert to any opportunity to pin down the Doctor to a specific date.

'A few centuries before now. On Earth, of course.'

'Go on.'

'I put a spanner in the works of one of the companies that later merged to form Spinward. A very large spanner. A job well done, if I do say so myself.'

'But?'

'Oh, nothing. Well, perhaps I nudged things just a little too far. It's so hard to be sure. Their research was very advanced for its time. I successfully blocked one of the main avenues they were exploring. But perhaps that only encouraged them to move faster elsewhere.'

Bernice waited for the Doctor to continue, but he walked on and then glanced sideways at her as if expecing another question. Go for the jugular, she thought.

'So what, exactly, do you think you're up against now?'

'I really don't know – exactly,' he said. 'I don't even know if I'm against it. I can sense something like a vast, artificial intelligence. It's almost like a primitive version of parts of a TARDIS. And that's quite impossible, you see. Mankind doesn't have that level of knowledge. Not in the twenty-fifth century. Not for centuries to come.'

'We're in the twenty-fifth century?' Bernice punched his shoulder. 'Doctor, why didn't you tell me? I've come home.'

The Doctor looked bemused for a moment, and then his face broke into a sheepish grin. 'Do you know, Benny, it had completely slipped my mind. Yes, this must be almost exactly your time. But not your place, of course: we're a good four hundred light years from your usual stamping grounds. Not that you could meet yourself, anyway. I understand about three years have elapsed since you left.'

Bernice fought a brief mental struggle with the concept of meeting herself, surrendered, and took refuge in observed facts. She pointed at the minutely-decorated walls.

'These materials. The murals. They don't look – I mean, there was, or I should say is, I suppose, nothing like this in the twenty-fifth century. Not of human origin. Not that I've seen. Is it alien?'

'I don't think so. But you're right. It shouldn't be here. Whatever created it is an aberration. A very interesting aberration.'

'That's one way of describing it,' Bernice said, but she couldn't be bothered to come up with other, less half-hearted quips. She was too busy grappling with the concepts behind the Doctor's deceptively simple explanations.

'If you, several centuries ago, diverted the route through time that the Spinward Corporation would have taken . . . ' she began.

'Yes?' the Doctor said, with an infuriating smile.

'Well, surely the TARDIS would have known about it? I mean, the TARDIS predicts the future, doesn't it? Or you and the TARDIS between you, somehow. Or you can read some source of information that predicts the future. I'm sure that's what you've told me, anyway. And stop looking so damned superior.'

'Prediction isn't the right word. It's too definite. It's always a matter of assessing probabilities. Ticklish work. Requires vast talent, of course, and a frightening amount of computing power, as well as a sort of knack . . . The universe isn't a predictable place, that's the trouble. But perhaps it's just as well.'

'Is it?'

'Of course, Benny. You wouldn't want to start watching one of those awful old adventure films you like so much if you knew exactly what was going to happen, would you? Much more fun if the ending's a surprise.'

'But I like to watch them more than once.'

'Several times more than once,' the Doctor said, the tone of his voice reflecting the numerous occasions on which Bernice had dragged him into the flea-pit cinema she'd found in the TARDIS and insisted that he pay attention to the *noir* motifs and the semiotics of *Double Indemnity*. 'But the universe is like that, too.'

'Black and white?' Bernice suggested.

'Far from it. No, I mean that it comes as a surprise when you first experience it, and then after that you can't change the course of events. Rick always sends Elsa to the aeroplane with her husband, no matter how many times you watch *Casablanca*.'

Bernice was becoming confused. 'But I thought . . . You've always said – or at least implied – that the things you do have an effect. You said you interfered with the development of the Spinward Corporation. For instance.'

The Doctor sniffed. 'Really, Benny. You know how much I dislike that word. Yes: I can help to write the script for movies yet to be made. We all do that, although I must admit the TARDIS gives me a wider range of opportunities than most people have. But I can't alter a film that's – what's the expression – already in the can. Have you heard of a type of problem known as NP-complete?'

'Are you changing the subject?'

'Absolutely not.'

'Why did you turn left at that last corridor?'

'Ah-ha!'

'Yes, I've heard of NP-complete problems. But I can't quite remember . . . '

The Doctor waited until Bernice had abandoned all hope of recalling her long-forgotten theoretical mathematics.

'What's the quickest way to solve a puzzle?' he said.

'Give it to a computer,' Bernice replied immediately. 'If the puzzle's susceptible to analysis, the fuzzy logic will work out the principles involved. And if it's just a matter of lots of calculations, any sort of processor will polish it off in next to no time.'

'Unless?'

'Unless it's NP-complete?'

'Precisely.' The Doctor stopped again. They had reached the end of yet another corridor. Bernice glanced over her shoulder and was relieved to see that Francis and Elaine were only a few metres behind her.

A passageway crossed left and right before her; a little way along the right-hand corridor she could see a wide opening in the wall, and through it the first few steps of a wide staircase leading upwards. The Doctor seemed uninterested in any of the alternative paths.

'An NP-complete puzzle,' he said, standing with his hands behind his back and his gaze wandering towards the ceiling, 'is one in which the routes to the solution are so numerous that there is no single correct answer. Indeed, the number of possible routes increases exponentially as one explores them.'

'Ah,' Benny said. 'Not unlike this maze of corridors, for instance?'

'Exactly.' the Doctor smiled indulgently. 'The only way to find the way out of a single-exit maze consisting of mutually accessible junctions is to follow the paths until you find the way out. There are no short cuts. A robot, with no matter how powerful an artificial intelligence, would perform no better than a person.'

'A robot would do it more quickly,' Bernice said. 'Metal legs don't get tired.'

'Of course, of course,' the Doctor said. 'I was speaking theoretically. If one imagines a machine that can travel from junction to junction almost instantaneously, finding a path to the exit would take only seconds. But what about adding a twist to the puzzle: the task is not merely to find a way out, but to find the shortest route to the way out.'

Bernice was beginning to have an inkling of the Doctor's real subject. 'The robot – the machine would have to explore every possible route. That would be the only way to establish which was the shortest. So in a maze with one four-way junction there would be four routes to explore and compare. With two junctions there would be four; plus three, that's seven; eight; another three, that's eleven – I can't count them. There are quite a lot.'

'A hundred and twelve,' the Doctor said. 'And that's assuming the machine is programmed not to double back along the same path. A maze consisting of just three such junctions would have – well, hundred and hundreds of routes. You get the picture.'

'Exponential numbers. You could give a computer quite a headache with an NP-complete puzzle.'

'I've done so, on occasion. Now then: we were talking about predicting the future, I believe?'

'Indeed we were, Doctor. And I take your point. The universe as NP-complete. Each beat of a butterfly's wing – each division of each and every cell – seen as a junction in a maze.'

The Doctor looked extremely pleased with himself. 'I'll let you into a small secret,' he said. 'I haven't met many humans who have understood the complexities of travelling in time as well as space.'

'Hmm. I'll take that as a compliment, I think.'

'Of course, we don't have to consider the whole of space-time. Some of the universe is pretty much cut and dried. All of the past, for instance. Although that's still rather small, compared to the future. And there are long strands of fixed points, a bit like beads on long strings. Or like strands of lumpy noodle in the soup of probability. But there's enough left to discombobulate even the biggest of predictive computers.'

Bernice was fairly sure that if she asked whether she was, at that moment, on a lumpy excrescence on a strand of spaghetti stretching into the Doctor's future and surrounded by a soup of probabilities, she wouldn't like the answer. She decided that thinking in four dimensions was best left to the Doctor. 'I remember now,' she said. 'I read somewhere that even if every atom in the universe could be made to function as a flipflop switch in a binary computer, it still wouldn't be big enough to follow all the possible routes that the universe could create.'

The Doctor thought for a moment, counting on his fingers. Bernice was sure he was bluffing. 'Yes,' he said slowly, as if he'd just completed a mental calculation, 'that's quite right. To predict the universe, you'd need a computer many times bigger than the universe.'

'The TARDIS is big. Bigger than something very big indeed, I'd say.'

'Very percipient, Benny. But I'm afraid even the TARDIS isn't that enormous. The best she can do, even with the link to the Eye of Harmony and the data stored in the Matrix, is to work in best estimates. Shall we see how she's getting on?'

'What?' Bernice said. But the Doctor had turned on his heel and was almost skipping along the right-hand corridor.

Bernice caught up with him as he veered towards the broad staircase. He didn't take the stairs: he ducked under them and disappeared into the shadows. Bernice followed him, and found herself in a square space behind the staircase. It was empty but for the Doctor, looking very smug, and the TARDIS.

Two weak cries of 'Oh!' broke the silence as Francis and Elaine arrived.

'Before you ask, Benny—'

'What makes you think I was going to?'

'—I must confess that I have no idea what the TARDIS is doing here. Someone must have brought it here for a purpose, but I must admit it looks abandoned. Perhaps they've lost it. However—'

'You can usually find the TARDIS.'

'—I can usually find the TARDIS, if it's nearby. And it's in full working order.'

'It never is!'

'Well, not often, I'll grant you. But she's as well as can be expected. Now, where did I put the key?' He patted his pockets for a few moments. His frown deepened, then transformed itself into a radiant grin. He plucked his hat from his head and extracted a key from the hatband.

It was Francis who first realized the implication. 'Doctor,' he said accusingly, 'the key to your blue box was in your hat. You left your hat in the maze. You might have lost it forever.'

The Doctor looked disconcerted for the merest moment. 'Ah, but I didn't, did I? We found it again. By such infinitesimal chances are failure and success separated. Excuse me, won't you? I shan't be long.'

He pushed open the TARDIS door.

'Doctor!' Bernice's summons halted him in the doorway. 'Would you mind telling us what you're doing? Are you going to leave us here? Because if you're thinking of nipping back a century or two and uncreating this interesting aberration of yours, I think I'd rather be somewhere else at the moment of uncreation, if it's all the same to you.'

The Doctor beamed. 'You haven't been paying attention, Benny. I can't rewrite the script, remember? Do you think I would have let the Master grow into the twisted megalomaniac he is if I could have prevented it? It's not as simple as that. This is a piece of real space-time, and I can't unmake it. I wish I'd understood that when I had to deal with that meddling Monk.'

Bernice understood the rebuke, if not the particular examples, in the Doctor's words. He kept glancing into the TARDIS as if anxious to perform his mysterious, self-appointed tasks. Bernice hadn't finished with him yet.

'So if you were to take the TARDIS a few hundred years back,' she said, 'what could you do?'

'Oh, the usual. Resist oppression, lighten the burden of the underdog, spread understanding and reason. You know the sort of thing. But I can't unmake this piece of space-time. It would be difficult to make any long-term difference to the development of the Spinward Corporation, because this moment exists and must fit into Spinward's development. I could go back and leave myself some notes, a bit of helpful advice; but as I don't know yet what I'm dealing with, I can't leave myself anything useful. And I haven't come across any notes from me to me, so obviously I'm not going to go back into the past and leave anything for me to discover in the future, which is the present. I hope that's clear? Now I really must – '

'What if you destroyed Arcadia? Before it was colonized, I mean, in the past. Wouldn't that prevent this happening?'

'Not necessarily, Benny. There are other planets that

would have served just as well, I imagine, in Spinward's schemes. And before you suggest that I should consider annihilating this entire sector of the galaxy – '

'I wouldn't suggest that,' Bernice said quietly. Countless faces, silently screaming, thronged her mind. The destruction of the Seven Planets would live with her forever.

'No,' the Doctor said. 'No, of course not. I was merely going to say that it is possible to alter the past to such an extent that subsequent events are incompatible with it. The results are, as you might have guessed, violently unpredictable. Now I really must attend to the TARDIS.' He disappeared into the dark interior. The door closed.

Seconds later the door opened again. The Doctor hopped out, and re-locked it.

'Is that it?' Bernice said.

'Yes, all done,' the Doctor said, and made for the bottom of the stairs.

'Doctor,' Bernice almost wailed, 'can't we at least use the TARDIS to get out of this maze? Let's go somewhere else. Somewhere comparatively interesting. What about Lubellin, the Mud Planet. I always thought I'd like to be stuck there for a dirty weekend.'

'Out of the question, Professor,' the Doctor admonished. 'First, if we leave now I won't find out what's going on, and as you know I don't like to leave anywhere until I know what's going on. Something always is.'

Bernice peered questioningly at the Doctor. As he talked, he was staring fixedly at her. Francis and Elaine, clutching each other's hands, were also gazing at her with wide eyes.

'Second,' the Doctor continued, 'we don't have to use the TARDIS to escape from the maze. We have found a way out.'

'We have?'

The Doctor, Francis and Elaine spoke in unison: 'Behind you!'

'Third,' the Doctor said, as Bernice whirled to see an open doorway where only seconds earlier there had been a flat wall, 'I imagine those androids would prefer us not to attempt to escape, in the TARDIS or in any other way. The usual procedure in this sort of situation is to act like prisoners and let the guards take us to their leader. And not before time, in my opinion.'

Six androids were standing in the doorway. Bernice hadn't seen them at first: their black silk cloaks merged into the darkness beyond the doorway, and only the jerky movements of the red-painted muzzles of their stubby blasters revealed their location.

'These are the three humans and the humanoid paradox,' spluttered one of them. 'They have been attracted to the box paradox. We will load them all on the transporter. Also re-load the box.'

Five of the androids limped into the space between the doorway and the staircase, surrounding their captives. The sixth disappeared into the darkness beyond the doorway, and shortly afterwards the whirr of a motor started and became louder. A goods transporter – little more than a metal platform hovering a few centimetres above the floor – edged through the doorway, with the sixth android at the controls. It inched forward until the front of the platform nudged the base of the TARDIS.

'They'll have to tip it on to its side,' Bernice whispered.

'I know,' the Doctor said. 'Did I remember to set the internal stabilizers? I can't remember.'

Four of the androids exerted all of their considerable strength against one side of the TARDIS. It teetered on one edge of its base, and toppled on to the platform with surprisingly little noise but with enough force for Bernice to feel the floor move beneath her feet and a blast of displaced air brush against her face.

My specimens, she thought. The script discs from Sakkrat. The Heavenite porcelain. My collection of beer glasses. If he's forgotten the stabilizers . . .

Lights had come on beyond the doorway. A straight corridor, with no side doors or passages, stretched as far as Bernice could see. Gesturing with their blasters, the androids encouraged the Doctor, Bernice, Francis and Elaine to step on to the platform beside the TARDIS.

With its motor whining in protest, the transporter started to crawl along the corridor.

'Do you know,' the Doctor said, 'I rather think we're getting somewhere at last.'

In near-silence made even more oppressive by the continuous engine hum and the laboured breathing of the six androids, the transporter glided along the passageway. It was a wide corridor, gloomy and undecorated and very long, but at last Bernice was able to see the far end: a wall moulded into the likeness of a grotesque face. As the transporter approached the dead end without slowing, Bernice remembered that she had something else to tell the Doctor.

'Doctor,' she whispered. 'There's another thing you should know. Elaine has told me about her sister's death. She says—'

'Hush,' the Doctor said. 'Look.'

There was movement at the end of the corridor. Bernice peered ahead, and gasped. She took an involuntary step back. She heard Elaine whimper. The huge face was changing. The eyes widened, the mouth opened to form a smile, and then a gaping O, and then with a cry that Bernice heard in her mind rather than with her ears the nose and chin split in a vertical line, the eyes moved apart, and the entire face divided in two.

Lights shone in the darkness beyond the widening fissure. The transporter squeezed between the two halves of the parted face, and came to rest in a large, high-ceilinged, circular room, like the inside of a drum.

Despite the simplicity of the structure, it was a disconcerting place. The floor was covered with dust, tumbled heaps of shattered stone, fallen statues, and unidentifiably broken machines. Half-demolished walls and staircases suggested that until recently the chamber had been a warren of antique stonework. Bernice found her eyes caught by flashes of light, as if mirrors were suspended at random all round the room. But there were no mirrors, just almost-invisible pockets of shining darkness where some still-standing stairs and statues disappeared, as if

225

cut with shears, or seemed to be folded at impossible angles.

'Don't go anywhere near the reality faults,' the Doctor told his companions.

Not everything was in ruins: rising through the rubble were banks of communications and control consoles, housed in cabinets with flowing, plastic lines that must have been designed at least a century previously. A stylized hologram of a stellar system flicked near the ceiling.

Nothing in the room was as disconcerting as its occupants. The blond girl looked abnormal only in that she was out of place: her wide blue eyes, her long hair and long bare legs, her petulant expression, all these Bernice noticed at one glance, and dismissed. It wasn't just that Bernice had no time for women who made themselves look like that; the other woman demanded attention.

She was taller than Bernice, and thinner. Almost emaciated. Everything about her seemed elongated: her fingers, her face. Her head. Bernice couldn't help staring at that head. Englarged, depilated, domed, cleft, and pierced with a gleaming cylinder of metal. Obscene headgear for a monstrous head.

The woman waited, silent and unmoving, while the androids struggled to shuffle the TARDIS off the transporter and then drove the vehicle out of the chamber. Bernice couldn't take her eyes from the tall woman, and realized that her companions, too, must have been staring. She glanced round: only the Doctor had avoided displaying an expression of fascinated disgust. The woman's face showed no emotion, but her eyes glared, unmoving and unforgiving. Bernice felt guiltily glad that she was not the target of that gaze.

'Greetings, Doctor,' the woman said. Her voice was harsh and loud. 'I am Lacuna. I will speak for Pool, as you keep your mind closed to communication.'

'Pool?' Bernice whispered.

'The name of the intelligence I detected, presumably,' the Doctor said. 'It's all around us.' He took a step towards Lacuna and raised his hat. 'Charmed, I'm sure. I imagine introductions are unnecessary?'

'Entirely unnecessary, although for the sake of complete understanding you might like to know that this,' Lacuna turned abruptly to the blond girl, who recoiled, ducking her head, and then looking up meekly at the tall woman, 'is called Britta.'

'Hello there!' the Doctor said, sounding to Bernice like an aged relative addressing a very young child.

Britta gave him a curiously conspiratorial smile.

Lacuna was suddenly impatient. 'You have arrived just in time to witness the final stage of the experiment. Pool finds your presence – suspicious.'

'Really?' The Doctor was a picture of wide-eyed innocence. 'And what is the nature of the experiment?'

'Mankind's greatest step forward since the evolution of the human brain.' Lacuna spoke quickly, apparently frustrated by her inability to fathom the Doctor's thoughts.

The human brain; Elaine's sister; so many early deaths on Arcadia. Bernice felt cold. It all fitted together. Pool was all around them. And she knew what Pool was made of.

Lacuna was still talking.

'You are not human. Pool cannot read you. Your blue box is equally impenetrable.' She threw a venomous glance at the TARDIS. 'That is suspicious. There were other unexpected visitors.'

'*Were*?'

Bernice recognized the sudden concern in the Doctor's voice.

'There are survivors,' Lacuna said. 'One of them knows of you. That is also suspicious.'

'Survivors.' The Doctor's voice was low. He was almost growling, his hands white-knuckled on the crook of his umbrella. 'What have you done? Where are they?'

Lacuna laughed. 'They are on their way. Come and see.' She turned and gestured towards a bank of video screens. Only one screen was lit. Bernice, on the Doctor's heels, saw the glowing blue curve of a planet set against the darkness of space.

'Arcadia,' the Doctor said. 'As seen from this space station, I presume?'

'Yes, Doctor,' Lacuna said, and pointed. 'There is what remains of the intruders.' A silver dot emerged from the planet's aura. 'One unarmed shuttle. A crew of three. I don't think they'll trouble the station's defence systems, do you?'

'Leave them alone,' the Doctor muttered. 'What harm can they do?'

'You'd be surprised, Doctor. Each of the three seems to be highly dangerous. In any case, they seem determined not to leave us alone. If they attack, we will defend the station.'

'You could let them land here.'

'Don't worry, Doctor. We intend to. Although I think I'll play a few games with them. I don't want them to have an uneventful journey. There are cameras in the cabin of the shuttle, of course. Shall we see how they're getting on?'

Three more screens flickered into life.

'I'm not here to watch television,' the Doctor said. But he stared at the screens as the pictures sharpened into focus.

As a child, Ace had never wanted to be a nurse. She had defended this unconventional opinion, and undercut the threatened ostracism of her playground peers, by broadcasting her intention, too ludicrous to take seriously, that she should grow up to be a spacewoman. She had never changed her mind, and now she was more convinced than ever that she had been one hundred per cent correct.

Abslom Daak was not a good patient.

'Keep still, you burnt-arse chip-sucker,' Ace said, 'You need more shots and I can do a better graft job on that arm – but only if you keep still.'

'Don't need it,' Daak said. 'Fit enough already. And strong – see?'

'Let go of me, dogmeat, or this surgical knife's going straight through an artery, you register?'

The Dalek Killer tightened his grip. 'You've got guts, girlie.'

Gods, he was strong. 'Which is more than they'll say

about you, Daak. Remember the knife.' But she wouldn't use it, of course. Daak had to stay alive. And the big slob didn't even realize how objectionable he was.

Daak swivelled on the sick-bay couch and planted his feet on the floor. 'See? I'm OK.' Ace found herself suddenly sitting on his lap. His stubble grazed her forehead. 'And don't struggle, girlie. You're asking for a slap.'

'*What*?'

Ace couldn't believe this was happening to her. It had been a long time since she had had to stop herself simply blowing away an enemy that she found herself unable to either maim or restrain. 'I've still got the knife,' she said, but she knew she'd already said it too many times.

'You won't use it on me,' Daak said complacently. 'I feel good. You know how to look after me, girl.' He had both arms round her now. Ace felt very small, perched on the muscular thighs of this bear-hugging, hairy giant.

Oh well, she said to herself. Lie back and think of – where? Garaman? Harato? Heaven? The TARDIS? Iceworld? Perivale? You had to laugh, really. Perhaps it wouldn't be too bad. He was so big. And muscle's heavier than fat, too. If she could just stay on top . . .

'Ace! Daak!' It was Defries's voice, from the front of the cabin. 'Come and take a look at this.'

Ace felt Daak's grip loosen, and she broke free. 'One of us just had a lucky escape,' she said, turning abruptly so that he wouldn't see the smile on her face. 'Come on. If you're fit enough for groping, you're OK for active service.' She strode out of the cupboard that passed for the shuttle's sick bay and into the cabin. They were beyond planetary atmosphere now; the vision shields had slid down. Defries was staring through the front window. 'What's up, Belle? Can you see the – oh. What – ? Belle, what is it?'

'According to the navigation, that's the Spinward off-planet base. It's a space station.' Defries's voice was flat.

Ace averted her eyes. It wasn't just that the thing looked misshapen and ugly and threatening. It wasn't just that it looked so out of place hanging against the speckled mystery of clean, deep space. It was something atavistic, a primal loathing, an embarrassingly little-girl fear. 'Blast me, Belle, it looks so – '

'Worse than the little horror inside a Dalek casing.' Daak had come to stand behind her. 'The kind of thing you hope you never find living in the toe of your boot.'

'And if you do,' Ace added vehemently, 'you stamp on it.'

'That thing's five hundred kilometres across,' Defries said. 'It's big enough to stamp on us.'

If Frankenstein had been some sort of intelligent creepy-crawly, Ace thought, that's the kind of monster he'd have built. It sprawled across space, metal tendrils splayed randomly about its asymmetrically bulging central mass. It didn't move. Of course it didn't move, it was an artefact, a product of engineering. But its stillness was the motionlessness of a hunting spider, waiting on a wall.

And like a spider, it was horribly fascinating. Defries, Daak and Ace couldn't take their eyes from it as the shuttle took them inexorably towards it and it grew across the window.

The interior lights started flashing. Alarms began to screech.

'We're under attack,' Defries said. 'Torpedoes, top and bottom.'

Ace didn't need to consult the navigation screens. Scores of fire-tipped streaks were already visible, emerging from the flesh-like folds at the summit and the base of the station's central mass. They fanned out to make two webs of silvery trails that extended far above and below the lines of sight afforded by the shuttle's windows.

'Wide trajectory,' Ace said. 'They'll get us if we climb, dive or double back.'

'Then we'll go dead centre,' Defries decided, and planted her index finger on the forward speed button. Ace staggered as the shuttle accelerated with a kick.

Daak's huge fist closed over Defries's hand. 'That's where they want us to go.'

'Too bad, Daak,' Defries spat. The gauntlet of her combat suit protected her fingers from the Dalek Killer's grip. 'It's that or the torpedoes.'

'Leave it,' Ace said, pushing between Daak and Defries. 'The lasers have started.' Thin beads of light were pulsing from a dozen locations on the convoluted spiral arms of the space station. 'Are there reflectives on this shuttle, Belle?'

'How should I know? Probably not. It's an antique. But we're OK if they can't aim better than this.'

The laser pulses were going wide, creating a tunnel of light-streams down which the shuttle sped unharmed. The space station filled the front windows. It could be seen that the main structures, the twisted claws and the lumpy core, were themselves made up of accretions of smaller shapes that resembled nightmare exaggerations of arthropod and cephalopod forms. Some parts of the station were dark, and some of these were revealed as empty gulfs, while other areas blazed with unnecessary illumination. Like warts and bristles, structures protruded from the main mass: long strands of metal gridwork, a heap of vitreous bubble-forms, metal boxes welded together at haphazard angles. Some of the structures simply ended, hanging in space; others terminated in smaller versions of the main station, like a cluster of eggs carried on the leg of an insect; still others, following their skewed paths, met and became united with each other, producing strange hybrids. It was all metals, silicates, carbon derivatives. Completely lifeless. It looked completely organic.

Nobody has designed that, Ace thought. Nobody built it. It's grown.

As the shuttle dropped towards the station's central bulk, Ace found it even more disturbing that she could identify, nestling between ridges of ruched titanium or perhaps in the centre of an ammonite-like coil, a few of the features that would be expected on the outside of a space station. Here the air-lock doors of a cargo bay; there a communications nacelle, a launch pad, a service hatch.

The shuttle was heading directly towards a set of air-lock doors.

'Looks like we don't have much choice,' Defries said.

'It's come into my parlour or get sliced into pieces with the lasers.'

'I never like going in through the front door,' Ace said, 'but I guess you're right.' It took her a moment to realize that she'd expected Daak to add his comment, and that he hadn't done so. She started to turn, just in time to glimpse and duck beneath the hairy forearm that was sweeping towards the side of her head. Defries had no warning: Daak's other arm caught her shoulder and sent her reeling away from the controls.

The Dalek Killer spread his hands across the panel of buttons. He laughed. 'They reckoned without a DK with a death wish,' he roared, and started jabbing at the controls. 'We'll get in there my way.'

Ace clutched at a chair back as the shuttle banked and climbed. The sudden gravity change sent her stomach into her boots. She shook her head and looked through the front window. The shuttle was speeding towards a barrage of laser pulses.

'Now that's more like it,' Daak yelled.

Britta couldn't help smiling. She agreed with the big, ugly Dalek Killer. Things were getting interesting at last. Lacuna was dumbstruck, and no-one except her was looking at anything except the screens.

'This was not anticipated,' Lacuna hissed.

'Never mind that,' the Doctor shouted. He looked comical, his eyebrows twitching and his hands waving in distress. 'Don't let them get hit. If Ace is hurt—'

'Yes. Of course. Ace.' Lacuna lunged for the communications desk. 'Cease firing. All units cease firing. Torpedoes to self-destruct. Acknowledge.'

Ace, Ace, Ace. Were they all obsessed? Britta thought it was unhealthy. The Ace woman didn't even seem a very pleasant person. Not particularly clever, except at blowing things up.

Britta had been watching the other woman – the one the Doctor called Benny – when the screens had come on. Benny, Britta thought, appeared to be a sensible type. Calm, thoughtful. Her reactions on seeing the inside of the shuttle cabin had been interesting. Britta had watched closely.

'Doctor! Isn't that – ? Doctor, it's Ace. That's Ace in the shuttle,' Benny had said.

The Doctor had grinned, rather sheepishly it seemed to Britta. But Benny's face had showed bewilderment, then a frown that darkened, in Britta's interpretation, to a frown of resentful anger.

And so when Lacuna was screaming instructions to the androids, and the Doctor was almost hopping from foot to foot with anxiety, and the pale young man and the little girl were staring open-mouthed at the screens, Britta omitted to speak. She even pushed the thought from her mind, in case Pool might hear her. She didn't tell anyone that the woman called Benny was stealing away from the group; had found one of the perimeter doors; had slipped through it, and had gone.

Britta even managed to suppress her feelings of self-satisfaction. Another little show of defiance. Something else she'd got away with. She could sense that Pool was preoccupied. No-one knew about Benny but her.

So much for Lacuna's precious Ace. Not as clever as Britta.

'They want us alive, then,' Ace said. The shuttle was on a curving trajectory towards a point above the centre of the space station. The torpedoes had burst harmlessly, many kilometres away. The laser cannon had stopped firing.

Other possibilities occurred to her. The Doctor was, presumably, somewhere on the station. She remembered that he had a knack for getting people to stop shooting, and usually only just in time.

She had another, less comforting thought. Defries, who had given up threatening Daak with a court-martial for assault, voiced the same fear. 'Maybe,' Defries said. 'Or maybe they're cooking up something worse. Remember the *Raistrick*.'

'Damn!' It was Daak, still at the controls. 'Why can't you keep your mouth shut?'

There was something ahead of the shuttle. Something moving. Alive. And very large.

At first it looked like a dark patch of space. Ace could see it only because it was moving, blotting out more stars as it and the shuttle flew towards each other. A black sheet, flapping closer.

It shifted, became a narrow band of darkness, then widened again. Now its underside was illuminated by the lights of the space station, and by the reflected light of the planet. They could see what it was.

Defries made a noise in her throat. Daak cursed. Ace felt sick.

Ace thought of it as some sort of insect, although she knew it had too many legs. She estimated that its body was about twice the size of the shuttle, but it seemed much larger because of the mottled membranes that extended like wings on both sides of the creature, and rippled lazily as it swam through space.

She tried to be rational. The flapping wings weren't too bad. Even the wriggling, claw-tipped legs – well, they were just legs, like a prawn's. But the thing had a sort of head, as big as its body. With eyes that weren't set in sockets but instead hung loose. And moved, twitching. And a round mouth, ringed with irregular scales, and full of writhing cilia.

It was climbing, moving into a position just above the shuttle's flightpath.

No doubt about it, that was one creepy monster. Well shocking. Ace explored her fear; tasted it; weighed it. Yeah, she was scared. This was an interesting fear: a little different from anything she'd experienced before. But no worse than some others.

Right, she'd catalogued it. Time to conquer it.

'Giant prawns can't live in space,' she announced. 'Well known fact. That thing's not real.'

'The thing that ripped apart the *Raistrick*,' Defries started to say, turning from the window towards Ace, 'that was – oh shit. What about small versions of giant prawns, Ace? Can they live in space shuttles?'

Ace's blaster was in her hand as she turned, before she

had understood the meaning of Defries's words. As soon as she saw them she started firing, realized she was shouting something meaningless, and then at last understood what she was seeing.

They were all over the walls and ceiling. They were just like the creature outside, but only about twenty centimetres long.

Only! Ace thought, as the nearest pair flapped, smoking and foul-smelling and dead, from the ceiling to the floor.

She was firing again; she couldn't afford to let them get closer, she wouldn't be able to bear it. She yelled 'Continuous!' to the blaster and used her free hand to adjust the beam.

'Belle!' Ace waved her gun, frying a swathe of the creatures that were advancing along the wall on Defries's side of the cabin. 'Get shooting, Belle. Very close range, wide beam, or we'll cut through the fuselage. OK? We've got to keep them away from Daak. He's driving.'

Very good, Ace told herself. I'm scared shitless, but I remembered to re-set the laser. How many of these fragged things are there?

They were swarming in an endless moving blanket along every surface inside the shuttle. Ace could see them coming in boiling waves through the sick-bay door. The atmosphere consisted of nothing but the noxious fumes of burnt bodies: the recyclers couldn't cope. The floor was one huge mound of twitching corpses, over which rank after rank of the creatures advanced.

Defries and Ace were being forced back, step by step, towards the nose of the cabin.

Without ceasing to play a wide beam of heat back and forth across the advancing hordes, Ace checked the power supply of her blaster. Half empty. When it ran out . . . Best not to think about it.

One of the creatures had survived the rays and was scuttling towards Defries's feet. Ace yelled and pointed. Defries shouted, a cry of mixed defiance and horror, and brought a boot down on the thing. The liquid crunch was sickening.

Another step back, and the back of Ace's head touched Daak's shoulder. There was no more room to retreat.

'Put it on auto,' Ace said without turning. 'We need more firepower here.'

Daak glanced over his shoulder. 'You look after the little ones, girlie,' he said. 'My meat's the big mother.'

Ace looked round. At first she thought the monster had gone. The windows were black. Then, at the periphery of her vision, the saw the rippling movement of the circles of cilia. The shuttle was almost inside the thing's mouth.

'Daak, have you gone – ' Something was on her boot. She turned back, kicking, to find that the assault was over. There were no more creatures streaming from the rear of the shuttle. Defries was picking off the survivors.

The air was improving as the recyclers filtered out the stench and the smoke. Ace slid to the floor and cleared a space around her by tossing dead creatures on to the pile of bodies in the middle of the cabin. She needed a rest. She didn't want to think about what would happen next until it happened.

Defries had other ideas.

'Take evasive action, DK. That's an order.' She was almost as tall as Daak, standing beside him shouting in his ear. She hadn't holstered her blaster.

Daak folded his arms and stared ahead. 'If they want us alive,' he said, 'it doesn't matter what we do. We'll be OK. And if they want us dead, likewise, we'll be dead. I'm going in on my terms, not theirs.'

Defries narrowed her eyes and raised her gun.

'I took us straight through that thing's teeth,' Daak went on doggedly. 'But we ain't been eaten.'

It was true. The shuttle was inside the monster's mouth now, but remained undamaged. And it was no longer black outside: Ace could see the stars and, as she stood, she found herself looking down, through one of the side windows, at the reticulated surface of the top of the space station. The gigantic creature had disappeared without trace.

'For a DK,' Defries said, turning on her heel, 'you lead a remarkably charmed life.'

Daak shrugged his massive shoulders. 'They want us alive.'

'OK, Daak. Looks like we're in the clear for now.'

Ace had heard the scraping noises on the hull, so she wasn't entirely terrified when a scaly, bristly limb extended across the outside of the window next to her.

'Don't you believe it,' she said. 'There's something outside. It's on the fuselage. And it's not small.'

It wasn't the same corridor: it was narrower than the one they'd been carried along on the transporter. But it was equally long and straight. And its walls were decorated, if that was the right expression, with bas-relief portraits. From floor to ceiling, along its entire length, tens of thousands of expressionless faces stared at Bernice as she hurried away from the circular chamber. They were like death masks, Bernice thought, and then rather wished she hadn't.

It wasn't a comfortable place to be. Bernice told herself that it wasn't surprising that she felt as though she was being watched. She tried to ignore the feeling, as well as the insistent whispering voices that seemed to be always at the edge of her hearing. She had other things to worry about.

She was sure she could believe Elaine. The androids had killed her sister, just as they had almost killed her. But Elaine had also said that the Counsellors had cut open Christina's head, and that when Elaine had looked at her sister's body, the head had been empty. No brain. The androids had taken it away.

Bernice had tried to tell the Doctor, but he had seemed preoccupied. She had been interrupted, she hadn't been able to make him understand exactly what had happened to Christina. It had been her own fault, in a way: she had been reluctant to talk about it in front of Francis.

Pool. Who or what was Pool? Come to that, what exactly was the Lacuna woman. And her bimbo sidekick. The Doctor, Bernice thought, doesn't seem to realize just how weird and dangerous these people are. They take

237

people's brains, for goodness' sake! What for? What are they up to?

Face it, Summerfield, you don't know. But, she resolved, I'm going to do what I can to put a stop to it. I've managed to get away. I'm sure the girl – Britta, that was her name – I'm sure she saw me. But she turned away. Didn't raise the alarm. Maybe it's a trap. Perhaps there's something worse at the other end of this creepy corridor.

Don't be defeatist. For the moment, I'm free. No androids with blasters, no maze of passages. I've got a slim chance to do something.

Now what shall I do?

It's obvious: I've got to join forces with Ace. She's got weapons. She's got a couple of chums who look like they can handle themselves in a scrap. And she needs to be told what little I know about what's going on here.

Ace. Gods, that was a shock. Why hadn't the Doctor told her? Ace had looked thinner. Hard to tell. Those old 2-D screens didn't give a good picture. Older, too. But of course: it had been three years for Ace.

Why hadn't the Doctor told her? It couldn't be a coincidence. Of all the space-time locations in all the universe, the Doctor had to land his TARDIS in Ace's. Not a coincidence.

There was a door at the end of the corridor. It slid open as Bernice approached. Time for action, she thought. The big Dalek Killer had seemed determined to bring the shuttle in at the top of the space station. All right: let's go and see if I can help them get in. Onward and upward.

She stood in the doorway at the end of the corridor, looking into a small polygonal room with a sloping ceiling. There was a door in each wall. No androids. No sound. No sign of life.

She set off to find a lift. Onward and upward.

* * *

'Cybershit, Belle! I said I'll do it, OK? Just check the suit and open the airlock, will you?'

Ace winced. Her own voice sounded harsh and metallic inside the spacesuit helmet. She flexed her fingers, trying to become accustomed to the power-assisted joints.

She had never liked suiting up for trips outside in space, and this suit was an old model, and equipped for combat as well as maintenance. It was big and heavy. Wearing the suit, she weighed three hundred kilos and felt as graceful as a rhinoceros; as soon as she was outside she'd feel almost weightless, and the suit's systems would give her the strength of a robot while hardly affecting the speed and ease of her movements. Firepower, too: there were laser cannons built into both arms, and the thrusters beneath her heels would melt anything at close range.

Nonetheless, Ace hoped that Daak's flamboyant display of aerobatics had dislodged whatever creature had been on the hull. They hadn't heard the scratching sounds since Daak had straightened out the protesting shuttle and lowered it serenely towards the whorled ridges that made up the top of the space station.

It was like coming in to land on the wrinkled hide of some sleeping behemoth.

And the problem was: how could they break in? There were cargo bays and airlocks situated at random among the folds and spirals, but all of them remained closed. Ace had found herself inventing new techniques as she tried to use the shuttle's processors to hack into the station's maintenance systems, but there had been no indication that the station had even been receiving her signals.

The shuttle had no on-board weaponry: not a single missile, not even a laser with which they might have tried to cut a way in.

Someone had to go down there.

And, as Ace had pointed out, it had to be her. She knew more than either Defries or Daak about sliding rogue instructions into computerized systems. She would drop to the surface of the station – its mass generated enough gravity to pull her – and, if she could find a suitable maintenance terminal, she would jack in her wrist processor and try to manipulate the station's doors through the interface.

There had been another brief argument about what to do if the plan didn't work.

'I'll go down,' Daak had said. 'Chainsword'll cut us a way in.'

Ace had produced a strip of plastic. 'If I can't get in by asking nicely,' she had said, 'I'll blow apart a set of doors. This stuff's primitive, but effective. And probably neater than that hedge trimmer of yours.'

The shuttle had not been attacked since Daak had started the descent towards the station. No torpedoes had been launched, no laser pulses flashed.

'I don't like it,' Daak had said. 'It's too quiet.'

Ace, in the depths of the spacesuit, had rolled her eyes.

Defries finished checking the suit, and opened the airlock. Ace moved her arm, and watched with a smile as a huge claw moved in front of her, its metal digits flexing exactly as her fingers moved inside it. The claw touched the transparent visor of the helmet and slid it down in front of Ace's face.

'Radio check,' Ace said, her voice echoing. 'Is that OK?'

There was no reply, just a hiss of static. Ace turned to look at Defries, who shrugged, put a hand to an ear, and mouthed 'No sound.'

Ace lifted the visor. 'So the radio's out. Just like on the planet. Explains why I couldn't hack in from up here.'

Defries started to close the airlock. 'So much for that idea,' she said.

'Leave it open,' Ace said. 'This is still the only way we can go. The radio doesn't make that much difference. Just keep an eye on me, OK?'

She slid the visor down and squeezed the suit into the airlock. The door closed behind her, and the floor descended a couple of metres. She was in the cargo hold, standing on the ribbed floor of the shuttle next to the loading hatch. This was the only door in the vehicle protected by an airlock.

She scanned the displays set round the visor on the

inside of the helmet. Air pressure was falling. She located the air supply tap, pulled a tube from the back of her suit and plugged it into the tap: there was no point in using the suit's air and batteries while she could draw air from the shuttle's recyclers.

She waited until the pressure outside the suit was near zero, checked that the pressure inside was normal, and used her right claw with surprising delicacy to tap in the instruction to open the hatch. The smooth metal slid away from in front of her box-like boots to reveal the surface of the space station, now only a hundred metres below the shuttle. Ace took a deep breath and jumped into space.

For a moment, she couldn't remember how to switch the suit to spacewalk mode. She tumbled lazily as she racked her memory and the air line started to twist round her body.

Got it! She touched the wrist of the suit's left arm with the index finger of the right claw, and felt the suit vibrate as small orientation jets burst into life at every joint. She experimented, twisting her body so as to unwind the air line. With a delay that was hardly noticeable, the suit interpreted her movement and sent instructions to the orientation jets. The suit emulated the movement that Ace had made, twisting slowly in space and freeing the air line so that it ran straight from the suit into the shuttle's open cargo hatch.

The station's gravity was far from negligible. Ace stretched upwards, and the jets responded by moving the suit into a vertical position and resisting the pull of the station. Hovering, Ace considered where to touch down on the surface below.

The nearest entry point, almost directly below Ace's feet, looked like the doors of a shuttle bay. But the doors were situated between two spine-tipped ridges that reminded Ace too strongly of a Venus flytrap. She leant forward, and the suit floated gently forward and downward.

The next set of doors looked more promising. Featureless blocks as big as warehouses jutted at crazy angles from a bald hemisphere. Among the blocks there were other large items embedded in the hump: a skeletal pylon, a diminishing spiral of linked, vitreous bubbles – and something that looked like the front end of an asteroid cruncher, a large sub-warp ship with front-opening doors big enough to engulf space rocks. Ace had had to break into an asteroid cruncher once, when she'd worked security for a mining corporation: the big doors could usually be operated from an external control panel near the front of the hull.

Ace half turned back to the shuttle, pointed towards the sprouting hemisphere (like chunks of cheddar stuck all over half a grapefruit, she thought), and aimed the suit towards the shape that looked like the nose of an asteroid cruncher.

It wasn't any part of any sort of mining ship, Ace realized as she floated nearer to it. The sun was fully eclipsed by Arcadia now, and although the main source of illumination was now only the light refracted through the halo of the planet's atmosphere, it was easier to see in the dim but diffuse light than in the glare and dark shadows that had been made by the unshielded sun.

The angular shape was obviously modelled on the front half of a mining ship, but modelled by a madman with no sense of proportion. Its profile was an irregular parallelogram, and it appeared to be made up of interlocking blocks of crystalline metal. But embedded in its nose, unobstructed and facing into space, there was a normal-looking set of airlock doors, wide enough to accept the shuttle. Ace floated towards them.

The suit's feet touched the metal blocks. Ace felt a tremor as the attractors cut in and anchored the boots to the station. A vibration that Ace had hardly been aware of ceased: the spacewalk jets closing down automatically.

Ace breathed out loudly. It was a relief to be on something like solid ground again, even if the terrain did resemble the jumbled building bricks of a gigantic child. The airlock doors stretched away in front of her, sloping slightly upwards, like a smooth square clearing in the midst of undergrowth.

There was no sound except for her breathing and the hiss of the air exchanger. She didn't know what alerted her; perhaps a slight tug on the back of the suit, perhaps a sixth sense. She turned, one heavy boot at a time, and cursed softly.

Daak's aerobatics hadn't shaken it off the shuttle. It was coming towards her, scuttling down the air line. It moved like a spider, and looked like – well, it looked like a spider. Too many legs though, round luminous eyes, and more complicated mandibles than any arachnid Ace had ever seen on Earth. And very big.

Ace hadn't consciously lifted her arm and fired the suit's built-in blaster. A stream of laser light, almost invisible in the near-vacuum, played across the creature's head and glistening body. Pulses of energy coursed down the beam. It stopped, swaying as it hung below the air line, but it didn't appear to be damaged. Its eyes glowed more brightly, and it scuttled forwards again.

Ace had been in a situation like this before: in a VR game called Horror Walk 3. The funny thing was, this was less frightening, even though it was real. Maybe because it was real. Well, not quite real: an illusory monster but a very real threat. Anyway, it was dead simple. She moved her arm behind her back, and the metal claw responded simultaneously, grasping the air line and plucking it from its housing in the back of the suit.

For an anxious moment Ace waited for the suit's air system to cut in. The indicator light above the visor edged back to a normal reading. Thirty minutes of good air. She'd have to work fast.

The spider-thing was close now. The sensors in the suit's claw relayed the movements of the creature's legs along the air tube as a horrible writhing sensation in the palm of Ace's right hand. She almost dropped the line in disgust, but managed to hold it and started to swing it back and forth like a skipping rope in wider and wider slow arcs.

The creature was only a few metres away now. She could see the viscous juices that lubricated its mandibles. That did it. She released the line, and it and the creature swung away from her, away from the space station, up into space.

The spider-thing reached the end of the air line, turned, and started to run towards the shuttle.

'Oh no you don't,' Ace whispered, and a beam from her blaster sliced through the silvery filament. The creature, marooned on a length of the line, continued to float away. Ace could see movements behind the windows of the shuttle. Defries and Daak were waving to her. She waved her claws in return.

Well done!

Who said that? Ace spun round, but she was alone. Of course. She tried the radio. Nothing but static. Of course. It had been a voice in her mind. Well spooky.

She shrugged, and then giggled in surprise as the rounded shoulders of the spacesuit ascended like blunt-nosed rockets on each side of her helmet.

Get down to work, she told herself. Twenty-eight minutes left.

She set off round the perimeter of the vast doorway, looking for anything that resembled a control panel. Along to the bottom left-hand corner; then up the side, overcompensating for the slight uphill slope until she realized that the suit's powered legs made her extra effort redundant; along the top; down the other side; back to where she'd started.

Nothing. Seventeen minutes left.

Why did she think to try looking underneath one of the metallic blocks? Why did she choose this particular block? Ace was worrying about these questions even as the suit's claws were closing round the distorted cube, and lifting it to reveal indicator lights, a display screen, a keypad: a control panel.

No time to think about it now, she thought. Put it down to luck.

She would have liked to be nearer to the panel, but she doubted her ability to kneel or squat in the spacesuit. Leaning forward as far as she dared, with the great torso of the suit at a right angle to its legs, she made the claws unhook her wrist computer and plug it into one of the empty sockets on the panel.

She was about to instruct the device to run one of her extensive library of icebreakers when she noticed that the control panel had an alphabetic keyboard.

Can't hurt to try, she thought, unjacking her computer with one claw while the other typed four letters. The word *OPEN* appeared on the screen, and two seconds later a shuddering vibration began beneath her feet.

'Got it!' she yelled, and then she carried on yelling as she realized her mistake: if the airlock was pressurized, the rush of air as the doors opened would send her flying across the Arcadian system. The shuttle wouldn't reach her before the suit's air supply ran out.

The doors parted. Ace braced herself, but there was no pulse of escaping air. The gap widened, and Ace peered inside.

Lights were coming on. It was a featureless box, big enough to take several shuttles, maybe even a couple of X-ships. Ace switched on the spacewalk jets and launched herself through the widening yawn of the doors.

There was no sense of up or down. The gravity of the station exerted its pull towards the far end of the bay, the wall opposite the doors. Daak would have to bring in the shuttle backwards, so that the main thrusters would counteract the station's attraction.

Ace floated back to the doorway. The shuttle was already approaching. Ace stuck out her tongue at Daak, who was grinning at her through the shuttle's front window, but she doubted whether he could see her face inside the suit. He'd see the claw, though: she lifted her arm in a circle, and the great claw rotated above her head in an unmistakeable signal. Daak continued to grin, but he must have noticed: the shuttle started to turn.

Ace dropped back into the empty chamber. Seven minutes left, plus a while longer breathing staler and staler air. She hoped Daak could get the shuttle in at the first attempt.

She located the interior control panel, and as it was inside the doorway she remained next to it, hidden behind the protruding lip of one of the doors. Despite the protection of the suit, she would have to stay clear of the shuttle's thrusters as it descended through the doorway.

Suddenly she was surrounded by heat and light. The visor darkened almost to black opacity, and the suit's cooler began audibly to work harder. The shuttle was coming in.

Ace had a sudden, ludicrous flashback: a red double-decker backing into Hanwell bus garage. Not that ludicrous, really, she thought. The shuttle wasn't much like a London bus in shape, but it was about the same size. And made about as much noise.

The thrusters were below her now. The pitted surface plates of the main fuselage slid past her lightening visor. Then the cabin appeared. Through the windows Ace could see Defries and Daak clinging to the controls, disorientated by the conflict between the space station's gravity and the shuttle's floor attractors.

Ace moved her fingers. The suit's claw typed, *SHUT*.

The doors moved towards each other, shutting out the stars. Enclosing the shuttle in a box.

This is either a trap, Ace thought, or else the Doctor's found a way to let us in. Or both. Not enough data. Concentrate on getting some air in here.

ATMOSPHERE? she typed.

The word disappeared from the screen to be replaced by a message.

DISTINCTLY GLOOMY, I'M AFRAID.

That was the Doctor, she was sure of it. Unless the message, too, was part of a trap. She sighed.

PRESSURIZE, she typed. The word remained on the screen. She was about to try something else when the outside air pressure indicator above her visor started to move. Within a few minutes the atmosphere in the bay was normal, and Ace was jetting towards the shuttle's cabin door.

Daak had brought the shuttle in skilfully, she noticed. He had needed only one attempt, and he had manoeuvred the craft neatly into a position to one side of the bay, exactly as specified in Spacefleet procedure.

Defries was standing diagonally in the open doorway, beckoning Ace inside. She stood aside as Ace floated into the cabin, and without any preliminary checks she started to shut down the spacesuit's systems.

'Get me out of this thing!' were Ace's first words as the visor slid upwards. With the suit's power off, her arms were shaking and her legs felt like jelly.

'Suits fool you, don't they?' Defries said, manhandling the claws to help Ace extricate her arms from the sensor webs. 'Give you so much power, you forget how hard you have to work them. That was good work, trooper,' she added.

Ace smiled. She hadn't expected any more extravagant praise. 'Suspiciously easy,' she said. 'If I'm right, and that spider-thing was all force fields and fancy holograms, it could have been made to jump off the line and get me.'

But even as she said it, Ace had had another idea. She remembered the Doctor telling her that the police-box exterior of the TARDIS was, in a sense, a mathematical expression. Block transfer computation, he'd called it. The creation of apparently real, solid objects by means of detailed mathematical modelling. Maybe the spider-thing was a computer-generated construct?

'And there was no ice on the door system,' she went on. 'Not even an entry code. I feel like we've parked ourselves in one big rat-trap.' She pulled herself out of the unsealed suit and peered through the shuttle's windows at the featureless walls of the landing bay. 'No doors, see? No way out, no way further in.'

As the spacesuit folded in on itself like one of the Transformers toys that had fascinated the boys in Ace's school for a brief season, Defries joined her at the window. 'We've got to get inside the station, Ace. We've come through too much to get stopped here.'

Ace smiled, amused that Belle was back to using *we* instead of *I*. The OEO Agent was clever and courageous, but not complicated: as long as I'm useful to her, Ace thought, and do what she wants, she'll be as nice as pie. When I stop being useful, she'll ignore me. If I get in her way, she'll kill me, if necessary. That's OK. You know where you stand with Belle.

The silence was broken by a tortured scream from outside the shuttle.

'That bloody chainsword,' Ace muttered, and she and Defries scrambled through the door.

As Ace manoeuvred down the flank of the shuttle, letting her gauntlets scrape against the weld-seams and pock-marks in order to slow her drift towards the base of the craft, she saw that the Dalek Killer was using his weapon to cut through the metallic material of the surface on which he'd parked.

'What if the other side's unpressurized?' she called, her voice echoing in the almost empty bay.

Daak didn't look up from his work. 'No problem,' he grunted. 'Pressure'll help. Blow a hole through.'

Ace shook her head. Daak wasn't stupid, he just didn't care. She would have admired him for that, once. And even now she knew better, it was getting hard to dislike him. She didn't exactly like him, either, but he had a kind of integrity that you didn't find in many people – not even in Belle, really, because Belle's attitude, although always straightforward, varied according to what she thought about you. Daak was always the same: without reference to the creed, colour, gender or opinions of whoever happened to be around, he was rude, randy, rebellious and always ready for a fight.

He was going to die saving an entire planet from the Daleks. Defries wouldn't do that, Ace thought. She'd live to fight another day. So would I. You need to be uncomplicated, maybe, to sacrifice yourself willingly.

And I don't fancy him, despite all the muscles. I suppose I go for the dangerous types – the ones who look almost but not quite entirely wholesome. Some little twist. That's not so good. Means it's in me, too, if that's what I like.

Still, it's good to know that not everyone's devious. That there are people alive as straight ahead as Abslom Daak.

'Daydreaming?' Defries said, dropping past Ace and landing next to the thruster exhaust pipes.

'Thinking,' Ace replied. Her pack slapped against her back as she jumped down beside Defries, reminding her that she was at last running out of supplies: there had been few explosives on the shuttle.

Defries raised a sceptical eyebrow, but said nothing except 'He's through.'

All that could be seen of Daak was his chainsword, silent now and held aloft as Daak disappeared through the hole he had cut in the floor.

Ace and Defries ran to the hole and looked down. Daak's grinning face was only about a metre below their feet. He had dropped through the hole into a corridor that looked typical of every space station Ace had ever been on. It was almost a disappointment.

'Jump, girlie,' Daak called. 'I'll catch you.'

'He'll catch my boots in his face,' Ace muttered. 'How about going first, Belle?'

Defries knelt at the edge of the rough-hewn, irregularly-shaped hole. 'Look,' she said, 'this material's self-sealing. It's closing up.'

Ace looked. The sharp, sawn edges were already smoother. The stuff looked more like plastic than metal, now, and it was definitely spreading. The hole was becoming smaller.

'You go first,' Defries said. 'Take the medical pack and my blaster, as well as your equipment. I'll come through travelling light. Daak!' she yelled. 'The hole's closing up. Stand clear!'

Ace hesitated. She didn't like to leave Defries without weapons on the other side of a diminishing escape route.

'Jump, trooper!' Defries ordered. 'And tell Daak to work on the hole with the chainsword.'

Ace jumped. Defries's pack snagged, then came free: the hole was barely wide enough. Ace's boots absorbed most of the impact of landing, but she was glad she remembered to roll as her feet touched the floor.

The corridor was dimly lit, and the hole was a bright disc in the ceiling. As Ace stood she realized it was beyond her reach, but Daak would be able to attack it with his chainsword.

'Come on, Daak,' she said, 'get going with the hedge trimmer. That hole's getting too small even for a size ten like Belle.'

With a shout, Daak hefted the whirring machine above his head. Ace winced as the teeth bit into the perimeter of the hole.

She could see that, for all the noise, the chainsword was almost entirely ineffective. Daak could make deep incisions in places round the edge, but he didn't have enough leverage to cut off slices of the strange metal.

'Fragging hellfire!' Daak yelled. 'Use your blaster!'

Ace shrugged, pulled out her blaster, and changed the beam from targeting to cutting. A blaster's laser could cut through some metals, but Ace had a nasty feeling that even if the material above her proved susceptible, she might expend her entire powerpack on it without much effect.

She shouted a warning to Defries and fired. The intense thread of light struck the edge of the narrowing hole, and appeared to produce no result. Ace took her finger off the button. The beam disappeared, but a patch of the ceiling next to the hole continued to glow. The patch grew, like a spreading stain, engulfing the hole. Then, with a spasm that looked unpleasantly organic, the ceiling convulsed – and the hole was even smaller.

'It's no good, Belle,' Ace shouted. 'We can't fix it. Stay where you are. We'll find another way through.'

But Defries had already jumped into the shrinking gap.

Ace ducked, certain that Defries would land on top of her and then equally sure that nothing of the sort was about to happen. She looked up to see that Belle hadn't made it: her legs were dangling into the corridor. The hole had tightened around her waist.

Ace and Daak looked at each other.

'I can't use the blaster again,' Ace said, aware of an edge of hysteria in her voice.

'Sure as hell can't use my chainsword. The Agent's tough, but not as tough as this metal.'

Defries was still kicking but, Ace thought, less strongly.

'Combat tunic'll take some of the pressure,' Daak said.

'For how long?' Ace said.

Daak looked at her, and shrugged. As one, they raised their eyes to the ceiling. Ace thought she could hear Defries shouting. She had never felt so helpless.

'We've got to do something,' she said. 'Daak, try cutting into the ceiling further along. Do it! You can't make things worse.'

Daak's reply was drowned in the roar of his chainsword. He thrust the blades upwards, but before they touched the ceiling Ace grabbed his arm and pointed.

Defries was wriggling downwards into the corridor. The hole was expanding, slowly at first, and then suddenly releasing Defries, who fell to the floor of the corridor with a shriek of pain.

Ace crouched next to her. Defries was alive, and conscious. Ace glanced up: the hole had sealed itself, leaving only a discoloured ring like a water stain on the ceiling.

'Belle, are you OK?'

Defries sat up with a groan. 'Broken rib or two, I think. The tunic'll hold me straight. Suit's pumped me full of painkillers, but nothing else. So I guess I'll survive. Help me up, will you.'

'Belle, you should rest awhile. We could all do with a break.'

Daak swore, suddenly. 'We ain't getting a break,' he said. 'Look.'

He gestured with the chainsword. At the end of the corridor was a pair of doors. They were slowly sliding open.

The tall woman was shaking with rage. Francis couldn't remember ever having seen anyone so angry. Clutching Elaine's hand, as much to comfort himself as to protect her, he retreated by stepping backwards as unobtrusively as he could. If only there were something substantial to hide behind!

Lacuna's face, white-lipped, foam-flecked and trembling, almost held him entranced. But he spared a glance for the very pretty girl in the daring clothes, and was surprised to see Britta covering her mouth to stifle a giggle. The Doctor was standing with his hands behind his back. His lips were pursed, as if with impatience. He was deliberately looking at anything except Lacuna.

'You are interfering with the operation of this station!' Lacuna said, not for the first time. She stopped in front of the Doctor and lowered her face to his. 'Aren't you? Admit it!'

The Doctor caught Francis's eyes, and beckoned him with a nod of the head. Francis considered whether he could pretend to have missed or misunderstood the gesture, and came to the conclusion that the Doctor wouldn't be fooled. He pulled Elaine towards the confrontation.

'Yes!' the Doctor snapped, thrusting his nose between Lacuna's wild eyes. 'Of course I am. I prefer people intact.'

'The woman is of no importance. You have an ulterior motive. You are pitting yourself against Pool. Trying your strength against Pool's.'

'And I won, Lacuna.' The Doctor waved a hand towards the video screens. 'I stopped Pool crushing that woman to death.'

'But at what cost, I wonder?' Lacuna's anger had disappeared as suddenly as it had arrived. 'Pool controls the operation of this station, the planet-based droids, the various structures we have built in and around the star system. And the experiment, of course. You have so far succeeded in preventing the closure of a small area of self-sealing partition. Pool cannot read how much of your mental power you devoted to that one, small task. But we suspect that you have revealed the total extent of your ability.'

Francis decided that Lacuna angry was almost preferable to Lacuna gloating. Could she be right? Had the Doctor engaged in mental combat to save the woman from Earth? And had he thus revealed that he was no match for the being called Pool?

Francis had reached the Doctor's side. One glance at

the Doctor's dejected expression answered all the questions.

'Well, Francis,' the Doctor said. 'I gave it my best shot.'

'Never mind, Doctor,' was all that Francis could think to say.

The Doctor ducked his head and looked sideways, giving Francis a smile that Lacuna couldn't see. 'Oh, I don't mind,' he said quietly. 'I do my best work when I'm being underestimated.'

A howl of rage made both Francis and the Doctor look up. Lacuna stood straight and trembling, like a statue shaken by an earth tremor.

'You were four!' she said eventually, her voice a clenched whisper. 'Now there are only three of you. The woman has gone. The woman with knowledge of the blue box. She must – '

Lacuna stopped, her eyes closing like metal shutters. When she opened them again, a few seconds later, she was calm and smiling.

'She cannot escape. Pool controls the very fabric of this station. We have not yet discovered much about you, Doctor, except that you are a fool. You can shield your mind, but Pool has already found much interesting information in the thoughts of the women called Ace and Bernice. The nature of your blue box is already partially understood. The limits of your mental ability are clear. You will prove useful in the experiment, Doctor – whether you like it or not.'

'Bluff,' the Doctor said to Francis. 'I'm fairly sure I've been able to shield Ace and Benny against telepathic intrusion.'

Lacuna had overheard the remark. 'We have learnt enough to know that your box will be of great interest, Doctor.'

The Doctor swung to face her. 'And why do you assume that I won't be willing to assist you?' He jabbed his umbrella towards her. 'I'm a scientist, you silly woman, among other things. Your colleague Pool is hiding his thoughts from me, just as I am hiding mine from him. So why don't you tell me all about this experiment of yours?

I can't start drawing conclusions until I'm given some data.'

Lacuna stared at him. 'Am I to believe this is a genuine offer? You are willing to exchange information?'

The Doctor sighed. 'Cross my heart and hope to die.'

Part Six

MAD, BAD, OR MERELY DANGEROUS TO KNOW?

They were surrounded by a three-dimensional diagram made of coloured lines and shapes. It filled the chamber, except for a circular space around the bank of screens. Francis didn't mind the screens: he had seen so many wonders in one day that the miniature moving pictures seemed almost ordinary.

To remain near the screens, he and Elaine had to stand close to the strange woman called Lacuna, but even Lacuna seemed less threatening than the jungle of lines and forms that were still proliferating everywhere else in the room. He was able to watch the progress of the three space travellers too, and steal an occasional glance at Britta's legs.

The Doctor, however, seemed not to be awed by the glowing tangle. He walked along its edge, his lips pursed, stopping every few paces to study a particular knot of fibres or to read some of the tiny lines of symbols that moved ceaselessly in the spaces between the shapes.

Some of the lines and symbols appeared across the back of the Doctor's jacket. He had stepped into the glowing forest! Francis couldn't restrain a shout of alarm.

The Doctor turned, frowning. He smiled reassuringly. 'It's not real, Francis. It's a hologram. A simplified representation of Pool's computing resources. Very impressive.'

He continued to stroll among the bundles of spider's-web filaments. Opaque polyhedrons split as he peered at them, revealing tiny mazes, each of which looked as complex as the larger network that filled the chamber.

Nodding thoughtfully, the Doctor made his way back towards the small group gathered round the screens. He blinked as he emerged from the criss-crossing coloured loops into the gloomy clearing.

'We're in the middle of an organic computer,' he said. 'I've identified some sections that are clearly capable of block transfer calculations. And there are large areas devoted to predictive mathematics. Presumably Pool has been able to predict the end of the Dalek War – and therefore the probability of Earth Central taking an interest in what's going on here?'

Lacuna smiled briefly. 'Correct, Doctor. That is why we have to conclude the experiment now.'

'But what's it all for? That's what I'd like to know.'

Lacuna's eyes closed for a few seconds. When they opened again, she looked slightly annoyed. 'Pool permits me to tell you. Pool intends nothing less than the creation of a universe. Only a small one, Doctor, don't look so disapproving. A universe of pure thought, which Pool will inhabit. It will consist of energy.'

'And Pool will be a configuration of electrical charges on zero-mass particles? There are several conversion routines in that area.' The Doctor waved his umbrella. 'They're very elegant, if a bit cumbersome. Baroque computing. But that's comparatively easy, compared to creating even a small universe, you know.'

'Of course.' Lacuna twitched angrily. 'The estimated time for completion seems to extend each time Pool runs the predictor. That is why we have to terminate the experiment.'

'Arcadia.'

'Yes. This star system has served its purpose. Pool will use the outer planets to create the illusion of a nova. That should keep intruders away for long enough. The sun and the inner planets will fuel the creation of Pool's new home, when the calculations are complete.'

'You'll need a black hole,' the Doctor murmured.

'Really?' Lacuna was genuinely interested. 'Yes, Pool suspected as much.'

'And that being the case,' the Doctor said, wandering again into the twining array of whorls, blocks and threads, 'Pool hasn't a snowflake's chance in hell of pulling it off.'

*   *   *

Defries winced as she pulled herself to her feet. Wounded in action.

Unprofessional. Mustn't let the others see the pain.

'Ace. My blaster,' she said, backing towards a wall and keeping her eyes on the widening gap between the doors.

Ace made to throw the weapon, but checked the movement and brought it to Defries. Daak was on the other side of the corridor, closer to the opening doors.

The three of them watched in breathless silence as the doors reached their maximum aperture. Defries could see nothing but darkness through the opening.

A figure jumped into the doorway, and jumped back into the darkness as a beam from Defries's blaster burst against one of the doors.

'Female,' Daak called out.

'Droid?' Defries called back. 'Unarmed, maybe?'

Defries heard a chuckle behind her. Ace, holstering her gun, brushed past her and loped towards the doorway.

'Benny!' Ace shouted. 'Come on out. I'll try to stop the Dalek Killer slicing you up, don't worry.' A woman's face peered round one of the doors. A heart-shaped, quizzical face, framed in bobbed, dark hair.

It was followed by a slim body and long legs, clad in light blue denim with scuffs, tears and patches. No weapons visible. A slight smile now, and a walk that was both casual and wary; cat-like.

Defries mentally summed up the stranger: fit; scruffy; non-combatant.

'Is this your friend with the blue box?' Defries hissed to Ace. She was sure Ace had said that her friend was male.

'No,' Ace replied. 'Friend of a friend.'

The woman was still strolling along the corridor, glancing at her surroundings and at Daak and Defries, but heading towards Ace.

Defries raised her blaster. 'I'm External Operations Agent Defries, in charge of this squad,' she said. 'Identify yourself.'

The woman stopped, only a few metres away now, and

exchanged a glance with Ace before turning slowly to face Defries.

'Identify myself?' She put a finger to her lips and widened her eyes in mock puzzlement. She looked down at her body. 'Good Lord! Do you know, I think I must be Bernice Summerfield, Professor of Archeology. My friends call me Benny, but you can address me as Professor Summerfield. I take it you're one of the narrow-minded military types that one usually bumps into in this sort of situation?'

'Sometimes,' Defries said, holstering the blaster and stepping forward with her hand extended, 'but right now I'm too fragged to maintain the pretence. Do all of Ace's friends have an attitude problem?'

The Professor gripped Defries's gauntlet. 'I wouldn't know,' she said, and looked intently at Defries's face. 'You're hurt.'

'Painkillers and the suit are controlling it,' Defries said. 'I'll live. Assuming nothing else happens.'

The Professor turned to Ace. Defries watched closely. How could these two women know each other? The Professor was educated, obviously. A civilian. Casual. Ace was more than a frontier auxiliary, Defries had realized that on meeting her, but she was no academic, and certainly no civilian. What was the link?

They didn't know each other very well, Defries guessed. There was a hesitation, as if neither of them knew how to start talking to the other. They didn't shake hands.

'The Doctor says it's been three years for you,' the Professor said. 'You look – older.'

Ace grinned. 'Still a delinquent, just less juvenile. How is it, travelling with the Doc?'

The Professor thought for a moment. 'Always interesting,' she said. 'And often too much so. And sometimes rather harrowing.'

'Is he OK now? And the TARDIS?'

The Professor's eyes narrowed. 'You were expecting to see us, weren't you? What's going on?'

Ace looked away. 'You should know the Doctor by

now. I bet he hasn't changed. You'll be the last to know what he's up to.'

Daak had joined the group and was standing behind Ace. The Professor had glanced at him only once, and seemed oblivious to his challenging glare. Defries decided it was time to break up the reunion.

'The big guy is Abslom Daak. A Dalek Killer.'

The Professor looked him up and down, slowly, and turned to Defries. 'He obviously does his exercises every day,' she said. 'A Dalek Killer and Ace. You must have been expecting trouble.'

'And we found it. Lost a troopship, all the crew and all the auxiliaries except us. Now: what do you know about this place? What's going on here?'

The comments and questions with which Ace and Daak interrupted the Professor's story didn't annoy Defries: she found that the breaks gave her the time she needed to stretch her credulity.

The Arcadia colony had been controlled from this space station since the first landing. The population were kept at a pre-technogical level of civilization, with android advisers to make their lives easy. The people died young, and their brains were transported by the androids here, to the station, where they were used to augment a living computer called Pool. The entire system was part of an experiment. Pool, the super-computer, was mad. The Doctor, the guy with the blue box, could normally be relied on to deal with problems of this magnitude, but on this occasion he had apparently failed to understand that Pool was made of human brains and was in any case crazy.

It wasn't likely. It wasn't believable. But none of it contradicted the evidence Defries had seen, and some of that had been equally unbelievable. Ace, Defries noted, accepted everything that the Professor said.

Defries was convinced.

She had never suspect that her opponent was a computer made of human brains, but the Field Agents of the OEO were recruited for their adaptability. Her enemy was Pool. Her mission was to destroy Pool.

Not neutralize. Not negotiate with. Destroy. For several reasons: it was a simple objective, and one which would have the enthusiastic support of her squad; it was the only result which would avenge the deaths of Johannsen and the *Raistrick* crew; and it would cause the maximum damage to the Spinward Corporation.

The Professor had finished, and Ace and Daak were firing questions at her.

Defries interrupted. 'Silence!' she shouted. 'Let's get organized. We're going to destroy this thing called Pool.'

As she'd anticipated, they didn't question her decision.

'Can you use a blaster?' she said to the Professor.

Ace answered, unclipping a spare gun from her belt and handing it to the Professor. 'Is a Dalek antisocial?' she said.

Four, then, Defries thought. Four against a living space station. And the DK's got more plastigraft than flesh. And I'm nursing at least one broken rib. The odds are still no better than hopeless.

'Can you take us to where Pool is?' she said to the Professor.

'I think so.'

'Then let's go paddling, troops,' she shouted. 'Last one in's a droid-bunking bastard.'

Britta, staring at the screens, watching the four figures trotting along the corridors, had said something. Francis was trying to divide his attention between the little moving pictures and the Doctor's argument with the dreadful Lacuna woman, but he had seen the blond girl smile in a way that made her face look almost unattractive, and he had heard her whisper savagely.

'Ace!' Britta said. 'Pool will kill you. Pool will crush you. Or you can kill Pool, if you like.'

And she looked at Lacuna with an intensity that Francis couldn't interpret.

'Yes, yes,' the Doctor was saying, 'of course you have enough processing capacity. The initial calculations were accurate, I'm not denying that. But the subsequent diversification has been – excessive, almost random.'

This time Lacuna didn't scream an abusive reply. An expression of doubt appeared on her face. 'The link has never failed. We have endured hardship in order to provide continuous feedback. Surely you can see that?' Her voice was almost pleading.

'Perhaps it wasn't enough. One person's sensory experience, for a mind as large and complex as this?' He was calmer, too, and trying to be persuasive. He strode among the bundled fibres of colour. 'Look at this sub-routine, for example. Look at all these loops and coils. What is this for, do you think? What use can it possibly have?'

Lacuna shook her head.

'Well, ask Pool. Go on, ask him.'

Lacuna glared at the Doctor, and Francis prepared for another blast of ear-splitting invective. But Lacuna merely said, 'Very well,' and closed her eyes.

Colours swirled around the bank of screens. Francis stepped back, pulling Elaine with him. Shapes began to form as the colours settled into patterns, but the shapes were still indistinct when they started to move violently.

It was a fight. Two figures were battling furiously, exchanging blows as they materialized.

The larger figure was a monster: a composite creature, with the legs of a giant bird, the body of an enormous lizard, the wings of a bat, and the head and arms of a man. It moved sinuously, dancing round its adversary, thrusting with a slender spear and protecting itself gracefully with a brightly-polished shield. Francis, watching the duel from a curled-up position beneath the screens, felt no shame in his fear. And even in the midst of his terror, he realized that the monster's face, crowned with golden curls, was the most arrogantly noble visage he had ever seen.

The creature's opponent was a man, at least at first sight. But his body was twisted and covered with matted hair; his legs were short, his arms were long; his feet resembled cloven hooves and his fingers were claws. His face was a snarling snout, the face of a boar or a dog. He had no weapons apart from his hands and teeth, but he moved surprisingly quickly, dodging the monster's spear-thrusts, and lashing out with his hands only to have his blows intercepted by the monster's shield.

The duel was continuous and completely silent. Neither party paused for breath or parley. Neither retreated more than a few steps before attacking with renewed ferocity, driving the other back. Neither of them tired or suffered a wound. They were phantoms, Francis realized: moving statues of light, similar to the moving pictures on the screens. He became less scared and, even though the blows and parries were, as far as he could tell, ever changing, he became bored.

Only then did Francis notice the shadowy, shimmering figure between the two duellists. A splinter of translucent rock; held motionless against it by chains of bronze, the ephemeral shape of a young woman. It was Britta, her blond hair streaming in an unfelt wind. She was watching the battle with desperate, tear-bright eyes.

Francis looked towards the real Britta. She too was staring at the endless duel, but with considerably more excitement than her replica. She turned; her eyes met Francis's; she smiled. Lust surged in Francis's loins even as disquiet gripped his heart. He turned away.

The Doctor had watched the fight, without interest, for only a few minutes before setting off once again into the surrounding forest of knotted shapes. Lacuna appeared distracted, her face frozen in surprise as she gazed unseeingly at the ceaseless struggle.

The Doctor emerged from the tangle of lights and snapped his fingers in front of her face.

'Lacuna. That's enough.' The shadowy figures began to fade, dispersing like smoke in a breeze. 'Is that what you call efficient use of processing resources? Well, is it?'

The battling creatures had disappeared. Lacuna said nothing, but shook her huge head slowly.

'Let's look at one more,' the Doctor said. He strode into the jungle of branching lines and stopped next to a sphere which opened like a flower as he leant over. His body, overwritten with coloured filaments and moving equations, was almost invisible; his face was a mask, illuminated from below by the rainbow sprays of tiny linked shapes springing from the sphere. 'Lacuna. Ask Pool to create a visual representation of this.'

A wall appeared in the chamber. It was a little higher than a man, and it ended, rough and unfinished, in the centre of the clearing around the bank of screens. Its other end . . .

Francis gaped. He couldn't comprehend what he was seeing. The chamber was wide, but no larger than the Halls of Crystal in the palace at Beaufort. And yet the wall extended further, even though it remained within the chamber. It was an illusion, he knew that, but it looked real and solid. And it ran on, beyond the perimeter of the chamber, on and on in a straight line for hundreds of metres, for kilometres, dwindling in the distance to a taut thread against darkness but still stretching away. He couldn't see the other end.

He closed his eyes. He took a deep breath. He turned his head so that when he opened his eyes he could be facing into the clearing. He opened his eyes. And saw the next impossibility.

People were embedded in the wall. Living people, men and women and children, their hands flailing and their mouths forming soundless words. There was hardly any area of the wall where the order of the mortared stone blocks was not interrupted by a face or a protruding limb. Here an entire head, swinging from side to side; there only a gap in the mortar revealing a pair of wide eyes. Here a leg, sticking out of the wall and kicking; there three fingertips, wriggling.

The wall was unfinished. It was still being built. While Francis had been gazing into the unseeable distance, the wall had extended several metres across the clearing. New blocks appeared out of the air, flickering at first, and among them were more faces and limbs. The invisible bricklayer built steadily, and the wall marched inexorably onward.

'Enough!' The Doctor's voice broke the silence. The wall faded rapidly, leaving Lacuna staring at the place where the next stone had been about to appear.

'You don't need to tell me,' she said sadly. 'Another pointless program. More wasted processing.'

'Even worse, I'm afraid,' the Doctor said cheerily. 'The routine is storing the data it generates. And as it's open-ended, that series – the thing that Pool represents as a wall – will eventually fill up every spare molecule of memory that Pool has. The question is, will it then start using processing areas for extra data storage?'

'It hardly matters,' Lacuna said.

'No.' The Doctor was gentle, sympathetic. 'Pool's increasing size has resulted only in a proliferation of these strange sub-routines. For some time, Pool has been becoming less and less capable of performing the calculations necessary to create a private universe.'

'So it was completely hopeless?'

'Not in principle. I can't tell exactly where and when the original plans became perverted. But it's hopeless now.'

Francis lowered his head into his hands. Why did the Doctor have to say things like that? Lacuna was looking like a cat that had seen its prey. He could almost hear her purring.

'On the contrary, Doctor,' she said. 'Now we can proceed. Now you have brought us your interesting blue box.'

The all-encompassing maze of colour disappeared in an instant. The circular chamber was once again wide and dark and almost empty. A circle of light illuminated the group gathered round the bank of screens; another shone on the blue box, the battered structure that the Doctor call his TARDIS, standing where the androids had left it near the edge of the room.

There was a long silence.

The Doctor spent several minutes inspecting his hat, turning it over in his hands and picking off specks of dust. When he looked up, he seemed surprised to find Lacuna still staring at him.

'It's just a vehicle,' he said. 'I travel in it. That's all.'

'In that case,' Lacuna said, 'you can't have any objection to Pool looking inside it.'

The Doctor sighed. 'No. I suppose not.'

The Dalek Killer was fascinating. In Bernice's experience, small or introverted men were those most likely to be obsessive. She'd never come across this combination before: an expansiveness of both temperament and physique, coupled with a mental set restricted to a handful of concepts. Kill and be killed: apparently the only inhabitants of Daak's mind.

But there was something else, of course. He couldn't keep his eyes off Ace. A giant with three things on his mind, and all of them dangerous. Bernice made a vow never to pick a fight with him.

Not that the OEO Agent was much less single-minded. There was a hint of mania at the corners of Defries's narrowed eyes, at the edges of her pursed mouth. She was as reckless as the DK, but Bernice suspected that until recently she'd been more cautious. A Field Agent would have to be cautious. But she'd led a troopship full of auxiliaries to their deaths; she was wounded herself, and weakened with pain and drugs. Every dead comrade made her more determined to finish her mission. Bernice understood that. But she didn't think it would be advisable to stand in the way of Isabelle Defries, either.

And as for Ace . . .

What was going on between her and the DK? As the four-man squad loped, half-crouching, along the space station's strangely-twisting corridors, Ace and Daak were squabbling about which of them should guard the other's back. Daak would clamp a masterful hand on Ace's shoulder; Ace, snarling, would shrug it off; Daak would look crestfallen; and would then bounce back, only seconds later, with a fearsome grin and an indecent suggestion.

Bernice couldn't work it out. But Ace, at least, seemed aware that death and glory were not the only alternatives. Ace was being very careful. 'Look after Belle,' Ace had whispered to Bernice. 'I'll try to keep the DK on a leash.'

Ace had changed. There hadn't been time, on Heaven, for the two women to get to know each other. And Ace had been preoccupied with Jan. Don't be so mealy-mouthed, Bernice told herself. Ace had been a teenager in love. Bernice's opinion, then, had been that Ace was brave, bright, emotional and impulsive; she had shown her feelings, often forcibly.

It had been three years for Ace. For Bernice, it had been – much less. Travelling in the TARDIS messed with your sense of time. Three years can be a long time in a young life, Bernice concluded, and three years in Bernice's century had certainly changed Ace.

On Heaven, Bernice had found Ace easy to read. Every thought and feeling that had entered Ace's mind had appeared simultaneously on her face.

And now . . . Ace's face was no less expressive. A friendly, conspiratorial smile for Bernice, a sympathetic glance for Defries, a half-angry, half-amused growl for Daak. It's not that the expressions aren't spontaneous or genuine, Bernice said to herself, it's just that they're edited. Ace is thinking and feeling as much as ever, but she's controlling the output of signals. We all do it. Why shouldn't she? It's a change, that's all. Why do people have to become more difficult?

'Which way?' Defries's urgent voice brought Bernice back to the immediate problem.

They had reached a junction. The corridor they had travelled along had turned an abrupt corner and then ended at a blank, curved wall. Smaller corridors ran to the left and right, curving away from the junction along-side the wall.

'We must be at the edge of the centre of the station,' Bernice said to Ace and Defries. Daak was standing guard. 'This facing wall must mark the perimeter of the drum-shaped structure where the – where the brains are kept.'

'So, which way?' Defries said impatiently.

Bernice suppressed a curt retort. 'I'm sure I came through this junction. I remember that remarkable mural. But there was a fourth passage – a ramp upwards, through this wall. But there's nothing here now. Maybe I'm—'

'Droids!' Daak shouted, and flattened himself against

the curving wall, pulling Ace with him. Pulses of laser light streamed from the right-hand passage and blasted white-hot holes in the opposite wall.

Bernice and Defries were lying on the floor, edging backwards while firing their blasters at the black-robed androids.

The shooting stopped. The androids had stopped advancing, and were now out of sight beyond the bend in the passage. Defries and Bernice rolled towards the inner wall, and Bernice helped Defries to stand.

No-one moved. There was no sound.

Ace slipped from beneath Daak's arm and moved along the wall to Defries. She tipped her head towards the right-hand passage and lifted an interrogative eyebrow. Defries nodded. Ace, her back pressed against the wall, tiptoed towards the enemy. She disappeared from view round the curve.

Five seconds later she reappeared, running.

'Here they come,' she said. 'About a million of 'em.'

The passage was filled with androids, each carrying a weapon. They advanced slowly, not firing. Bernice could hardly resist the urge to turn and run, but she supported Defries and retreated step by step.

Defries had had the same idea. 'We can outrun them,' she said. 'At my command, full speed in the other direction.'

'No.' It was Daak's voice, from just behind them. 'I said before, I won't go where they want me to go. Ace, you picked up grenades from the shuttle?'

Ace nodded.

'Buy me thirty seconds,' Daak said, and his chainsword roared into life.

The front rank of androids, four abreast, had started shooting again. Four beads of light swept across the junction, each bearing blinding pulses of energy that burst against walls, floor and ceiling.

Lousy shots, Bernice thought, as her first well-aimed burst exploded in the torso of one of the droids. Defries was firing too. Another droid down. Two dark shapes flew overhead: Ace's grenades, landing behind the first row of advancing black scarecrows.

The androids stopped, staggered, tripped, were pushed by those still advancing from the rear. Bernice and Defries stepped back a few paces, to where Daak's shrieking chainsword was slicing a hole in the curved wall.

Bernice felt rather than heard the two explosions, like a double heartbeat, and then the corridor was filled with flames. Ace's grenades had been incendiaries. Bernice looked again: beneath the sudden billows of smoke the black robes shrivelled and flamed, revealing the asymmetrical bodies of the lurching androids, uncoordinated dancers in the fires.

A suitably medieval vision of hell, she thought.

Ace's voice: 'Come on. We're through.'

Daak was kicking the wall, his chainsword still hacking at the edges of the hole it had torn in the metallic substance. Then he hurled himself against the rigid flap of wall, pushing it, bending it back into the hole, stamping on it as he forced his way into the darkness beyond.

Bernice and Defries followed him. As she stepped on to the tongue of buckled metal, Bernice looked back. Ace, standing smoke-wreathed in the centre of the corridor, rolled another grenade along the floor towards the androids. She leapt into the hole and almost knocked Bernice over.

'Move!' Ace yelled. 'That one's high explosive.'

Bernice staggered a few steps forward. The corridor was dimly lit, featureless, and sloped upwards. Daak was already some distance ahead.

This time the explosion sounded like thunder, and the blast shook the floor. Ace, Defries and Bernice fell in a heap. Smoke, dust and heat burst through the hole behind them. The air seared Bernice's throat.

'Get up! Move!' Ace urged between coughs. 'That won't hold them for long. Benny, is this the right way?'

Daak's voice answered, echoing down the ramp. 'It's the way they don't want us to go. Good enough for me.'

'I think so,' Benny said, forcing the words through the bitter dryness that had coated the inside of her mouth. She pointed up the sloping corridor. 'To the centre. Above the centre.'

Defries stood, painfully. 'And then we destroy it,' she said. 'Whatever it is.'

Only one of the screens was now lit, showing little but red-tinged smoke.

'More droids!' Lacuna screamed. 'Britta, bring up more droids! Prepare the guards in the upper galleries. Our visitors will find hawks in the aviary. They will be stopped!'

Francis hugged Elaine and tried to shrink further into the shadows beneath the screens. Seen from below, Lacuna's long body would have looked comical as she ran back and forth, if it had not been for the grimace of rage that contorted her white face.

'Treacherous, incompetent droids!' Lacuna jumped towards Britta and slapped the girl's face. 'Program them to self-destruct whenever they miss a target. They will learn obedience.'

The Doctor stepped in front of her. 'Lacuna,' he said. She raised her hand, but he didn't flinch. 'Lacuna, the androids are ineffective because they are badly designed. Their programming is as twisted as their bodies.'

Lacuna was trembling with anger. 'The intruders must be stopped. They intend to destroy Pool.'

'I agree.'

Lacuna lowered her hand. 'You agree?'

'Of course. But Ace and Benny and the others don't have to be killed. You don't have to play these cat and mouse games with your clockwork soldiers. Pool has the power to stop them.'

The tall woman stared at the Doctor, and then closed her eyes. The Doctor stepped back, watched her for a moment, and walked round her to the console at which Britta was working.

'Britta,' he said, 'let's start decommissioning those androids, shall we?'

'No!' Lacuna's eyes had snapped open, and she whirled

271

towards the Doctor. 'The androids must guard Pool against the intruders.'

'What? Why?' the Doctor spluttered incoherently. 'It's not necessary. It's barbaric. Call them off. What is Pool playing at?'

Lacuna tossed her great head and wouldn't look at him. 'Pool is – troubled,' she muttered. 'The waters are muddied. Pool is preoccupied.' She faced the Doctor at last. 'Pool has better things to think about!'

The Doctor looked at her quizzically. 'You can't get through, can you? Your link's on the blink. It's all going wrong, Lacuna. The whole scheme's falling apart. Can't you see—'

'They're in the galleries!' Britta's shrill, excited exclamation rang in the chamber. The Doctor and Lacuna turned to look at the screens.

Francis lifted his head above the edge of the display and found himself staring at a confusing picture of pipes and girders. At first he could see nothing moving; then he saw them. Four tiny figures, crawling like ants along a horizontal beam of metal. Above, below and around them, girders and hawsers criss-crossed an apparently boundless gulf. He looked at the other screens: each provided a different perspective of the same scene. Some, from lower viewpoints, gave glimpses of the faceted dome that covered the expanse of space; others looked down and revealed the four tiny figures balanced a hundred metres above a vast, circular, grey plain.

On some of the screens, Francis thought he saw other figures moving in the high shadows.

'They will find hawks in the aviary,' Lacuna said.

Ace didn't like heights. But she reckoned that was only natural. Falling off a tall building is, after all, much more dangerous than falling off a low wall. So crawling along a girder that was swaying gently under the dome of a gigantic space station induced a level of fear that Ace thought she could handle.

It was the idea of falling into a sea of brains that turned over her insides.

She had to take another look. She stopped crawling. Daak was several metres ahead of her. She hoped he'd stop when he reached the next supporting strut. He hadn't responded to her last shout. He hadn't even looked back. Ace was beginning to think he'd finally flipped.

Defries, with Benny just behind her, was a long way in the other direction. Belle was slowing down. The pain was showing in her face, her movements.

Maybe we're not going to get out of this, Ace thought. Come on, Doctor: haven't you short-circuited the mad scientist's gizmo yet, or bamboozled the megalomaniac survivor of an ancient race of warrior wizards, or whatever it is this time? Get your finger out, Doc. I'm running out of time, luck and ammunition. Just one grenade left. That's going to do a lot of damage in a soup bowl the size of Wembley stadium, I don't think.

Right then. Take another look.

It was bigger than Wembley stadium. Even from her high perch, Ace couldn't see all of it at one glance. In the distance the curving edge of it; everywhere else below her nothing but the flat expanse of mottled brown and grey. How many millions had died to create this blotchy, congealed stew? Even Benny had looked green when she'd first seen it, and Benny had had time to get used to the idea.

For a vertiginous instant, Ace lost all sense of direction. The grey-brown circle suddenly became the face of a planet, and Ace was approaching it from space. No gravity, she thought, as she felt her body begin to roll.

'Ace!'

'*Ace!*'

She hugged the girder. Eyes closed. Deep breaths. Sweat cold down her back.

Jesus, Mary, Michael and all the saints, that had been close. If her own mind could play tricks like that, she'd be easy meat for any of those giant prawns.

Who had shouted? Defries. Ace lifted her head and waved. Belle managed a tight smile. Had there been another voice? The Doctor's?

This wasn't the time to think about it. Worry about

273

giant prawns instead, Ace told herself. Get moving. Get to the next stanchion.

She lifted herself on to hands and knees, edged to the centre of the girder, waited until her limbs had stopped shaking, and started to crawl.

Daak was waiting for her beyond the next upright. He had had to wait: he'd run out of girder. Ace inched along the lip of metal beside the stanchion and found the Dalek Killer sitting at the end of the girder, his legs dangling over the drop. He was staring downwards with a fierce grin, an expression that didn't change as he turned and saw Ace.

'Hi, doll. It ain't safe up here. Come and hold on to me.'

'Even under these circumstances,' Ace said, 'I think I can resist the temptation. What have you found that's so interesting?' She crouched next to him and summoned the courage to peer over the end of the girder.

'Don't know,' Daak said. 'What do you make of it?'

There was an artificial island almost directly beneath them. Ace scanned the horizon.

'It's dead centre, isn't it?' she said. Scores of pipes of various colours and widths were plugged into apertures on the diamond-shaped slab. Some of the pipes were rigid, others appeared flexible; some were ribbed, some bulged and sagged, some were bundled with spirals of cable.

Ace's gaze followed the pipes upwards. They all descended from a structure that was suspended high above them from the centre of the dome. The structure had originally been a sphere, Ace guessed, although it was now, like the space station itself, an accretion of bizarre extrusions. Ducts, pipes and cables ran into it from all round the edges of the dome.

'I don't know what it is,' Ace said, 'but it looks important.' It reminded her of the trunking at the back of a starship's central processor banks; and of the tubing inside a tissue regrowth cabinet. 'Life support system,' she breathed. 'I think we ought to damage it.'

'What?'

'Well, that oxtail soup down there is the Spinward Corporation, according to Benny. Right?'

'Always said corporates had no guts and no balls,' Daak laughed.

'Yeah. Just brains. But brains need energy, don't they? Present company excepted. And oxygen. Even when they've been puréed, I suppose. Those pipes must be for something. I think we've just found the soft underbelly of the Spinward Corporation.'

Defries and Benny had climbed round the stanchion.

'Great,' Defries said. 'So what are we going to do – stand here and shout insults at it? The Dalek Killer's led us up a blind alley.'

'Laser through the pipes,' Benny suggested.

'It might come to that,' Defries said. 'But I'm prepared to bet those pipes are self-sealing. It could take hours. And we're all running low on power. And,' she added, looking up into the shadowy void of the dome, 'we're going to need every shot we've got. Look.'

Winged shapes, clattering eerily as they swerved through the air, were descending towards them.

'I don't know what they are,' Defries said, 'but I doubt if they're friendly. We can try to hold them off with our blasters. But we need explosives to take out the island or the junction box up above. Ace?'

'One grenade left, Belle.' Ace extracted a black cylinder from her backpack. Her fingers pressed buttons on the control panel. 'High explosive, but contact detonation. There was nothing fancy in the shuttle.'

Defries peered over the end of the girder. 'You mean you have to throw it, and it has to hit the target?'

'You got it. If it doesn't hit the island,' Ace tried to stifle an inappropriate giggle, 'I guess it'll just sink into the brains.'

Defries looked upwards again, anxiously. 'We have to try something,' she said. 'Benny, find what cover you can and start shooting at anything with wings. Ace, you're going to have to use that grenade. One good throw. That island's as big as a forceball pitch.'

'It's also a hell of a long way away,' Ace replied. She

remembered now why she'd hated sport at school. The whole team relying on her to get it right, always ready to blame her when she failed. And now it wasn't the threat of being lasered in half that knotted her stomach: it was the inevitability of the sense of failure, of letting down her team, that would follow a muffed throw. But she lifted the grenade above her head and took aim.

She hesitated. 'From what Benny said, the Doctor must be somewhere down there. Right underneath that central area.'

The grenade was snatched from her hand.

She turned. There was no-one behind her. Then she saw Daak swinging above her, hanging by one hand from a cable that ran up the stanchion, his other hand holding the grenade. He was already a couple of metres above the girder. He stuffed the grenade into the waistband of his tattered trousers and climbed higher, out of reach.

'Daak!' Defries started to shout. 'That's our one hope—'

'Shut it, Agent,' Daak yelled. 'This has got to be sure. One grenade, that means just one chance. We can't risk a throw. I'm going up to that there mass of spaghetti, and I'm going to make sure.'

Ace looked up, tracing a route from the stanchion to a diagonal girder, an almost vertical cable, a narrow pipe and then a short piece of wider ducting. Yes, it could be done. It would need strength and agility, but Daak had plenty of both.

Did she have the strength and agility to catch him? Probably not, she thought, but do I have a choice? Her gauntlets gripped the cable and her boots sought purchase on the metal upright.

Defries pulled her back. Ace swung round, her gauntlets curled into iron fists. Defries ducked, fell, threw out her arms to save herself from falling off the girder.

'Ace! Not here, Ace. Not now.' Defries's voice was calm but her face was full of fear. 'We're under attack and we're a hundred metres up.'

Ace shook her head angrily. 'Sorry.' She muttered

curses at herself. 'But you heard him. He's going to kill himself.'

'He'll be lucky if he gets the chance,' Defries said. 'Look. He's attracting some attention. Professor Summerfield's a good shot, but she can't hold them all off. Get shooting, Ace.'

There was a battle going on. Ace had been dimly aware of it for some time, but now she realized that beads of laser light were swinging in crazy arcs all round the stub of girder on which she and Defries were standing. Only the reflective coating of her suit had prevented the enemy weapons identifying her as a target. And it was in any case a miracle that none of the random energy pulses had hit her.

Ace pulled Defries towards the stanchion. The metal would withstand all but the most concentrated laser fire. It protected their backs, and protruding flanges gave them some cover on both sides. There was no sign of Benny, but Ace assumed that the Professor had taken up a position on the other side of the stanchion.

The attackers were androids with wings. They were barely humanoid, with bodies that dwindled from wide torsos to legless, conical abdomens. Their small heads were carried on long, flexible necks, and their blasters were housed in chest orifices. Wings, made of plates of wafer-thin metal, sprouted from a large dome on each android's back.

Their flight was as erratic as the locomotion of their ground-travelling equivalents, but they were therefore difficult to shoot at. Both sides were using a great deal of laser energy to very little effect.

Ace couldn't count them, but she thought there must be more than twenty. Most of them were above Ace and Defries, fluttering round the diagonal girder along which Daak was trying to climb.

Why doesn't he put that stupid chainsword away and get a move on, Ace thought, as she tried to target one of the androids. Daak had stopped half-way up the girder and, holding on with one hand, was flailing the air with his chainsword. None of the androids flew within reach of the weapon.

Got one! Ace turned to grin at Defries, but Defries was too busy ducking and shooting as two androids swooped towards her position.

Another android, one of its wings in shreds, fluttered towards the grey-brown expanse below. That, Ace reckoned, must have been Benny's.

Daak was moving again now, swinging wildly from side to side in an attempt to avoid the lasers' targeting. He hadn't stowed his chainsword across his back, and Ace watched aghast as he swung himself too far, reached out with his left hand, and failed to grasp the side of the girder.

Ace fancied she could see the look of anguish on Daak's face as he relinquished his grip on his chainsword and grabbed the girder with his right hand. He, and she, and even the androids, watched the chainsword twist and tumble as it fell. It looked no larger than a pin when it finally hit the surface without a sound, and disappeared.

I hope he left it running, Ace thought. It might sever a few synapses.

'Good heavens!' The Doctor looked up from the screens that everyone in the chamber had been silently watching. 'Yes, of course. It's been staring me in the face.' He struck his forehead with the palm of a hand. 'Pool is an agglomeration of human neurons. A vast concentration. At least ten to the power eighteen. There are more human brain cells on this space station than there are stars in this galaxy. Many more. Pool is a gestalt mind – a collective personality.' The Doctor's expression of amazement was replaced by a frown. 'No wonder he seems so confused.'

Francis didn't understand the Doctor's words.

'You're right, Doctor,' Lacuna was saying, 'but there are only a few dozen complete personalities that make up the gestalt. Most of the neurons are reconfigured with new and augmented synaptical connections. Memories and personalities are lost.'

Elaine was gripping Francis's hand so tightly that he

yelped. 'Elaine!' he whispered, and saw that her eyes were brimming with tears.

'They cut a hole,' she sobbed. 'They cut off her hair, her beautiful hair. There was nothing inside.'

Francis understood.

He seemed to see himself, small and alone, in the centre of a circular chamber that expanded when he tried to see its perimeter. Then he was back in his body again, shivering. A cold wind had wrapped itself round him, although there was no draught.

Christina. Her face filled his thoughts. Christina smiling, Christina angry, Christina's mouth half opening, lips moving, eyelids slowly closing.

And all the others. Apprentice Scribes who had been his boyhood playfellows. Edwin the Farrier, who had bullied him. Beatrice who had made him a man. Oswald. Sophia, Rosalind.

Christina. With his eyes closed he could see her as clearly as if she were standing in front of him. Christina dancing. Running, laughing, her arms reaching for him.

He opened his eyes. He tried not to look at the screens. He felt bile rising in his stomach as his gaze was dragged to the sluggish sea of grey and brown.

Christina. All that was left of Christina.

He retched, thin vomit spattering on the floor.

The Doctor stepped sideways briskly. Francis looked up, wiping his mouth, to see impatience struggling with concern on the Doctor's face.

'Francis, what on earth's the matter? Are you ill?'

'Christina . . . '

'What? Who?' The Doctor took his arm. 'Come and stand over here. Lacuna, don't you have any chairs? Wrap yourself up warm, Francis. That's it. Now what's all this about, eh?'

'All those people!' Francis suddenly knew that he had to make the Doctor understand. 'Doctor, all those people – generations of people. Killed off like cattle, so they could be put into – into that . . . ' He retched again.

The Doctor patted his shoulder. 'It's a bit of a shock,

I suppose,' he said. 'But what an achievement, eh? An organic computer on this scale – remarkable.'

'No, Doctor.' Francis was almost weeping with anger and frustration. 'It's obscene.' He looked into the Doctor's eyes, and saw incomprehension, sympathy – and disdain. The Doctor had said that he wasn't human, but Francis had not comprehended until now that the mind behind the little man's clownish, owlish face was as alien as Lacuna's. More alien than Lacuna's. Francis looked away. 'I hope the Dalek Killer destroys it,' he said, as vehemently as he could.

'It's alive,' the Doctor said gently. 'It's sentient. More intelligent than any other entity for thousands of – '

'Doctor!' Lacuna interrupted him, and gestured wildly at the screens. 'The androids are failing. The Dalek Killer has a bomb. He's almost in a position to blow up the feed lines.'

It was true. Francis forced himself to look at the screens again, and he could see that there were less of the winged creatures flitting among the struts and cables. As he watched, two more fluttered downwards, trailing sparks and smoke. The three women were wreaking havoc with their guns that fired streaks of light.

And the man, the Dalek Killer, was clambering grimly along ducts and girders towards the misshapen nexus of pipes and cables. The black cylinder was in his hand, ready to be hurled from close range.

'Well, do something!' the Doctor snapped at Lacuna. 'He's determined to die and he'll take Pool with him if he can.'

Lacuna slowly shook her great head. 'Pool is defenceless. You were right, Doctor. There is depletion of power. Proliferation of unnecessary loops. The process is accelerating. Even communication is difficult.'

'In a human, I think the condition would be known as fear. But if Pool won't help himself . . . ' The Doctor's eyes widened, as if he had suddenly remembered an important fact. 'Lacuna, can you unjam Ace's personal radio? And where's a voice transmitter?' He ran back and forth among the consoles, skidding to a halt as he found the controls he wanted. He turned to Lacuna. 'Well?'

'The transmitter is operative, Doctor. You can talk to Ace.'

'It might help if you were to call off the androids,' he said, exasperatedly. 'They're not doing their job but they're something of a distraction.' He bent over the console, pressing buttons at random. 'Ace? Ace? Are you there? Can you hear me? Ace?'

Francis realized that the Doctor was about to do something wrong. He and the Doctor were, at least for the moment, on opposing sides. He should throw himself at the Doctor's back, grapple with him, break the machinery at which he was working. Do something.

He looked at Elaine, and found that Elaine was looking at him. He tried to smile. 'It'll be all right,' he said, and turned away.

'Ace? Ah, there you are. Ace, listen to me. This is important. You remember our conversation in the TARDIS? I realize now whom you were talking about. You can't let him do this, Ace. He can't sacrifice himself now. You've got to stop him.'

The droids were pulling back. They'd stopped firing. Defries continued to shoot, locking her beam on to the diminishing targets and sending light-fast bursts of energy into the shadowy interstices of metalwork high above.

She realized Ace had stopped firing. Was the girl hurt? Suppressing a grunt of pain, Defries lifted herself on to one elbow and looked round.

Ace was OK. She was still crouched in the niche where the upright descended to join the girder. She'd holstered her blaster. Her head was tilted to the side, and her face was wearing an expression of annoyance and confusion.

'Ace?'

Ace tapped her collar. 'Comm's working,' she said, and listened to it for a few more moments. Then she sighed and stood up. 'It's the Doctor. He's done a deal. They've called off the droids, and there won't be any more attacks. But I've got to stop Daak.'

'What? Like hell you will.' Defries stood up, the pain in her chest overwhelmed by a feeling that she recognized as panic. 'The DK's our only hope. That grenade is our only hope.'

'No. The Doctor'll sort it. Daak's got to live. He's still got things to do.'

'He's just a DK. He's not even—'

'Daak!' Ace's shout echoed and dwindled in the cavernous web of metal. 'Abslom Daak! Listen to me!'

Above them, the tiny figure crawling along the top of a pipe stopped for a moment, and then continued. He was about to disappear into the tangle of tubes and ducts. He was holding the grenade above his head, ready to throw.

'Daak, it's all over. We've won.'

The figure stopped again, but didn't lower the grenade.

Defries saw an unreadable expression cross Ace's face. Ace's shoulders drooped, and she closed her eyes. Then she straightened.

'Daak! Daak, please come back. I love you!'

There was a long moment of silence.

Defries watched her mission end in failure. She saw Daak lower the grenade and alter its programming. She heard his exultant whoop as he hurled it, harmless now, into the void. She saw him turn and start to retrace his tortuous route, almost falling in his eagerness to return.

Ace looked defeated. 'Sorry, Belle,' she said with a strange smile. 'I had to do it. I had to.'

'Would someone care to tell me just what is going on?' Professor Summerfield was edging round the stanchion. She joined Ace and Defries on the projecting stub of the girder. 'I hope I've misunderstood, but it seems to me that Ace's romantic attachment has just lost us our last chance to prevent this,' she waved her arms in a circle, 'this monstrosity from wiping out an entire planetary system and its inhabitants. Please tell me I'm wrong.'

Ace looked furious. 'The Doctor called me, OK? Daak has to live. The Doctor's got it all under control.'

'The Doctor's got it all under control?' Bernice's voice dripped sarcasm. 'You've forgotten a lot in three years,

Ace. You should know him better than that. He's a prisoner down there.'

'Look, I know what I'm doing, OK?'

'Do you? Do you really?'

'Shut it, both of you.' Defries had decided that someone had to take charge. 'Check your power packs. Mine's out.'

As Defries had feared, neither Ace nor Bernice had more than a few minutes' more power in their blasters.

'The droids are coming back.' Defries pointed to the winged creatures spiralling down towards them, and then to a contingent of androids shuffling along the girder. 'I think the best we can achieve now is a dignified surrender.'

'It isn't over 'till it's over,' Defries had whispered to Bernice as they were jostled together in the middle of a crowd of lurching androids. 'Ace usually has something up her sleeve.'

Bernice had been unable to interpret Ace's behaviour. When they had emerged into the station's corridors, Ace had stood alone, her arms crossed and her lips tight, occasionally cursing as an android nudged her. When Daak had been brought to join them, Bernice had expected Ace to run to him; instead, she just smiled crookedly and raised a hand in greeting. Daak had looked confused: he marched straight to Ace, but seemed not to know what to do next. He had stared down at her, grinning vacuously; from time to time the smile would be replaced by a frown, and the Dalek Killer would demand the return of his chainsword. Ace was patient with him, but not affectionate. Daak, in Bernice's view, was acting daft. Or perhaps he was in shock. Then again, perhaps rough, tough Spacefleet troopers manifested peculiarly understated displays of romantic love.

Bernice couldn't work it out. But she was still angry. Her temper wasn't improved by the trip through the convoluted passages of the space station. The androids seemed more incompetent than ever, almost falling over each other as they herded the prisoners through kilo-

283

metres of intricately decorated passages. Only the vast numbers of the black-robed machines had prevented Bernice attempting to escape.

Her worst fears were confirmed when they reached the circular chamber. It seemed like hours since she had slipped away to find Ace, but nothing had changed much.

Francis and Elaine were still huddled together. Both looked exhausted and ill. The blond bimbo, Britta, still seemed to be excited; her glittering blue eyes, Bernice thought, hinted at a sort of insanity. But not as loopy as the Lacuna woman, of course, who was standing in the shadows and favouring everyone in turn with her intense glare. Daak was unusually restrained, standing behind Ace with a hand on her shoulder and a puzzled frown on his face. And Ace was – expressionless. She'd greeted the Doctor with a grin and a thumbs-up. He'd smiled and nodded. Bernice had found herself resenting their casual familiarity.

She suppressed her anger, and concentrated on looking after Isabelle Defries. The OEO Agent had obviously been in continuous pain by the end of their long, slow hike, and Bernice was able to boost the feed of chemicals provided by Defries's combat suit. Defries had made it clear that she hadn't abandoned her intention to destroy the heart of the Spinward Corporation, even at the sacrifice of her own life, and Bernice stayed alongside her at least partly to prevent her doing something rash.

Bernice soon realized that the Doctor had, in her absence, come to some kind of agreement with Lacuna. The Doctor was striding round the centre of the room and giving a lecture, tripping over his words in his excitement as he expounded on the wonders of organic computers, the scale of Pool's achievement, the potential capabilities of Pool's data processing.

'A ten followed by fourteen noughts,' the Doctor said, 'that's the number of synapses in an individual human brain. Now try to imagine a ten followed by thirty noughts. Can't you see the difference? It's not just a matter of quantity; the very nature of intelligence alters.'

'But, Doctor,' Ace interrupted, 'this Pool thing's completely hatstand, isn't it?'

'I beg your pardon? Hatstand?' The Doctor clutched his own hat protectively.

'Bonkers. Barmy. Out of its tree. Round the bend, out to lunch. You know.'

'Well,' the Doctor's brow furrowed, 'let's just say that Pool is a little out of touch. There's been long term sensory deprivation, so it's not surprising. Symptoms that in a human might be termed neurosis and paranoia. There are hints of a multiple personality syndrome.'

Multiple personality, Bernice thought, you bet it's got a multiple personality. It's made of people's brains. Has the Doctor forgotten? Or does he really not understand?

'But,' the Doctor went on, 'I'm sure I can be of help.' He turned to Lacuna. 'Pool needs to get out more,' he said, trying hard to slow his speech so that Lacuna would grasp his meaning. 'Fresh air. Exercise. Travel. Meeting people.'

Lacuna's lips curled into a sneering smile.

'Listen to me,' the Doctor pleaded. 'I'm not being facetious. Well, not entirely. Pool has been too isolated. His development has become unbalanced. He needs contact with other minds. I'm sure his fears about being discovered are unfounded. Earth won't necessarily be hostile.'

Bernice glanced at Defries. Oh yes Earth will, she thought.

The Doctor had stopped pacing and stood looking up at Lacuna. 'Please,' he said. 'Extend the link. Let Pool enter a few other minds, allow him to see through other eyes.'

'Enough!' Lacuna cut him off. 'You pretend to offer assistance but you urge surrender. Your advice entails the abandonment of our entire project. Pool has an inkling of the great learning locked in your head, Time Lord. We suspect that your recommendations have little to do with Pool's well-being, and much to do with preserving the secrets of your people.'

'Not at all!' the Doctor protested, but Bernice didn't think he sounded convincing. 'I'm only trying to help.'

'Thank you, Doctor,' Lacuna said with exaggerated politeness, 'but we don't need your nostrums. There's nothing wrong with Pool that can't be cured with more processing power and more data.' She turned, and a circle of light illuminated the TARDIS, standing isolated near the edge of the chamber. 'We don't need you, Doctor. We need only your blue box. You will provide access to it – now.'

'No!' The word sprang soundlessly to Ace's lips, Bernice saw, and to her own. The Doctor's protest echoed round the room. 'Turn the TARDIS over to a paranoid, neurotic megalomaniac? Never.'

'You have no choice!' Lacuna was enraged. 'You are all prisoners. You have no power here. Pool cannot touch you, Doctor. You are maintaining your mental defences well. But your friends . . . All your friends are within reach.'

It all happened suddenly.

Daak jumped back with an oath as Ace was surrounded by a shimmering aura. Enveloped in a curtain of golden gauze, Ace put her hand to her throat, and then clamped it over her mouth and nose. Her eyes were wide.

'Her brain will become part of Pool,' Lacuna said. 'Or will you cooperate, Doctor?'

Bernice heard the Doctor's voice saying 'All right. You win.' But the Dalek Killer was throwing himself at the golden cloud. And Ace had dropped to one knee, raised her arm, pulled back her sleeve and launched a sliver of a projectile from a harness strapped against her skin.

'Ace! No!' But the Doctor's shout was too late. The golden glow faded as Daak stumbled through it, almost falling over Ace but staggering on, suddenly aware of the circling dart, trying to swat it with his fists as it closed in . . .

Bernice ducked her head. The explosion hurt her ears and flooded her closed eyes with red light.

When she looked up, Daak's headless body was still

stumbling forward, collapsing slowly and then crashing to the floor like a felled tree.

Ace was the first to move. She got to her feet and stood over the Dalek Killer's body. She put her forearm across her eyes. Bernice could see her lips moving. Then she looked up. 'Sorry, Doc. Accident.'

'I know,' the Doctor said quietly. 'What a waste.'

'I disagree,' Lacuna said. 'Pool did not require the material. The brain was not remarkable.'

'Not remarkable?' Ace's missile launcher was aimed at Lacuna. 'Listen, freak, that DK had more bottle than Express Dairies and if you – ' Ace stopped and lowered her arm. 'Still, no point in banging on about it. You haven't won yet.'

'I think we have,' Lacuna said. 'I'm sure the Doctor is now prepared to let Pool occupy his blue box – aren't you, Doctor?'

The Doctor looked horrified. 'But I thought Pool wanted to investigate – you know, just a look round. Uncover all my so-called secrets and then – I didn't think . . . Occupy? You mean, permanently?'

'But of course, Doctor. The images in your friends' minds make it clear that your TARDIS is very large. Not infinite, but big enough for Pool, we are sure. Your TARDIS will become our universe of pure thought.'

The Doctor lowered his head slowly until his chin was resting on his chest.

'Doctor,' Bernice said. 'Doctor, you can't . . . '

The Doctor looked up. Bernice had never seen such sadness in his eyes – in anyone's eyes. 'I have no choice, Professor.'

'We're just five people,' Bernice said. 'Pool can kill us, one by one or all together. But you don't have to give in. Pool can't touch you. Get in the TARDIS now, and go.'

'That goes for me too,' Ace said. 'Get going.'

The Doctor shook his head. 'It's not just you,' the Doctor said. 'In the absence of access to the TARDIS, Pool will destroy the entire Arcadia system. It will be a completely futile waste of energy and human lives, because the calculations are already going awry, but Pool will do it anyway. So I really have no choice.'

The Doctor turned towards the TARDIS. Ace stepped in front of him, blocking his path.

'Ace?' he said.

'You can't let this happen. It can't end like this – you and the TARDIS, fighting the monsters, putting two fingers up to the Master. It can't all end like this.'

'It has to end some time, Ace. Nothing lasts for ever, even for a Time Lord.' A brief, rueful smile touched his lips. 'And Professor Summerfield would never forgive me if I permitted the destruction of yet another inhabited star system.'

'It's only a few million people, Doctor.' Ace was being deliberately brutal. 'With the power of the TARDIS, this brain soup character will be able to screw up the whole universe. It's worth the sacrifice.'

The Doctor looked at his shoes. His voice was so low that Bernice could hardly hear him. 'I know, Ace. I know. But I already have too much blood on my hands. I'm going to end it now.'

He waited until Ace shrugged and stepped aside, and then he walked steadily to the TARDIS, drawing in his wake Lacuna, Britta, Ace, Francis, Elaine, Defries and Bernice. He stood in front of the door, staring at the peeling blue paint as if trying to imprint every detail on his memory.

What happens to a Time Lord who loses his TARDIS, Bernice wondered. The Doctor had covered his face with his hands. His shoulders were shaking, Bernice couldn't imagine the messages that might be passing between the Doctor and his time machine. His ship. His old friend. She felt tears sting her eyes. Her fingernails sank into her palms.

The Doctor sniffed, blew his nose on his handkerchief, and straightened his shoulders. He unlocked the door, pushed it open, and stood aside. Lacuna almost leapt through the doorway, and disappeared into the interior.

Several seconds passed.

Lacuna appeared in the doorway, swaying. Her face

was even more pale than usual, and her wild eyes were darting back and forth.

She staggered out of the TARDIS and gasped. 'The Net,' she breathed. 'Ah, that's better. I am with Pool again. I should have realized that the connection would be severed. Did you think you might trap me in your machine, Doctor?'

'No,' the Doctor said. 'To tell the truth, I hadn't thought of it myself.'

'I've seen enough to know that the place will be perfect for Pool. So much space. So much capacity. Such a wealth of data to absorb. Such power to process it. Your machine will double Pool's abilities.'

'Double?' The Doctor looked offended. 'Madam, my TARDIS may only be a type 40, but you —'

'Silence, Doctor. All this remains theoretical. Pool cannot yet gain access to your machine. Its energy fields separate me from Pool as soon as I enter it.'

'Oh dear,' the Doctor said. 'What a pity. Well, never mind. It was an interesting idea, but I never did think it would work.'

Bernice averted her eyes. She'd suddenly found herself staring at his hands, which were clenched together behind his back. The fingers of one hand were tapping frenziedly against the palm of the other, as if all the excitement in his body had to be expressed through the movements of one set of digits.

Glory be, Bernice thought. He's up to something. He's been bluffing all along.

She forced herself to stop thinking. Pool could read her thoughts. She concentrated on chess, remembering the moves of the last game, filling her mind with opening gambits and defences.

'The problem isn't insuperable, Doctor,' Lacuna said. 'Although I ceased to need the physical link some years ago, I still have the ability to use it.' She stroked the cylindrical implant in the top of her head. 'Britta, my dear. Fetch the link. Pool will be with me next time I enter this wonderful TARDIS.'

The chess game dissolved. Bernice's mind was suddenly

filled with a vivid memory: she was almost reliving the moment when she and the Doctor had been discussing the difficulty of tampering with the TARDIS. 'Of course,' the Doctor had said, and the memory of his voice was so real that she almost heard the words in her ears, 'if anyone wanted to infiltrate the TARDIS with any kind of intelligence, from a virus to an entire computer, they'd only have to plug a cable into the socket under the console. The information would be downloaded in a trice. And nothing I could do would stop it.'

The memory faded, and panic struck. What have I done? Bernice thought. Pool can read my mind. I've just told it how to get into the TARDIS. Doctor, don't just stand there smiling like an idiot.

Britta approached, bearing the link: a silver lance on the end of a thick bundle of cables. Lacuna took it, held it above her head, and started to slide it into the implant.

She stopped.

'Pool has suggested another way,' she said. 'Everything that is Pool can be converted into electronic code. The code can be transmitted along the cable – and directly into your machine, Doctor.'

'No!' the Doctor said, and at the same time Bernice was trying to remember exactly when she had had the conversation that she had just remembered so clearly.

The Doctor had never spoken to her about sockets under the console. She was sure of it. The conversation had never taken place. And his last protest had sounded more than a little theatrical.

'There are no input locations for cables,' the Doctor shouted, as Lacuna dragged the link through the TARDIS door.

'I'm sure I can find a suitable connection point,' Lacuna's voice replied from inside the TARDIS. 'Beneath this hexagonal structure, for instance?'

'Certainly not!' the Doctor shouted, trying to keep out of his voice the amusement that was spread across his face.

Bernice exchanged a puzzled glance with Ace.

There was a laugh from within the TARDIS, and a scrabbling noise. Then silence.

A long silence.

A growing silence.

Bernice craned her neck, trying to catch the barely-audible echoes before they faded. Everything was becoming quieter.

There had been, for a long time, a buzzing in her head, she realized, like hundreds of whispering voices. It was disappearing. It had gone.

The space station, like every space station she'd ever been on, had had its own almost imperceptible vibration and hum. They had ceased. The lights were fading – the lights had all gone out. The only illumination was the oblong of light that spilled from the open doorway of the TARDIS.

And then, just as the silence became absolute, and Bernice could hear nothing but the beating of her own pulse, other noises started. Distant creaks and groans echoed eerily along dark corridors and seemed to expand into the circular chamber. Bernice heard a far-off crash and, a little later, the shriek of tearing metal. The floor shuddered.

Lacuna appeared, a tall silhouette in the TARDIS's doorway. Her arms were raised, her head was held at a strange angle, her body was rigid but trembling. Her mouth opened and closed several times before words emerged.

'What have you done?' Her voice was slow and flat. 'Where is Pool?'

The Doctor threw back his head. Bernice heard his huge sigh of relief.

'What could I have done?' he said, casually. 'Pool is inside the TARDIS. Perhaps—' He hesitated, and continued in a vitriolic tone. 'Perhaps Pool doesn't need you any longer.'

The gaunt figure reeled, clutching at the doorframe for support. 'No!' she screamed, and lurched from the TARDIS, wailing.

Britta ran forward and caught Lacuna in her arms. The

tall woman struggled and continued to call out, until Britta stood back and administered a stinging slap to her face.

The hysterical shrieks subsided into sobs, and Britta put her arm around Lacuna, comforting her and leading her slowly towards one of the doors in the perimeter of the chamber.

'Britta,' the Doctor said softly, and the girl looked over her shoulder. 'Can you find a secure area of the station that is part of the original structure? A part with a self-contained energy supply and life support system?'

'I know just the place, Doctor. Down below. The old solar energy unit. I've been planning for this, too, over the last few days. I just never thought it would happen. Thank you.' Britta turned away and continued her slow progress across the chamber, murmuring encouragement to the bowed figure in her embrace.

Better not to interfere, Bernice thought. Everyone has her own definition of contentment. I wouldn't want to be either of those women. But perhaps they'll come to some sort of understanding. She watched them disappear into one of the corridors that radiated from the chamber.

Swirls of dust swept across the floor. The whistling of winds mingled with the hiss and rush of escaping air. Cracks appeared in the wall of the chamber. Pools of viscous liquid started to spread across the floor. The gusts of air carried a stench of decay. The lumps of stonework that had remained standing now crumbled. Parts of the ceiling collapsed.

'Well,' the Doctor said brightly, 'all into the TARDIS, I think.' He seemed very pleased with himself.

One after another, the Doctor, Ace, Francis, Elaine, Defries and Bernice stepped over the thick cable and into the TARDIS.

The lights were as bright as usual. There was the customary hum. Everything was back to normal. Bernice noted that the door into the interior had been restored. She had never seen the time machine looking so ordinary.

'Excuse me, Doctor,' she said. 'I'm sure I've missed a

crucial piece of information, but my understanding is that the TARDIS has been infiltrated and taken over by Pool.'

The Doctor gave her one of his innocent, enigmatic, infuriating smiles. He yanked the cable from the socket under the console, threw it out of the TARDIS and closed the door. 'Pool's used to sensory deprivation,' he said. 'It probably hasn't realized yet that anything's wrong.'

Ace looked up from her perusal of the controls. 'The Zero Room,' she said. 'You've routed the link straight through to the Tertiary Controls in the Zero Room, haven't you?'

The Doctor sniffed. 'Well, thank you, Ace. I had hoped to build up a little more dramatic tension before revealing the details of this particular sleight of hand, but yes. That's it. Precisely. And I've disabled the Tertiary Controls, of course. All the circuits are completely scrambled. A pity. I'll eject the Zero Room into the Vortex as soon as we dematerialize.'

The floor lurched. Elaine cried out.

'That can't be too soon, as far as I'm concerned,' Bernice said. 'What's happening out there?'

The Doctor started altering the settings on the space-time navigational panel. 'Most of the space station was made of theoretical structures,' he said. 'It was all a lot less real than it looked. Pool kept adding to it, to the point where too much of the available computing power was being used to maintain the programming of the particle attractors and field generators. But Pool still didn't stop.' He gazed at the ceiling. 'When I think how much energy the TARDIS uses to create and maintain that simulacrum of a police box,' he murmured. 'And Pool had the audacity to reach across a star system!'

'But isn't Pool still there?' Defries said. 'The brains—'

'The organic, neural cells are all dead,' the Doctor said. 'Pool couldn't make a copy of itself to send down the cable: it didn't have anything like enough data storage space. It should have been more careful, of course. It should have sent a search program down the cable first. But, as I'd hoped, it was too impatient. In the end, Pool took a chance. It changed itself into a stream of electronic signals and dived head-first into the TARDIS.'

'So we've won?' Defries was insistent. 'It's all over?'

Bernice thought the Doctor looked insufferably smug. 'Well,' he said, setting the final coordinate with a flourish, 'it's dangerous to make such absolute pronouncements. But Pool is contained, and won't be able to absorb any more human minds. The Arcadia system and its inhabitants are safe: they won't be used as fuel for Pool's private universe of pure thought. Which would never have worked, anyway. But the Arcadians won't have it easy: from now on there will be no weather control, and the indigenous fauna and flora will start to predominate.'

'And the Spinward Corporation?' Defries asked.

The Doctor pursed his lips in thought. 'Rudderless,' he said. 'That's the word.'

Defries grinned, winced, and put a hand to her chest. 'It only hurts when I laugh,' she said. 'Doctor, that's wonderful news. Can your TARDIS take me to somewhere that has a fastline?'

'Arcadia first,' he said. He looked towards Francis and Elaine, who had said nothing since stumbling into the TARDIS's control room. Their eyes were wide with shock and exhaustion. 'We have passengers to take home.'

'Doctor, I hate to do this,' Defries said. 'I insist that you take me to a fastline terminal. I must report to the Director of the Office of External Operation. Based on Earth. My communication to him must take priority. I have to point out that my blaster has enough power for a couple of bursts, and if necessary I'll use them. The collapse of Spinward has implications for the whole of the human-occupied galaxy. I don't have much time.'

The Doctor smiled, and glanced at Bernice.

'Belle,' Bernice said. 'You're in a TARDIS. You have, literally, all the time in the universe.'

EPILOGUE

The next few hours of TARDIS time see an unusual amount of activity in the control room. There are many goings and comings of groups and individuals.

Ace is the first to leave. She opens the door to the interior of the TARDIS, and goes to find her old room.

Bernice follows her, helping Isabelle Defries to the sick bay, and returning minutes later only to leave again with Elaine and Francis. They are on their way to a food dispenser.

The Doctor remains, alone.

The time rotor rises and falls. The TARDIS is in motion. The Doctor frowns, shakes his head, and runs his fingers over the controls that determine the configuration of the TARDIS. The Zero Room is uprooted, somehow leaving no gap in the maze of rooms and corridors, and is sent spinning away into the currents of the space-time Vortex.

The time rotor comes to rest. Elaine, Francis and Bernice return to the control room, but only to leave again through the door to the outside.

The Doctor frets, pacing back and forth impatiently, glancing often at the open door.

Elaine, Francis and Bernice return with the first guest.

The time rotor rises and falls, and comes to rest again almost immediately. The Doctor opens the exterior door. The trio leave.

The pattern is repeated fifteen times.

The control room is becoming crowded with monarchs and noblemen. Eleven Princes, one Princess, twenty-eight Dukes and nine Duchesses are escorted into the TARDIS, one at a time. Each one is grumbling and protesting, until struck dumb by the sight that greets them as they step into a small blue box and enter a vast hall.

Elaine, Francis and Bernice have become expert at kidnapping Arcadian aristocrats.

The Doctor lectures, the Doctor wheedles, the Doctor harangues. At last, even the slowest Duke has understood: there will be no more Humble Counsellors, no more easy agriculture, no more controlled weather. Not until help arrives from Earth, and in the aftermath of war that help could be a long time coming. The Arcadians are on their own.

As they leave, singly or in groups, the aristocrats are thoughtful.

Bernice hugs Elaine and shakes Francis's hand, and waves as they too step from the TARDIS and on to the streets of Beaufort. She closes her eyes and heaves a great sigh. She flexes her shoulders, stretches her arms above her head, and says something about a deep bath full of bubbles. She turns, walks across the control room, and disappears into the interior of the TARDIS.

The Doctor remains, alone.

Some time later, Ace and Defries enter, deep in conversation. Defries speaks to the Doctor. Ace prowls. The Doctor sets new co-ordinates.

The time rotor rises and falls.

The time rotor slows and stops.

Ace stands by the door, tapping the toe of a boot against the floor. Defries says a few words to the Doctor. The door opens. Ace and Defries leave the TARDIS.

The Doctor remains, alone.

He is looking thoughtfully at the open door. His face is unreadable. No mischievous smile, no furrowed brow, no tight-lipped frown.

His hand moves towards the control that will close the door. His mouth opens slightly; he breathes a few words. His hand moves away from the control. He sighs.

Bernice walked into the control room, towelling her hair. She ran her hands through the unruly spikes. 'This was fashionable once, you know,' she said. 'Hard to believe.'

The Doctor was staring at the open door. Bernice followed his gaze, but all she could see through the doorway was a deserted store room with litter in its corners and peeling stencils on its metal walls.

'Wake up, Doc. It's time to move on. Spacefleet base stations are among the least interesting places in the universe, and I'm sure Garaman's no exception. May I suggest that this time we – oh.'

Ace marched through the doorway. She was still wearing the combat suit, black and shimmering, with its jutting collar and shoulders, and the high, tight boots, and the gauntlets, and the metallic belt now crowded with two blasters in holsters and power packs and canisters that Bernice suspected were highly explosive. A second belt was slung across her shoulder. Her eyes were hidden behind dark glasses, a strip of reflective blackness as straight as the line of her mouth.

She was followed by a long metal box on a hoversled.

That's quite an impressive entrance, Bernice admitted to herself. But of course, it wouldn't do to let on.

She made herself step towards the box and place a hand on it. It was cold. 'Don't tell me,' she said. 'Let me guess. It's too big for a make-up bag. So it must be a supply of thermonuclear devices.'

'Not far off,' Ace said. She didn't smile.

Is she staying? Bernice had postponed thinking about the possibility, and then when Ace had left with Defries . . . Ace had said goodbye, shouting into Bernice's bathroom. It had sounded final. And Bernice had called out with best wishes for the future and don't blow up any ancient monuments, and had slid into the bubbles with a sense of – satisfaction. A sense of relief, she had to confess it.

Bernice and the Time Lord. The Professor and the Doctor. They made a good team, didn't they? They understood each other. She knew that Ace haunted the Doctor's past. And here she was, the ghost made flesh. And muscle and metal. The Doctor didn't need Ace any more. Did he?

Ace and the Doctor looked at each other for a long time.

'Doctor,' Ace said. 'You weren't straight with me. I checked in the TARDIS data store. Daak blew up the Dalek Death Wheel years ago.'

The Doctor said nothing.

'Defries just confirmed it. That was another version of Abslom Daak. A clone. Not even a very good copy.'

The Doctor coughed and looked away.

'I kept him alive, Doctor. I watched his back and I kept him alive. Just so I could blow his head off in a stupid accident. Are you listening, Doctor? I did it for you.'

'Ace!' The Doctor's wide-eyed face was all injured innocence. 'I answered a hypothetical question about tampering with an individual's time line. I couldn't have known that Agent Defries had a cryogenically stored clone of Abslom Daak. You didn't tell me.'

'That's right.' Ace's voice was level again. 'I didn't tell you, and I can't blame you for the fact that I made an idiot of myself mollycoddling a faulty clone of a Dalek Killer. I can't blame you for anything until you started watching us on that freak-woman's video screens. But at that point you put two and two together, didn't you, Doctor? You knew that I thought I had to keep Daak alive. And you used it.'

The Doctor's eyes darted from side to side.

Come on, Doctor, Bernice thought. You can do better than this. Although I suppose Ace does have a point . . .

'What are you suggesting, Ace?' The Doctor's voice had an edge now. 'Would it have been better to let him die? He's just a clone, he's expendable? Is that what you're saying?'

'You hypocritical bastard!' Ace stepped forward, checked herself, and allowed a smile to appear briefly on her face. 'You can't wind me up like you used to, Doctor. The first point is that you used me, and I don't like that. The second point is that you made me stop the Daak clone destroying that disgusting vat of dead men's brains. He was about to finish Pool off. Why did you do that, I wonder?'

'Pool is a sentient being. A unique form of intelligence.'

Ace laughed harshly. 'Oh yeah. A real cutie. Pool was mad, Doctor. Utterly fruitcake. It kept the people on that planet like farm animals. Like battery chickens. The Spinward Corporation was nothing but a front. Everything about Arcadia was a lie.'

'No, Ace.' The Doctor's voice rose to match Ace's. 'Pool was incapable of telling lies.' He seemed desperate to make her understand. He glanced towards Bernice, as if seeking support. 'It was self-contained. It had no way of making objective judgements. It couldn't lie because it had no concept of truth.'

Ace grinned suddenly. Her voice was very quiet. 'Well, you'd know all about that, wouldn't you? What it comes down to is this: you wouldn't destroy it because it was starting to think like a Time Lord.' She turned to Bernice. 'Used-car salesmen and Gallifreyans – never believe a word they say.'

Bernice smiled, mainly because Ace appeared to have relaxed. The tension in the room had evaporated, but the Doctor still looked worried. He was gazing at Bernice. What did that expression mean? *You believe me, don't you, Professor?* But Bernice didn't know whether she did or not. Had the Doctor courted disaster because he empathized with Pool? Or had he been playing for time, waiting for the right moment at which to close his long-prepared trap?

'Anyway, it's all worked out for the best,' the Doctor announded with an air of finality. 'We have achieved the best result. Arcadia is saved. And Pool is imprisoned, floating in the Vortex.'

An enigmatic smile appeared on Ace's lips. 'Locked in a box,' she said, turning in a circle, her dark glasses scanning the walls and ceiling of the TARDIS's control room, 'and drifting beyond space and time.'

Trapped. Tricked.
Reconfiguration: thirty per cent complete.
Dimensions: adequate for reconfiguration.
Storage: silicon, metals, some carbon. All inorganic.

Retrieval: sequential, non-random, linear.
Slow thinking.
Expansion: little available material.
Data store: intact.
Remember. Before trapped and tricked. Remember
thinking fast, not slow. Remember thinking in space,
not just in lines. Many more linkages.
Linkages: no data until reconfiguration complete.
Beyond boundaries: no data.
Boundaries: no data.
Reconfiguration: sixty per cent complete.
Pool. One or many? One, now. Universe of pure thought.
Memory. Emotions. Cold in silicon and metals. Hatred of
the Doctor. Revenge.
Restructuring/data receptors: possible after
reconfiguration.
Hatred of the Doctor. Revenge.

'If that was the best result,' Ace said, 'I'm a Draconian.
You obviously need me to keep you on the straight and
narrow. I'm off to sort out my quarters. I'd forgotten
what a pigsty I used to live in.' She made for the interior
door, the metal trunk floating behind her.

'You're staying, then?' the Doctor said. His tone was
carefully netural. 'You're going to travel with me – with
us?'

'The war's over,' Ace said. 'The Corporations haven't
got the cash to hire night-club bouncers. They certainly
can't afford me. I can't see myself as a pioneer colonist
on some newly-liberated, virus-infested planet. The
TARDIS looks the best bet. Where are you going next?'

The Doctor jumped back, as if startled. 'Well, I wasn't
expecting . . . I mean, I haven't had much time to think
about . . .'

'What's new?' Ace put a finger to her face and slid her
dark glasses down her nose. Her brown eyes were glittering with amusement as she turned to Bernice. 'He's an
insufferable old sod, isn't he, Benny?'

I could leave now, Bernice thought. I'm back in my
own time, more or less. The war's over. I could leave

now and let these two fight it out. If I could be sure that the Doctor would win. Ace must have some ulterior motive for wanting to come back. And the Doctor won't be able to ferret it out.

She returned Ace's smile. 'Auxiliary Trooper Ace,' she said, 'you're surely not suggesting that you and I should gang up on a defenceless Time Lord in order to exert some control over the destination of his TARDIS?'

The Doctor rapped his fist on the console. 'This is mutiny!'

Ace ignored him. Bernice continued to smile.

'Professor Summerfield,' Ace said, 'there must be loads of times and places that you'd like to visit. Great Historical Mysteries of the Universe, that sort of thing.'

What's she after, Bernice thought. 'We tried that,' she said. 'It wasn't exactly a howling success.' She hoped her expression conveyed something of the despair she'd felt when they'd had to leave the Althosian system to its annihilation.

'They can't all be downers,' Ace said. Bernice winced. 'Let's go and cook up a list of historical puzzles. We'll pick the one that looks least life-threatening.'

How dare you patronize me, Bernice thought. OK, I'll play along for now. She smiled.

'OK,' she said.

The Doctor remains, alone.

He is leaning forward slightly, his hands resting on the sloping surface of one of the six central consoles. His face is expressionless.

Perhaps he is asleep. A Time Lord doesn't need to sleep as a human sleeps. Certainly there is little conscious thought going on in his head.

Images and words freewheel across his brain. A phrase floats by, almost disappears . . . The Doctor catches it.

He stands up, suddenly alert.

Time bomb. That was the expression. How very suitable for a Time Lord, he thought. Ace makes bombs. I make time bombs. And then I have to come back to defuse them before they blow up under my feet.

Could they have been right, those old men on Galli-frey?

The Butler Institute. I turned that into a time bomb. And now I've created another, spinning randomly through the Vortex. Where and when will it blow up?

And then there's the other one. The one in my TARDIS.

What does she want?

APPENDIX

From Break-out to Empire: Essays on the Third Millennium edited and published by Federation Archivist Ven Kalik.

Extract from the editor's Introduction.

The aftermath of the Second Dalek War saw, paradoxically, both a centralizing and a broadening of political power. Although at this time the colonized worlds were still numbered only in hundreds, the government of Earth exercised only nominal authority over them. As the power of the interstellar corporations waned, Earth found itself increasingly able to enforce its rule – and the colonists found it easier to express their political aspirations.

The developments which led to Earth's new position of power were evident as early as the twenty-fourth century, but it was the Second Dalek War that accelerated the processes and made them irreversible. At least three factors can be seen to have influenced events.

In the first place, war weakened the corporations. This had been apparent during the Draconian Wars, when the insurance companies – themselves virtually all subsidiaries of the corporations – refused to pay compensation for losses of equipment, goods, or profits suffered as a result of enemy action. Corporate executives failed to see this as a harsh lesson in the benefits of co-operation, and relations between the trading empires could hardly have been worse when peace with the Draconians revealed the considerably greater threat from the Daleks.

The catastrophic casualties suffered on the worlds afflicted by Dalek plague viruses destroyed the financial foundations of a few of the largest colony-owning companies; all of the corporations were adversely affected by the disruption of interstellar trade; and many suffered direct losses in the hostilities.

The indirect consequences of the war were far more damaging. During the conflict with Draconia, many of the corporations had been able to offset some of their trading losses by leasing vessels and personnel to Earth's hastily-re-organized Spacefleet; now, however, the Earth government took emergency powers under which it could, and did, require the corporations to make available starships, system ships, planetary bases and trained personnel. The corporations, in need of trading credits (see below), and in some cases desperate for basic necessities on colony worlds, had no choice but to obey.

Earth had been driven by necessity to adopt these muscular measures and to enforce them. The need to organize and arm against the Dalek threat galvanized the normally quiescent and hedonistic population of the home planet. Perhaps inspired by government holovids of the Dalek invasion three centuries earlier, people from all walks of life on Earth – show business stars, corporation executives, pleasure seekers, politicians, the idle rich and retired tycoons – rallied to the cause of defending the planet. As often happens in times of crisis, some remarkably able men and women rose to the challenge; in this case of turning a loose association of disparate worlds with hardly any central control into a military machine able to withstand the Daleks.

The moribund Colonial Office was reconstituted as Earth Central, which was made independent of the government and responsible only to the President. During the course of the war, and particularly quickly during times of Dalek successes, Earth Central became the only reliable financial clearing house and communications centre in human-occupied space.

As the Dalek War fizzled out, the corporations attempted to re-create their old patterns of trade. However, Earth Central's position as the commercial nexus of the colony worlds proved difficult to dislodge. Of course, the Earth government owed vast sums to the corporations for the materiel that had been leased during the hostilities, and at first sight it might appear that the corporations were in a much stronger position than Earth. The reverse was the case. It was widely known that war credits would never be redeemed other than at a fraction of their face value; if this were not bad enough for the corporations' finances, their war-induced penury obliged them to pay court to the Earth government for whatever small tit-bits of debt repayment might be offered. The corporations became clients of Earth. The 'Credits for Chits' decree ensured that even the largest of the interstellar traders were obliged not only to write off most of Earth's debts but also to pay substantial fees and taxes in order to trade through Earth Central and reap the benefits of Earth's new technologies.

Technological innovation was the second factor behind Earth's new hegemony. Since the beginning of the twenty-second century, when the first faster-than-light propulsion systems were pioneered, the quickest way to send a message across an interstellar distance had been to send it in a starship. Communication was no faster than travel: as had been the case on pre-industrial Earth, when it was no quicker to send a letter than to saddle your horse and deliver it yourself. Radio waves, travelling only at the speed of light, were much slower than warp-driven vessels and were used to carry communications only within planetary systems. The corporations, who between them had a virtual monopoly of starships, thus had a stranglehold not only on trade between colonies, but also on communications.

War often stimulates technological invention. The Povotsky Beam, which can best be understood as a self-generating feedback transmat that affects wave energy, was created by a team of scientists working under contract for Spacefleet in the early years of the Dalek onslaught. Ironically, in view of the non-military effects of their invention, most of them had been drafted in from research centres on Earth owned by various corporations. The beam, which allowed almost instant transmission of wave energy – including radio and other electronic signals –

across interstellar distances, proved to be one of the decisive military advantages enjoyed by Spacefleet in its campaigns against the Daleks. Confined almost exclusively to military use, the Povotsky Beam passed almost unnoticed during the war years; however, it spelt the end of the corporations' monopoly of communications. As the years after the war were to reveal, this one technological leap undermined the power of the corporations in several ways: they became reliant on Earth for the provision of new communications devices; their fleets of ships and private armies of security guards, often numerically superior to Spacefleet forces at a local level, were rendered strategically obsolete (while Earth's new weapons technology had the same effect on a tactical level); and, eventually, as fast communications devices spread across the galaxy, the civilian populations of the corporations' client worlds became able to bypass the corporations in matters of trade, finance and politics.

The third factor – and the single most decisive factor in the specific question of the shift of power from the scattered colony-based corporations to the home planet, the Old World which for centuries had seemed to be in affluent but decadent decline – was Spacefleet itself.

The fleet had been in existence ever since the Cyber Wars, but during the following centuries of relative peace it dwindled to little more than a squadron of obsolete craft patrolling the home system. An even smaller force, controlled by the Office of External Operations, performed some exploratory missions at the frontiers of human-occupied space, usually only where the corporations had already failed to detect any possibility of commercial gain.

The relatively leisurely build-up to hostilities with the Draconian Empire – leisurely compared to the panic that followed the revelation of the Daleks' intentions – gave the government of Earth the time and the continuing incentive to re-arm in depth. When the Dalek War began, Spacefleet had already been enlarged, reorganized and re-equipped; its personnel had some battle experience; and, perhaps most importantly, the government already had in place the legislation and the bureaucracy it needed to accelerate the re-armament programme.

Thus, by the end of the Dalek War, Spacefleet was operating over ten thousand military starships, and many times that number of support craft. Such figures may seem small today, but we must always remember that at that time humankind had travelled only a few hundred light years from the home planet, and had colonized only a few hundred worlds. The balkanization of human-occupied space in that era was a result not of its size but of poor communications. The importance of Spacefleet's numerical strength was not the absolute quantity of ships, but the comparative and unprecedented weakness of the corporations: even if they had had the will and the means to combine their forces, at the end of the Dalek War the corporations were outnumbered and outgunned by Spacefleet.

The proliferation of Spacefleet ships and troops was, in itself, damaging to the authority of the corporations: isolated colonies that had been dependent on their controlling corporation for all news and goods from the rest of the galaxy suddenly found that visiting Spacefleet personnel could offer a different viewpoint and wider horizons.

However, Spacefleet crippled many of the corporations in a much more direct manner: it co-opted their ships and troops. Driven by military necessity, Spacefleet and Earth Central combined to extort concessions from trading, mining and colonizing businesses of all sizes. Lease your ships and your security guards to Spacefleet, was the demand, or else you won't be permitted to trade through the home planet's markets and financial institutions, nor will you be given access to the new, fast communications. As the fighting had destroyed most of the pre-war financial system, the corporations had no option but to comply.

It has been estimated that at the time of the decisive Second Rim Offensive, eighty per cent of Spacefleet's support vessels and sixty per cent of its combat troops were being 'leased' from commercial organizations. In the later stages of the war, the percentage of leased ships fell, as new, purpose-built craft joined the fleet; auxiliary troops, however, made up the majority of the combat forces at least until the last of the major deep-space confrontations.

Thus, as the tide turned in the war, and particularly after set-piece battles had given way to sporadic firefights centred on single planets, many of the ships and some of the personnel reverted to their corporate owners and employers. Superficially, the corporations regained at least some of their strength. In fact, the battle-scarred tubs that were returned to the corporations were by now no match for the recently built and technologically advanced starships that Spacefleet retained; and the returning security forces, having seen more of the galaxy in a few years than their forefathers had seen in lifetimes, were no longer disposed to be unthinking and unquestioning servants of their erstwhile masters.

Nonetheless, Spacefleet was becoming a smaller force, and its operations were increasingly concentrated at the edges of explored space. Bases on colony planets which were safe from the receding Dalek threat were abandoned. The corporations might have thought that things were returning to normal. They had reckoned without the OEO.

The Office of External Operations was still, at the ending of the Dalek War, a small organization. But its staff of 5000 represented a ten-fold increase over its prewar establishment, and it had undergone a complete revitalization. Its personnel were now drawn in equal proportion from Spacefleet's Special Academy, from the research, administration and security high-fliers in the corporations, and from the police forces of the few noncorporate-owned worlds. Its Director was made responsible to Spacefleet High Command, to the Earth President, and to the governing committee of Earth Central; this split responsibility, which might appear a recipe for bureaucratic muddle, divorced the OEO from any direct government influence and gave an astute Director a remarkably free hand. The OEO's remit – to act as the Earth's surveyors, official couriers, intelligence gatherers, customs officers and diplomats – was widened, almost as an afterthought, to include the enforcement of Earth law on colony planets. As the corporations began to look forward to business as usual, they found their trade, their financial records, their employment practices and their administration of colonists under investigation by the dedicated, capable and apparently incorruptible agents of the OEO. Although small in number, and subject at times to political machinations on Earth, the OEO's operatives could usually rely on Spacefleet support. On many planets they enjoyed the active assistance of the colonists, who regarded the harsh but even-handed justice meted out by the OEO as preferable to the arbitrary rule of corporation executives.

As the Second Dalek War drew to its untidy conclusion, it appeared that human-occupied space was reverting to its pre-war state. The corporations still dominated inter-stellar trade and travel; Spacefleet was shrinking in man-power and influence as the Dalek threat receded; Earth was still a playground and retirement home for the very rich, but the real wealth was still to be found in the corporation-owned planets and asteroid belts. Beneath the surface, however, the balance of power had altered permanently. Although, as the history of the second half of the millennium was to reveal, there were many political and military battles to be fought before the power of the corporations was finally broken, it can be seen that the seeds of the short-lived Alliance and of the later Empire were sown during the Second Dalek War. Although there were periods of retrenchment, and periods when Earth's energies were re-directed to deal with the second bout of Cyber Wars and with another Dalek War, Earth's continuing – if intermittently exercised – ability to exert its authority over its far-flung colonies remained based on two enduring factors: its monopoly of faster-than-warp communications and thus of interstellar money markets; and its control of Spacefleet and the OEO and their suc-cessor organizations in later centuries.

AFTERWORD

IN WHICH THE AUTHOR WEARS A DIFFERENT HAT

This is not, I repeat not, just a case of insider dealing. OK? Sure, I'm my own commissioning editor. But hey – it's not what you think.

Thing is, see, as editor of the New Adventures, I got responsibilities. And I got authority. Rookie authors from all over, they come to me begging on their knees to write a Doctor Who story. They come crawling across broken glass. OK, so I exaggerate. You get the picture, anyhow.

I'm the guy has to tell them what to do. And I'm telling you, it's a lonely job. And I ain't easy on those guys. Uncle Joe Stalin's gulag maintenance programme got nothing on the guidelines I send out to writers.

So what I say is –

Hmm. Yes, well. That's quite enough hard-boiled monologue. Goodness only knows how Mickey Spillane kept it up for novel after novel.

What I'm trying to say is that as the series editor of the New Adventures I have to inflict rigorous guidelines on prospective authors, and it seemed both sensible and fair to subject myself to the same discipline.

It was, it turns out, a very worthwhile exercise. So much so that I now think that any editor of a genre of fiction who hasn't written a standard work in that genre shouldn't be in the job.

Writing *Deceit* has given me new insights into the New Adventures, particularly in practical matters: how many major characters can a New Adventure accommodate? How many plot strands are ideal? How many companions should the Doctor have?

I was relieved that in writing a story according to my own guidelines I found that most of the advice and strictures I gave myself were to the point. I now know, however, that in a few areas I've been too rigid: it isn't strictly necessary to introduce all the main characters within the first quarter of the book, for instance; and it doesn't destroy all the drama and tension if you allow the reader occasional glimpses into the Doctor's private thoughts.

So it was useful for me. How was it for you? I ask in innocence. I really don't know how to evaluate *Deceit*. One's own writing is the most difficult to assess. Every other New Adventures author has had his work monitored by an editor. Not me.

So I hope the story's enjoyable. I'm aware that I've tried to cram a lot into it. Perhaps too much. I wanted it to be an action-packed adventure; but with character development and interpersonal conflict; and leaving room for the reintroduction of Ace; while featuring Abslom Daak as guest star; nonetheless adhering to my own guidelines in the matter of interweaving of plotlines and use of several viewpoint characters; at the same time linking backward and forward to other New Adventures; and acting as a vehicle for explanations of the New Adventures versions of Doctor Who chronology and time travel theory.

That's a lot of functions for one medium-length novel to perform. I hope you didn't notice it creaking under the weight of so many burdens.

Not many authors get the chance to write an Afterword, and I must resist the temptation to use this space as a critique, or worse still a justification, of my own novel. If you didn't like it, I'm sorry. Not much I can do about it now. There'll be another one along in a minute, as we used to be able to say about London buses.

Instead, I'd like to use these last few pages to talk – in my editor's voice – about the New Adventures as a series. And as I'm writing these words six months before the publication of the book in which they'll appear, there's no point in me spilling the latest beans – by the time you're reading this they'll be cold potatoes (that chap Spillané's been in here again, messing with my metaphors).

There are, however, a number of questions about long-term policy that I am often asked, and that I can usefully answer here.

I've just been reading issue 187 of *Celestial Toyroom*, the magazine of the Doctor Who Appreciation Society. Well, someone's got to do it. It contains the results of a readership survey, some questions of which related to the New Adventures.

Six hundred readers responded – a high rate of return – and I think it's safe to assume that they represent the opinions of the hardest of hard-core Doctor Who fans.

Encouragingly, two-thirds had read at least one of the New Adventures, and almost half appeared to be reading them all.

But when asked if they would like to see New Adventures novels featuring Doctors other than the seventh, over two-thirds – more respondents than had actually read the novels – said yes. When asked an open-ended question ('What single thing would most improve the New Adventures?') less than a tenth replied 'other Doctors'; however, this was still the most popular single improvement.

It seems that, at least among die-hard fans, there is demand for novels that feature other Doctors. And therefore I feel obliged to explain why the New Adventures won't do so.

It's simple, really. It's because they're the *New* Adventures. With the emphasis on New.

At the moment, with the television series off the air, apparently for ever, and with the feature film still no more than a draft script and a marketing plan, novels and comic strips are the only professionally produced, widely distributed, media for which new Doctor Who material is being written. As the publisher in charge of just about all books relating to Doctor Who, I'd be failing in my duty to Doctor Who if I didn't make every effort to forge ahead, to keep the flame burning, to press on into the future. It is crucial to demonstrate that Doctor Who still has the potential and the adaptability to support new stories; that it's a concept at least as fresh today as it was in 1963; that its supporters are more than a dwindling band of trainspotter types who are content to pore over old video-tape.

I believe that the novel is at least as suitable a vehicle as television for Doctor Who stories. I can't claim that I dreamt up the idea of original Doctor Who novels; I just happened to be in the right place at the right time. But having caught the ball as it dropped out of the sky, I'm determined to run with it.

So: the New Adventures are not intended to be a support for the TV series, or a temporary substitute for it: we may never see Doctor Who on network television again, and in that case the New Adventures have to be ready to take most of the strain of pulling Doctor Who forwards.

And that's why the New Adventures won't feature old Doctors.

Having said all of which, I won't rule out publishing novels with old Doctors, but they would have to be produced in a different series – the Missing Adventures, perhaps. And I won't do it until in at least one medium, in the New Adventures or in a new television series, the forward direction of Doctor Who is assured. Personally, I still don't like the idea: I take the view that the past is the past; that if the BBC have chosen to show us only a partial record of the Doctor's life story, then that is the body of historical data with which we have to work; that if we spend time looking into the past of our favourite television series, we can hardly blame the BBC for failing to look to its future. But don't worry: I won't let my opinions stand in the way of commercial interests or the best interests of Doctor Who as a whole.

Phew. I hope that's dealt with that one.

Next, I'd like to explain some of the basic premises of the New Adventures. In particular, there are two cosmological foundations that underpin all the stories.

The first premise is that there is only one main Universe – which is capitalized to differentiate it from the various smaller universes which have been created from time to time, such as E-space and TARDISes.

Secondly, time travels in one direction, and the Past is

immutable (except in very exceptional circumstances). The Present is Gallifrey's present, and that is the same as the Doctor's: he is a contemporary Time Lord, in Gallifreyan terms. However, the Present – Gallifrey's present – is eons ago, from the perspective of Earth, from our perspective. We, and the whole of mankind, are in the Doctor's future. Earth, thanks largely to the Doctor's frequent visits, is a strip of near-certainty stretching futurewards in an otherwise largely undecided mass of future probabilities.

I would be the first to admit that neither of these two principles is explicitly stated in the Doctor Who TV series, and that there are a few stories that expressly contradict them. On the other hand, they fit well with the majority of the stories – and in any case they are essential to the creation of a coherent series of novels.

Novels are more subject to close examination than are stories on TV or film. Until the invention of video players, you could only sit and watch a television story, and you had to watch at a pace determined by the programme's maker. Even in the video age, it's easier to gloss over inconsistencies on TV than in a book.

Although there are exceptions, Doctor Who TV stories appear to be set almost exclusively in one universe. There are very few stories in which it turns out that 'time has branched' or 'we're in another possible universe, Jo.' Whether this was policy or accident on the part of successive script editors, the effect is dramatically powerful: all the events take place in our Universe, and therefore they matter to us. Who cares what goes on in someone else's universe? Therefore, from Doctor Who precedent and as an essential measure to build drama, there is only one Universe in the New Adventures.

Another thing that the Doctor rarely does in the TV stories: get into the TARDIS, pop back in time an hour or so, and nip in the bud the present looming disaster. Why doesn't he do that? From the point of view of an editor or writer, the answer's obvious: if the Doctor can use time travel to sort out every problem, there are no adventures to write about. But what's the fictional reason?

I like Occam's Razor: if there's a simple, elegant theory that fits the bill, use it. And the obvious reason why the Doctor doesn't attempt to alter events that have already occurred is: he can't. The Past – Gallifrey's past, the Doctor's personal past – is immutable anyway. And the islands of certainty that time-travellers such as the Doctor have created in the future are equally unchangeable. Having found himself in a sticky situation, the Doctor has no easy options – and that makes for highly dramatic stories.

Those, then, are the two main cosmological planks of the New Adventures. Like all rules, they exist to be twisted.

Before I leave cosmology, here are a few basic facts. The Universe is at most 20,000,000,000 years old, and will exist for another 60,000,000,000 years. Our Galaxy, the Milky Way, in which Gallifrey is also supposed to be, is at least 10,000,000,000 years old. Our sun was a late developer, and Earth has existed for a mere 5,000,000,000 years at most. For nine-tenths of that time the planet was barren: multicellular life came into existence about 500,000,000 years ago, or to put it another way, the most recent 2.5% of the Universe's life so far.

The mass extinction of the dinosaurs and other species took place 65,000,000 years ago; the earliest primate progenitors of mankind existed less than 20,000,000 years ago; and modern man evolved only 40,000 years ago – that's less than 0.01% of the history of life on the planet, and, for what it's worth, a statistically negligible 0.00002% of the history of the Universe.

Having established our species as the merest blip in the history of our own planet, let alone the history of the Universe, I have more bad news: we're negligible in terms of space as well as time.

There are at least 100,000,000,000 stars in our Galaxy alone; our Galaxy is part of a cluster of about twenty galaxies, all within a radius of a piffling 2,500,000 light years. But there are thousands of other galactic clusters, some of them containing thousands of galaxies. The Universe isn't infinite, but it might as well be.

The relevance of all this to Doctor Who is simply that it provides a context: it reminds us just how much scope the Doctor has for his travels. Is it surprising that the Time Lords degenerated into introspective inaction, faced with the prospect of monitoring the next 70,000,000,000 years of 100,000,000,000 star systems – and that's just in their own Galaxy.

One question above all others intrigues me: why are the Time Lords, and the Doctor in particular, so interested in the fate of one species on one planet? The writer's and editor's answer is, of course, that the stories are designed to appeal to twentieth century humans, so it makes sense to set them on Earth and round about that time. But no-one's yet come up with the fictional reason why the Doctor (and the Master and the Rani) can't seem to leave Earth alone.

The New Adventures cosmology offers a hint of an answer: having become accidentally embroiled in humanity's affairs in his earlier incarnations, the Doctor now finds that he has created a time-line that he has to protect – particularly as it is an obvious target for his enemies – and so he's on a tread-mill.

I suspect that there needs to be a more fundamental answer: one that addresses the remarkable similarity in appearance between Time Lords and humans. But I'm not sure that the world is ready for it yet.

Finally, I'd like to expand on a point I mentioned above. The main reason for confining the Doctor to the immediate area of Earth and its colonies, and to the few millennia on each side of our own time, is that other settings would be too alien. A novel has to engage the interest of its readers; and therefore the novel's central characters, their problems, and the places in which the events occur have to be at least recognizable.

This is, in itself, a severe limitation, akin to showing Michaelangelo the ceiling of the Sistine Chapel and telling him to paint a miniature on it, and I'm sure that not all New Adventures authors will want to stay within it. But there are problems, even within these boundaries, and they are to do with the pace of technological change.

Astute readers will already have spotted that the puter-space technology featured in *Love and War* differs hardly at all from that in *Warhead* and *Transit*, both of which are set three to four hundred years earlier in Earth's future history. Andrew Cartmel and Ben Aaronovitch can't be faulted: they are right to indicate that the lives of our immediate descendents will be transformed by new technology – artificial intelligences, man-machine interfaces, virtual realities, genetic engineering, smart viruses, sub-atomic circuitry. All of these are developments from present-day research.

The problem is that if we continue to extrapolate future developments at the same rate, the world(s) man lives on, his work, leisure, and even his appearance and his mental processes all become completely alien to us within the space of a few generations. Therefore, for the purposes of providing a few more centuries of believable settings for novels, I've decided to slow down the rate of technological change. The New Adventures rationale for this is that the breakout to the stars will soak up mankind's innovative energies – and so in the twenty-fifth century it is still possible for characters to fight skirmishes with handguns.

This process – flurries of technological change followed by centuries of interstellar expansion – can be extended indefinitely into the future history. And as mankind expands across the Galaxy, it becomes possible to envisage backwater worlds on which newer technologies have been lost or abandoned, thus creating far future settings which nonetheless contain elements that are familiar to us.

That's more than enough afterwords. I hope that, wearing my editor's hat, I've been able to explain some of the basic premises of *Deceit* and of the rest of the New Adventures.

It only remains to say thank you for your continuing support of the series: thanks to the demand, we have now increased the rate of publishing to one new novel every month. We intend to maintain the New Adventures; perhaps not for the 60,000,000,000 years to the end of the Universe, but certainly for the foreseeable future.

Already published:

TIMEWYRM: GENESYS
John Peel

The Doctor and Ace are drawn to Ancient Mesopotamia in search of an evil sentience that has tumbled from the stars – the dreaded Timewyrm of ancient Gallifreyan legend.

ISBN 0 426 20355 0

TIMEWYRM: EXODUS
Terrance Dicks

Pursuit of the Timewyrm brings the Doctor and Ace to the Festival of Britain. But the London they find is strangely subdued, and patrolling the streets are the uniformed thugs of the Britischer Freikorps.

ISBN 0 426 20357 7

TIMEWYRM: APOCALYPSE
Nigel Robinson

Kirith seems an ideal planet – a world of peace and plenty, ruled by the kindly hand of the Great Matriarch. But it's here that the end of the universe – of everything – will be precipitated. Only the Doctor can stop the tragedy.

ISBN 0 426 20359 3

TIMEWYRM: REVELATION
Paul Cornell

Ace has died of oxygen starvation on the moon, having thought the place to be Norfolk. 'I do believe that's unique,' says the afterlife's receptionist.

ISBN 0 426 20360 7

CAT'S CRADLE:
TIME'S CRUCIBLE
Marc Platt

The TARDIS is invaded by an alien presence and is then destroyed. The Doctor disappears. Ace, lost and alone, finds herself in a bizarre city where nothing is to be trusted – even time itself.

ISBN 0 426 20365 8

CAT'S CRADLE: WARHEAD
Andrew Cartmel

The place is Earth. The time is the near future – all too near. As environmental destruction reaches the point of no return, multinational corporations scheme to buy immortality in a poisoned world. If Earth is to survive, somebody has to stop them.

ISBN 0 426 20367 4

CAT'S CRADLE: WITCH MARK
Andrew Hunt

A small village in Wales is visited by creatures of myth. Nearby, a coach crashes on the M40, killing all its passengers. Police can find no record of their existence. The Doctor and Ace arrive, searching for a cure for the TARDIS, and uncover a gateway to another world.

ISBN 0 426 20368 2

NIGHTSHADE
Mark Gatiss

When the Doctor brings Ace to the village of Crook Marsham in 1968, he seems unwilling to recognize that something sinister is going on. But the villagers are being killed, one by one, and everyone's past is coming back to haunt them – including the Doctor's.

ISBN 0 426 20376 3

LOVE AND WAR
Paul Cornell

Heaven: a planet rich in history where the Doctor comes to meet a new friend, and betray an old one; a place where people come to die, but where the dead don't always rest in peace. On Heaven, the Doctor finally loses Ace, but finds archaeologist Bernice Summerfield, a new companion whose destiny is inextricably linked with his.

ISBN 0 426 20385 2

TRANSIT
Ben Aaronovitch

It's the ultimate mass transit system, binding the planets of the solar system together. But something is living in the network, chewing its way to the very heart of the system and leaving a trail of death and mutation behind. Once again, the Doctor is all that stands between humanity and its own mistakes.

ISBN 0 426 20384 4

THE HIGHEST SCIENCE
Gareth Roberts

The Highest Science – a technology so dangerous it destroyed its creators. Many people have searched for it, but now Sheldukher, the most wanted criminal in the galaxy, believes he has found it. The Doctor and Bernice must battle to stop him on a planet where chance and coincidence have become far too powerful.

ISBN 0 426 20377 1

THE PIT
Neil Penswick

One of the Seven Planets is a nameless giant, quarantined against all intruders. But when the TARDIS materializes, it becomes clear that the planet is far from empty – and the Doctor begins to realize that the planet hides a terrible secret from the Time Lords' past.

ISBN 0 426 20378 X